C000108027

Chateau Lafite 1953
(and other stories)

Malcolm Gluck

IndePenPress

© Malcolm Gluck 2010

All rights reserved

No part of this publication may be reproduced, stored in a retrieval system, or transmitted in any form or by any means, without the prior permission in writing of the publisher, nor be otherwise circulated in any form of binding or cover other than that in which it is published and without a similar condition including this condition being imposed on the subsequent purchaser.

This is a work of fiction. Living individuals appear, but strictly in the roles they have in life. Every other character herein is based on no-one alive or dead. Any resemblance to such a person is, therefore, a freak accident.

First published in Great Britain by Pen Press

All paper used in the printing of this book has been made from wood grown in managed, sustainable forests.

ISBN13: 978-1-907172-94-6

Printed and bound in the UK
IndePenPress is an imprint of
Indepenpress Publishing Limited
25 Eastern Place
Brighton, BN2 1GJ

A catalogue record of this book is available from the British Library

Cover design by Jacqueline Abromeit
Cover photograph by Malcolm Gluck

To: all those thousands of Guardian and Superplonk readers who made being tied to a column for fifteen years a delight.

Contents

Penfolds Grange Hermitage 1982

The e-mail was the last of a group of nine and it was the most laconic.

"You must die. Your crime is too great. From: one who hates."

Paul Hobbs smiled, briefly scanned the screen again to see if he knew who had sent it, but did not recognise the address. He put the computer to sleep and went out to lunch. Mr Hobbs liked to lunch. He was old-fashioned in spite of the silvery iMac on his desk.

The next day he accessed his server as usual before the midday feed and in the middle of a group of thirteen e-mails there was this: "You must die SOON. Your crime is too great. From: one who still hates."

Mr Hobbs now felt a slight irritation. He could remember no-one he had recently upset. He wasn't in the business of upsetting people. This was a silly joke. He deleted the message, read the rest of the e-mails, quickly replied to one, leaving four others to address when he returned from Chez Albertine, where the consultancy that designed the firm's brochures had booked a table. His boss, naturally enough, ate with the ad agency that created the TV commercials. You've seen them, of course. They are the ones with the porcupine and the elephant in subtitled conversation about savings and mortgages.

Friday's threat was yet more elongated still. It arrived in the late afternoon, after a sandwich lunch (for athletic reasons Mr Hobbs did not eat formally on Fridays).

"You must die SOONER than you think. Your crime is too great. From: one who still hates more than ever."

Mr Hobbs printed this one out and sent an immediate reply: "Please do not bother me further with your childishness." Mr Hobbs packed up for the day; for the weekend. Mr Hobbs was packed himself into that somewhat anonymous cusp between middle and senior marketing management of a large building society, which had dithered for years over whether it should remain a mutual society or become a bank. Having been passed over for promotion to managerial board status on at least four occasions (that he could remember), he was perhaps – and in his more lucid moments he confessed as much to himself as well as to his closest friends – fated to stay where he was or leave. But pastures familiar and well-chewed, even after twenty-three years, contain a charm that greener fields lack. Besides, Mr Hobbs had a routine that a new job would inevitably disrupt. Friday evenings was always tennis; tennis at the Indoor Centre with the same opponent, holidays and foreign trips permitting (Mr Hobbs' regular Friday tennis partner travelled widely).

Unusually, Mr Hobbs lost 7-5 6-3 for the first time in ages. Had those stupid e-mails gotten to him? He didn't mention it to the victor or show him the print-out in his tennis bag, on the grounds it would appear he was trying to concoct a preposterous excuse for the unaccustomed loss. The victor, Raymond Hawkes (yes, *the* Raymond Hawkes), felt all his dogged work on his second service was at last paying dividends.

By the time of the next match between the two men, Mr Hobbs had received not only an unpleasant e-mail each day but several such a day. Each said more or less the same thing. He felt he now had to mention this to his right hand, Vera, who shared his affections and secretarial workload with Donald Thynne, who ran the marketing training programme for new branch staff. Her first thought was that Mr Hobbs, whom she called Paul, must have a secret life about which she knew nothing. Vera had removed the accent over her second syllable since becoming British but she could not erase her dark mittel-European suspicions about life and these suspicions attached accents, cedillas, graves, umlauts and underlinings to every word and gesture. Vera pointed out that the e-mail, the one he clicked up on his screen and showed her, came from an internet café. Mr Hobbs felt no mollification at this discovery, only a determination now to discover who or what lay behind it. Who had his personal office e-mail address? He could not begin to count – it included the 3,781 employees of the branches for a start, not to mention HQ staff and suppliers. In an inspired moment he thought it might be Ray, plotting to destroy his tennis concentration, but when the nasty e-mails arrived on Monday and Tuesday, when he knew Ray was in Perugia judging a wine competition, he knew this to be a wild and uncharitable notion.

Mr Hobbs' boss had to be told, since Vera pointed out that perhaps other members of the Society had been receiving similar missives. The boss, Hugh Parris, contacted the police, being of that generation which conceives of modern society as being based on the principle that all wrongs can be righted, all sins redressed, all injustices revoked, simply by finding the organisation expressly set up to remedy them. Thus Mr Parris would not talk face to face with a noisy neighbour but would telephone the council's Noise Hotline. In the case of the Hobbsian e-mails he was pleased to discover that Scotland Yard had a small department, staffed by specialists, devoted to solving computer crime. Mr Hobbs was asked to send copies of the e-mails to a Sergeant McHarries who, by Thursday afternoon, was able triumphantly to inform Mr Parris and Mr Hobbs that each one of the e-mails had been despatched from a different internet café and that in his opinion it was all a daft prank and would peter out, especially if ignored, within a fortnight. If this did not happen, Sergeant McHarries promised, his analyst would carry out a survey to see if there was a pattern to the location of these cafés. Quite what this would achieve Mr Hobbs could not appreciate, but Mr Parris took it to mean he had been taken seriously. It was enough for him.

But not enough for Mr Hobbs who had to serve and volley (well, let us say serve and *try* to volley) during another straight two-set defeat – this time 6-2 6-3. The fear ran through him that if this continued Ray might decide he was too feeble an opponent to continue the relationship. Apart from the tennis (and it must be said that Mr Hobbs was a far better stylist than Hawkes could ever dream of being), there was the fact that he liked having a famous wine personality as his tennis partner, almost, he thought, as a friend. Of course, it was Mr Hobbs who paid for the courts every time, and who was the member of the Centre (an exclusive establishment where the annual membership cost £1250). In spite of his celebrated palate, his occasional appearances on the Trev & Tracey show, and his weekly column in The Weekly Nation, Hawkes was a relative pauper as pleased to accept regular free tennis courts of the lushest indoor green as regularly to receive free bottles of wine of the richest red and white. Mr Hobbs could afford indulgences. He was unwed and childless. Hawkes had a wife somewhere, and child, but these, like ugly rumours, were never referred to openly.

Their friendship, if that is what it was, had begun when Hawkes had been invited to address the Speckshall & District Wine-Tasting Forum, of which Mr Hobbs was president. For a modest fee of seventy-five pounds (paid directly from the Hobbsian pocket), Hawkes had talked for an hour about Australian wine, his particular field amongst all the vineyards of the world to which he travelled and about which he wrote, and when Mr Hobbs had given him a lift home afterwards, since Hawkes was in no condition to drive or indeed as it transpired in no condition to even own a vehicle, the talk had turned to tennis. That was seven years ago now. Mr Hobbs had, last Christmas, totted up how much his membership of the Centre had cost during that time; the number of courts he had booked and for which he had paid; the amount of cans of tennis balls he had stumped up for; the gallons of petrol expended running Hawkes home; and he concluded that he could have spent the money on stocking up his modest cellar with a fair bit of *en primeur* first growth claret which he would dearly love to be able to collect. But Hawkes was a personality. A man of wine. A man who knew about wine. Who even spoke French and Italian (it was rumoured). Mr Hobbs considered it an honour to thrash him on a tennis court. It was useful preparation for the games he played on Saturdays and Sundays at the outdoor tennis club on the edge of town, between his bouts in the kitchen and his twists of the corkscrew. His was a full life. He was especially fond of Puccini, Mozart and Verdi. Now and then he persuaded a mixed doubles partner to accompany him to a performance, but these outings were rarely repeated with the same partner. Mr Hobbs preferred Puccini alone; Mozart with feminine company; Verdi in a group (when he could manage to get one together). He had no idea why he had these preferences and did not examine the proclivity further.

"After the first three games I simply fell apart," muttered Mr Hobbs, sipping his usual mineral water and Rose's lime juice.

"Don't you think, Paul old chap, that my second service has become mightily improved?" said Hawkes.

Mr Hobbs could think of no shred of evidence for this belief.

"Oh yes," he said bitterly. "Mightily."

Hawkes beamed.

ooooo

The two men had showered and changed and were refreshing themselves in the room adjacent to the main bar, set aside for adults who did not want to watch TV or to endure the families stuffing themselves in the cafeteria next to the bar. The room was always sparsely tenanted at this hour and it was Hawkes' chosen post-match drinking post although Mr Hobbs would have preferred the main bar so that anyone from the outdoor club who happened to see him there would spot him in company with a wine personality. Naturally, Hawkes was not a member of the outdoor club. It had an annual membership fee of £350.

A young woman, whom Mr Hobbs knew to be called Lola, came into the room bearing a parcel and a carrier bag. Lola would love Verdi, thought Mr Hobbs. Hawkes, who had given up on young women, sniffed as her perfume impinged on his senses and his eyes took no account of her startlingly glossy mane of black hair.

"A member asked me, Mr Hobbs…"

"Paul."

"He asked me to give you this. There's this letter too."

Lola left. Mr Hobbs opened the envelope and a finely woven and watermarked sheet of personal notepaper emerged with a gothic typeface announcing a local address of some opulence. The letter writer apologised for his nerve and asked Mr Hobbs, in his capacity as president of the Speckshall & District Wine-Tasting Forum, if he would taste the bottle of wine in the carrier bag and see whether it was advisable for him to invest in six cases of it. Each case was available at a knock-down price of £4500 but the decision had to be made that weekend. The seller was, apparently, desperate for cash. Mr Hobbs did not recognise the name of the writer. He handed the letter to Hawkes, who sighed.

"Oh dear. What we connoisseurs have to put up with! Some dreadful old claret, is it?"

"Let us see, shall we?"

The box in the carrier bag was a standard cardboard single bottle container and inside, once Mr Hobbs had peeled away the tape, was a white polystyrene tube, its two halves neatly slotted together. Mr Hobbs lifted off the topmost half of the tube and a bottle of red wine was revealed. He placed it on the coffee table between himself and Hawkes. The ugly, almost wilfully crass typography of the label instantly struck them.

"My God!" murmured the wine personality.

The jaw of the president of the wine forum dropped.

"Grange 1982," he said.

"Perfect drinking," breathed Hawkes. "Miraculous year."

"A bargain at £375 the bottle?" wondered Mr Hobbs aloud, his brain instantly doing the conversion.

"Buyer must be desperate for cash. Auction price would be nearer £500, I fancy, for this vintage, maybe twice that. Well, you'd better prepare something special for Saturday night to go with it. You lucky blighter."

Yes I am, thought Mr Hobbs. He picked up the bottle and examined the neck to see how deep was the gap between the bottom of the cork and the top of the liquid. This gap, called the ullage, tells the thinking purchaser how much of the wine has evaporated through the cork seal. In this case, there was negligible evaporation, suggesting, if the cork was not faulty, that the wine was in tip-top condition.

"Of course," muttered Hawkes, "if you'd like a second opinion on the wine, now if you like, I'm only too happy to share the burden with you. But I wouldn't want to spoil your weekend fun."

The greedy beggar, thought Mr Hobbs. He said nothing, torn between wanting to keep the wine for tomorrow (and maybe sharing it with a doubles partner) and accruing the prestige of being able to say to the letter writer that he had consulted with the famous Hawkes. Hawkes, sensing this dilemma, rummaged in his tennis bag and came up with a corkscrew. He waved it in the air. It advertised on its side the name of a famous champagne house. A freebie, thought Mr Hobbs, like everything else in Hawkes' life.

"The restaurant has some decent glasses, I take it?" continued the wine personality.

Mr Hobbs looked at Hawkes and saw him properly for the first time. The man was positively gagging for a taste of the Grange. For a rich moment, Mr Hobbs breathed in Hawkes' lust and felt revolted. He fought with himself. He lost.

"I'll go next door and see what I can find."

When he returned, Hawkes had opened the wine. Another piece of cheek, thought Mr Hobbs. Hawkes proclaimed the cork to be in fine condition, unusually so for one eighteen years old, evidence that the wine had been well cellared. He passed it to Mr Hobbs who put his nose to the top of the bottle. The smell was of a wine in highly drinkable condition. An elderly woman member came in, stared at the two men for a moment, and went away. Legs like a flamingo, thought Mr Hobbs.

He poured out the wine into two of the largest glasses the cafeteria boasted. Then the two men picked up a glass in unison, looked at the wine, and stuck in noses. After several seconds, they exchanged expressions. Mr Hobbs' was serene; Hawkes' joyous. Now they sipped, gargled, swallowed, breathed deep, sighed, smacked lips; unspoken phrases hung in the air.

"Colour's a bit bright for a wine of this age, isn't it?" said Hobbs.

"Yes. Odd that. Not as orange around the rim as I'd expect," said Hawkes.

Mr Hobbs felt himself moving on to a different level of wine-tasting as the men traded their impressions, just as Hawkes, though he could not admit it, moved into a different class when he walked on to a tennis court with Paul Hobbs. Those e-mails had truly taken their toll on the Hobbsian serve and volley technique.

The elderly female member with the phoenicopteric calves and thighs thought the two men must have dropped off when she returned to the side room with a copy of that day's

Telegraph which she had finally laid hands on. It was only when she approached closer, to hide herself away in the corner and read, that she noticed that one of the men, the portlier of the two, had his glass lying sideways on his stomach and the wine had dribbled all over his shirt. The thinner man's glass had slipped his grasp altogether and had smashed on the coffee table. Were they drunk? The elderly member was outraged. Then she saw that the tongues of the two men were moving and starting to protrude from their mouths. These organs of taste were turning blue. The men's eyelids were bulging, as if some force was inflating the eyeballs. With mounting horror, she witnessed convulsions starting in the chests of the two men and she began to scream and scream and scream.

No-one heard her; the muzak was omnipresent in the bar outside. But a sober member did see her gaping mouth and flailing arms and he saw her collapsing out of view on to the floor. He rushed in. He rushed out. Two doctors, known to be on court somewhere, were summoned. When the police and the ambulance medics arrived, both within fifteen minutes and both within a minute of each another, two bodies had, what flesh was visible to the naked eye, begun to turn blue and green and to exhibit an unholy ghoulish glow and a third, a collection of pink bones, was hyperventilating on a sofa. The elderly member was quickly revived but she was never brought back wholly to life and soon retired from tennis altogether.

Sergeant McHarries was also summoned, by his dyspeptic superior Chief Inspector Nuffield, who put it to the sergeant that a little foresight might have prevented the murder of Paul Hobbs, since the murderer had given plenty of notice of his (and the chief inspector thought only in terms of male pronouns) intentions. There was also the unfortunate second murder (or was it technically manslaughter? the sergeant wondered) to take in to account. It was exciting. Computer crime had its first corpses.

Within twenty-four hours the case was wholly assigned to another department run by sleuths who didn't puke, as had Sergeant McHarries at the sight of discoloured, murdered human flesh. The investigation had a simple aim: to discover what poor Mr Hobbs had done to merit the devoted attentions of a fiendishly cunning and resourceful avenger. Find that, agreed the hardened sleuths, and we have the net to snare the culprit.

The poison, the laboratory employed by Scotland Yard thrillingly revealed, was the rarely seen Belladonna-QV7. It is a post-war poison, developed by two South African chemists in the grip of gold offered and fear exercised by an Apartheid government minister anxious to find modern ways to dispose of opponents of the regime. It was developed not from the common European Deadly Nightshade plant, *Atropa Belladonna*, but from *Amaryllis Belladonna*, more commonly known as the Belladonna Lily, which is native to the Cape. It is not normally considered poisonous like its European cousin but in combination with certain chemicals, not plant derived, a stunning weapon had been created – odourless, tasteless, crippling within four minutes, lethal within eleven. Belladonna-QV7 also has the unique property of biodegrading and becoming harmless within forty-five minutes of the liquid element into which it is introduced being exposed to air. And it has to be diluted since in its pure state it oxidises and becomes useless within ninety seconds of air contact. It is illegally available at $150 a millilitre in Johannesburg and Cape Town.

It had been injected into the wine, via the cork, with a hypodermic syringe. This was revealed when the cork was examined by a spectron microscope. The thin channel was clearly revealed running right through the cork. It was a masterpiece of clandestine ferocity, that bottle, the sleuths conceded. What had Paul Hobbs done to get up the nose of so dangerous, so formidably well-equipped, an enemy?

ooooo

Vera Szabolcsi had become Vera Slocombe by marriage. Divorce, four years later, did nothing to change this. Her mother had brought her to England as a child when Hungary became invaded by Russians. They were from Debrecen, a very pleasant and historic city (when left to its own devices) some one hundred and thirty miles from Budapest. Naturally, Vera was a suspect for some days in the Hobbs case, *cherchez la femme* being a police mantra in certain homicide cases, until the hardened sleuths found nothing to incriminate her.

The letter was a fake, though someone certainly lived at the address. It had been typed on a word processor of Dell manufacture. The person who gave Lola the bottle to bring to Mr Hobbs was described by its carrier as a member she had never seen before, but this was nothing remarkable with so many members, and she could remember only vague details of his appearance. He was tall and had long hair. Was it a wig? Who could tell? Members were quizzed but no-one could shed any light on who the long-haired member might be, though true member, of course, he was not.

The bottle, after analysis, was stared at by one or other of the sleuths for the first few weeks of the investigation, then forgotten about and stored. Naturally, its provenance was investigated, but in the absence of any back label with a modern bar code and batch number on it, it proved impossible to trace it to any merchant. One hardened sleuth in particular, Detective Constable Turnbull, read up on the wine and discovered that it was indeed a rare and sought after artefact of great value, in spite of a label that appeared to indicate a pharmacological liquid which might be used for the alleviation of boils or perhaps a cure for snake bite. Penfolds Grange Hermitage, DC Turnbull discovered from a library book, is not only Australia's most legendary shiraz, but is a piece of Australian history. He would have liked to taste it, but did not dare to in spite of the lab assuring him that its poisonous element was not now lethal; besides, when he put his nose to the open top of the bottle, it smelled of vinegar. In spite of these off-putting indications of the death of this particular bottle – and all wine is destined to become vinegar in time – DC Turnbull discovered that a magnum of the '79 Grange had been sold, in March 1998, for several thousand pounds at a Sotheby's Bond Street auction. Turnbull did the rounds of the internet cafés and assembled descriptions of a thousand tall customers with long hair. But who could possibly trace which one of them had sent e-mails to Paul Hobbs? He went to Mr Hobbs' funeral, a bleak affair, but did not think to attend the cremation of Hawkes, which was a far livelier event with many smiling faces. The turnout from the Circle of Wine Writers was considerable; everyone wanted to be able to say that s/he had attended the last rites of the first wine critic to have died from drinking from a bottle of Grange. Penfolds' PR company was briefed in case of any adverse publicity but no-one blamed the wine. It was unfortunate, Hawkes' friends observed, that he had been so unlucky as to have been in the same place as a poisoned bottle intended for someone else.

Paul Hobbs would have liked to have collected first growths. Vera Slocombe *née* Szabolcsi collected something far more valuable: first impressions. She believed her Paul incapable of committing a crime, or even a perceived misdemeanour, of a calibre sufficient to inspire a murderer possessed of so creative an appetite for diabolical revenge. She said as much to Turnbull but he brushed this aside with "no-one truly knows another person or what they are capable of" and so Vera suffered in silence.

But not for long. A week passed at the office, her routine was permanently disrupted, but no-one said she should secretarise for anyone else and so Thynne was happy to give her more responsibility for visiting branches. It was noticing an internet café opposite one branch that had aroused her instincts for justice.

She discovered nothing. Then the editor of the Society's monthly magazine – which went out to savers and mortgagees (the members) as well as employees – e-mailed her and asked her if she knew who could take Paul Hobbs' place writing the wine reviews.

Vera instantly she said she would. The editor was delighted, unaware that Vera had little interest in wine, knew nothing about it, and drank it infrequently. The only wine she liked was the sweet stuff from Germany. Mr Hobbs' column, a 250-word ramble through whatever vinous nicety was currently taxing his imagination, had been written with great feeling and no little enthusiasm for its subject. By consenting, for a fee of £20 a month, to take her ex-boss's place, Vera felt she was only doing her duty. She now had to find out more about wine. The last bottle of truly delicious wine she had drunk had been when Paul had taken her to The Magic Flute and they had had a pre-concert supper beforehand in the West End. What was that wine called? She regarded herself in the ladies lavatory mirror, where she had gone after e-mailing the editor, to scold herself for her presumption and stupidity. She took off her glasses to better focus on what she saw. What stared out at her was a regular featured face of a woman in her early forties with green eyes and the suggestion of a cleft in the chin. She liked her face, and often wondered why it was not more popular amongst men. Was it the large glasses?

Paul had never got fresh or made anything like a pass. The Mozart became a one-off. Mr Hobbs never knew that Vera loved him more than a little. Sublimated passion had always been her way; a way at ease with itself, content in non-consummation, resolved to simply wait. Now his death had robbed her of that future, unlikely though it might have been.

Who had killed her Paul? *Why* had they killed her Paul? She thought she knew. Vera also concluded that if the police were too dense to see the obvious, she would have to act unilaterally. Now she was going to write regularly on wine, she thought she had the means to pursue her goal.The first thing to do was change her glasses. She removed £350 from her building society account and purchased a pair of the latest Danish lightweights with the indestructible frames. She added an inch to her heels. She went to the library and consumed several books on wine. She haunted the Society's press office and read every published wine writer, in the Saturday dailies, the Sundays, the women's magazines. She subscribed to Decanter and Wine magazine. She perused back copies. She purchased bottles containing the major grape varieties but could discern little difference, red and white apart, between them. How could she pull this off? She had no palate, or even enthusiasm for wine. She must, she thought, approach this like an odalisque facing a caliph with halitosis. Her real feelings must be buried behind a beautiful mask of knowledge and false respect. How else would she find Paul Hobbs' murderer?

The list of suspects grew with every journal, every book she read. Soon, as her knowledge expanded with the precision of her memory, she would be able to make the move towards the lion's den. What made a wine memorable? It was not just finding it provocative as a liquid it was also the circumstances in which it was drunk. She recalled the name of the wine at the pre-concert supper. She found it in a Thresher's. It was called Hans Muller-Grimm Rheingau Riesling, from Germany. She took it home, found it totally different from the one she remembered, and thus made an important discovery. It was all in the mind. It was all a figment of the imagination. It wasn't like music, like learning to read notes, and then translating them, via a highly practised technique on an instrument, into a sound the composer would recognise as his design.

She now knew as much about wine as she needed to.

What she wrote in her column attracted letters from readers. Paul had never received a letter from a reader in his entire occupancy of the column. This was because he had approached his job in the belief that he was talking to an audience wholly composed of Pauls. Vera took the line that wine was extremely boring to read about and therefore she should not only be entertaining and unstuffy but provide down-to-earth guidance. She did this by extolling the virtues of the cheapest wines possible and with a flair for the language she did not know she possessed. The letters began to pour in. She was permitted to answer them in the firm's time since she was seen to be doing a valuable public relations job. The director of communications Thynne complained to about his secretary's increasing submergence in correspondence and wine matters was not only unsupportive, but enthusiastic about Vera's new role.

Perhaps it was the new glasses, or possibly the higher heels, or most likely her acquisition of a wine memory: a widower on the board asked her out to lunch. They went to Thierry's and he handed her the wine list although he had, he said with the suggestion of a wink, a cellar in his house in Berkshire and was very keen on wine but obviously not, he added soberly, as "up on it" as her. She ordered a very expensive burgundy and sent it back the moment she smelled it. The waiter bought a fresh bottle and agreed it was superior to the first. The director's eyes shone with regard.

Can it be this easy, thought Vera? There had surely been no difference between the bottles whatsoever.

Her list grew. It would have excited too much attention to have had it pinned up in her tiny office so she kept it at home, in her kitchenette, a red magic marker hanging on a string beside it. It now had fifty-nine names on it.

It was time to take the next step. The lion's den was only one, or perhaps two telephone calls away.

From a helpful young woman at Wine magazine she was given the e-mail address of an organisation called The Circle of Wine Writers. She had come across its existence in the wine magazines, which now and then credited a contributor with belonging to it. These individuals went on the list and received the honour of being so inscribed in capital letters. Vera's interest in Moravian cooking and German beer dwindled. As did her bridge evenings and the Sunday hikes in

Epping Forest. Paul's murderer had made one huge error, so obvious the police were blind to it, and Vera had no doubt she could succeed where they had failed.

The reply from the honorary secretary of the CoWW was prompt: "If, madam, you are a published author or a writer on wine who can provide published evidence of one or the other, we would welcome you as a member. I cannot send you the membership list as requested until the enclosed application form is completed. You will require two referees to become a member, and fee details are also enclosed, but this will be no problem to arrange if, as you say, you write on wine for a monthly magazine with a circulation of four and a half million. I don't mind telling you that if this circulation figure is true it makes you the best-read magazine wine writer in the United Kingdom. Our next new members election meeting is next week."

Vera sent four back issues of the society's magazine with her application form duly filled out and soon after this arranged, upon being telephoned, to meet the honorary secretary and a colleague for lunch. Naturally she paid and paid handsomely. The honorary secretary suggested the Tate, and it cost Vera two hundred and ten quid (a good deal more than the annual membership fee).

The two men, agreeing to be proposer and seconder, drank three bottles of excellent burgundy, Vera pretending to enjoy just three glasses of it, and very soon a membership card arrived with her picture on it. The membership list of the Circle soon followed.

She had stepped inside the lion's den.

As she went to sleep that night, feeling slightly groggy from the cognac after the lunch, she murmured to the list on the wall, which had swelled to its full extent of one hundred and twenty people, "All for you, Paul, all for you" and she never slept better in her life. She could get a taste for that old cognac, but the burgundy she wouldn't have fed to a pig being fattened for seasonal slaughter.

Thynne was outraged when Vera presented him with her first expenses bill but the director of communications was unruffled. Indeed, he promptly transferred her to his own floor, told Thynne to find a new secretary, and Vera had soon doubled her salary and was now called a communications officer second grade. Scandalously, she dared, just for a second, to entertain the notion that had not Paul been so careless as to get himself murdered she would still be typing up reports for him and Thynne. She had a manicure to celebrate and joined a gym. All these incursions into eating and drinking were beginning to show around the midriff and, she thought, under the chin.

And still the only wine she *really* liked was the sweet stuff from Germany.

ooooo

It was astonishing how old, even decrepit, some of the members were. And so many duffers! She cut great swathes through the list of names and out went several dozen luminaries of the Circle who were, she decided, after attending two meetings of the organisation and enduring regular wine-tastings with its members floridly on display, utterly incompetent at anything above fixing free lunches. The younger ones she also eliminated – a couple of good-looking male writers on the Telegraph and the Observer and the starveling girl on The Sunday Times who looked like a retired model – and she was left with nineteen names.

She approached the editor of the Circle's newsletter, having decided that he knew everything she did not, and asked him out to lunch. He had been taken off the list long ago. He was, she thought a peculiarly ugly fellow with a face like a Mexican bandit, all angry teeth, and he had great furls of facial hair like the off-cuts of a fluffy bedroom rug. It would be unpleasant to face him over food and watch him eat, but how else would she find out what she wanted to know? In the absence – shocking to her ordered mind – of an archivist in the organisation, she had to resort to bribery. And what more luxurious bribery than Manoir aux Quat'Saisons?

ooooo

"This is my first visit to this restaurant. Such a thing as this has never happened to me before," he was saying, spearing a piece of asparagus and a shred of truffle.

She attempted to pour out more of the Von Schubert Riesling, which she quite liked, but a waiter rushed up and almost reprimanded her for daring to do his job. The editor – his name was Max Bye – closed his eyes as he sipped and chewed and Vera thought he looked almost human in that pose. She sighed. They had been there an hour – it was Wednesday lunchtime – and the first course was still only half-consumed. Quite a bill was going to be run up. Would the director of communications swallow it as generously as he done the others?

"Such a thing as this?" she purred. "Surely you've had Moselle like this with asparagus before? Or do you mean the truffles are an innovation?"

"Well, they are. No, no. What I meant was that no new member has ever taken me out to lunch before."

No old member had ever taken him out to lunch either, but he thought better of admitting to this. He didn't, of course, need to. Vera had him taped pretty well. She felt a little sorry for him. It was obvious he had trouble making ends meet (he had the same problem with the ends of his trousers and the top of his shoes).

She ordered a bottle of burgundy. It was always expensive burgundy that made men go ga-ga, she had discovered. Expensive burgundy – and the one she'd asked for was a René Engel Vosne-Romanée – was the perfect whore of the wine world, a fantasy that made men go weak at the lips. Bye was surely no different.

By degrees, as Engel's wine went down with the lamb (Vera splendidly concealing her repugnance at the bouquet of long-hung game), Bye, the fount of all knowledge, trickled, then poured, then gushed.

ooooo

There were now just three names left on the list. Bye – dear Max, as she now felt able to call him – had discovered that there *was* such a thing as a free lunch and not just lunches stolen under the guise of being a wine taster whom nobody, his own newsletter apart, published. He had felt obliged, it is true, under that torrent of marvellous pinot noir and then those glasses of incredible Calvados, to repay Miss Szabolcsi for her unique largesse and he felt better than he had in a long time. After all, he was an officer of the Circle and editor of its newsletter; shouldn't it now become a rite of passage for every new member to wine and dine him? He wondered how it would be possible to achieve a resolution to this effect at the next annual general meeting but then he reflected that if it were to be enshrined as a custom then the competition for his job, unwaged and often uncongenial, would become intense. In future, he thought, he would approach new members privately as soon as they joined.

No-one, he thought, had been so keen to hear, and so fascinated to listen to him explain in such convoluted detail, all the stories about the more colourful members, the ones who were published, the naughty ones, the ones who were loathed, the ones who were loved, the ones who were having affairs with wine company PR girls, the ones who bore the deepest grudges. He had been indiscreet. But then he had been unable to resist indiscretion. He had been particularly eloquent in unravelling the complex tapestry woven by the late Ray Hawkes. Just who would not mourn his passing and indeed just who would relish his descent to hell – and he had been adamant that this was Hawkes' rightful destination – Max had enjoyed revealing.

A six-hour lunch. It was a record. Even for the editor of the Circle of Wine Writers' newsletter it was a record.

Poor Vera had a hangover that kept her out of the office the next day (as the lunch had kept her out of the office all afternoon). This price was worth the paying. The list had shrunk to manageable proportions. Two men, one woman; their names, as the evening light of the day after the lunch began to fade and her hangover to lift, were all capitalised and Vera set about making notes of everything the effusive Bye had said. She eliminated two names, and she was now beginning to feel the breath of the lion or lioness on her. Could it have been the woman? She was unable to completely believe it or discredit it.

She had to proceed with delicacy and cunning. One of those three names would have already been wondering about the new member and perhaps already planning a further homicidal outrage if Vera's joining proved to be more than mere coincidence…

The solution was so simple that when it came to her, she wondered why it had taken her so long to think of it.

ooooo

It was the day of the Tesco tasting. Most of the old soaks were there since Tesco always laid on a good lunch and the central London location was easy to find. These conditions to ensuring the success of a wine-tasting – and indeed how a wine retailer was perceived by professional tasters – had astonished her. In her innocence, even with all that she had learned and amassed in her collection of first impressions, she had thought that the wines, the quality of the wines, was what mattered above all. But not entirely. It was also a matter of presentation. That was the great secret of the world of wine, just as it was in every other walk of life. Shallowness, masking itself under a luxurious patina of looking-the-part, was the key.

She went up to the woman first and introduced herself. The woman knew her name, had seen her at tastings over the past few months.

"I wonder, Mrs Vandyke-Price," said Vera, "if I could tempt you to give a tutored wine-tasting at my offices? The Chiswick & Richmond Building Society – we're the fourth largest in the world you know. The fee—"

"My dear, you must call me Pamela. I'd be delighted."

Thus Vera was able to eliminate the woman at a stroke.

The first of the two men, the immensely scruffy and anorexic radio wine critic Will Grover, was dismissive at first and Vera's heart leapt. But then he came up to her – as she was furiously trying to concentrate her mind on tasting Tesco's chiantis – and whispered in her ear: "Just how much of a fee exactly?" and Vera's shoulders slumped as she eliminated him too. She had been inclined to do this before she had even spoken to him, purely on grounds of his limited intelligence, and now she felt desperate. Could the one name left, the man standing imperiously by the champagnes, be the person she was looking for?

He looked formidable. He looked vaguely attractive even. He radiated intellectual fervour and distain. She knew the murderer had to be cold-blooded; also highly intelligent, highly creative.

How dumb of the police, she raged inside herself as she spat out sangiovese, not to see what was as plain as day.

But what if Sheridan Piggott was not the murderer? What then? If he wasn't, her whole world crumbled. She could not approach him as directly as she had done the others, fobbing them off with "I'll get back to you with dates in the new year". She could not bear the thought that he could just as easily disprove his candidacy as announce it the moment he said, perhaps clutching her arm, "My dear young woman, nothing would give me greater pleasure than to give a tutored wine-tasting at the Chiswick & Richmond Building Society."

Well, it might be worth it just to hear him say "my dear young woman" but then he might just as smoothly say "Fuck off" and wouldn't the unreasonableness of this just as strongly discount him?

Vera had reasoned that the murderer would baulk at the thought of going anywhere near the Society's offices. The murderer had known a great deal about Paul Hobbs and had poisoned him for blatantly obvious reasons. Those reasons Max Bye had disclosed over lunch, though he had had no idea of it.

Vera trembled. She had waited many weeks for this eventuality to come to pass. Sheridan Piggott was looking in her direction. She had looked up and caught his glance. She had not spoken to him before. Now that she came to think of it, he always avoided her or certainly seemed to move away from whatever wines he was tasting when she came close. Coincidence? Her paranoia? She wondered.

"Mr Piggott. May I ask you something?"

She had strode over to him, glass in one hand, clipboard with the tasting sheet affixed to it in the other, just as his head had been declined to expectorate into the adjacent spittoon. She had caught him when he least expected it. He was taller than she felt comfortable confronting, though she liked tall men (Paul had been six feet two inches). His lips parted in a surprised gesture he could neither contain nor conceal. She forced herself to look directly in to his eyes, though she could hardly escape noticing the heavily stained teeth from the red wines he had earlier tasted. She introduced herself, apologising for not doing so before she had put her first question to him. He did not answer. His face was frozen. Only the lips possessed mobility for were they not trembling?

"I wonder if you would be interested in giving a tutored wine-tasting at the Chiswick & Richmond Building Society? Do you know it? We're the fourth largest in the world."

He slowly put down his glass. He ran his tongue across his lips.

She gently took his arm.

"The fee would of course be commensurate with a wine critic of your standing."

She could feel sudden heat through the sleeve of his brown suiting. She knew she had her man.

He knew he was sunk.

ooooo

They were married a little less than six months later. Sherry, as he was called by his intimates, showed her the pile of press cuttings in which Ray Hawkes had poured out his bile on Piggott's books over the years: those volumes devoted to the classic grapes of eastern Europe, the pinot noir producers of the New World, the great wine families of the Cape. Hawkes and Piggott had feuded for fifteen years but what finally drove the latter to murder the former – and to disguise his real objective by seeming to target a building society employee – was the virulence of the scorn poured on The Sheridan Piggott Wine-Tasting Class, three video tapes plus an extensive manual. Hawkes had critically savaged it to the extent that Sheridan – poor Sherry, thought Vera, I do understand you so well – had tried to initiate legal action but had found no lawyer ready to consider personal abuse actionable.

Piggott had followed Hawkes regularly, so he confessed to Vera, waiting for a chance to kill him but had found that as each opportunity presented itself he wavered, unable to visit naked physical violence upon his adversary – not only (he further confessed, his new love making him unusually candid) upon grounds of a personal aversion to violence but a fear of being easily found out since he would be the prime suspect. He discovered that Hawkes and Hobbs played tennis on Friday nights and slowly the idea of how to concoct the perfect murder developed after a visit to South Africa to do research for one of his books.

It was a horribly perfect idea. How could anyone think that anyone but Hobbs had been the target? Only Vera had tumbled to it. Not even the most forensically minded of Circle members – experienced barristers like Julian Jeffs, for example – could conceive of Piggott being the cause of Hawkes' demise since it was deemed to be an accident. He had been in the wrong place at the wrong time. The lethal bottle of wine, that legendary Grange, was deliberately chosen, even down to the vintage.

"You know, Vera. I actually purloined that bottle. I never paid for it. I stole it from a Penfolds tasting held at the Avenue restaurant in St James's Street. I knew that greedy swine would be unable to pass it up. Oh Vera! I've led such a lonely life. To have found you at my stage, at my age. I don't feel guilty in the least about getting away with…with murder."

Vera said nothing. She thought what an enormously stupid person he was. From where had he found the ingenuity to kill her Paul? To carelessly kill the only man she had ever loved? She felt she knew. She knew exactly where those resources had come from. She possessed them herself. It was almost, she felt, as if her desire for retribution was greater than her Pauline love. Indeed, that this retributive desire *was* love.

"You worked it out. You knew."

"I knew. I knew no-one could possibly have a motive for murdering Paul. The police thought I was crazy. They will never know the truth…now."

"Oh, but you are crazy, Vera! How else could you say you love me? I've done a terrible thing. How do you know I won't bump you off?"

"You couldn't kill anyone you love. We were fated to meet. You do realise that, don't you?"

The glass of Clos de Vougeot Le Clematis 1962, which Sherry had so proudly poured from his single rare bottle kept for a rare occasion, she sipped with a beautifully enigmatic smile of pleasure. To her, the wine smelled hellish.

"To think that I have found someone who loves me, who can forgive me everything, someone with whom I can share my love of wine, who loves wine as I do. Someone who loves me enough to let me get away with murder."

Oh no Sherry dear, Vera thought as she contemplated the years ahead of them, I'm the one who's going to get away with murder, not you.

ooooo

Chateau Cheval Blanc 1947

"It's a yellow 'un," said Tarrant to Steadman.

Identifying the colour of the envelope was like a man yelling *Fire!* when the flames could be seen and the heat felt: it confirmed the bleeding obvious but, more richly, acknowledged the talismanic power of the circumstances. Custom dictated that yellows must be delivered to their addressees within the hour.

"More strictly ochre," said Steadman, Tarrant's manager. "You know what to do with it."

He placed the envelope, bulging with importance, into the relevant section of Tarrant's trolley. Steadman, his emaciated features lit, made almost rich, with the pleasure of seeing his underling so charged with duty, thought that a yellow one in the hands of Terry Tarrant was as good as delivered. He considered Terry to be the boy with whom he had the least trouble, and watched him leave the mail room with an easy eye.

Waiting for the lift, Terry took out the envelope and sniffed it. He detected the usual papery smell mingled with the faint odour of tobacco and some unidentifiable perfume, possibly musky in origin. Terry never knew why he sometimes smelled things; things of no seeming or indeed seemly interest to a nose.

Terry Tarrant's nose, as a physical swelling, was nothing extraordinary. As in all animals it was the only part of his anatomy open to the brain (though he had never given this consideration a moment's thought). The organ advertised its vulnerability with two holes set either side of a membrane called a septum, which lead to filamented chambers enclosed in a protuberance of flesh which, in Terry's case, was smooth and shiny but with age would, as with so many others, become hairy, crinkly, veined (or as Macbeth's gatekeeper has it, painted) and, in certain extravagant specimens, furuncular. These chambers connected to Terry's cerebral cortex and provided it with essential information. He took this, as he took smells, for granted.

His nose was not at an advanced stage of development. It could be said to be a virtual virgin (as its owner was, in another respect, a total one). His nose was, then, nondescript; in outward show banal. It had emerged from the womb nondescript. It sat in the middle of a nondescript face and provided his black-framed National Health spectacles with a handy prop. In assassins, confidence tricksters and mail boys, however, nondescription passes for an asset.

Terry Tarrant followed the least sensational of these ancient trades. His ability to pass without comment was an attribute to a person who trod the corridors and lifts of Atlas International armed only with a mail trolley or, as now, occupied with a single bulky envelope of above average importance, a fact confirmed by its yellow hue. Atlas occupied a seven storey block on a half-acre site in New Fetter Lane, that historic artery between Fleet Street and Holborn Circus where stands Prince Albert's least visited memorial – apart from the pigeons which obliged the regal cranium with regular excretory libations.

Ashley Armitage, the person to whom the ochre envelope was addressed, was the head of the TV department and it was a name Tarrant was forever to revere. For it was through Mr Armitage's good offices, in that gentleman's octagonal office itself that Tarrant's rebirth occurred – and that banal bifurcated canal sited in the centre of the Tarrant face was transformed into a dynamic engine of reconstruction.

Tarrant left the trolley outside the department's main door. He felt a little naked without it to give him distance from people. He also liked the support it provided for his hands. But this was a special mission. Yellow envelopes, international missives, had to be delivered immediately and took precedence over mere trollied correspondence. With no trolley, he would have to negotiate the bevy of Personal Assistants – who were dotted about the open plan section of the department – gripped by a slight queasy feeling in his knees. These PAs were secretaries in truth but had arrogated to themselves the fancier Capitalised title. Tarrant often reflected on this anomaly, unique to the TV department in Atlas, but had never dared ask a TV PA why she was so called. Equally, he did not understand why other junior members of staff said, usually with a sneer, that P.A. stood for Public Address. Tarrant could not explain either why these PAs were all blondes, all mini-skirted, all affected sunglasses of the same intense degree of blackness, and smoked the latest menthol cigarettes.

Tarrant padded across the department in his winkle-pickers, the one sartorial extravagance discernible in him, let alone permitted in the rules of dress for the lowest order of clerks. His face was arranged in its usual unquestioning state and seemed for all the world intent solely upon its duty of directing the gaze of its owner to the appropriate desk to which he was headed.

However, Tarrant was not unmoved. He noted Jill Seelig's exposed throat with its shadow of a cleft as it dipped to the breasts. And he did not fail to note Carole Threasham uncrossing her legs and leaning forward to extinguish her cigarette.

He moved around the desks and reached the one of the most feared PA of all, Linda Bigmore, who was A.A's secretary. She was not there. Had he not been preoccupied with cleavage-spotting he would have noted this inescapable fact as he entered the department.

Ashley Armitage liked to be referred to as A.A. – especially on memos, of which he received a daily pile. In the days when the Automobile Association had as many members as could fill an average third division football ground and Alcoholics Anonymous was as obscure and as frightening a bunch of nutters as communists and vegetarians, A.A. carried some rhythmic kudos. Who else in the department would have his name inscribed on a yellow envelope?

With no Linda to bark at him, Tarrant cheekily peered through the glass oblong inserted into Armitage's door and saw the head of television, head bowed, reverentially addressing a large glass of what he took to be wine. Armitage was acting most interestingly. He was agitating the reddish purple contents of the huge glass (or was it a vase?) and breathing in its fumes as if it were a vaporiser for blocked sinuses. Inaudible but expressive sighs escaped from the ample Armitage lips.

The man gave the impression, as Tarrant stared, of hallucinating. Maybe Armitage was smoking those weird cigarettes Tarrant had heard about and which it was rumoured were popular (indeed, rife) in the TV department after dark. But no smoke could be seen. In fact, now that Tarrant thought about it Armitage didn't touch cigarettes, unlike his staff who could give the impression, huddled in a corner during a tea-break, gossiping and belching smoke, of a distant prospect of Midlands heavy industry.

Tarrant knocked and went straight in. The mail room manager gave clear instructions in circumstances like this: all mail staff delivering a yellow envelope may knock and open any door even when the addressee's secretary is absent.

Ashley Armitage looked across at Tarrant. He pursed his lips, gargled the contents of his mouth, swallowed, rolled his eyes to heaven and then returned his face to his wine glass.

Tarrant, sheltering within his underling status like a snail before a blackbird, advanced unchecked across the carpet and agitated the ochre envelope as if sending semaphore. Armitage let out a fusillade of gentle sighs.

Tarrant became aware that a wine bottle was on the desk in front of the head of TV. He leaned forward, as far as he dared, and placed the envelope against the bottle. He turned to go.

"Excuse me," said Armitage. "What do you think you are doing?"

Tarrant felt utterly incapable of answering this question. He simply couldn't imagine what Armitage was up to: praying to a wine bottle?

"You…*you*…have dared to let this junk mail come into contact with the greatest bottle of wine you will ever be in the same room with. Take this vile missive and place it in Linda's wastepaper basket. I do not have one." He twanged one of the straps of his red braces. Armitage's dark navy, brass-buttoned jacket hung behind him on a hook and it nestled on its owner's black, brilliantined scalp as he leaned back in his swivel chair.

Tarrant felt he had to say something. Was Armitage serious?

"Aren't you going to open it? Sir?"

"It is enough for me to have opened this." Armitage stood up and gestured over the neck of the bottle. He picked up the envelope, gave it a glance as if to confirm his worst fears, and thrust it in Tarrant's direction. "It's only a script from that imbecile in Milan. It won't hurt you. Take it. Take it back to your post room and send it back to Milan marked 'address unknown'."

"It's…it's a yellow…an ochre 'un!"

"I know that, you idiot. I'm not colour blind. If I was I'd never have got aloft and they'd be a good few more Germans alive today, I can tell you." He paused, swallowed this delicious reminiscence, then a sip of the wine, which he chewed. "But I will have nothing to do with recommending a British feature film director for those ridiculous Italian commercials. Take it back. If Linda's off chin-wagging somewhere give it to…to Carole. Tell her I told you she should bloody well deal with it."

Tarrant took the envelope and caressed the flap. So much for the ritualised importance, demonstrably hollow, of its colour. He would enjoy confronting Carole with a yellow 'un. He put it in his jacket pocket. That way he could stand over her desk and regard her coldly before he produced the envelope with a flourish and commanded her to "bloody well deal with it".

But of course he also knew he would do no such thing.

Armitage smiled as Tarrant professionally patted his pocket where the envelope nestled. In eighteen months of mail-boying at Atlas Tarrant had picked up one or two tricks.

"Good," said Armitage. He sat down and poured himself more wine. Or rather, Tarrant considered, he didn't pour the wine so much as lovingly transfer it to the glass in which, Tarrant also thought, several goldfish could safely have swum.

"Still here. What are you staring at? Never seen a glass of wine before? I thought you lot in the mail room spent every lunchtime in the pub. Or El Vino."

This man's barmy, thought Tarrant. Has he any idea what a mailboy earns? And as for El Vino – didn't you have to be a member?

"I suppose you'd like a sip. Is that it?"

It wasn't it at all. Tarrant didn't care for wine much. He found it insipid.

"Er…um."

"Get yourself a glass then. Over there."

Tarrant felt he was in a dream. Had Ashley Armitage, a board director, ex-war hero, really asked him to have a glass of this wine? But that was hardly the most pressing question. What did he do when he found the wine to be as engaging as cats' piss as usual? Dare he accept this wine? He put his hand on the smallest glass.

"No, no, no, young man. You need a proper bucket-sized job for a wine like this. Don't worry. I'm not stupid. You're only going to get a teeny bit. Can't have the backbone of Atlas roaring round the corridors drunk, can we? Your modesty does you credit."

Tarrant found the twin of Ashley's glass on the shelf and picked it up. His forearm felt as if it was manoeuvring a gymnastic implement for muscle accretion. He handed it to Armitage, who picked up the bottle, which was dusty and appeared hardly the sort of container from which pleasant things could emerge, and bringing the glass to its neck he poured a measure of wine. Rather than filling the glass, it barely lined a portion of the tapering bottom. Tarrant's expression again misled Armitage.

"You are old enough to drink this, I take it?"

This irritated Tarrant.

"I'm sixteen, sir. Well, sixteen and a half."

The admission of the half irritated Tarrant further.

The affect on Armitage of this sum of years, however, was even more dramatic.

"Then this day was ordained, um…Tebbitt. It is Tebbitt, isn't it?"

"Tarrant…um…sir…Terence."

"And stop that dreadful sir. Makes me feel I'm back in the bloody air force. Do you realise the wine in your glass is the same age as you are? Give or take a bloody half? Look. D'ye see? 1947. Year you were born."

Quarried rather than born, thought Tarrant, echoing his father's standing joke. But then what happened next crushed all parental jibes. Tarrant raised the wine to his lips, thinking to get the matter over with quickly, but such was the girth of the glass his nose could not escape catching the rim and the fumes rose up. Tarrant's head giddied. Yet his lips had not touched the wine. He smelt the liquid again. It coursed through his nose, seeming to drown even the taste buds in his mouth; the very top of his head, Tarrant could swear, was vibrating.

Had his hair stood on end? Yet still he had yet to let his lips touch the wine.

"That's right, Tarrant. Let the proboscis get to grips with it first. Marvellous stuff, eh?"

Tarrant saw how Armitage twirled the wine in his glass and gingerly he did the same, careful to use both hands (unlike Armitage, for whom practice allowed the use of one). To Tarrant's delight, not a drop was spilled; instead, the wine, deep red to regard when still, took on brick and damson hues as it spread itself thinly over the lower concavity of the glass. Tarrant reinserted his nose and was rewarded with more massive doses of perfume.

"Awe-inspiring, isn't it?" he heard Armitage say. "I'm jolly pleased you appreciate it so much. Like some kind of rare, rich meat. How did anyone coax grapes to smell and taste like this? The texture is so...well, velouté! Like bloody velouté!"

Tarrant grappled with trying to define what this amazing aroma was. It was as if every single pore of his body was straining to catch it. Can merely smelling alcohol make you drunk, he wondered?

"Are you picking up the ripe blackcurrant and cigar box?"

Tarrant turned in panic and regarded the carpet. Had something been spilt? What was Armitage asking him to do now?

Armitage now seemed to have his whole head in the glass. Or so it appeared. Tarrant thought the time had come to leave. At last he let the wine touch his lips and he took a sip. Instinctively, and it was a gesture he was not to forget, he did not immediately swallow the wine but let it wash around his teeth. Armitage made strange gurgling noises and furiously nodded his head in approval.

Tarrant sucked in air through his teeth and then slowly let the wine trickle down his throat. He felt his body, suffused with satisfaction, soften to velvet. He could feel his free hand trembling. He had to sit down or fall down. Slowly he lowered himself on to Armitage's sofa.

Before he passed out he heard Armitage yell, "Keep that glass upright!"

Concerned that his visitor might stain the furniture, or shatter the glass, Armitage failed to notice that the grit had just dropped in to the oyster's shell.

ooooo

"Mum, is there any wine in the house?"

Anita Tarrant, grilling her husband's tomatoes and bacon, turned in shock. She stared at her son, registering that indeed it was he who had addressed her, and dropped the end of her cigarette in the puddle of cold tea at the bottom of her cup. Tarrant caught the fumes of the bacon but felt no salivatory response. He'd never liked bacon anyway and now it seemed more malodorous than ever.

"Under the sink. Why?"

"Funny thing happened to me today."

"I thought something was up."

"I look different, you mean?"

"No. Course not. You just seem different. Also, you've said more to me since you've come home tonight than you normally say in a week."

"Yeah?"

"Yep. Straight. You haven't found some poor girl to fall in love with, have you, Tar?"

Tarrant, who nobody seemed to call Tell let alone Terry, got up from the green formica-topped table and went across to the sink. He opened the door beneath and rummaged inside. He liked it when one of the family used his nickname. He had learned that his mother had called him Tar from birth because he'd had "a real tar baby" head smothered in gleaming black hairs like an oil slick – for the first two years, at any rate.

Bert Tarrant had qualms about Terry being really his until the customary Tarrant frizz had finally asserted itself.

"Where?"

"Where? What?" Mrs Tarrant turned, sighed, left the bacon and tomatoes to sizzle untended and she threw her arms up. This was a difficult feat. Her globular alabaster limbs were heavy instruments, except where they tapered to the fingers, where there was evidence of finesse.

"The wine, mum. Where?"

Anita Tarrant drew in a deep breath and reluctantly approached the sink. It was spilling over with plates and dishes, cups and knives and forks. Just by looking at the sink Tarrant could tell it was Tuesday. No washing up got done on a Tuesday unless Tarrant could be prevailed upon to do it or Bert did it before he went off to night work. Tarrant's brother Ronald and his wife Barbara, who lodged temporarily in the spare bedroom, never did washing up because they ate sandwiches in their room most nights and besides, Barbara demonstrated cosmetics, just to help save for the deposit for a flat, and couldn't be expected to spoil her soft hands. As for Anita, she played the piano for the over thirty-fives' keep fit class on Tuesdays and refused to get her hands red and raw in hot greasy water prior to public display. Wednesdays saw no diminishment in the pile in the sink, either. It was the under twenty-fives' keep fit class then and they expected jazzy tunes and Anita had to keep her finger joints out of harm's way for that lot. Thursday was a day of rest, it is true, but the construction of a mountain of steel and china and glass can become a compelling pastime.

And then Fridays it was The Bridge Inn for three hours and, though the pub regulars were undemanding in their choice of music and could not have worried less about the state of the pianist's hands as long as she knew the white notes from the black, the washing up nevertheless stayed where it was; by the end of the week it resembled a range of low-lying hills, a minor fortification, spread right across the sink and the draining boards either side. Come Saturday every dish and glass in the place was dirty and even the Tarrants could see the wisdom in doing the washing up rather than going out to buy new crockery.

Though, as Anita would have been the first to point out, they could have afforded to go out and buy new. Every member of the household worked. Five adults, all bringing in loot. The Tarrants were the richest family in the street. (Even Ronald and Barbara, saving their deposit between every slice of bread they ate unbuttered, contributed their share.)

"There Tar." She pointed to a dark bottle cowering behind the cobwebbed washing-up liquid and floor cleaner. "You don't need new glasses already, surely?"

Tarrant shuddered. He hated any reference to his spectacles. He'd only been wearing them since he left school. The travelling educational authority ophthalmatist who'd checked his sight three weeks before he had finally given up the secondary modern, a year and a half ago now, had been shocked. "How did you ever see the blackboard? How long has your eyesight been this poor? How is it no-one examined your eyes before? Didn't you realise you were severely myopic, presbyopic and astigmatic?"

"This is Sanatogen, Mum." He pulled out the bottle and showed it to Anita.

"We'll both have a glass. Oh…yes…okay then, two cups."

All the glasses were in the sink. Tarrant poured the tonic wine into two mugs and handed one to his mother who was rescuing smoking bacon from imminent immolation by fire.

"Where's your dad? His breakfast'll spoil. Thanks, Tar. Cheers. Ah. That's better. No, not another thank you. Mustn't get too merry for the over thirty-fives."

ooooo

Tarrant lay on his bed half undressed and wondered whether to masturbate. He took off his glasses so he didn't have to see and what little desire he had in his lower loins left him. He felt a little light-headed from the Sanatogen. Ugh, it was horrible stuff. He heard the front door close and his father coughing on the front step. A moment later the Anglia started up and the car, never liking to be in reverse, slowly grunted its way out of the car port, built over two weekends by the male members of the Tarrant family under the belligerent eye of Anita, whose piano money paid for the timber and cement.

The Anglia's headlights lit up Tarrant's small bedroom as they had done every weekday night for the past two years, except in summer when even sidelights were unnecessary, and the car spluttered up the street. The noise was the signal his dad was out of the way, out of the house, on his way to play whist all night as he gave the nod to the car accessories passing along the assembly line. Anita had left for the keep fit class after giving her husband his breakfast and Ronald and Barbara were at the Young Conservatives playing table tennis and drinking elderberry wine. And trying, Tarrant had once remarked (to himself), to keep their aitches off the lino by talking posh. Ronald said they only went to the Young Conservatives because they had two match play tables and a plentiful supply of new balls, unlike the Labour Club where the only table was pitted with the craters caused by fag ends and where one ball was expected to last a whole evening.

Tarrant, who had fostered a loathing for playing sport since he had first been invited to kick a football, scorned this explanation. His older brother was keen to get on. Tarrant saw nothing wrong in that, he simply couldn't understand why Ronald didn't come clean and admit that was the real reason he hobnobbed with the YCs.

ooooo

The neighbours had also joined the conspiracy of silence. Tarrant could hear himself think. He was grateful for that. He wasn't always so when left to his own devices in the house, which was frequently since Bert had started night work when Tarrant was eight, Anita had begun her evening ivory tickling, and Ronald had been conscripted. Tonight, though, was in the nature of a special occasion. He didn't even feel much hunger as yet, unable to tackle the supper Anita had left in the oven ready to warm up.

He fingered the lump in his trousers, caused by the thought of that terrifying but sexy Seelig girl lurking naked on the edge of his brain, but his erotic senses were held in check by the more splendid memories of that wine he had drunk at midday. Had he really keeled over and fainted on Armitage's casting couch? The shock, the delicious shock, of the wine had been all-enveloping, as though not just smell and taste but all his senses had been trapped in it.

What had Armitage said of it? *Vel-ou-tay*. What did that mean? Was it French? The wine was. He'd look the word up in Ronald's old school French dictionary. Only clever sods possessed old school French dictionaries. Ronald was the clever one in the family all right. Look how he had latched onto bright Babs. Look how bright Babs had been happy to be latched onto when she had only to crook a painted finger to rustle up a bloke. Consider how Ronald was the one to see himself serenely through the eleven plus while Terry couldn't even see the words on the blackboard that directed candidates to their exam classrooms.

Oh yes, Ronald was the clever one all right. Married at twenty-three and a nice flat, maybe, in Park Side in a year or so; a car after that; a spot of promotion when he qualifies; then a semi somewhere in Kent and the kids would follow as night follows day. Okay, so it wasn't ideal living with Bert and Anita and the mountains of dirty dishes, and Tar creeping lugubriously around the place, but that deposit had to be accumulated and both Ronald and Barbara thought so-called easy money like gambling on the horses and the dogs unwise if not immoral.

Where *was* Ron's French dictionary? Tarrant stood up. His standing presence in the pokey bedroom made it seem completely full; certainly there was hardly room for another human. The room boasted one small single bed with a wooden head, a small single wardrobe and matching dresser; the veneer apologetically peeling on each one. The walls were bare. It was a box room. Ron and Babs had the big bedroom. Tarrant, however, had an illicit key for this – stolen from a pair that had once been on Ronald's key ring. Tarrant always enjoyed the feeling of power possessing that key gave him. He went out and inserted it in the lock.

He opened the door and turned on the light. The room was doused in a sallow green from the bulb in the spinach-coloured shade in the centre of the room. The curtains were half-drawn but he ignored the usual precaution of drawing them fully as he sneaked around his brother's room. The books were on the shelf formed by the cornice that housed the three-bar fire. His hand fell on the French dictionary immediately, though he had never showed the slightest interest in it before.

He unearthed the word he wanted between 'velours' and 'velu'. It was not quite spelt the way it sounded. *Velouté. 1. a. Velvety; soft as velvet; downy. 2. s.m. Softness (of material); bloom (of peach).* Tarrant said the word softly to himself as Armitage had spoken it – v-e-l-o-u-t-a-y.

To his astonishment he felt his nostrils and mouth fill with the smell and the taste of the wine. It *was* like velvet; and it was also downy, the down of the sort most gloriously glimpsed back-lit on a fair skinned girl's forearms as her fingers played with a glass or an earring. It was like a peach's touch, with the incredibly subtle fuzzy skin of the fruit caressing and barely tickling the throat as it slid down. His nose filled with more complex sensations; blossomed with the wine's aroma.

Armitage was right. It was blackcurranty and cigar boxy – or what Tarrant imagined the mustiness of a cigar box might smell of. But none of these images did the memory of the wine justice. What words could? Most importantly, how could he acquire more sensations like it? He ran his index fingers along the sides of his nose. He'd never felt his nose before. He'd never even thought about his nose before. He looked at the word again. *Velouté.*

He pushed aside a single brown stocking on the crumpled counterpane and sat on the bed. Funny to think of this word existing hidden away in this book in this room he knew so well. *Like velvet…* But that didn't describe the smell so much as the feeling of the wine as it passed the gullet. It was the smell that had him hooked; the word was merely the trigger.

Maybe this worked for other things. Maybe there was a whole world of smells out there of which he knew nothing. He was only dimly aware that he did sometimes hold the envelopes and packages he delivered up to his nose. What did he hope to discover when he did this? He couldn't say. It was just curiosity.

What more exotic aromatic experiences, he wondered, were just around the corner? Were they as accessible as simply reaching out and touching them with his nose?

He looked at the bedpost with its curl of green knicker and he blushed. He had seen Barbara cross the landing once from the bathroom to the bedroom dressed in only a short towel and the bits of naked wet flesh he had glimpsed had not seemed repellent. Most times, whilst recognising that she was pretty, he found her distant and preoccupied. Her Leicester accent, though becoming gently south Londonised, cut through him like a knife. He knew this was ignorant prejudice but he still loathed her for it: loathed her for taking up yet more space in the house he hated in itself for being so inhospitable.

He reached across and took the knickers. He thought of the time Barbara had crossed the landing and he twisted the undergarment and tried to force it into a ball in his hand. He held it in both his hands and stared at it. Nothing. His penis did not so much as flicker. He raised his hands to his face and choked on the green frills. He closed his eyes and inhaled deeply, receiving nothing but the smell of *Nuits de la Rose* scent, five bob at Woolworths, and Boots talcum powder. It was all rather unappetising and completely unarousing.

"So this is what you get up to when we're out. You disgusting little pervert. How did you get in here?"

Tarrant looked up at Barbara standing in the doorway. She had taken off her green shiny mac and was dressed in calf-length white boots, a black and white skirt of modest knee-length and a vermilion coarse-knit jumper with a v-neck. Her words, despite their content, held no hint of menace.

Tarrant felt a giddying panic grip his guts. Where was Ronald? Ronald would kill him. He tried to stand but he was also trying to push the knickers away. The incriminating evidence stuck, like glue, to his hands.

"It's all right. You needn't worry about Ron. He's still at that boring club playing boring ping pong."

Barbara bent down and unzipped her boots and flipped them on to a heap of other shoes by the wardrobe. The wardrobe, equipped with full-length glass doors, caught the reflection of the boots as they described an arc. She smiled at him.

"So you like the smell of my underwear, do you, Tar?"

Tarrant had never seen Barbara like this before; she seemed someone else, or rather it *was* Barbara but someone else was speaking through her. Someone he didn't entirely recognise.

"It's flattering to think you like the smell of my knickers."

"Barbara, this is…I'm…I…"

"I must say I never realised you had such hidden depths. How long have you been doing this? Ever since I moved in here, I suppose? A year. Well, ten months. Ten months! And I never suspected a thing."

Barbara was now standing over him. He couldn't get up if he wanted to.

"Well, you've got more going for you than your big brother. You dirty little pervert! What do you think he'd say if he was to catch you doing that with his wife's knickers? I ought to tell him, Tar. I really should."

But Barbara was not acting like someone threatening to spill any beans. She was not even giving the impression of being angry, or upset, or even scandalised. Rather, it was as if she was excited.

"Now I think you should enjoy the smell of the real thing. If you really want to know what I smell like why don't you just…well, why don't you just go ahead and breathe me in…"

It was no use Tarrant protesting that was not his desire or his purpose in being there. Frantically he searched for the French dictionary amongst the bedclothes so he could reveal the reason for his presence in the bedroom.

Barbara stood there and unzipped her skirt. It fell in a tiny heap and she kicked it away. She unclipped and then rolled down her stockings and ignored them as they slid to the floor. She discarded various bits of patterned webbing to which Tarrant could not give a name. He stared at the bare flesh of her lower legs and thighs but he couldn't keep his eyes away from the tight red flowery knickers pinching her skin white. She took his hands in hers and placed them on her thighs.

"Come on, Tar. This is your fantasy come true. Don't sit there like your brother would."

This is very strange, thought Tarrant. I thought she loved Ronald. He felt an odd surge of sibling affection. Didn't he resent Ron's hegemony over parental emotions and pride, living space, rations, and, it seemed, the very air in the house? He sometimes had a dream in which Ron was incapacitated whilst on National Service, but he was never sent anywhere dangerous, like Malaya or Cyprus, not even to the impotent old enemy Germany, but instead spent his uniformed two years as a corporal accounts clerk in various UK supply depots.

"Barbara, this isn't right. I shouldn't be in this bedroom. I was…"

Barbara had no ears to listen. Lifting Tarrant's hands to the edge of her knickers she used them to roll the undergarment as far as her knees. From there it fell to the floor. Tarrant felt the erection career in his trousers. He had to stand and get out of here, three-legged and freakish as he now was.

But that pubic hair, that triangle of closely-knit fuzz: instead of horrifying him as he'd always suspected it must, he felt unable to resist kissing it. As he did so he felt Barbara grab him with both hands round the back of the head. Her legs parted and a thick wisp of wet hair brushed him on the lip. The smell of her was like damp grass and hot roses and rancid sweet fruit. And, quite unnervingly, there was, ever so subtly, the gamy taste that Armitage had alluded to in that wine. What was the phrase? "Like the smell of some kind of rare, rich meat."

"Put your tongue inside. Go on. All the way. Go on… please…"

Tarrant felt as if his head was coming off. Barbara showed no sign of relaxing her grip. She was frenziedly twisting and turning his head as if attempting to unscrew it. She reached a climax with a scream he had never heard her emit during the sometimes percussive lovemaking sessions that went on in this bedroom. She was gasping and flinging her own head to and fro in unison with the manipulation of Tarrant's. He sensed a feeling of warmth spread through his body like a religious conversion, or at least a feeling engendered by a heady session in a heated religious environment. As she unhinged herself from him and looked down on him, she picked up her fallen knickers and wiped his mouth. She sat on the bed next to him and he saw that her face was bathed in sweat.

"I dreamt of a man doing that to me. Who would have ever dreamt it would be you, eh?"

Then he felt her hand on his trousers and her fingers unzip the fly.

"We can't make love, Tar. Understand that. I'm married to your brother and I'm going to have his children some day. But we can have our little secret, can't we? Just until Ron and I save enough for that deposit."

Tarrant ejaculated the moment Barbara had him in hand.

ooooo

When Ronald got home, face still shiny from the ping-pong, Tarrant was sitting at the kitchen table eating sausages. Barbara was doing her nails opposite, the pot of varnish parked by a steaming pint mug of tea. Mrs Tarrant came home ten minutes later and before they all went to bed they had a quick game of pontoon for half-a-crown a player, max.

They could only play pontoon when Bert was out of the house. Being a skilful card player he despised naked games of chance and made rude remarks if anyone dared to play them under his roof. The Tarrant household was a strangely complex tribe under its outward skein of normality.

ooooo

The war hero was standing by his PA's desk waving her cigarette smoke away when Tarrant came in with the mail. It had been over a week since the incident with the wine. As Armitage turned to go back to his own office, Tarrant spoke, conscious that seven days ago he would not have dared even cough in the man's presence.

"Mr Armitage, can I ask you something?"

Armitage liked the question. He saw right away that the boy would not speak in front of Linda.

"Come into my office. Less poisonous there."

Linda stuck out her tongue at the retreating back of her boss. It was a gesture not so much in response to his jibe about her addiction to nicotine as his removal of the mailboy from her presence – she was going to be deprived of secret intelligence. What on earth would a little guttersnipe like Tarrant want with Armitage?

"It's about that wine, sir…"

"Now stop that bloody 'sir' nonsense. Carry on."

"Um, what wine was it? It was wonderful. I didn't like wine. I still don't. I had a glass of red at The Crown and—"

"The Crown? I'm surprised they even had a bottle of wine on the premises. My dear boy, there's all the difference in the world between a glass of Chateau Cheval Blanc '47 and a tumbler of vin rouge from a bottle which has probably been opened for a week and left to fester behind a bar."

"That's what I wanted to know! What that wine you gave me was called."

Armitage began a slow tour of his office, all the while rubbing his chin in a gesture he did not know he possessed. Tarrant, asked to sit on the sofa he had fainted upon, leaned back and felt strangely at ease. Usually he was terrified in directors' offices; terrified he was going to break some law of etiquette without knowing even what it was. Indeed, he could never get used to the fact that an oik like him was even allowed to talk to such people in the first place. Bert had instilled in him such a notion of Them and Us, which school had only reinforced, that he had not expected to land a position in an office at all. Ron had received the brains in the family, said Bert, and you got the… But Bert never filled in this silence and Tarrant never asked. The man at the Employment Exchange, where Anita had taken Tarrant two days after he'd left school, his new spectacles perched uneasily on his nose, had put it to him thus, without ceremony:

"Heavy industry? Or light industry? We have an office position, but…"

Light sounded easier work. He said light. Anita pooh-poohed this. Light or heavy, neither was what she wanted for her younger son. She demanded to know about the office position, but or no but.

Hence Atlas; though both Anita and Bert regarded it as a miracle their son had got the job. Tarrant had been sullen and withdrawn, even more than usual, during the tube journey to Holborn and Anita put it down to nerves. His silent fury was, in fact, due to his impotence at failing to persuade Anita not to accompany him. What Tarrant never twigged was that he only got the job because the mail room manager was so impressed with the mother. Tarrant obviously came from an honest family. And honesty, in the eyes of the mail room manager, counted for more than anything. And so he was saved from light engineering. Anita was happy. Her younger son had made it to office employment in one bound.

"Can you write it down, Mr Armitage, please?"

Armitage handed Tarrant a notepad and a pencil.

"Write it down for yourself. The other bottle's in the rack. Be gentle with it."

ooooo

"Something," said Anita gravely, "is up with Tar. He's acting very odd. He got a book from the library the other day."

Bert, polishing off the grilled mushrooms and tomatoes he had as a breakfast special before he faced the rigour of an evening's (and half a morning's) whist, tried to shrug in ignorance but found he couldn't do it with a knife and fork in his hands. He gave up the gesture, which was lost on his wife, and cocked his head at Barbara who, unusually for this time of day, was enjoying a cup of tea with her in-laws. Barbara saw the gesture and totally misconstrued it. Surely Bert could not have guessed?

"Always keeps himself to himself your younger son," she mumbled.

The last of the buttons and a slice of local hot-house grown tomato disappeared down Bert's gullet. The top of his hairless head shone silver from the centre light. He nodded vigorously in agreement as though Barbara's answer made further discussion of the point redundant.

"Bert, why don't you and Terry go and see Crystal Palace play no more? You used to go lots."

"Not been since I started nights, Neat. Not the same team any more. 'sides, Tar lost interest. He lost all interest in sport when he was ten."

"When his eyesight got so poor," said Barbara, pouring herself more tea. It came out of the pot like lemon squash. Why do southerners take their tea so weak? she thought. "He couldn't see the football, let alone tell one side from another."

"What? How do you know that? He's only had glasses eighteen months. Since he left school."

Barbara wished she had kept her mouth shut. She tried now.

"Well, Barbara, what d'ye mean by that?" insisted Anita.

Bert kissed his wife on the cheek, nodded yet again at Barbara, and took his car key from the hook next to the pantry. He said bye bye and gratefully fled from the inquisition.

"Did he tell you that, Barbara? Bloody little liar."

Barbara felt she owed Tar something. He had done her beautifully over the past week.

"He told me, yes. I didn't know you didn't know."

"I know what the opthalmiwatchyoucallhim said when he tested his eyes. I was there. He said Terry's eyesight must have been poor for some time. But Tar never told me. He never said either that he gave up watching football because he couldn't see the ball."

"I reckon," said Barbara, enunciating as clearly as she could, "that Tar's eyesight troubled him all the time he was at senior school."

"Did he tell you this? Don't tell me Ronald told you. He wouldn't have known if Tar had grown two heads."

Barbara nodded. Anita looked at her in astonishment.

"Let me make you some more tea," she offered admiringly. "I'm glad to hear Tar talks to someone. He surely never talks to me. Well, not since…since…"

"Since he was ten years old or so."

"You're right. Ten years old. I lost him when he was ten years old. He just disappeared inside himself."

Anita took a boiling kettle and poured the majority of its contents into the teapot. Barbara winced. Maybe, she thought, she should reveal more and ask for maybe a few more teaspoons of tea in the pot. In the event, she felt she had said far too much already.

"Barbara, you're a surprise. How did you get Tar to open up like that? I thought he…well…you know…"

"Hated me?"

"Yeah, something like that. Jealous of you. Taken his brother away from him."

"Anita, thanks for the tea. There's something I must do upstairs. Shouldn't you be getting ready for those old biddies at the keep-fit?"

So much, thought Anita, for being considerate towards Barbara and heaping the teapot half full of tea. Some of those old biddies were younger than her.

ooooo

Barbara went upstairs feeling edgy. But when she flung open the door of the bedroom, closed it, sat on the unmade bed and brushed the sheets free of the crumbs from last night's sandwiches and ran her fingers through her crop of hair, she felt suddenly elated. It was a feeling she had never had before. It was to do with knowing something others did not; something that, if they found out, would electrify them. She rather liked the feeling now she was out of the kitchen. She wished she could pour herself a stiff drink, but the only bottle of spirits in the house was in the pantry and it was Bert's whisky kept for the occasional sinew-stiffening. Barbara and Ronald had given up spirits in order to accumulate the house deposit – until then she was stuck with mild and bitter and the odd glass of lager and lime. Neither, however, was available in the bedroom.

What *was* she doing with Terry Tarrant? Was it sexual boredom with Ronald? Was it sexual hunger from an over-sexed libido? Was it, perhaps, to do with this new discovery of the illicit excitement involved? Was the seduction of a teenage virgin part of the thrill? (She ignored the consideration that his virginity, in technical fact, remained an unaltered state.)

Was the key attraction the bizarre nature of their erotically restricted and tightly defined relationship? Was it the dare-devilment of doing it, whatever *it* was and however it could be defined, in that bedroom? Could she have done it with anyone else but her husband's brother? And, most oddly, how long had she harboured the desire to have a man do that to her? Would the touch paper of this particular firework have ever been lit had not she come across Tar with her knickers in his face sitting on this very bed?

There was a confused but very satisfying jumble of questions in Barbara's mind and none offered a straightforward answer. The only thing she did know was that what was going on between her and Tar was not going to stop quickly, unless he suddenly ended it. It had only just begun, after all, but it was getting better each time and Tar was becoming tender, expert and versatile; both clitoritic and vaginal orgasms were bestowed upon her by his increasingly exploratory and ecstatic tongue and he was content merely to accept her hand in response. He seemed genuinely eager to please. Maybe that was all he imagined he could hope for – from any woman. But maybe he was also changing in expectation and ambition as rapidly as he was gaining in prowess. He was certainly talking more.

She wasn't experienced at dwelling on things. She felt like a different person, merely crouched there indulging in speculation. Life wasn't to be deeply thought about. There had been obvious (and not to be reflected upon further) choices now safely behind her. These included having to get married to escape two inhumanly dull parents so introspective they were barely past the pupal stage of their development, along with the need to get away from their damp two-bedroomed council maisonette with its outside toilet; but she had made this choice concrete by grabbing the first lance corporal she could find who came from somewhere south of Watford. This wasn't difficult. Ronald had been a pushover.

She heard the front door go. It was Tar. Ronald always whistled when he opened the front door. Always the same tune, too, which, quite incredibly now that she thought about it, always crescendoed as he stepped inside the hall. Was this coincidence? Practice? How many renditions of the tune did he get through once he alighted from the bus in Hive Lane? (Assuming, of course, that he didn't sit on the bus whistling away and entertaining the other passengers.) And when did he begin the last rendition so that it would unfailingly start to climax as the key turned in the lock? The tune was "Oh, for the wings of a dove".

Tonight Ronald was at his double-entry book-keeping class in Dulwich. He wouldn't be back till half-past ten or so as he had to change buses twice. She heard Tar reach the top of the stairs and pause. She was familiar with that break in his step. She was unable to stop herself from springing up and opening the bedroom door. What, she wondered, was this book Anita said Tar had got from the library? She beginning to suspect it was The Kama Sutra or somesuch manual. The sort of forbidden volume she remembered got dog-eared and dirty from being passed amongst all the girls in class before it was confiscated by a teacher who was as ignorant of the more outrageous of the book's suggestions as the girl from whom she had snatched it.

"Hello, Tar."

Tarrant was a little red-faced, Barbara noted. Surely not from the walk upstairs?

"I passed Mum at the top of the street. She said she was glad I was getting on so well with Barbara. You, I mean. She… she…er…she…don't…doesn't…?"

"No. Course not."

"I was dead flummoxed, I can tell you. I didn't know where to put my face."

"Oh, Tar. You know exactly where you can put your face. What's the book you've got under your arm?"

Tarrant reached into the top pocket of his jacket and took out his glasses. He habitually removed them two stops from his local station in case anyone should see him wearing them. He couldn't recognise a neighbour, or an ex-school mate, from twenty-five yards away without them, but he was prepared to run the risk attendant upon the failure to spot such an acquaintance by sheltering behind the peculiar security myopia conferred, as sand on the eyelids is said to serve the same purpose for the ostrich. How could he face the embarrassment of their unfailing "Oh, I didn't know you wore glasses" or, worse, "Hello, giglamps" or "four-eyes" or, in one awful encounter with his old gym teacher, "Ah, Tarrant. The dodgy pupil with the dodgy pupils" ?

ooooo

It had no cover. She expected that. Library books never had covers. Or did they? She'd never been inside a library, or borrowed a book, so she was unsure. It was better without a cover, anyway. How could Tar read it on the tube otherwise? He'd never have the nerve to sit there on the Northern line with The Kama Sutra emblazoned on his reading matter. Wasn't it a banned book, though? She'd heard that from the radio; or had she read it in the Daily Sketch? Wonder how Tar smuggled such a book out of a public library?

She followed him into his bedroom. She'd never done this before. Tarrant wondered why she wanted to take the book from him. She took it in her left hand, the one she always used on him though she was right-handed. She didn't so much as glance at it.

"It's great you getting this book out of the library. I'd like you to know I think that."

"I want to know more."

He adjusted his glasses, took off his jacket. He was feeling contented. He was always keen on Tuesdays anyway because it was Anita's senior keep-fit session and Ronald's accountancy class, and Bert never missed a night off work; even during the 'flu epidemic or the worst of the smogs he'd made it to the factory with the decks of cards in his knapsack as unruffled as his health. Usually Tarrant had the house to himself for a while, Barbara normally doing overtime and not back till tennish. He stared at his book in her hand. He was slowly picking his way through it and it was only out for a fortnight. He prayed no-one else wanted it so he could immediately renew it. He'd have liked to continue reading it. He was at a crucial stage of chapter fifteen, so much so that he had forgotten to take off his glasses until he reached the ticket collector and old Eldritch, who kept chickens in his back garden two doors along, had greeted him and fallen in step with him and Tarrant had endured his company, waiting for a "How long have you worn those things?" that never came.

Barbara must be keen to be back so early from her cosmetic demonstrations on a Tuesday, he thought. She stroked the book in her hand. She smiled.

"Yeah, I know. I should be doing the overtime tonight. That's thirty bob that won't be going into the deposit."

Tarrant didn't know what to say. Didn't know if he should say anything. She looked angry, just for a moment. He wished he could have his book back. He did want to get on with it.

Barbara loosened the belt in her skirt with her free hand. She went to kick off her shoes but remembered which bedroom she was in and merely stood out of them. The four-inch heels made egress easy. She had no stockings on. She gestured at him with the book.

"I'll look at this while you…you…"

She's gone loopy, thought Tarrant. He looked at her bare legs. He felt the swelling in his groin. His mouth went dry. Barbara flopped on to the bed and slipped out of her knickers.

"We've got lots of time tonight. Let's do it lots of times."

He let out a sigh and mentally jettisoned his book for the evening. He unknotted his tie and unbuttoned his shirt, white like the ones he always wore to Atlas. Barbara liked him to take his shirt off. She said she liked to feel his shoulders on her legs. He obediently lay down beside her and moved to part her legs but she took his head in her knees and gently agitated his ears. He found this not unpleasant. She lay back and opened the book at random.

There was an oath followed by a yelp of dismay.

"Oh bloody hell! Tar!? What is this? 'There is one growth of Saint-Emil…lion, that of Chat…eau'…Chateau Bastard?… no, 'Chateau Balestard…Chateau Balestard…Balestard-la-Tonnelle…which has had the signal…' – signal? – '…honour of inspiring a poem of Fran…Fran…Francois Vill…Vill…on…in its…'"

"It's A Book of French Wines. By a bloke called Morton Shand. Only book they had on wine in the whole library. 1928 it came out, so it's a bit dated but…"

"Be quiet and concentrate. You little bugger. I thought you'd borrowed The Kama Sutra…!"

She gasped as Tarrant bent his head to his task. She threw the book to one side. He stopped after two minutes and raised his head, squinting at her through the bunched ends of her blouse pulled up over her stomach. He could feel she was coming. He'd never known her so abandoned. He felt, not for the first time, that he was becoming more than a little fond of her; maybe genuine affection was setting in. Well, it was only natural, wasn't it?

"The Kama Sutra? What's that?"

"Oooh…that's…ummm…uuuuuu!"

She reached a clitoral climax and hugged his head but didn't pause to take breath for the question:

"So what's a signal honour when it's at home, Tar?"

ooooo

Tarrant was happily surrendering to his obsession with wine. Not just the memory of the bombshell in Armitage's office, with that glass of Chateau Cheval Blanc 1947, but the other wines he had managed to taste over the few weeks since. None of these wines compared with the White Horse, as he now called it, having discovered what the French words meant from a merchant's catalogue he had dared to ask for whilst passing a shop in Holborn. He had not thought to look the words up in Ronald's French dictionary in the belief that brand names didn't appear in reference books.

He had also finished Mr Morton Shand's book on French wines. But he wasn't satisfied. He wanted, when all was said and done, to *drink* the stuff and dry history was no substitute for a dry glass of it even though he was beginning to acquire a taste for the myths and legends that surrounded almost every bottle he experienced. These bottles, for the most part, were scant in number and thin in reputation; nevertheless they swelled his knowledge.

One Friday, back pocket swollen with a week's pay, he had persuaded three members of the mail room staff to accompany him to El Vino's. He had not dared to enter alone, having heard of its Masonic clublike nature and refusal to serve men not wearing jackets and ties and women, whatever their dress, in any circumstances; and even with a trio of colleagues, one in his early twenties, he still felt nervous as he followed them through the door of Fleet Street's most infamous bar. It was not mere safety he sought in numbers, or even companionship; it was value. With four to divi up, maybe he could persuade them to go quarters on a couple of bottles of expensive wine and not the resinous or vinegary plonk the pubs served.

He was flattered when Duncan, the mail room undermanager, handed the list to him and said that he didn't understand it but maybe Tarrant did. Tarrant suggested they drink a bottle of white first and follow it with a bottle of red, and then grab a quick spaghetti at the *ristorante* on the corner of New Fetter Lane before their lunch hour was up. Everyone fingered the lump in their back pockets, looked at the prices of the Meursault and the Clos La Madeleine Tarrant plumped for, and then they quickly worked out that they could get out of the *ristorante* for four bob each. The smile was only wiped off Tarrant's face when Duncan said that it was now up to him to go to the bar and order the wines: *to speak their names.*

Tarrant couldn't let the side down now. Not with their triumphant acquisition of the only spare table in the place (which wasn't as posh as Tarrant had feared – he failed to see what all the fuss was about).

Tarrant fled to the bar clutching the wine list and shouldered his way through the pin-striped throng. The barman looked at him fiercely, for a moment thinking to ask if the customer was old enough to be in the place but then let the thought perish under the consideration that no customer, in the whole long history of the bar, had ever been asked such a stupid question before.

"Bottle of Meursault and a bottle of Cl…Cl…Clos de la Madeleine…we're sitting over…"

"What?"

Tarrant repeated himself.

"You'll find salt at the end of the bar," said the barman.

"No, the wine. Meursault," shouted Tarrant.

The barman twigged. He asked what the other wine was called again. Tarrant shouted it out and went bright scarlet. The barman said the bottles would be brought over.

"How many glasses?"

Tarrant didn't quite catch this and thought the bastard was making a joke about his specs. The barman repeated himself. Several pin-striped bodies turned and looked intently at Tarrant. He squirmed and retreated to the table.

ooooo

Tarrant recalled this incident as he lay on his bed before supper. He had hoped the awful embarrassment he'd experienced when he asked for those wines would have abated under the encroachment of the rich pleasure drinking them had provided. As he lay there reliving the taste of the wines, he could feel his face burn for a moment in physical remembrance. How was he going to learn about wines with only books for a teacher and the occasional bottle as a blackboard? If the wines he read about weren't French, with its slimy and impossible to handle language, they were German, which was as coiled and lethal as a cobra, or Italian and Spanish; only Portuguese wines were handily English sounding but he wasn't yet experimenting with these – largely on the grounds of their high alcohol content and their cost. Who wanted to go quarters on a bottle of vintage port for lunch? The lunch at El Vino's with the bottle of Meursault and the Clos de la Madeleine had occasioned comment, later that afternoon, of the "Who's a bit pissed then?" sort from old Steadman, so fortified booze like port was definitely ruled out. Tarrant was also conscious that he wasn't, for some months anyway, legally able to enter licensed premises and personally order alcohol. The only solution to the problem was to get a job in the wine trade. There he would pick up the way to pronounce the wines and get to taste many more – certainly more, he reasoned, than he could afford to buy under normal circumstances.

"Tar! Your supper's on the table!"

"An' it's not gettin' any warmer!" added his father, who had yet to leave for the night shift.

The voices were transmitted at a frequency between a scream and a shout – that indeterminate and personal area of auditory transmission which practice makes sufficiently perfect to carry up stairs and pierce a doorway yet insufficiently sharp to suggest the caller is hysterical. Tarrant picked himself up off the bed and opened the brown paper carrier bag that was lying on the floor. He took out the bottle of Valpolicella he'd paid nine shillings and sixpence for in the Peter Dominic shop he'd discovered up in town, and hoped it would go with whatever his mother had prepared. He was interested in learning something about Italian wines and the man in the shop said this was a bargain and "The Beaujolais of the Veronese". Tarrant did not let on that he had no idea what the man meant although Morton Shand had covered Beaujolais.

Outside the shop Tarrant jotted the phrase down in the notebook he had acquired, hoping he'd spelled Veronese right, whatever it meant, and that the Valpolicella did come from Italy and not France. He confirmed this by unwrapping the wine there and then and studying the label. It was a very confusing business, he was beginning to discover. The notebook was a great substitute for a yet untrained memory; he could remember tastes and smells but hard facts had trouble sticking.

He came through the kitchen door with a smile on his face and the Valpolicella in his hand. He waved the bottle at his father.

"Like a glass of wine before you toddle off, Dad?"

"Blimey, Tar," said his father, "you think you've got something to celebrate?"

Tarrant thought for a moment and said nothing. He rather thought he *did* have something to celebrate; but how was this remotely communicable to his parents? Exactly what was *this* in any case? He couldn't explain it. He didn't know quite what was happening to him. He only knew it *was* happening and it involved a side of himself he had never suspected. No-one had ever, in his life up till now, said anything which provided the smallest clue that what was taking place might be perfectly normal.

All his life he had accepted what was on offer, without question. He didn't quarrel with the way things were. He didn't question the cards he was dealt. He didn't consider it his place to demand a reshuffle let alone rearrange the deck himself.

He sat there, finishing his lamp chop and boiled cabbage with Oxo gravy, and wondered how he could have gone through four years of secondary school and never seen a word written on a blackboard. Not only had no-one, certainly no teacher, ever cared to ask why he never knew the answers to questions in front of his nose, but they hadn't even stopped to think why the boy always fought to be in the front row of any class room (where at least he stood a better chance, with the more emphatic wielders of chalk among the staff, of reading what was on the blackboard). Why had the boy always squinted? It was a question as meaningless as asking why he always wore scuffed black shoes.

Tarrant had never once complained that he couldn't see. But now… Now, as he sat there with the remains of a thoroughly unsatisfactory Valpolicella in front of him, he would, and could, ask why. He could discern differences and act upon them. He could bitch loudly and long and say: throw out the deck. He could even demand that a different game altogether be played. And he realised that this was not just true of wine, but of more fundamental things.

He looked across at the morning paper and saw the advertisement he had seen so many times before, read so many times before. "I was a seven-stone weakling!" it shouted.

Tarrant smiled and thought he would tell that bloke at Peter Dominic's, if he ever passed the shop again, just what he thought of his Valpolicella. He finished half the bottle nevertheless. He fell asleep at the table, his head resting on a pillowed pancake of cold, flattened greens.

ooooo

Was he awake? There was the smell of decaying vegetable matter, previously boiled, along with the crudely yeasty, slightly farty overtones of the stale Oxo gravy. His nose twitched. It was perhaps sensing the future; for many a white burgundy would, in the years to come, give a fair aromatic impression of the plate of greens and gravy his head was lying on; but by then he would be able more accurately to identify it as hydrogen sulphide. But there was another sensation. It was that of a snail crawling through his hair. Had the creature lived in the greens? Had it survived the forty minutes' boiling Anita habitually gave all green vegetables (as if in revenge for growing in the first place and requiring such fiddly cleaning and cooking)? He started up in panic. Barbara was stroking his head.

"Ron's gone straight upstairs to bed. I only came down for a glass of water."

She picked up the half-empty Valpolicella bottle.

"You drink all this by yourself?"

Tarrant yawned and realised he urgently needed to wash his face. He looked across at the sink but there was no chance of inserting his head between the tap and the pile of dirty crockery. He wanted to douse his face in violent cold water. He could feel cold gravy on his cheek. Barbara picked a dried green lump off his hair. He lifted up his head. The newspaper was still there, the ad smirking at him: Charles Atlas with his black-as-tar hair and pregnant upper arms daring the reader to become a real man. "Ten minutes a day and Dynamic Tension can give you a body like mine!" it bawled.

He grabbed Barbara round the waist and kissed her on her lips. They didn't quite make a matching pair. The bottom lip was fully protuberant and comfortingly half-moon shaped but the top one was a shadow of this. It was thin and flat as though inscribed by a dab-handed cosmetician. But there was nothing hard about the lips. They opened, there was a polite, suppressed "uuhh" from deep inside his brother's wife, and then he was properly kissing her. He was actually kissing her; lips were grappling with lips, not in simple implanted mutual affection, but in a febrile exchange of passion. Tongues joined in and he found himself kissing a woman for the first time in his life. Barbara clung to him and let her tongue vibrate inside his mouth and her hands swept through his hair, greens or no greens, and his own hands were somehow inside her blouse.

They fucked one another on the cold linoleum of the kitchen floor, Ron's distant snores ignored, Anita's imminent arrival discounted. He had his penis inside her and she was writhing and moaning and he didn't climax immediately but managed to hold himself back while she came three times before he did and she could not stop herself screaming out and rolling about so violently that she ended up on top of him.

It was then that he heard hurried feet descending the stairs at the same time as the front door latch, on its Yale sliplock, let off its distinctive clunk as Anita's key opened it.

You've really gone and done it now thought Tarrant and a silly grin spread slowly over his face. And in that instant, as his teeth thrust themselves against his lips and the unstoppable smile formed on his face, he stopped being a child. He stayed where he was on the floor and ejaculated with a great roar. As Ron stepped inside the room and became a frozen, mute image of the helpless horror-struck cuckold, he was witness to his younger brother Tarrant finally throwing aside childhood. But of course Ronald didn't quite see it like that.

ooooo

Le Consommé House Red £18

The devastating revelation arrived simultaneously with the waiter. The latter's face had already caused Theo to question the truth of the observation that a man's history can be read in his facial appearance and as the tiny pots of herb-infused cold broth (*amuse gueule* between the artichokes and the sea-bass) were ceremoniously placed in front of the two diners, and the mysteries of their contents oleaginously saxophoned by the waiter's quaint English, Theodore had time to consider again how such a youthful countenance could harbour such ancient grief. But the quiet yet numbing declaration by the person whose guest he was drove such reflections from his mind.

"How is it possible? She stinks."

It was a fatuous response and he was perfectly aware of it. He considered the pot of consommé in front of him, the renowned delicacy of which had made both restaurant and chef famous (and indeed given the restaurant, part of a small hotel, its name), but felt that eating it, or indeed sipping it, was out of the question. But Iris had no such inhibitions – though she was not reeling with shock and emptiness as was Theo; instead, along with the extraordinarily concentrated consommé, she was experiencing inward delight at the anguish she was causing him. How cleverly had she chosen a great restaurant, one of London's most august, and not waited to give Theo the news as she paid the bill but as he was dipping in to the famous consommé. She delighted in torturing her contributors, especially ones habitually late with copy, routine with inspiration, and with fanciful notions of their own importance.

How can a restaurant build a reputation, and acquire hatfuls of restaurant guide stars, on the basis of a mere consommé? It was equally fatuous to believe what he had just been told: he, Theodore Hook, was losing his job as German wine correspondent of Clos Encounters. And losing it to Beryl Smith. The very name of the woman spoke of her dreary provinciality! My God, she had learned her German at Nottingham and probably spoke it, he raged, with an accent like David Herbert Lawrence (someone else he loathed). Whilst he, a product of Balliol, had connections, like that despised author of Lady Chatterley via his wife, with Germanic aristocrats whose families predated any Smith by centuries. He even knew Eddie von Richthoven, whose great aunt had been the floozy Lawrence had run off with.

Theo tried to be demure and controlled. He nosed the glass of rare Moselle riesling he had chosen but it smelled like shit.

"Of course I shall ask you, if you agree, to contribute the odd article on your speciality…but just as German wine is changing, so must the magazine. It is often forgotten that we are the biggest selling wine magazine in the world, with substantive sales not only in all English-speaking countries but all over Europe and South America. We even have subscribers in Russia."

You mean, you ignorant bitch, wailed Theo internally, substantial, not substantive. God, even the editor was a semi-literate; no surprise really in a world of technology-sodden semi-literates.

Iris's speech was a further turning of the screw. It reminded Theo of what he was losing. She sipped the glorious old Moselle. One thing to be said for lunching with Theodore Hook was that the wines were impeccably chosen, whoever was footing the bill. Her publisher-in-chief would raise an eyebrow at the expense of this one but she could defend the extravagance on the grounds that it was the only civilised way to get rid of the old stick-in-the-mud. And wasn't it the publisher-in-chief who had suggested the present course of action? After twenty-eight years in the job it was time to get a German wine correspondent who didn't resist the idea of covering all the new-fangled wines coming out of that confused and depressed wine land. It was what the advertisers wanted, after all. And Beryl *was* an old university chum.

Iris Wagstaffe was just ten years older than Theodore Hook's tenure and enjoyed looking at herself critically in a mirror. She was always rewarded with a smile. Today she was wearing a cream trouser suit with an ample cleavage, which Theo had noted and sighed over, and her abundant blonde hair would have been sexy on a head twenty years younger. She suppressed a giggle. She was thinking of how devastated the ex-German wine correspondent looked as he tried to enjoy the wine in his glass.

He must have cut quite a figure in his youth, she thought. Well, he cut quite a decent one now, with his willowy frame, the elegant crinkly hair, the yellow silk handkerchief spilling over the top pocket of the grey jacket which, though frayed, had been tailored to grace the Hook anatomy. What Iris did not know was that it was not Theo's anatomy it had been designed to fit but Maurice Hook's. Theo had inherited the dapper suiting from his elder brother, who'd died five years ago after a prostate operation went awry. Theo and Maurice had often been taken for twins though there had been seven years between them.

Iris leaned across the table to give him a better view of her beautifully toned brown breasts and was rewarded with a flicker of interest. She felt like patting him on the hand and saying there there, but if she dared do this he might take it the wrong way. The wrong way being the way that would lead him to suppose there was some other possibility on the agenda apart from the food and the wine…and the sack. Or rather not the sack but dismissal, and as the pun sank in she could hardly control her giggling and had recourse to the napkin to cover her mouth.

"The Germans won't like it, you know," he said miserably.

The German Wine Information Service will be thrilled, thought Iris, gasping with suppressed laughter. They had steadfastly refused to spend a penny on advertising in Clos Encounters while Theodore Hook ranted about the appalling atrocities being visited upon the wine shelves of Britain by modern abominations like Fire Mountain and Devil's Rock and, worst of all, Bend in the River Riesling. Theo felt himself rather radical for his predilections, which caused him to worship the traditional face of German wine. He was at home with the wild Gothic monsters of Teutonic wine labelling and he saw no good reason to make pets of any of the tame, modern creatures he saw posturing as wines.

"Hot in here," said Beryl, and jiggled with her lapels to distract herself from the fit of giggles. Theo was afforded more mammalian overview and for the first time in their ten-year acquaintanceship it struck him what a considerable double page spread his editor, his *ex*-editor, could display in this department. She added a further lie: "The Germans will be as sorry to see you…er, your role lessened as will I…"

"Not to mention the readers."

"…but I have a duty to the years ahead, Theo. We are in the third millennium. An editor who has only a duty to the past has no future." She liked that last thrust. It was lifted from the biography of a famous denizen of Fleet Street.

"Having said that," she went on, seeing that Theo was biting his lip, "this wine is quite magical."

"One of the greatest white wines in the world. Much more concentrated and fascinating that any Meursault or Montrachet…let alone some Australian…confection."

He sighed. Iris thought it was because of the present situation but it was regret that so much of the rest of the world did not share his appreciation of old German riesling. His German friends' popularity had fallen disastrously on world markets, but especially in the UK. The Germans struggled to make ends meet when once they had been leaders. Only a fortnight before he had been in the Moselle and discovered that one of his oldest friends, Rudy Buscher-Langendorfer of Weingut Dr Buscher, had been reduced to hiring a large van every weekend, filling it full of his delectable spatlesen and auslesen, and driving off to Cologne and Hamburg and knocking on people's doors. Rudy's humiliation was not unique, many growers did the same, but it was still galling and now Theo could relish a similar loss of supremacy. What doors could *he* call on now? He was losing his legitimacy: the right to call himself a wine correspondent, *the German wine correspondent* of the most influential wine magazine in Europe, possibly the world.

"That numbskull Smith believes Germans should experiment with malolactic fermentation. Make their wines more modern. Fatter. Did you know this, Iris? Is this the sort of person you really want as a German wine correspondent?"

Iris, who wore fake tan all year round to save herself the dangers of encountering the real thing and attracting wrinkles, buried her nose in her glass to hide her confusion. Although she was editor of Clos Encounters and thereby presumed to be an expert on the field she lorded it over, she was in truth no such thing. She had studied French at Nottingham and that was all the credentials anyone ever much cited in her favour when they considered her expertise, and thus it was assumed she knew her onions; but in fact all she really knew, as she would admit to herself in her more candid reflections in a glass, were her *oignons*. The malolactic ferment bit always confused her. What was it exactly? She knew about the alcoholic fermentation where yeasts eat grape sugars and convert them into alcohol and slowly commit deliriously happy suicide but *le malo*, as her French friends called it, was something of a mystery. With some effort, she recalled that it was not something the Germans went in for but why she couldn't say. Luckily, Hook could, and was in full flood on the topic.

"The history of inhibited malolactic fermentation in Germany is a long and honourable one…"

The first course had been cleared away and the sea-bass (whole, for two, £25 supplement) arrived with a truffle oil and fennel sauce which Theo had said could only be tamed by the Spatlese they were now finishing. He stopped talking and ordered a second bottle. Iris felt annoyed that he did not defer to her, and nearly said "I'd much prefer red wine if you don't mind", but he was babbling away about malolactic fermentation with the enthusiasm, and bitter recrimination, that some people reserve for discussing their failure to get elected for Parliament in spite of a recount. The fish, though, was marvellous.

Theo also felt annoyed by the time he had finished his viva on malolactic fermentation. How had he got sidetracked like this? With its mild alcohol level (barely 9.5 per cent) and "metaphysical minerals" (one of Theo's riper aphorisms) encouraging easy consumption, the second bottle soon began to look the worse for wear and it was time to consider fresh ammunition. He asked for the wine list. Iris pursed her lips and drew the lapels of her jacket together.

"It was that bloody Smith woman who got us going on malo," he snarled.

"Please! Theo! Beryl Smith is an excellent writer. Knows her wines. Speaks fluent German."

"I can see nothing in what you have just said that elevates her candidacy above my own tenure…twenty-eight years…"

He got his third bottle. Or half-bottle at least: a trockenbereenauslese – too young in his view but outrageously expensive enough – to go with dessert.

The oasis had now been reached. All meals between acquaintances find accommodation there after travelling the *hors d'oeuvre* and the *premiers plats*. It is the pausing place; the spot to water the horses of discourse; the site where the traveller can, for a moment, relax, having journeyed and jockeyed with words, issued and received, before embarking on the third stage of the ordeal – the trek to the reaching of the final destination: the presentation of the damage, the settling up, the retrieving of the coats, the kissing on the cheeks, the goodbyes as posteriors disappear into taxis or round corners. Plus, of course, that dreadful anti-climatic sense, prompting weird late-night dreams, of having been a participant in a game where the rules were obscure if not wicked: just what *was* all that meal in aid of?

Iris knew. It was in aid of her delicious ego and *amour-propre.* It was this self-confidence that had gotten her the job, at the comparatively tender age of twenty-eight, when she confessed (to herself only) that she knew little enough about wine but possessed a consummate appetite for consuming it. The publisher-in-chief felt he had been promised her body in return for giving her the job – over the heads, and indeed bodies, of more richly qualified candidates after the incumbent, Albany Swift, had drowned in Chateau Labastide de Figeac's swimming pool after a drunken orgy to celebrate the end of the great Vinexpo wine fair in Bordeaux – but he never received this due.

She could muse on this now. Just as she could sit there soaking up Theo's discomfiture. It gave the wine an added piquancy.

She threw a smile and a measure of cleavage across to the other side of the oasis. Hook caught both, tested one for smugness and the other for size, and kept his counsel.

Theodore Hook, *the* Theodore Hook, having ordered dessert, was thinking he must now complete his book, thirteen years in the gestation, on the oldest and greatest wine estates in the world (all German, of course, since Germanic efficiency ordained that records were not only kept up but never considered surplus to requirements so that several German wine families could legally trace their vineyard's lineage to the time of Charlemagne and one grower could even go back to 742 and wave the evidence of Pepin, Charlemagne's father, in your face). He surely had time for this book now.

Surplus to requirements! This was him now. Was this all

he was going to get after twenty-eight years? Sea-bass and a few bottles of riesling?

The dessert went gloriously with the honeyed trockenbereenauslese and Iris began to feel she might be nearing the frontiers of her vinous capacities.

'When," he ventured, "when, exactly when, do you want me to…relinquish the reins? I have articles planned for the next year…notes, you know…trips organised."

Iris looked sharply at him and felt another surge of annoyance. She drew the lapels of her jacket together.

"I thought I had made it plain…"

"Plainness, my dear Iris, you have never suffered from."

But fools are a different matter, she thought, saying: "The current issue is your last…I mean I don't require anything more from you…for a while…"

"But…then Beryl has already submitted her copy for the next issue, July's, and doubtless, August's…but for that to be so…then she must have known of her appointment months ago. Three months back, in Baden, we – she and I – were together on a trip with those Michelin chefs. She must have known then. Surely not, Iris? Don't tell me, please, that she had the promise of my job then."

Iris was silent. It spoke volumes. Theo felt like crying. A waiter wheeling a chariot appeared.

"Cheese, sir? Madam?"

Madam made her uninterest plain with a wave of the hand. Theo, boiling inside, felt rather dizzy and he snarled his requests, in his quaint French, and was rewarded with a plate heaped with yellow and white oozing lumps.

"I must have a bottle of red wine," he said. He asked for the wine list.

Enough is enough, thought Iris. I can't drink any more and the bugger will doubtless order some horrifically pricey claret. She barked, as the waiter turned to go, "We'll have a bottle of the House Red", annoyed at herself as the words left her mouth that she had said them in English.

Theo was too slow to rescind this order; he could only stare at Iris and let the poison the woman had engendered work its way around his system. He poked at his cheese.

The waiter returned with the wine and two large glasses.

"Not for me," said Iris.

"I think you're wrong there," said Theo, as the waiter opened the bottle and began to pour a measure in Theo's glass.

"What?" said Iris.

Theo ritually smelled the wine in the glass and nodded. The waiter bowed and departed.

"This wine is wholly for you, my dear Iris."

Theo stood and took the bottle and poured the contents over Iris's head, neck and shoulders. She froze in utter astonishment and two-thirds of the bottle had already emptied themselves over her before she attempted to stand and push Theo away.

Waiters came running. Lunchers on several other tables sat back in mixed delight and disgust. Wine was dripping off her nose and ears, her chest was soaked, and the trouser suit was turning a rich shade of blotched crimson. Theo was particularly delighted to see some of the wine had run down the inside of her arm and emerged at the cuff-end, where it trickled on to her mobile phone. As Iris stood and wildly tried to slap away her ex-German wine correspondent, Theo calmly tossed the empty bottle to the nearest waiter.

"Unforgettable lunch, Iris, unforgettable," was his parting shot. "You should wear red more often."

Domaine de la Romanée Conti 1978

The voice at the end of the phone was like oil, unguent and cloying.

"Mr Dupré? I got your number from the Guild index. Happy new Millennium! I am so pleased to have got through to you so quickly. I had wondered if a man in your position might not surround himself with the usual phalanx of assistants and secretaries, not to mention, of course, that bane of modern living, the answering machine."

A man in my position? Dupré, sitting half-dressed on the side on the bed, stared at the considerable hole in his sock in the much-repaired area of the left large toe. He mumbled. It passed for grudging acknowledgement of the caller's presence. Then, as the voice on the line spoke again, Dupré's uncombed hair crackled. Something, one of those senses beyond the conventional five, bade him sit up straighter. The voice had a certain familiarity. Charterhouse, thought Dupré, definitely Charterhouse, or, at a pinch, Haileybury (though Dupré had not been to a school remotely like either).

"My name is Alec Saunders. You won't know me. But you will know the great man I work for, His Highness Prince Zayn Mussire al-Din, the world's fourth richest businessman…"

Saunders permitted himself a subtle clearing of the throat

to allow time for the richness of this particular oily drip properly to ooze into the Dupré consciousness.

"What," said Dupré, brightly, "can you, or His Highness, want of me?"

He leaned down and tore off the offending sock, pressed it into a black ball and hurled it at a wastepaper basket in the corner of the bedroom. He missed the basket by some margin. With his large toe he pulled down the other sock, also fraying, to his ankle and slowly began to slide it to his toes, preparatory to turning it into a second disposable missile.

ooooo

The history of that pair of grey and black socks was as colourful as the socks were not. Dupré retrieved them from the carpet, both having missed their target, and chided himself for his marksmanship and extravagance. They were surely worth further reparation however promising-of-riches Saunders had sounded. He returned them to the socks drawer, the left-hand side of which was reserved for injured pairs, and selected a woolly couple from the right side. Like all his socks, they came from Marks & Spencer – the busy branch on the corner of Orchard Street and Oxford Street. He felt pleased Saunders had caught him so early, before he was fully dressed and had gone out for the day. Early meant 9.30am for Dupré. The wine palate, he was fond of pointing out, is at its sharpest from ten.

The black and grey pair had, though Dupré did not recollect this as he folded them in half further to differentiate them from the wearable pairs which were balled up, accompanied him on two trips to Australia, one to New Zealand, fourteen to France, eleven to Italy, seven to Spain, one to Chile, five to South Africa, and they were the pair he was wearing when the plane he was travelling in on an internal Romanian flight skidded at Iasi Airport near the border with Moldavia and caused disarray amongst the passengers, who included an intrepid band of British wine writers. Those socks were as worn out, though only half as old, as that plane.

They had also been the pair he was wearing when he had at last seen off Paul Hawksmere, at the final show of hands, and Hawksmere's chairmanship of the Guild of Writers on Wine had reached its bitter end and his own tenure of the honorary position began. It was the defining moment of his life and he was still basking in it, for that final showdown had taken place only six months previously.

Thank the Almighty he had persisted in his determination to oust the odious Hawksmere. He congratulated himself. Would he have received such deference from Saunders if he'd been merely an anonymous committee member of the Guild? No indeed. Would he have even received that call? Probably not. Thus he could now conjecture that his holding of the chairmanship might lead him to achieve his other life's ambition: a small cosy place somewhere warm to which he could permanently retire when his time was done.

ooooo

Dupré's real name was Reg Harris – coincidental with the legendary English cyclist. Dupré's father, a Solihull electrician, was a bike fanatic and hoped the naming of his one and only son would encourage development along the lines of the racing Reg's fantastic pneumatic thighs and calves; but of course Fate intervened long before and bequeathed to the spindly youth, now a rotund 59, a grammar school place and no interest in sport of any kind, though Dupré did spend several hours once observing a stage of the Tour de France because it passed through the town he was staying in as part of his French degree at Birmingham University. Pierre Dupré was, however, the name he had deliberately adopted for professional use; it was how everyone, except his mother, addressed him. It was the name he had subsided into. France – French wine and French food and French manners – was his obsession. His father had disowned him when he glimpsed his son on black and white television cheering the goal scored by St. Etienne that put West Bromwich Albion out of the Inter Cities Fairs Cup in 1959.

Reg Harris became Pierre Dupré some three years after this, when as a graduate he got a job on a wine trade magazine. The metamorphosis into Frenchification was already so superb that Londoners would often remark how excellent, if a little quaintly regional in places, his English accent was. He became a leading light, or as he sometimes joked "a leading heavy", of the Guild of Writers on Wine when that organisation was barely five years old. In satirical moments, the Guild referred to itself as WoW! but even the chairman thought this was stretching irony a little far.

ooooo

Dupré's mobile phone rang as he was sauntering past the Lansdowne Club in Fitzmaurice Place, which runs into Curzon Street where he was expected for lunch. He had walked from his basement flat in Luxborough Street, just off the Marylebone Road. It was two weeks since the oleaginous Alec had first contacted him and Dupré was feeling deliciously lubricated and looking forward to further massage.

In fact, Dupré's phone did not ring, it pulsed. It was a sign, he felt, of how sensitive an individual he was. Loud ring tones would not be tolerated at the wine-tastings he frequently attended – though of course it was the gossip exchanged in loud ringing tones by Guild members at the lunches afterwards which were the social highlight of such events – and so he had been thrilled to find a mobile phone that could be switched to vibrate in his breast pocket when an incoming call was received. He wore an earpiece permanently attached to his left orifice even when he nipped round the corner from his flat for a newspaper. How could he be available, for discreet advice, to his PR clients at a moment's notice any other way?

Naturally, he kept the fact of this multiplicity of clients as close to his chest as the phone, especially since his campaign to become chairman of his beloved Guild had so brilliantly succeeded. True, the Guild tolerated a certain amount of light PR activity by its members, who all referred to themselves as Wine Writers and carried around a little card with the proof of this inscribed, but Dupré's PR involvement, though sporadic and meagrely remunerative, was considerable and his only source of income, apart from the odd wine trade article he was commissioned to write or a piece on wine futures for a Far Eastern economic review. The Guild had long ago recognised how impossible it was for anyone to subsist on the scrappy shekels brought in by the writing of consumer wine journalism.

"Pierre Dupré."

It was a confident voice and, with no apparent phone on view, it convinced the woman coming out of the Lansdowne Club doorway that she was being sworn at and she took a hasty step backwards. Thus did the Guild chairman continue on into Curzon Street unaware of the fright he had caused an innocent Oregonian.

"Alec here, Pierre. You're not sitting down yet then? I can hear traffic. Good…I…"

"Good morning, Alec. Just coming into Curzon now."

"Fine. Look, I'm going to be delayed a little. His Highness has asked me to solve a little domestic problem and I can't join you for half-an-hour or so, perhaps a little more. But please go ahead and enjoy yourself. His Highness would want you to order a bottle of something interesting while you wait. I believe that the restaurant has several years of Domaine de la Romanée Conti…"

Dupré's intake of breath was audible.

"…so long as you save a glass for me. I can't take more than a glass at lunch. I'm afraid I'm not like you gastronomes…"

Dupré laughed. He could not quite believe what he was being offered here.

"It's rumoured there's even the '78 of that vineyard on the list," said Dupré, as off-handedly as he could. 1978 was possibly the year of the century for this most legendary of all French vineyards.

"Then order a bottle…" ordered Saunders.

"Oh come, it's…"

"It's essential. My employer's sense of hospitality insists that his guests always have the very best. If I am being forced to be so rude as not to be punctual for our lunch he would insist that you, as a great man of wine, as chairman of the renowned Guild, enjoy the very best bottle La Cuillère Graisseuse has to offer. I must go. Order whatever you like, Pierre. But just remember this. As we start so shall we go on."

Dupré's head spun. As we start so shall we go on? My God, he thought, if we pull this contract off we'll have Krug '85 to clean our teeth in.

ooooo

"The wine list, Mr Dupré."

It looked like an archive. Dupré took it, sighed, and looked around him. La Cuillère Graisseuse had long been a famously imposing establishment, had then fallen upon hard times, lately to be rejuvenated by a TV chef-entrepreneur. The wine list, representing a capacious inherited cellar richly expanded, was rumoured to be immense and as comprehensively stunning, and as regal, as Le Gavroche's. Dupré now had the weight of the evidence of this in his hand, or rather his two hands. He put the list down; fingered his bow-tie, stroked his chin; wondered, just for a second, if Saunders would turn out to be, and to look like, the middle-ranking ex-army type he anticipated. Prince Zayn Mussire al-Din he could put a vague face to because he had checked up on the man. His Highness was indeed seeking to build the greatest holiday resort in the world and so what more natural than that he should require a wine consultant, on an appropriate annual retainer, to advise on the wines for the complex's rumoured seventeen different restaurants. Dupré picked up the list and turned to the Burgundies.

Already it was apparent this was a restaurant *de luxe ultra*. He had been addressed as Mr Dupré from the moment he had entered the place and given his name, Saunders having insisted on booking the table in Dupré's name because "it would ensure we get the best table and I never book in His Highness's name". Dupré was flattered, even felt a twinge of pride that the masquerade he lived behind could possibly convince the private secretary to the world's fourth richest man that the name Dupré carried weight at London's most opulent eateries. Though whether the corner he had been shown to could remotely be considered a "best table" was open to doubt.

Nevertheless, here he was, clutching La Cuillère Graisseuse's wine list, leafing through the white burgundies, through the red, until he reached the place exclusively given over to the wines of Domaine de la Romanée Conti. It was an awesome collection of wine at awesome prices from the world's most awesome grouping of small vineyards – the one of Romanée Conti itself being a mere four and half acres producing just five thousand bottles of the world's most expensive pinot noir, the world's most expensive wine forsooth. Dupré had tasted it on less than half-a-dozen occasions; even as chairman of a Guild of professional soaks it was not a wine one encountered often. It had never been less than interesting, perhaps sometimes overrated, but then the years he had sampled had not always been of the greatest. But the '78 was reckoned to be totally marvellous, possibly the vintage of the century for Romanée Conti, and at twenty-two years old it would now be at its most drinkably succulent, aromatic, and lingering. It ought to be, Dupré thought, a wine to die for.

He stared at the wine's name and vintage on the list. He felt a trifle giddy. He sensed a sudden flicker in his heartbeat. The price rose up from the page like a hideous perfume. It had to be the highest priced single bottle on the list, possibly the highest priced single bottle on any restaurant wine list in London.

Eleven thousand pounds.

It could be worse, he thought. It could be guineas. But £11,000! It was slightly less than he'd earned in the whole of last year. It had been a particularly harrowing year. He shifted in his chair. He licked his lips, sensing the sudden dryness on his palate. £11,000! Could Saunders have the remotest idea that the wine could cost so much? No employer, however munificent, could possibly tolerate an underling's lunch expenses for two people with £11,000 of it spent on a single bottle of wine. Or could they?

Dupré smiled, and turned the page; sipped his glass of mineral water. He examined other regions of the world and noted the colossal prices of even a humble bottle.

"Have you chosen, sir? Can I be of any 'elp?"

The sommelier was at his shoulder with, it seemed to Dupré, something like disdain in his eyes. Dupré stared up at the man; closed the wine list with a bang. Dammit, he was not going to be brushed off with something like a vin de pays from Narbonne at £35 the bottle. This was a business lunch, wasn't it? A lunch held at the behest of the world's fourth richest man. What if it led to nothing? What if the conditions attached to the possible consultancy were too onerous? What if others were in the running, of whom he knew nothing? He ought to get something out of this lunch, make it unforgettable. Saunders had said he should order the Domaine de la Romanée Conti and the 1978 vintage to boot, so what did he have to lose? It was Saunders who was picking up the tab and the fourth richest man in the world who was…

"Sir?"

"Apportons-nous une bouteille de La Romanée Conti '78, s'il vous plaît," Dupré barked.

The sommelier blinked, took the wine list from Dupré's grasp, hesitated a second; then he bowed low.

'While I decant it, Mr Dupré, shall I bring you a glass of champagne? On the 'ouse, bien sûr."

ooooo

Dupré had always fretted about his hair but it had, over the past five years, acquired a distinguished grey tint, which compensated for its lack of depth on top. His was a jolly face, much commented upon. As if, a client once remarked, one had requested central casting to send along the perfect token middle-aged Frog, a man in anonymous middle-management who always enjoyed two-hour lunches. The lips, the Dupré lips, were, as his dad's had been, like utensils designed for the manipulation of food. In short, Pierre Dupré looked like the sort of man – and indeed he effected to dress the part – for whom ordering great bottles of wine in great restaurants was not merely routine but a duty. That the suit was seventeen years old, the shirt eleven, and the bow-tie twenty-two was irrelevant. There is such a thing as understated style and neither money nor a trendy modern label can guarantee the conferring of it. It would be uncharitable to remark that this style was strictly only discernible when the object of it was sitting down, but then Pierre did spend most of his time in that position and so the tightness of the shirt around the neck, the unfashionable cut of the trouser turn-ups around the ankle, the sagging pockets of the jacket hugging the waist, and, were he foolishly to remove that jacket, the undulatory wrinkles of the trousers across the buttocks, were only noticeable to assiduous voyeurs of such niceties. These details passed without comment in the chambers of the world of wine-tasting, since it was a world whose denizens were largely poor and mostly wretchedly dressed. Elegance of manner and of expression are what counts in the true assessment of a gentleman, Dupré had once remarked to Paul Bocuse, and Monsieur Bocuse had entirely agreed with him. True, the shirt did bulge uncomfortably with the mobile phone in it, as though he had a wen beginning to sprout on his chest, and he had noticed this morning that the pocket was fraying again. He was, though, in spite of a pair of hands like indian clubs, a deft needleman.

He moved to switch the phone off, remembering where he was. His glass of complimentary champagne was now empty, the sommelier was advancing smoothly across the room carried along by that spectacular deeply woven carpet and in his fist was a decanter of red wine affixed to the top of which, by a sliver of lead capsule, was the cork from the bottle.

His phone pulsed just as he was about to turn it off and the sommelier was arriving with the wine.

"Pierre, it's Alec, I've got the most horrendous problems here. I can't join you for an hour or more. Please eat. No, no... please go ahead...order whatever you fancy...and if that wine's all gone by the time I arrive, well it'll just be my hard luck... I'm most frightfully sorry, old man...but you go ahead and enjoy yourself. You did order that Romanée Conti, I hope?"

Dupré experienced a tinge of irritation at this tardiness and then, as the sommelier placed the decanter on the table and his assistant appeared holding a vast globular burgundy glass, felt nothing but contempt for this Saunders fellow who was merely a fartcatcher for an Arab prince. Dupré thought of remarking that he would do his best to contain his excitement until Saunders's arrival but the sommelier was at his shoulder.

"I have everything I need, thank you."

The phone went dead. Dupré switched it off and removed his earpiece. He had quite forgotten he still had it in. The sommelier poured a measure of wine into the glass, whirled it around and placed it adjacent to Dupré's hand on the tablecloth. Dupré took it, whirled it again, and placed his experienced proboscis over the rim. He smelled wild raspberries, truffles and a touch of sweet farmyard earth. Not bad, for openers. He looked up at the sommelier, who was gazing at him with rapt attention. Whatever contempt Dupré might have fancied the man's eyes exhibited had vanished, to be replaced with something more congenial, perhaps even worship.

"C'est parfait, le vin," muttered Dupré matter-of-factly.

"Monsieur. Merci." And the sommelier annointed the glass with a little more wine, smiled at Dupré, and turned on his heel. Dupré called him back and asked him to tell the waiter he would like to order from the menu in three minutes.

The assistant returned with the empty burgundy bottle and placed it on the table, apologising for the omission when he brought the glass. Dupré studied the label and then placed the bottle where the nearest neighbouring table could see it. Where was the glory in drinking eleven thousand quid's worth of wine if its provenance was anonymised by a decanter?

Gervaise Gilroy-Carstairs! It was no less than he waving at him from a table, getting to his feet, and coming over. Dupré affected not to see and turned his nose into the glass of burgundy, thinking what a stroke of good fortune it was that the biggest gossip in the wine trade was bearing down on him when he had not yet been joined by this Saunders character. If Dupré did swing this contract it had to be discreetly handled since it conflicted with his involvement with the Warrington Russell bijou hotel chain. But what had that brought in last year? Eleven assorted free nights in three hotels and barely £1500's worth of consultancy fees.

"Well, Monsieur Dupré, *mon vieux*. How are you, Pierre? Congratulations on the chairmanship. Hawksmere is still seething." He dropped his voice to a whisper. "Well, he only has himself to blame. Fancy openly touting for PR business at a wine fair. Totally unethical."

"An abuse of his position, Gervaise. I'm fine, thank you. Enjoying this rare treat."

"You had no choice but to bring it up before the committee...."

Dupré frowned. Someone at that private Guild meeting, at which he had provided the evidence that had scuppered Hawksmere, had obviously been talking to Gilroy-Carstairs.

"I cannot comment on that."

"Of course. Your discretion does you credit. Well, I'd better get back. I'd ask you to join us but I see you're laid for two... my God! I see what you mean by rare treat!"

Gilroy-Carstairs' tier of expensively acquired chins trembled as he picked up the bottle of Romanée Conti.

"The '78!" he breathed. "That blasted Léoville-Poyferré '89 is costing me a packet with that pair of merchant bankers I'm having to schmooze but it's ditch piss compared to this. My God, Pierre *vieux fruit*, this is...who in God's name is standing you lunch today?"

"What makes you think anyone is sharing this wine with me?" said Dupré smoothly. "Can't a chap take himself out for lunch and enjoy a little burgundy?"

The waiter to take the Dupré order now arrived and went to hold the chair out for Gilroy-Carstairs to sit, but the wine merchant restrained him.

"Just one at this table, I fancy. Well, Pierre, I'll sit over there and envy you and if you get lonely and want to share a glass...oh, lawks, let me just smell it, would you?"

Dupré handed Gilroy-Carstairs the glass. He inhaled the aroma, pretended to take a gulp, and then, with a theatrical sigh, handed the wine to the waiter to pass back to Dupré.

"Bloody awesome. You jammy beggar! I'll see you at my Alsace tasting on the 29th and you can tell me how the whole bottle performed."

"Be my pleasure, Gervaise. See you then."

Dupré thought that if he didn't receive at least four telephone calls from old friends tomorrow and get at least a dozen e-mails, then Gilroy-Carstairs would have to be considered to have lost his touch. Dupré ordered the Bresse pigeon with wild mushrooms and truffles, with the *paté de foie gras* to start. He asked for a glass of Monbazillac to go with this. The burgundy would be swamped by the foie gras.

The goose liver dispensed with, he was halfway through the pigeon, and the bottle of wine, when a man with a dark blue brass-buttoned jacket and pale red tie entered the restaurant and Dupré almost waved; but it was prudent he restrained himself because the man was soon swallowed up by the clutch of tables at the far end of the vast eating area and Dupré felt relieved – to his surprise. He didn't really want to share a single drop of this wine with Saunders. He felt sure that the one-glass-a-lunchtime secretary would finally turn up when dessert was on the table, or perhaps he might make it in time for the cheese.

But Saunders made neither. The red wine had all gone, finished off with *petite rondelles de brie au truffe* and then it was the sweet course and Dupré, thoroughly pleased with life, acknowledged Gilroy-Carstairs' wave of departure and ordered the *soufflé aux fraises sauvages* and half a bottle of Chateau Climens 1962 – a snip at £275.

Cigars were being run under noses on far tables (to be lit upstairs), and the *chariot de liqueurs* was doing the rounds. Dupré ran a finger around the soufflé bowl and licked it, unashamedly relishing the last morsel of the signature dish. He finished his glass of the marvellously nobly rotted Sauternes, almost chewing on the fungoid grapes, which had bequeathed to the wine its extraordinary bouquet of spiced *crème brulée* and the honeyed succulence of its fruit. Where was this dratted Saunders? This was becoming a little intolerable. He selected the '37 Depissier-Rayneau Grandes Fines Champagne Cognac from the trolley and the waiter poured a generous measure.

Half an hour went by and the restaurant was empty except for the Birmingham electrician's son, nosing a second glass of the stunning cognac. Waiters re-laying tables threw him discreet glances. Dupré already knew that he had been, and still was, the object of veneration and awe amongst the younger commis staff who, unaware of his sharp ear for anything expressed in French, however rustic the accent, had passed whispered comment on the burgundy.

Now it was the chef's turn to pay his respects. The TV chef's most notable protégé, the formidably stubbly Brian Peploe, was bearing down on him, pushing the *chariot des liqueurs* to the evident discomfiture of the sommelier.

"I hope you enjoyed my cooking, Mr Dupré. May I offer you another glass of the cognac before you depart? On me, of course."

"Phlease…um…please! Join me. Remarkable meal, er, Mr Peploe."

Dupré could read the man's name on his immaculate white top, kept specially crisp for customer relations. He had heard the name before. Wasn't he the genius tipped to be one of the few British-born chefs to soon acquire Michelin's third star? The sommelier rushed up and poured out glasses of the brandy. The chef and the sommelier exchanged glances.

"Shall I organise *l'addition*?" said the chef, clinking glasses with his customer. Dupré wondered if the chef had not been deputed to this task but then, as he regarded the young man's bristly features and massive forearms, he thought that no-one, not even his televisual boss, would dare ask him to do anything so eccentric in so formally a regulated world as that of *grande cuisine* cooking.

Dupré clinked his glass against Peploe's.

"Organise the bill? Certainly, old sport. Do you mhean, I mean mean, you'd like to settle it yourshelf…self? Once my dining companion turns up it'll be settled…where is the bugger?' Dupré looked at his watch. It was half-past four. "My God," he muttered. "It's terribly late. I had no idea…er…"

"Organise the bill for Mr Dupré would you, Serge? Mr Dupré, I'm pleased you like the food here. I hope we have the pleasure of your company again. Fantastic cognac this, eh?"

Peploe disappeared as the bill, disconcertingly rapidly, arrived and Dupré stared at the silver platter it was lying on and felt a sudden shiver of horror pass through him. They weren't…they surely weren't expecting this bill to be picked up by him? He wasn't even going to look at it.

"Anything the matter, Mr Dupré?"

It was the restaurant manager. His moustache was like two skipping rope handles, thought Dupré.

"I am waiting for the man who booked this table for lunch, Alec Saunders…to arrive. Ah! Of course. I switched my phone off. Let me just shh…um, see."

Under the Mona Lisa smile of the manager and his athletic upper lip, Dupré manipulated the phone out of his pocket, switched on the message finder, but was surprised to see no calls recorded.

"Is there a problem, Mr Dupré?"

"No problem. This lunch, which was for two, was arranged by a business associate. He booked the table. He rang me earlier to shay he was gloing to be a little delayed…well, where is she…er…he?"

"Where indeed, sir? Would you excuse me?"

The manager turned on his heel and Dupré searched in his pocket diary for the phone number Saunders had given him. He had never had occasion to use it as yet but now he did, dialling it with exaggerated care.

"This number has not been recognised. Please check or dial again."

Dupré cursed his hammy digits and redialled. He got the same message. He dialled twice more and again got that irritatingly smug android voice.

"Mr Dupré, there appears to be a little confusion here." It was the manager.

"Eh? Yeshyes, you're right. My bloody phone won't work."

"You say a business associate booked the table, Mr Dupré. But it was booked by you. In your name. You rang and confirmed the booking yesterday."

"I didn't book the bloody thing…it was…someone else. Look, didn't you get a contact number? You always ask for that, don't you?"

"Indeed we do. In your case we didn't use it because, as I just said, the table booking was reconfirmed yesterday. If I ring the number you left…"

"I didn't leave any number! I didn't book the table or reconfirm it!"

The man gestured and whispered in a waiter's ear. The waiter sped off. The manager put both his hands on the table.

"But it was reserved in your name. For two people, yes. But booked in your name, sir. Mr Dupré. And Santoro over there distinctly remembers your conversation with Mr

Gilroy-Carstairs when you said to him you were eating alone and didn't want to share the Romanée Conti with anyone."

He leaned down and pushed the silver platter bearing the bill towards Dupré, who felt a sudden chill grip his entrails. He remembered what he'd said to Gervaise. He had tried to give the wine merchant the absurd impression he wasn't on yet another freebie lunch – at a table patently set for two. He bit his lip. The waiter returned, shaking his head. He muttered something inaudible to the manager.

"Surprise surprise. The number you left is not recognised by the telephone company. Doesn't exist. Just like your dining companion."

Saunders! Where was the bastard? He would clear up the whole thing in a flash of a gold card. In desperation, Dupré held out the phone and his diary to the manager.

"Then dial *this* number for me, would you? I can't seem to get through. I assume it's not the same one given you by whoever called and booked the table who I have every con… confidence was a Mr Alec Saunders."

The manager looked at the number in Dupré's diary.

"Doesn't exist, that number. We've just tried it. Er, sir, the bill. May I ask you to…?"

"To what? I've told you. It isn't my bill. I was invited here to lunch by a business associate who booked in my name. It is *his* bill. I must go to the loo now."

Dupré launched himself across the deep-pile and down the stairs. When he had finished his long piss and wiped his hands on the deep-pile towels emblazoned with La Cuillère Graisseuse in imperial purple, he came out of the lavatory and could not fail to notice two of the younger and brawnier waiters idling outside. They escorted him back to the table.

He stared at the bill on the platter. He picked it up. With a "15 per cent discretionary service charge" added on, the total leapt out at him like the final figure in a set of annual accounts: £13,517.76. He slumped back in his chair. He lacked the funds to even pay the service charge: £1705. It was beyond belief.

He waved the manager, who was standing by the liqueur trolley, to come over. The establishment was now empty of customers except the wine writer.

"I can't possibly pay this, you know."

"I rather feared as much, sir. Shall I summon the police?"

"What? But…."

"Well, sir, we have been deceived, have we not? A lunch, a rather expensive lunch, has been enjoyed by you under false pretences. It is fraud."

"But I haven't defrauded anyone. I was invited here…"

"So you say. But where is this man who you claim booked the table? Does he exist? His phone number doesn't. Do you play this game often? Very clever."

The manager clicked his fingers and a commis waiter arrived and removed the half-finished glass of cognac, as though the manager could not bear this final outrage, this final fraudulence. The chef now appeared, out of uniform. His arms, thought Dupré, were like Parma hams protruding from his tee-shirt. He sat down at the table. The manager sat down at the table.

Dupré slumped in to the napkin in front of him. The chef leaned over and, taking the chairman by the hair, gently lifted his head up.

"My boss is quite clear about people like you, you bleedin' swindler. We want our money for the wine and food you're trying to steal. Shall I cut a little finger off, Antonio, just for a start?" He flourished a vast sushi-chef's implement. Dupré wondered where he could have been concealing it.

This was, surely, just a bad joke. Someone had set him up, this was beginning to seem clear – but these theatrical threats were over the top. The joke was getting out of hand.

Two commis waiters arrived and held Dupré by the shoulders as the manager leaned across and extracted the wallet from Dupré's inner jacket pocket. He took out the Barclaycard he found there, handed Dupré his wallet back, and strode away. There was silence as the chef, one palm resting on the knife handle, and Dupré, his head resting on his shaking hand, regarded one another.

"Look, this is all a terrible mistake. I had no intention of trying to get a meal for free…that wine…"

"You've had a right old guzzle and feed at my expense, you cheating shit, and if Antonio doesn't return and tell me the credit card's gone through okay, I'm going to chop bits off you…starting with the little pinkie you raise so hoity-toity when you drink."

Dupré stared at his right hand little finger. Did he raise it when he drank? Like some dowager duchess in a piece of Wildean tea-party theatre? He would have liked to laugh but his breath, the very air, was feeling like cotton wool in his chest. The manager was returning, waving the card.

"This card is in the name of Reginald Harris. Is it a stolen card? Or is Harris your real name?" He threw the card on the table. "Over the limit anyway. Useless plastic. We have a con merchant here. Best get chopping, Brian."

"But…no! Stop trying to frighten me. Dupré is my professional name. Look, my friend Gervaise Gilroy-Carstairs, the man who was eating here, he will vouch for me…"

"I'll ring him now, shall I?" said the manager. "Will he pop round and settle this bill for you?"

Peploe raised the knife and, grabbing Dupré's hand, brought the knife towards it. Dupré screamed, the manager gasped, the commis waiters turned their faces away. The knife descended, at the last second to veer away from Dupré's hand and strike the credit card. With a faint shucking noise the knife severed the credit card in two. Dupré had gone completely ashen. The chef pushed the knife aside, and held up the two pieces of the Barclaycard.

"See that? How many chefs in London can do that? Look! Look, you miserable effin' fraud. Look! Not a scratch on the cloth, is there? Not even an indentation. That's what you're paying for here: chef skills of the highest effin' order. And you want to walk out of here without sticking your hand in your pocket." He raised the knife again. The manager made a feeble attempt to restrain Peploe's arm for it seemed that nothing could now stop the amputation – especially as the incensed chef shouted:

"I'll stick your hand in your pocket for you. Just like this."

Dupré could not move his hand from the chef's grip and he saw the knife flashing through the air on to his hand and then…nothing. He had closed his eyes. When he opened them he saw that the knife had stopped exactly on the ridges of his knuckles and though it was sharper than any razor, the damage caused to the skin was no more than if a blunt instrument had rested there.

"Not another chef in London, in Europe, can do that. That's what you pay for here. That's why this is the greatest restaurant in Town. Antonio, call the boys in blue. Let's prosecute this con artist."

The chef stood up and walked out. Dupré began to tremble. He examined his hand. It was frozen. He slowly unpicked the fingers one by one. The hand started to tremble again. How had he allowed himself to be suckered in to this horrific situation? It wasn't as if any of the wines, the Sauternes apart, were remotely worth the money.

He grabbed the only remaining glass on the table, holding the restaurant's own brand of mineral water, and gulped the contents down.

"Somebody set me up, Antonio," he muttered feebly.

The manager sighed and wandered off. He was thinking that this would make a marvellous story for Londoner's Diary in the Evening Standard. It would make the restaurant even more deliciously notorious. It was only a pity that this Dupré fellow was a nobody. A good row with a Hollywood film star was what really made the headlines. How had he not noticed Dupré was a common or garden con-man the moment he entered? The manager had already instructed the girl on cloaks, Bernice, with whom he had recently struck up sleeping arrangements, to call the police but they declined to intervene. The affair was a civil one and was not police business unless violence or tangible theft had taken place. The manager wished Dupré was not so damned ordinary, but then he thought of the man who had come over to the shyster's table. Gervaise Gilroy-Carstairs was a known wine merchant; he had supplied the restaurant with many of its Alsatian and German wines. Was Dupré something in wine? He went back to Dupré's table. Dupré was staring at the two halves of his credit card as if hoping they would suddenly be miraculously rejoined.

"Do you have a business card I could see?"

"That's more like it," said Dupré, glimpsing hope. "Look. Here." He extracted his Guild of Writers on Wine membership card. Under his name was the imposing word Chairman but as he looked at this card and thirty years of shenanigans, double-dealing, bribery and arse-licking passed before his febrile intelligence, he realised that it would be disastrous if this situation became known to this colleagues. He would have to resign as chairman. Not even the Guild, which tolerated all manner of mountebanks, would stand for a chairman publicly disgraced. The man he had replaced, not to mention that ex's cronies, would have a field day. Dupré would be forced to go whether he liked it or not. And what of his PR clients? He would surely lose them. And what about His Highness Prince Zayn Mussire al-Din? He could kiss goodbye to him, too.

He laughed. He felt his chest tighten. There was no private secretary called Alec Saunders. He didn't exist. Someone had set him up. He returned the card to his wallet and put it in his pocket.

"No, I don't have a business card. Sorry."

"That was a card you just took out. I insist on seeing it."

"I'm going now. I'm leaving. I'm sorry you have been misled, but so have I. You cannot forcibly keep me here and you cannot possibly get that amount of money out of me because I don't have it."

He stood up, a trifle unsteadily. He felt, however, a little braver now that horrendous chef had disappeared. His heart was bursting against the immobile mobile phone.

"Please wait until we have ascertained your true identity. I shall telephone Mr Gilroy-Carstairs."

The sound of the wine merchant's name burned like hot coals in Dupré's head. He began a walk, which he hoped contained some vestige of dignity, towards the door. He had to escape. No waiter stood in his way as he fled the restaurant. He ran down the street.

He was soon, to his relief, engulfed by a narrow passageway in Shepherd Market. He desperately felt he must have a coffee. No-one from the restaurant had followed him. He stood against a wall and passed a handkerchief across his forehead.

"You look like you need someone like me. Anything I can do for you?"

It was not an uncultured voice and she was not dressed like any tart he had ever seen, even the discreet ones who operated behind the *Rue des Rosiers* in Paris. Dupré put his hand on his wallet. He had fifty quid in it for sure. It was to last for the week, and it was only Tuesday.

"Yes. Yes there is. You don't know…anyone…called Alec Saunders, I suppose?" he said breathlessly.

The young woman, able to discern intentions in eyes and gestures like some people can read hieroglyphs, put a hand on his arm. She could feel the heat of the body and the trembling of the limb.

"You don't look like the sort of bloke who likes men. Fifty quid straight sex, seventy-five a blow job, hundred if you want me to dress up, hundred and fifty for bondage or anything exotic."

"You know," said Dupré, looking her up and down and taking in the comparative elegance of the pink high-heeled shoes, the short black skirt, and the cheese-cloth shirt with its vivid *crepe de chine* waistcoat, "I've been well and truly fucked once today already. But I don't mind…"

"Round here, was it? Where? This is my beat."

"One sixty-one Curzon Street."

"What? I don't know anyone worked out of there. Above that restaurant, yeah? "

She was no girl, this one. Dupré thought her rather restrained for a prostitute. Twenty-five years old or so, short fair hair with black roots, big lips not over-made up, nose in keeping with the narrow eyes. She was a big improvement on the ghastly battle-axes whom he had had to wheedle – in some cases actually wine and dine – in to voting for his chairmanship of the Circle. That ghastly Scots journalist, whose sole *raison d'être* was to prance around wine-tastings showing off how many corked bottles she could detect, he'd almost been compelled to sleep with.

He leaned off the wall and fingered his bow-tie. It was constricting his throat. His chest felt so tight it was as if it was being stretched. The woman was about to go, puzzled by his inertia. He caught her hand and as she responded to this positive possibility of business, Dupré fell sideways across her and collapsed and she was far too frail of stature to prevent him folding up and keeling over on to the ground. He was dead before he hit the cobblestones, though she did not know this. She was out of the alleyway and off into White Horse Street within seconds.

ooooo

The cremation at Kensal Green cemetery brought out a healthy contingent of wine scribes, PR women, wine merchants, wine association employees, a German wine grower, an ex-wife no-one knew about, several restaurateurs (though no-one from La Cuillère Graisseuse) and Reg's widowed mother, who took the coach down. Those who came face to face with her marvelled at Mrs Harris's deportment for a woman of eighty-five. Other mourners, upon being presented to her, wondered where on earth *la mère* Dupré had acquired such a pronounced Midlands accent. The ex-chairman of the Guild of Writers on Wine, Paul Hawksmere, gave a moving oration, his skills as an ex-TV commercial voice-over artiste fully deployed. There was a sob in his voice as he spoke of the great job Pierre would have done had the Great Sommelier in the sky granted him the time.

Pierre would have turned in his grave had he had one. But he was a heap of ash and would only be able to turn in an urn that would, at some point, be presented to his mum.

Though Pierre Dupré had, let us not forget, achieved his life's ambition: a small cosy place somewhere warm to which he could permanently retire when his time was done.

ooooo

Sainsbury's Own-Label Sicilian Red 1999

They put health warnings on cigarette packets. In America, they put health warnings on wine bottles. But baby daughters are born without health warnings. This is a major medical omission. Florence, my baby, slid free from between my legs, slippery like a seal pup. And after the midwife had done her bit my husband, misty-eyed, handed Florence to me and said, "I believe this belongs to you". How little he knew. In reality she was going to belong to him. They should put health warnings on baby daughters. They should be born with a notice around their angelic necks: *"Beware. Fathers fall in love with their daughters."*

Brian and Florence became inseparable. Not at first, you understand. At first he was merely elated, proud, fulfilled. More or less the parallel emotions he got from his job. I know this because he told me. I saw him at work, knew what he did there, because that is how we met. I left university with French and Spanish determined to work in travel but ended up at Sainsbury's buying wine. Brian is Fine Wine Director (it actually says this on his calling card), or rather was when I met him, of an international wine importer. He earns a fair slew of money, or rather did; makes lots of friends, or rather did; has a lot riding on his shoulders, and I suppose that bit's still true. I thought I was the peasant girl who married the prince when I woke up one day and found him not only in my bed but, more dangerously, in my affections. Those affections stayed intact, became strengthened when Florence was born, dipped as our lovemaking dropped off drastically for six months whilst I was breast-feeding her, and then got back to something like its old self, but not quite, as she began to walk at ten months. Then sex died almost completely as she threw off her nappies during the day at seventeen months but never learned to sleep at night. At twenty-five months, she learned to talk like a machine gun. Finally, at thirty-eight months, she took my husband away. Not only from me, you understand. She's also taken him away from his job. Now, at seventy-two months, he's the one at home looking after the house, taking her to school, picking her up, and I'm the one at work. He's become a new man alright, and it makes me sick.

I remember how it began, so innocently. He took Florence to a meeting at the office. This was considered a wacky thing to do in a stolid business like wine importing (and his company was very stolid and large) and she went down a bomb, gurgling, apparently, at all the right moments. He took her again, and again, and again and again, before she started nursery school. Then he began to insist on taking her to this new school himself, staying while the name-call was taken, and then on picking her up when school was over. He got to the office late, he left early. The office got miffed at this. Where was he, I was often asked by some frantic salesman or other, as they rang around trying to trace him. I didn't dare say at first. At first, I thought it was cute. It was wonderful having a husband who was so doting on his daughter. Besides, it left me free to catch up on a few things. But there is only so much that a woman needs to catch up on. *Cute!* Can you believe that? In the end there was no job left for him to do. Pushy underlings took it over.

Florence is a little vampire. She sucked me dry of energy and interest in normal pursuits for all those early months and replaced the master of the universe I thought I'd married with a sexless, exhausted, trite, puerile wimp who gets up in the night to attend to her least nightmare whilst I, my vagina wet yet unexplored, remain in suspense until I go back to sleep knowing I have to be out of the house by a quarter to eight to attend a tasting panel for our new range of own-label Spanish and Italian wines. I leave the happy couple at the breakfast table, Florence's pink plastic lunch box bursting with the sandwiches he's made for her lying beside her plate with her bus pass on top, and Brian nose deep in some medical handbook which he believes will get him closer to understanding Florence's slight back rash and irregular insomnia. *Bus pass!* Can you believe it? My husband has one too. Can you believe, can you really believe, that he drove a Porsche 911, admittedly vintage but still cool, with CD stereo and a turbo charger before he chucked in his job – or rather got fired. I'll give him credit for that. He did wait to get the bullet and he received a year's money as the smallest golden handshake they could contractually give him. But they took the Porsche back, and the Volvo that I had on the same deal, and now I putter off to Sainsbury's on the tube.

"Bye, Mummy."

"Bye, darling. Kiss!"

"Mmmmm."

"Bye, Brian. Bye, Brian. Brian! Bye-bye!"

"Oh yes…bye, darling…see you."

As a normal husband he's dead for me now. His transformation from old man to new is complete. He's proud of being a new man. Of treating women with the same offhandedness he treats men. Of having come to terms, as he puts it, with the feminine side of his character. Of being involved with child-rearing like a woman would. Can you believe such drivel? I'm lucky Sainsbury kept my job on hold. Well, almost. I'm doing what I used to do before Florence came along but of course I don't get to travel to France and Spain any more.

"Get back to where you were," Brian had said smugly, "and then get to the top. I'll be behind you all the way." I hadn't planned to go back to work so quickly. I certainly hadn't in my worst dreams imagined that I would be the main bread-winner. Oh, true, Brian does some consultancy work. A bit here and a bit there. He fits it in between the number 18 or 31 bus ride to Kensington High Street to get Florence to school by nine in the morning and the same ride back at three in the afternoon. He does small things for those fringe boutique wine merchants that can't afford full-time input. He makes peanuts, of course. He used to make caviar. He buys his shirts at Marks & Spencer. They cost £14.50. Well, he's only bought one, a short-sleeved number, but he hardly needs long-sleeved shirts any more and, besides, he has thirty in his wardrobe and most of them say Paul Smith or Agnès B on the inside collar. Three months before Florence was born he spent £700 on shirts and thought no more of it than if he was forking out the cash to buy a paperback book. Now he compares the prices at Tesco and Lidl since my employer's nearest branch is a car drive distant. Now he has his Oyster card. Now he has Florence.

Many women think it's wonderful what he's doing. We go out with friends, me having finally cajoled him into the belief that Emma may be only nineteen but she's a perfectly competent baby-sitter and yes, she does cost £15 and that's a week's worth of bus tickets but it's worth it, and the men consider him at worst genuinely deranged or, at best, faintly dotty. But the women think I've managed some new feminist miracle. I'm out to work all day, sometimes some of the evening, doing a glamorous job (ha, ha) which more than pays our mortgage, and when I get home the hoovering's been done, the washing machine has churned out my undies clean, and the dishwasher is emptied. Everyone says Well done, Amanda! Clever old Amanda! Crafty Machiavellian Amanda! But I'd rather take credit for Florence than any brilliant scheme to have turned my wonderful normal husband into a so-called new man. It's not the money. Please believe that. The money, or the lack of it, is only a minor factor really, though I do miss that fortnight we took every year at his international wine merchant's expense in Sardinia. This year we're going to Cornwall where a friend has a house and a boat and they're letting us have it for £200 for two weeks. The house we stayed in Sardinia cost £2000 a week.

I suppose Florence comes off best. She has a doting father. And she is a doting daughter in return. He spends hours on her reading and her drawing and, of course, her music lessons. She perceives, as far as I can tell, nothing extraordinary about the relationship at all. Why should she? Maybe it's the way it ought to be. Maybe I'm the one out of step. I yell at him a lot more, which only makes me feel worse and more guilty since what do I have to yell at him for? Lack of money? Yes, but we get by with a struggle. Lack of sex? Yes, and we barely get by and there's no struggle. Sex isn't what it was. That's another health warning they should print on new-born babies. "God,

I'm tired," Brian says as he flakes out forty-five minutes after Florence has been put to bed.

The incredible thing is that I've let this state of affairs develop under my nose. Unfortunately, or perhaps I should say inevitably, things have now reached crisis point. I emptied the waste basket in the spare bedroom where Brian does his consultancy dreaming and discovered a crumpled letter three weeks old. It was from one of the biggest wine e-tailers and they were confirming in writing an earlier telephone conversation in which this company urged Brian to change his mind about the job they wanted to talk to him about. Seventy-five grand a year! I went, I'm not ashamed to admit, completely potty.

"Why didn't you tell me about this…you…you…"

I waved the crumpled letter under his face. He was sitting on the Conran sofa with the suede cushions. Couldn't afford to buy the castors now, let alone the cushions, let alone the damn sofa. He had just put Florence to bed after reading her, no doubt for the fiftieth time, *Wind in the Willows* which he was actually trying to get her to read herself. The child's barely six years old, for heaven's sake! He had his half-moon glasses halfway down his nose. God, I wanted to smash those glasses!

"I'm tired. I don't need to justify…."

"Brian, we're broke. We're just about surviving…"

"Florence needs me. I'm not going back to full-time wine merchanting."

"But what about me? What about *me* doing the job they wanted to talk to you about? I'm not talking about *you* here, I'm talking about *me* !"

"But you…you couldn't…you…"

"You phoney bastard! You're about as much a new man as I am! It never even crossed your mind. You never even considered that I could do the job of Buying Director for Virgin. I could do it standing on my head. I could do it...do it..."

"I never thought."

"*I never thought.* What happened to your 'I'll be behind you all the way'? You're behind no-body but yourself! "

I saw the look in his eyes. Behind the tiredness there was contempt. The contempt of the winner for the loser. I was his wife. That meant a secondary role whether he went to work or I did. Nothing had changed at all. I was forever condemned to secondary status whatever the circumstances and I hadn't even my daughter to confide in. That's when I tore the glasses off his surprised, stupidly surprised, face. Tore them off and stamped on them and then hit him with a bottle of my new own-label Sicilian red, the one I'd personally blended for the company. *I never thought.* He's never thought. New men don't. They just want to be children, so they make sure they spend all their time around children. I left him bleeding all over the suede cushions and walked out.

You see, I could stand losing the housework. I could tolerate not seeing as much of Florence. I could accept the loss in our sex life. I could even get used to never seeing that Sardinian villa again. But I couldn't bear living with the thought that my husband never even for a moment considered that I could have done that job for Virgin. All he had to do was tell them that they couldn't have him but they could have me. Would they have bought it? Maybe. If Brian had put the idea to them right. Sure they would. I could bear all the losses, but not this final one. The one that said your husband doesn't even think of you as his equal. Doesn't even put you in the same league as him.

I never thought. Those were the last words I ever let him utter to me. He sat there dazed as the blood ran down his face and globs of Sicilian red seeped on to the rug.

He looked at me without comprehending. Was he still conscious? Who cared?

"Get yourself a new token wife. This one is *quitting*."

And I made sure I woke Florence with the noise of wardrobe doors groaning, and bathroom doors slamming, and I humped a suitcase down the stairs and left. As the front door crashed behind me I'm sure I heard a voice saying "It's alright darling, Mummy's just nipped out…for…"

I never heard another word. But the word was of course *good.*

ooooo

Le Mesnil Grand Cru Blanc de Blancs Champagne 1949

1.

At half-past five that Friday afternoon a thorn was due to drop from Alexander Sturtin's side. He had borne its barb with discomfort for twenty-two years. The most ingenious surgery had failed to dislodge it and in celebration of its removal he had descended to his cellar one week previously, carefully extracted the last bottle of Le Mesnil Grand Cru Blanc de Blancs Champagne 1949, and taken it to his office. He was going to be magnanimous. After the thorn had been drawn and seen off the premises he was going to treat his fellow directors to this last bottle of great champagne, which his father had given him when his son had succeeded into the position. There had been only eight bottles and the last one opened, the seventh, had been quite extraordinary, as had been the daughter whose birth it celebrated, though Sturtin craved a boy.

From the triple-glazed window in his office he could see the factory clock. It dominated the machines, high above the clatter, like an android tennis umpire: impartial, implacable, the unswerving arbiter. Sturtin checked its time with his watch. Both agreed on five twenty-five.

The clock had an incurable eccentricity Sturtin admired. The large hand did not slide from minute to minute with the remorseless precision given to Swiss mechanics. It stood guard at each minute notch for sixty seconds; only, at the last moment with British abandon, to hurl itself forward with a stumble and a clack.

Just like Mr Sturtin senior, Alexander's father, as now and then he picked his way about the works (for old times sake). However, only freight trains were rarer visitors nowadays. The weed-swathed railway line had once connected the factory with ports to the far-flung markets of the empire. Sturtin & Hardy Metal Casings Limited, though still one of the neighbourhood's bigger employers, was not the force it had once been.

It was a fact of life frequently on Sturtin's mind. He liked exquisite champagne. It was necessary to do shrewder business if he was to continue to fund such tastes. Occasionally he thought new avenues might open up and fresh opportunities beckon, but always he faltered. Yet wasn't this a new decade, a new era? Wilson, that closet libertarian, had been sent packing, along with his blasted pipe and pipsqueak socialist puppies. Heath had been in Downing Street for a couple of years now but where was the fresh air, and fresh hope, this promised for the rejuvenation of the less dynamic members of the Confederation of British Industry? The firm soldiered on; in the manner of an ancient yet handsome spinster of whom it is said by legend was a real wild 'un in her youth.

On this particular afternoon Sturtin felt the invigorating breeze of opportunity stir once more. Indeed, he told himself, at the very next hooting of the clock's klaxon, the very second the minute hand slumped into the half-hour notch and the hour hand groped nervously towards the six, his agony was due to end and, perhaps, a glorious dawn of fresh management initiative would break.

At half-past five that Friday afternoon, Harry Maddren was going to retire after thirty-three years with the firm; twenty-two years of which he had been shop steward. The last bottle of Le Mesnil Grand Cru Blanc de Blancs Champagne 1949, waiting in his secretary's office in an ice bucket, was a fitting libation to this end of an era. Sitting next to it was a second ice bucket in which cooled a bottle of Cremant d'Alsace.

2.

The man in the shadow of the press turned to his mate leaning over the adjacent cutter. Both machines gnawed the ears with their din, the cutter screeching, the press groaning, yet the two men had over the years achieved the precise pitch at which conversation was possible. Even so, their interchanges tended to be strained and short with the machinery on and their earplugs out.

The less careworn of the two nodded approvingly at the clock as its hands slouched reluctantly on to half-past five. He took a cigarette packet from his overalls pocket and rattled it.

"Soddin' things!" he shouted. "Do me a favour. Take me last one. Tonight I'm back to Capstans. Sticks of chalk. That's all these are."

The cutter laughed and took the last cigarette. "All in a good cause," he reminded the presser.

"Fifty million coupons. Unbefuckinglievable."

"Harry'll like what we got. You wait and see."

The presser twisted his lips in his skull. It was neither grin nor grimace. The cutter knew the expression well. He sympathized with a look of his own.

Expertly, the presser hurled the empty cigarette packet in to a swarf bin some twenty feet away.

3.

"Surprising our workforce should show such imagination," Sturtin remarked to Henry Corke, who was sitting the other side of the desk.

After a pause, as if to allow a moment in history to collect itself before passing on, Corke nodded into his whisky glass.

"Astonishing Maddren never guessed. Every worker in the place smoking the same brand of cigarette must have seemed rather odd."

"They asked Roberta, you know, to join. They were most piqued at her refusal."

"Your secretary is beyond reproach, Alexander."

"She did the right thing."

"Well, she actually gave up smoking five years ago."

"They asked her because they were several thousand coupons short. Fifty million, I believe, they contracted with the cigarette company. I wonder what they got the old bastard?"

But the response in Corke's breast – "his own nuclear missile perhaps?" – was not allowed to surface. The geriatric clock, giving the nod to the klaxon, reached half-past five and the employees and directors alike enjoyed a ten-second blast in F falling to A. As the democratic wail subsided, the managing director and the director of personnel partook of a ritualised adjusting of their neckties. Sturtin went off to the boardroom. Corke smoothed his hair and headed slowly to the men's washroom next to the jig store.

4.

With the klaxon's wail fading the howl of the machinery died. Harry Maddren stared at his mechanical master. He touched the wheel of the bore. It had not changed its convex gleam in years. No amount of sweat or oil had impressed it. He wiped it nevertheless. He scraped a fingernail along its only scar: a quarter-inch long groove made by a piece of once stuck then hot flying metal. The apprentice who had forgotten to both lock the jaws and shut the guard had been badly hurt in the chest. But that was fifteen years ago and more modern safety regulations made such a repeat of the accident improbable.

Maddren breathed deep. The factory smells permanently encrusted his nostrils. The most powerful being the coolant's. On his first foreign holiday, ten years ago now, he had passed by a brass-turner's workshop in Marbella and the reek was so redolent of his machine and the factory that he had been subdued for an afternoon. Joan Maddren thought he must have been stricken by a food-bug.

His short legs took him into the gangway. As his balding head, crouched on his shoulders like a half-sleeping bird's, appeared from behind his machine, a great cheer greeted him. Even the women, whom he had occasionally infuriated, touched him and laughed. Flora, who stitched the leather cladding for the decorative rods and nursed enmity like a sick child, condescended to smile and throw him a kiss. The men slapped his shoulders. It wasn't difficult. He was only five feet four.

Maddren reached the jig store where three gangways converged and there the crowd was. Someone sang "For he's a jolly good fellow". But if Harry was moved he didn't show it. Shepherds acquire a certain stoicism with regard to their flock, though this metaphor was not one of which he approved. He led no animal to slaughter; he merely tried to control the ticks, those damn parasitic managers.

In the washroom men stood aside to let Harry reach his basin. The younger ones regarded his passage with envy, wondering how many years it would be before they could walk into the jig store washroom at knocking-off time, when nigh on eighty men would throng the five basins, and know that space and time would be granted them by others to wash without queuing.

"He's washing his hands of us now. For good and all."

The jokes flew thicker and faster than the wet lumps of loo paper. The towels rolled black and greasy to the floor. A capstan-lathe setter who should have known better scrawled "Maddren Rules, O.K.?" with thick green industrial soap on a mirror. It slithered into a mess on a sink.

Henry Corke edged his way into this assembly with the fastidious horror of a vegetarian who miraculously finds himself in an abattoir. The washroom fell silent and wary.

"Can't let you go without a token of our esteem, Mr Maddren. Mr Sturtin and the board…that is, we, would be honoured if you would join us before you go on to the celebration I know you have planned."

There were fresh jokes now, and when Corke and Maddren, shoulder to shoulder as never before, finally pushed their way out of the washroom, the party had already begun. A rolled-up ball of loo paper struck the personnel director provocatively on the back. If he felt anything he gave no sign.

5.

Corke held open the boardroom door and Harry acknowledged the toothy smiles of the directors and contrasted them with the expressions on the same faces not six months back. He allowed himself to look pleased. Was he really feeling happy at retiring?

He supposed he was. Though in the past month or so he had begun to realise that he was not so much leaving something old as going on to something new. But what was this other, this unknown, this new something?

Sturtin regarded the entrance of the great barb with satisfaction. He felt his heart fluttering. He could swear his pulse was racing. He could feel the tweezers – no dammit, the pliers – encircling the barb ready to tug it free. Or was the operation already over? That was what they were celebrating, wasn't it? Sturtin spoke without thinking.

"The champagne, Roberta! The champagne."

Roberta, who secretly admired Harry Maddren, nodded. She entered her boss's office, adjoining the boardroom, and tried to remember which champagne cooler contained the right bottle. It was the right hand one, wasn't it? Both had white washing-up cloths draped over them. She picked up the left one and checked the bottle. The label, its ancient glue shaky in its loyalty, had slipped off the bottle but the word champagne was still visible on the neck if she put on her reading glasses. She examined the other bottle. It was the cheap Alsatian bubbly she had been specifically instructed to transport. Sturtin had gone through the arrangements that afternoon. But then hadn't Mr Sturtin said, just a few seconds ago: "The champagne, Roberta! The champagne"? Surely he had. Roberta raised an eyebrow. She removed her reading glasses. She let a flicker of a smile play on her lips, which she had recently lipsticked. She picked up the left-hand cooler and re-entered the boardroom.

"It'll just go round six glasses, er, seven…I mean," said Sturtin, remembering to include his secretary.

Roberta put the cooler down on a mat on the old mahogany boardroom table. Sturtin himself was doing the honours. He had been asking Maddren what his plans were now that he had no workers to incite (that was what Sturtin would have *liked* to have said, but it came out differently). Maddren had shrugged his shoulders, as he always did when addressed by Sturtin.

The bottle was flourished from the cooler and handed to Sturtin. He tore away the foil and untwisted the wire and began the speech he had prepared thick with reminiscences of the wars the two men had fought and how it was now time to let bye-gones be bye-gones. Maddren felt quite thirsty. He felt, in fact, utterly empty.

The personnel director brought the tray with the glasses, Roberta bringing the seventh herself. The other four members of the board, all dressed in what seemed to her identical striped suits and club or sporting ties, murmured sagely with Arctic hearts behind their tropical smiles. Each one of them nursed a detestation of the diminutive creature who stood before them as ferociously as they would a murderer of a member of their Sunday golf four. The sales director cursed the missed orders Maddren's intransigence had frustrated; the works director remembered the lost hours never made up; the finance director mourned the lost revenue; and the export director, who had learned his German from his prison camp guards, lamented the export markets the firm had failed to sustain. He was due to retire himself next year and he could hardly wait for it and to do slightly less than his duties required of him now.

Sturtin let the personnel director pour out the wine and as he saw the bubbles settle in the glass and the rich straw colour of the wine became apparent, his face changed. When he smelled the wine in his glass, as he was extruding from his mind (as stubbornly as a strip of tempered steel) the platitude that "the board and I have never had anything but the greatest respect for your principles as a leader of men, Mr Maddren", he was forced to grit his teeth all the harder. He turned on Roberta in a fury.

She had anticipated this. Why should this mean old bugger get away with fobbing Maddren off with a bottle of Cremant bought from Cullens the grocers in the high street?

"Something wrong, sir?" she said.

"Wow! This is generous of you, Alex!" said Works, as he nosed his wine.

"This is the champagne!" ground out Sturtin.

"That's what you said to bring in, Mr Sturtin. That's what you said to bring in."

Sturtin stuttered a routine toast. The directors sipped. Harry Maddren downed his glass in one gulp and smacked his lips. Sturtin's eyes bulged. Like traffic lights, thought Export, remembering with a shudder that Sturtin & Hardy was once the major producer of traffic light hoods, produced by machines still extant in the works: power presses forced into short time working and then expensive refit by this very same Harry Maddren because they were declared unsafe by a joint decision of the union and the works health & safety committee. All because an imbecile of a Pakistani had lost two fingers of his right hand due to his misunderstanding of English!

"I s'pose," said Maddren," there isn't any more of this stuff, is there? I could get used to bubbly like this."

"This stuff!" raged Sturtin in his heart. "This stuff! A single bottle of this stuff costs more than a month of your wages!"

An image of the Le Mesnil vineyards, to which he had once made a pilgrimage with the protesting Isabel, floated in to his brain. That rare patch of earth! Those reluctant, majestic vines! This unique champagne they created, the most expensive in France! 1949 was its greatest vintage of the century and even his father, who had endured the trenches of 1917 and '18 (rising to the heights of captaincy and the Military Cross) in order to keep such vinous treasures out of the hands of the Boche, had never been allowed to purchase more than a single case a year.

It made him sick to see Harry Maddren treat it as if it was lemonade.

6.

They let him go after eleven minutes. Sturtin was too choked with emotion to say much more. In Maddren's hand was a barometer of gothic pretentiousness with a plaque endearingly inscribed.

When he examined the memento at the works party he discovered the milled ornamental balls on the casing had been ground and polished in his very own section. He said nothing to Joan when he brought the monstrosity home. She'd be upset that the old men had bought him something at trade from an established customer.

7.

"They didn't give it to you just to sit in and brood, y'know," said Joan Maddren coming through the garden shed door with a cup of tea.

She looked reproachfully at Harry and then glanced accusingly round at the small and tidily arranged agricultural tools hanging on the walls. They were pristine and shiny. Been like it for two weeks. She handed him the cup.

"My retirement, isn't it?" he shot at her.

Joan shuffled her feet in her slippers. She was bigger than Harry. And with him perched on an exotic terracotta flower pot (5000 coupons), she appeared even larger. She was already finding it difficult to adjust to a husband who didn't work any more; who only seemed interested in going out on alternative Saturday afternoons and on Wednesday nights to the Labour Club for billiards.

"If only they'd asked me," she muttered. "I could have told them you hated gardening."

Harry sipped his tea. His world had shrunk to the dimensions of this garden shed and he wanted to wallow in the poverty of his domain. Joan recognised the expression and moved towards the door.

"Get a bloomin' part-time job. Like me. Won't interfere with your pension if you work it right."

So that's what's on her mind, thought Harry, raising his eyes to hers. The wooden slatted door slammed shut behind her. Maybe she had a point.

After two weeks of retirement he was aching for some kind of action. He was almost jealous of Joan's part-time number, which she refused to give up. Maybe he was too young to go out to grass after all. He finished the tea and glared at the fork beside him, the gleaming tines rebuking him for their disuse. Wasn't there some cricket on the telly this afternoon?

8.

For several decades Joan Maddren had only ever seen her husband in a grey-green cap, a tweed jacket the colour of strong tea, and a pair of brown trousers. She was not unused to seeing him in aquamarine pyjamas. And if City reached a respectable stage of the Cup she would shake the moths off a maroon and black scarf and he would wear that with pride.

Coming back unusually early one afternoon from her school canteen due to a dispute over cooked peas she was, then, rendered speechless, as she came through the bedroom door, by the sight of Harry examining himself in the full-length wardrobe mirror.

He had on a knee-length yellow mackintosh and a black peaked cap with a yellow band. In his hand, like a lancer on parade, he gripped a pole with a red disc on top. He turned, wary. She stared, stunned.

"Didn't expect you for another hour," he murmured.

Joan came closer and playfully tapped his cap.

"Haven't seen you in a uniform since VE Day. You said never again, remember?"

Harry's and Joan's hands, obeying an old force, touched. He put down the pole and took off the cap. They stood, arm in arm, seeing themselves in the mirror.

"Not bad nick for sixty-two," he said to her approvingly.

She smiled and rested her shoulder on his. She regarded the stiff, wiry body of her husband reflected in the glass and thought: you're not in bad shape yourself for sixty-five. Top of the head was showing through the hair, which was frost-like above the ears, but she could affectionately relate the image in the mirror to the demobbed figure she had met at Clacton Beach Holiday Camp. Maureen had been conceived during that fortnight. Joan had been grateful that Harry had done the decent thing. Now she felt suffused with an accumulated subcutaneous satisfaction. As if the bones held the memories in the marrow and, leaning her skeleton against her husband's, feeling her hip joint against his, she was summoning up past images simply by pressure. She made no further comment about his new outfit; though, for the moment, she could not quite place what occupation it kitted him out for.

9.

The town Council had been fearful of ever finding the right person to cover the dangerous stretch of road between the junior school and the west edge of the golf course. They knew the elementary mistake they had made in not putting down slip roads when they had built the school. The road was the only route to the dual-carriageway available to the residents south of the golf course and these residents were among the town's notables. Luckily for Council peace of mind such residents sent their kids to schools other then Berkeley Junior, which was reputed to be rough. Local worthies could comfortably motor by and regard the little horrors as they might goldfish, through glass, and gain further comfort from the thought that thank God little James and Sarah didn't have to mix with that lot.

Harry took up his appointed position at 7.59am. Rain was fizzing down and he was pleased to have found a practical purpose for the green rubber boots (15,000 coupons) that had come with the shed.

At eight-o-one he made his first professional decision. He could have let the old Ford Zodiac through before the kid reached the kerb to cross but Harry felt concern for the bedraggled youngster with the over-large football boots across his shoulder (hand-me-downs from an older brother) and he stepped in the road with pole bristling. The kid, as if on rails, never averted his downward gaze, never lifted his head or said a word, just plodded across. He'd obviously been sent out of the house early. If the father was on night work and the mother had a job it would be one time they could enjoy a bit of peaceful nooky. Harry stared sympathetically at the football boots as the kid vanished out of sight down the alley to the school. Then the Zodiac's tetchy horn started up and Harry realised he was still standing in the middle of the road. As he moved out of the way he was treated to a glare of hatred from the driver.

10.

Alexander Sturtin's partiality for overbearing timepieces was quickly evident to any visitor to Birch Lodge, easily the most imposing of the houses visible from the seventh and twelve tees. The grandfather in the hall was massive and ticked like a lumberjack working off a grudge. In the dining room, where he was finishing breakfast, hung a clock so corpulent that dinner guests could feel the reverberant chimes enter their bowels as they chewed Mrs Sturtin's speciality venison dish.

Each morning Alexander checked his clocks with the incongruously up-to-the-minute watch around his left wrist. It was a very modern quartz timepiece and guaranteed to be accurate to within three seconds a month. Satisfied with the monster on the wall, he kissed his wife and left his copy of The Times by her bread plate. He went in to the hall, onfirmed the grandfather's fidelity, and picked up The Financial Times, which lay folded on the wine table. He opened the front door and recoiled at the rain. The chauffeur in the Rolls

Royce in the drive was out of the car and standing beside the porch with an opened umbrella in less time than the guaranteed monthly accuracy of Sturtin's watch. Sturtin got in the car, opened his FT and settled back in the old leather. By the time the car had reached the end of the drive he had already checked that no disaster had struck the family's considerable share portfolio in prime British stock.

He had followed this procedure, more or less without deviation, for over two decades. The chauffeur could set a chronometer by the precise second his employer's front door opened in the morning. It was twenty minutes to nine; not nineteen; not twenty-one; always, teeth-on-edge-settingly, twenty. Sufficient time to allow the chauffeur to appear with his cargo at the weighbridge by the factory gates at nine o'clock precisely. The gatekeeper would check his fob as the maroon limousine purred through. The goods-in personnel (who started at half-past eight) would consult their watches. The time clerk, who looked after the workers' time cards, knew no surer way to congratulate his brass chronometer on its accuracy than by Alexander's Sturtin's arrival for work.

Sturtin liked to think of himself as Halley's comet: predictable, unswerving, a real ball of fire.

Wrapped up with, and not a little concerned by, the newspaper's prophecy of an impending and considerable rise in oil prices, it was some moments before Sturtin realised that his car had hardly been travelling for two minutes before it was stationary for a similar lapse of time. He chewed his lip and raised his eyes over the paper's doom-laden rumblings.

"Get a move on, Barker," he said softly. He had no need to use the intercom to talk to his driver. He allowed the sliding-glass glass partition between the front and back seats to remain open when he travelled alone. A modern touch, he thought, in keeping with the more open style of management he was considering introducing now that the barb had been extracted.

"They've got a lollipop person, sir," said Barker, pointing out the sulphurous-coloured sentry. (And quelling the thought that it was about bloody time. His Terry went to Berkeley Junior.)

Sturtin looked at his watch and tutted. "Hooter?" he suggested.

"It's a bloke, Mr Sturtin."

"What?"

"The lollipop man. It's a man."

"I know it's a man. Hoot the blighter and let's be on our way. We can make up the minutes we've lost if you put your foot down."

But Barker was spared the trouble of hooting. Behind Sturtin's Roller at least eight other cars were strung out and as one driver pressed his horn so they all did. The yellow figure turned around, water dripping off his cap. He pulled the peak more firmly down around his eyes and motioned the children to continue crossing.

"This is intolerable, Barker."

Barker kept a tight rein on his lips, the steering wheel, and his emotions. "Yessir," he agreed.

Harry didn't see why these kids, many of them indifferently protected against the rain, should stand and get soaked while motorists swept by dry and warm. After a moment, when his next customers were a good thirty yards away, he finally stood himself and his pole aside. The cars cruised through, splashing his boots. The maroon Roller seemed familiar from somewhere, but it hardly mattered.

Inside that particular car, however, something was very much the matter. Its passenger quickly forgot distant oleaginous controversies to fume at the bare-faced disruption to his schedule. The arrival of Sturtin's car at three minutes past nine flabbergasted the gatekeeper. Had not his transistor radio recently announced the time he would have considered his fob to be faltering. Like thoughts occurred to the goods-in personnel. And the time clerk was out of his office and frowning at his clock when the gate-keeper put him straight.

"I don't believe it, Alf," said the gatekeeper. "Sturtin three minutes late."

"First time for everything," shrugged off the time clerk.

"Eeee...I feel quite dizzy..."

And the two men laughed with the joy of a pair of astronomers who've just confirmed that the moon is made from green cheese after all. But no laughter was heard in Sturtin's office until after the managing director had enjoyed an especially soothing lunch, brought to him, as always on a Monday, by Barbara, the only real cook the office canteen boasted. It was usually steak and chips, and with it Sturtin enjoyed a half-bottle of Monthelie, one of the lesser burgundies; but then Monday lunchtime was, gastronomically, one of the lesser days.

That morning, however, was merely a foretaste of what was to come; a simple canapé to a complex repast.

The next morning the rain was still around and so was Harry. Sturtin, forewarned, ordered Barker to put his foot down and sweep through before the Rolls could be stopped. Barker, mindful of his un-unionised position, did as he was bid, dousing the yellow sentinel and a group of kids with a lovely tsunami that penetrated Harry's socks.

Harry stared grimly at the back of the speeding Rolls. Maybe there was something to this job after all.

Which he proved to his satisfaction the morning after. He saw the Rolls coming two hundred yards away and he was in the middle of the road in a flash, impervious to Barker's hooting. He let the Rolls idle for five minutes before he stepped back to the kerb. The car crept through, its maroon sheen going nicely with the facial colour of the passenger in the back seat.

Sturtin's secretary of sixteen years' standing, dear Roberta, was ready to hand in her notice by lunchtime in spite of her boss working off his rage on a member of the town council he had telephoned. If this had any effect it was not apparent in the lollipop man's surly demeanour. Sturtin was several minutes late for work the next morning in spite of heeding his wife's reasonable advice to leave home five minutes earlier.

"How is it I can get a treasurer booted out yet can't shift a wretched lollipop man?" he complained to the councillor with whom he played Sunday morning golf.

"Big things are easy, Alex. You know that. Little things are tricky. That lollipop man who is an inconvenience to you is, in the view of many of the people who voted for me at the last election, an absolute Godsend."

"Godsend?" screamed Sturtin, teeing off expertly into the trees.

ooooo

The week that followed took five years off Sturtin's life. (It might have been ten years. These things are difficult to pin down precisely.) The effect the matutinal skirmishes had on the life of the lollipop man was equally dramatic.

He asked his wife if she'd like to go to the cinema that evening.

It had been seven years since he had last made such an outrageously spontaneous suggestion. They saw the James Bond film and Joan noticed Harry laugh twice.

Two more than Sturtin managed the next morning. Realising that he faced a determined adversary, he planned an outflanking manoeuvre. Barker was told to turn left at the corner of the golf course instead of right. Barker did so, but quickly found himself facing the dangerously narrow Spring Street, which was one-way in the opposite direction.

"Drive on," commanded Sturtin.

Barker hesitated but did as he was told, only for probationary constable Zealous to turn out of the drive of number eleven having just returned a stolen garden gnome. Fortunately for Barker's licence and Sturtin's reputation, P.C. Zealous was pleased with himself for having single-handedly solved the case and so, at fifty-seven years of age, Sturtin was treated to a lecture by the nineteen-year-old, but nothing more dramatic than that.

They returned whence they came, the tail of the Rolls between its legs, to the conventional route and the merciless Maddren.

The gatekeeper won fifty pence from the time clerk for betting that the managing director would be more than six minutes late that day. Roberta, poking round the cocktail cabinet, looked at her watch and considered but did not take a stiffening swig of sherry.

ooooo

"Why on earth don't you try talking to the man?" offered Mrs Sturtin one morning. "Butter him up," she added briskly, reaching for the toast.

Alexander, chastened by such obvious good sense, thought on this. He chewed his toast ruminatively. Then, with a suddenness that startled a wife inured to his studied demeanour, he rushed out of the house, forgetting even to check his clocks.

Had Isabel Sturtin a covert wish for early widowhood, perhaps? Her suggestion certainly helped peel a few more years off her husband's allotted span and it rattled Fate's grip on Harry's.

ooooo

Now adept at Roller-spotting a mile away, Harry let the car get closer than normal before he pushed his pole into the road. Barker screeched to a halt and Harry let a delightfully lengthy and animated crocodile of children clump slowly across. He was quite unprepared for the tap on the shoulder. He turned and stared up, transfixed, at the head of Alexander Sturtin. A wave of something like horror mixed with impotent rage gripped him. He felt his pulse-rate quicken. And his nostrils were assailed by the reek of industrial coolant, which was remarkable considering the man he faced wore nothing more aromatic than bay rum shaving astringent.

"May I say," began Sturtin, "what an excellent job you are doing here ensuring that future generations will flower unmolested by traffic? Only the other day I was on the phone to Walter Farmilow telling him how...how conscientious our new traffic guardian is..."

Sturtin saw the loose jaw and the wide eyes and wondered if he wasn't talking over the man's head.

"Walter is head of the council department which employs you," Sturtin supplied usefully. "He agreed with me you were doing a first-rate, ahem, job. May I, however, make a small suggestion?"

Sturtin never stayed on his feet long enough. Harry took

off his cap and when Alexander saw that uncovered skull with its white hair like fur above the ears, his jaw sagged lower than Harry's. His eyes rolled like marbles. He reached for Harry's pole for support.

"You! You!? The man who made my life hell for twenty years! The swine who drank two glasses of the last bottle of Les Mesnil 1949 in the world as if it was lemonade!"

Failing to reach the pole, the managing director crumpled like an emptying flour sack. For the first time in his life, Harry found himself supporting Alexander Sturtin.

Barker, who took Alexander's mother on trips, kept smelling salts in the glove compartment and they quickly brought the quenched ball of fire to its senses. Conscious that the Rolls might now be an ambulance, Harry checked the children and let the car speed away.

Sturtin took the rest of the day off. Harry, fifty-one years of toil having licensed all his days off, went home and sat in the garden shed drinking strong tea and nibbling ginger biscuits. He didn't feel especially pleased with himself.

Isabel Sturtin's next suggestion will seem to cynics convincing evidence of her complicity in a plot to lay premature hands on Alexander's life assurance.

"I can't stand the thought of facing Maddren every morning before I reach the office. The prospect is mortifying," Sturtin had admitted, convalescing around malt whisky and extremely old Medoc that weekend.

"I wish he'd never retired," he added, "and if someone had told me I would ever say that, I would have wagered our shares in ICI against it."

Isabel ruminated. This new sherry Alex had bought really was too dry.

"Men," she said emphatically, "can never see the wood for the trees. What was it you and Henry were talking about the other night? Quite boorishly, I might add, since it was supposed to be a night out for Queenie and she was not in the least charmed by your industrial banter. Wasn't he going on about persuading some skilled men to retire early or work part-time? Something to do with teaching the apprentices? Though why anyone needs to spend five years in indentures to turn out a brass spindle is beyond my understanding..."

"So is your drift beyond mine, Isabel."

"My drift is this: why not offer that little man his job back?"

Alex looked dangerously close to a relapse at this suggestion.

"Alex, think about it. He'll have no political power. He'll just be a part-time instructor. Besides, didn't you say the new union official is already putty in your hands? An acned adolescent who studies knitting at the Open University, you said."

Alex smiled and Isabel knew that smile. She knew she'd hit home. Maybe now she could also cajole him into sending back the rest of the sherry and order her regular poison, or at least some decent oloroso.

11.

"It's half-term next week, y'know," said Joan. "You'll have nothing to get up for for a couple of weeks until school comes back. Why not give it a try until then?"

Harry had showed her the letter from Sturtin and Hardy. He could smell the coolant on the envelope but it wasn't altogether putting him off. Maybe he wasn't keen because Sturtin was obviously behind it. But maybe he should go back. He couldn't torture road travellers for ever, and rainy weather was a real grind. So what if that crafty bastard Sturtin wanted him off the road? Better back in the works, even if it was only for a couple of mornings a week. When term started again, he could go back to lollipopping, couldn't he? Or would he find the Council had given the job to someone else? But there wasn't anyone else. So: did he give Sturtin what he wanted? Or did he do what was in his own best interests? If it amounted to the same thing, so what? The old days were over. Surely he'd be cutting off his nose to spite his face if he turned this opportunity down.

"Maybe they'll take their present back as well," he said hopefully.

12.

Having lived in the shadow of Harry Maddren for so long, Lewis Shore, once elected shop steward, was quick to demonstrate that he was of the new school. He appreciated the managing director's avowed intention to introduce a more open style of management and to "reward initiative in the most effective way, in the wage packet".

To prove his faith and to show his more flexible frame of mind (having indeed studied at the Open University, not knitting, as Sturtin had so cruelly suggested, but dialectical philosophy), he had already made certain concessions to the management which the union and workers had accepted in return for a promised share in the increased productivity that would inevitably result. He was rather intrigued to see Maddren back. He had never forgotten the older man's contempt for his intellectual studies. Perhaps a parade of the new-style flexible approach, his small but definite move in the right Hegelian direction, would prove to Maddren that a disciplined and schooled mind was not "a soft thing only good for arguing the toss with vicars" but a force for working-class prosperity. He was among the first to shake Harry's hand when he arrived.

Harry merely remarked how strange it was to come to work an hour after everyone else and not have to use a clock card. More damning proof of how firmly Maddren was entrenched in the past could not be provided, thought Shore. Harry sniffed the air and thought: so what's new?

He found the answer while demonstrating the intricacies of a Schliffen meter (or a Kaiser's arse, as it is affectionately known to older operators) to a pair of priceless ha'porths who called themselves Sniffer and Buster. Harry found both names irritating.

He'd not enjoyed watching City regularly once the players had picked up the modern habit of referring to each other by silly nicknames. That and all the kissing when a goal was scored.

He looked at the clock with a weathered eye and noted the minute hand slump exhausted into the quarter-past notch. The hour hand stood at eleven. He automatically wiped his hands on a rag, preparatory to moving on to the canteen but no Pavlovian klaxon sounded.

"Klaxon's busted, eh?" he said to Sniffer.

"Nah. Don't sound no more. Not for tea-breaks. Trolley comes round between quarter-past eleven and quarter to twelve."

"You mean…no canteen? You don't visit the canteen for tea? You sit in this filth for ten minutes and drink it?"

"Done away with tea-breaks, haven't they? Drink the piss while you're working."

Harry let the heresy sink in. It had taken him years to get a decent amount of time for tea-breaks, morning and afternoon. Not to mention the construction of a clean canteen to drink it in. He left the boys playing with the Kaiser's arse and went over to the men on the press. He wasn't altogether sure that the apprentices weren't having him on.

He spoke to the press operator, who afterwards said he'd thought Maddren's Adam's apple was going to burst through his windpipe.

Harry threw his rag in a bin and went through the wire gate to the adjoining section. He could see Lewis Shore standing philosophically regarding an old Huddersfield made lateral multi-drill.

"Should have been replaced years ago," said Shore as the ex-shop steward came up.

"It's good for a lot longer than you, son. Are you responsible for re-negotiating the tea-breaks? Do you realise..."

Shore was taller by a head than Maddren. He was also the man who carried the can. No-one carried it for him any more. Maddren was out to grass. Shore felt none of the compunction he would have a few months back.

"Don't lecture me. Mr Maddren. Harry."

Harry bridled at that Harry. He studied Shore's hair, which was like plaited rope, his pebble glasses worn so far down the nose they threatened to fall.

"Isn't it enough that human beings work in this filth without having to drink tea in it?"

"Tea! Tea! Tea doesn't oil the wheels of industry, Harry. Incentives do that. The more you put in, the more you take out. We've swapped tea-break canteen privileges for a new productivity deal."

Harry laughed.

"You fool! Sturtin tried for ten years to get me to buy that one. Have you got it in writing? Have you got a written guarantee of access to the books so you can see where the profits go?"

"Have you ever heard of trust? Give and take?"

"You traitor! You've got no guarantee of anything, have you? You've thrown twenty years of my work out the window..."

"Progress, Harry, progress. You stick to instructing. I'll stick to shop-stewarding."

Harry was past sticking at anything except what his instincts commanded. The spirited conversation of the two men had attracted quite a crowd, which soon found itself taking sides. Old memories revived. By the time the minute hand of the works clock had trudged up to noon, three sections of the factory were switching off their machines and throwing their tea in swarf bins.

ooooo

Henry Corke was pleased the hereditary Lothian redness was showing in his managing director's cheeks again. And it was not due to the late morning malt they were enjoying.

"Irony. Supreme irony."

"You said it, Henry."

"Did you know the time clerk was made quite unwell by the irregularity of your morning appearances? Took a day off. Got a doctor's certificate."

Alexander liked that. Liked to think the humblest of his employees felt his presence, or lack of it, so keenly.

"I'm getting the best of both worlds now. A man of Maddren's experience passing on something to our apprentices is invaluable. He's so conversant with all that old machinery! And he's off the streets and off my back. One of my better ideas, I think."

It was then that he sensed the unusual tenor of the factory machinery. It was slowing down. In spite of his double-glazed office he could sense something was wrong. He went across to the window and raised a slat of the Venetian blinds.

"Good Lord, Henry. Two of your lads are racing down nine aisle on a tea trolley."

Corke smiled and thought how they were *his* lads when something was awry and Sturtin's when they were turning out brass rods at a record rate.

"My God. Henry! The whole factory's at a standstill! The main compressor has been switched off. Look, there's a bunch of your men round the blessed thing… and…Henry! Lewis Shore is being forcibly restrained by two of his fellows. He is yelling at…at…Harry Maddren. Maddren…?"

He turned away from the window, the bloom leaching from his cheeks. Roberta came through the door waving a sheet of paper and her sudden entry, unannounced by the customary tap, caused the whisky glass to fall from Sturtin's grip and roll across the carpet. Henry took the paper from her hands and waved her out. He read. He sat. He poured himself another malt.

"Well?" muttered Sturtin.

Corke creaked like an oil-less engine. "It was your idea to have Maddren back. It was never mine. You can never charge me with that insanity."

Sturtin snatched the paper and scanned it. His heart dropped to his boots with a louder thud than the whisky glass's. His felt a violent stabbing pain in the chest.

"Never! Never! They'll never get their tea-break privileges restored! Over my dead body they will! Whose idea was it to have that devil back? My idea? Mine? Who cares whose it was! Ha! Ha! Ha!"

He was still trying to laugh when the ambulance arrived. His last coherent vision in this life was of two champagne flutes, bubbling over with the last remaining drops of Le Mesnil Grand Cru Blanc de Blancs Champagne 1949, going down the gullet, like lemonade, of Harry Maddren.

"He looked after every ticker but his own," remarked Isabel to the cardiologist when she was summoned to the hospital some hours later. She would, she thought, order some oloroso when she got home and immediately cancel the FT.

ooooo

Domaine Chivrun Oak-Aged Bulgarian Merlot 1999

Jo Robinson was discovered missing when the rest of the party got back inside the minibus. In itself, this was not especially strange; she was a tardy creature at the sunniest of times. "She only puts pen to paper the day of the deadline," protested the subs at Clos Encounters.

"Any one seen Jocasta?" said the interpreter, holding the door open and addressing the inside of the bus. She removed the malodorous Sobranie from her bottom lip and crushed it under her shoe (even though a sign said, in several languages, that smoking was forbidden anywhere inside the monastery complex, which included the car park). The rest of the party breathed a sigh of relief. They had only tolerated the interpreter on the condition she smoked outside and this condition was being narrowly observed.

"Perhaps," said Trevor Pfister, "the saintly Jo has been so overcome with sanctity she has decided to apply for permanent residence."

The interpreter snorted. "Impossible," she said. "This is religious community for men only."

Pfister could have kissed the hairy-upper-lipped interpreter for the opportunity this rejoinder offered.

"It would be easy to confuse her sex. Especially in the

heat of religious fervour," he said. As the interpreter pondered this, Pfister was treated to a look of distain from Ally Kingrove and Mandy Weiss – though not, significantly, Lucas Belgrove. The lack of regard Pfister had for Jocasta Robinson, which was heartily reciprocated, had occasioned Ally and Mandy to elicit a promise from him that he would, on this trip, refrain from any behaviour designed to upset her. He gave them a look which said "she isn't here to hear that, so where's the harm?"

Fifteen minutes later the interpreter returned from a search of the grounds.

"Most strange," she reported.

"What did I tell you?" exclaimed Pfister.

"Several people say they saw a woman answering Miss Robinson's description getting in to a car with three men and a woman. This was an hour ago, soon after we first arrive here. They all agree on the orange blouse and blue trousers – which I told her was not correct habiliment for a visit to a holy shrine. I wonder what is afoot?"

She said something to the driver in Bulgarian. He started his engine.

"Hold on!" said Mandy Weiss. "How can we be sure that it was Jocasta these people saw? She might still be here."

"We must move on," said the interpreter. "We are due at the Gevrobrechen winery for lunch. We are now forty-five minutes behind time already. I must make phone calls."

Lucas Belgrove felt his stomach. "Not good to keep a winery waiting," he remarked.

"Should you not talk to the policeman by the car park entrance?" said Mandy. "We can't just drive off and leave her here…if she is still here."

"I talk to the policeman already. He was one of the people who saw her being…er, getting in to the car."

There was a silence, more resonant than the throbbing of the engine. That 'er' hung in the air like an executioner's axe.

"I want to talk to that policeman!" said Mandy stoutly. "What's going on? What did that policeman say? Please let me out."

The interpreter rattled off instructions and the driver put the engine into gear and drove out of the car park. The policeman gave them a wave as they passed his wooden hut.

"How dare you ignore me like this, Miss Vengerov!" screamed Mandy Weiss. "What are you not telling us? What has happened to Jocasta Robinson?"

There was a loud guffawing noise from Pfister. He was looking at Belgrove when he spoke.

"It's obvious. She's been kidnapped by that grotesque gang of thugs we saw yesterday. The ones who terrorised the waitresses at the Mildov Hotel. Didn't you tell us, Ludmilla, that there were lots of gangs like that? Ex-wrestlers and weightlifters no longer supported by the State to win Olympic medals. They probably want to interrogate her about all the rubbish she writes about wine."

Belgrove was ready with a dutiful laugh but, like the rest of them, he could not fail to be checked by the sight of the colour draining dramatically from Ludmilla Vengerov's dark cheeks and her beautiful almond Bulgar eyes clench as if ready to leak tears.

"Mr Pfister," she whispered, moving down the mini-bus to take her seat as the vehicle accelerated on to the high road, "you are most perspicacious. That is exactly what has happened to Miss Robinson." She extracted a mobile phone from her bag and began a series of animated conversations in which the name "Jocasta" and "Robinson" were the only words any of them understood.

Even Pfister shut up. Belgrove had closed his eyes and was seemingly meditating. Ally and Mandy, veterans of all manner of unscripted wine trips to foreign parts, gripped their respective sets of knees (protruding from the skirts they had deemed correct for the visit instead of their habitual trousers) and wondered what kind of joke was being played here. But then on the evidence of the two days they had already spent with Ludmilla Vengerov, they knew she possessed not a scintilla of a shred of a sense of humour in the whole of her ample body.

ooooo

A week before this incident they had buried Alexei Turnov. He was the victim of an unfortunate motorcycle accident. These are not uncommon in Balkan countries and neighbouring lands, especially when the machine is an old Russian-designed Jezevski, with its appallingly greedy two-stroke engine and badly conceived supposedly-hydraulic braking system. Were such bikes thrown on the scrapheap after two years of abuse, or five thousand miles (whichever arrived sooner), then the population of these countries would not, annually, be reduced by the deaths of young males and old men on Jezevskis ten, twenty, thirty, and sometimes, as with Alexei Turnov's, thirty-nine years of age. Bulgaria is a living, and dying, museum.

The fact that Alexei was buried without a penis, and a few other things, was not noticed by the friends and family who paid their last respects to the nineteen-year-old. Alexei gave no sign of mourning his missing member either. He was clothed. He was partially shrouded. The mortician's assistant who cut the penis off, complete with testicles, and put it in a formaldehyde-filled screwtop jar, had no idea why his infrequent friend Max should ask for such an object and he didn't care to enquire further. He had haggled over the price he was prepared to accept for risking his livelihood in this way but in the end he asked for, and got, a million leva.

It is doubtful whether Jocasta Robinson, some hours after waking from her drugged sleep, was aware that £330 was the going price for a dick and balls (plus a few other things). When the severed organ was waved in her face she screamed and then fainted. Precisely the reaction expected. She hadn't seen a man's tackle for some while. In her dusty Maidstone flat she lived a celibate life and the last such fleshy excrescence she had seen had been connected to a fellow mature student, in his late twenties, who had failed to marry her.

They let her lie for a while on the bed. To cool down. She was only a mile from the airport where she had originally landed three days before but she felt she was in some nightmare on some faraway planet. These people were aliens. Even the woman, who spoke English, had muscles – even, Jocasta swore, in her lips. The magnificent Rila monastery from where she had been abducted, which she had so looked forward to visiting, was a distant memory. She had hardly seen any of it before being dragged off.

The woman came in to the room. Behind her the man who had waved Alexei Turnov's paraphernalia in her face waved at her. He made to follow the woman in. But she, in a theatrical gesture, waved him out.

"I sorry," she said. "My friends are crude. But when someone does not cooperate with us…" And she made a cutting motion with her hand.

Jo felt herself shivering. It was, though, not cold in the windowless room from which she could hear the occasional roar of an aviation engine. She screamed.

"Let it all come, Mrs Robinson. No-one can hear you."

Jo hated this title.

"I'm *Miss* Robinson."

"Shall I call you Jancis then?"

"What?"

"I'm sorry. We are informal here, Jancis."

"I'm not Jancis Robinson I'm Jocasta Robinson."

The woman smiled.

"The famous Australian consultant, to whom you were partly introduced an hour or so back, tried to tell us he wasn't who we knew him to be. We know, Jancis, your value."

"My first name is Jocasta. Look, it's on my passport." She looked wildly around for her bag.

"There is no passport in your handbag. We've been through it."

Jocasta remembered.

"I left it in the hotel," she murmured weakly.

"Time for you to speak on the telephone, Jancis. You could be out of here by this evening if do the right thing. Or shall I invite Hristo back in? He can show you a long gone Australian's right hand if you like."

"No! No! What do you want? I'll do whatever you want!"

"Good. Without ears, or a nose, who would wish to look at the famous Jancis Robinson ever again?"

Jo wondered: which of the Australians she knew to have been advising wineries in Bulgaria was now a eunuch? And why had the story not reached the newspapers, let alone the British wine press?

ooooo

After this display she was putty in her kidnappers' hands. Given the telephone by the smallest of the musclemen, who seemed to speak no language at all let alone his presumed native Bulgarian, she gave a hysterical performance. The president of the winery she was connected to, who was acting chairman of the Bulgarian Vintners Association, needed no convincing of his guest's plight. He agreed seventy-five million leva after only five minutes' haggling. Even if this gang had got the wrong Robinson, he could not refuse to pay the price of the wrong Robinson's freedom. Besides, the European Bank of Reconstruction had already loaned his winery fifteen billion leva so what was seventy-five million out of that? He thought the price cheap, considering it was the wrong Robinson. He had begun to bargain, of course, but gave in when his secretary delivered him a package, clearly marked to be opened only by him, which had just been delivered by a motorcycle messenger (whose Jezevski was of a comparatively recent vintage).

The man at the other end of the phone knew all about this package. The acting chairman opened it. A toe fell out (male, but how was the acting chairman to know that?). The acting chairman felt the gorge rise in his throat.

"You don't," said the man at the other end of the phone, "want to lose any more of her do you?"

Seventy-five million leva it was.

ooooo

"A glass of wine, Jancis?"

A bottle of Domaine Chivrun Oak-Aged Bulgarian Merlot 1999 was placed beside a plate of meats and cheeses.

"I told you. I'm Jocasta Rob—"

The woman snarled. "It said J. Robinson on the guest list. There is only one J. Robinson, a woman, in the world of wine. You are a famous wine personality, Jancis. It is an honour for us to entertain you. You have co-operated splendidly. You could be released in an hour…if the money is delivered to our associates in Plodiv."

Jocasta fell silent. Would she lose weight because of this experience? She couldn't eat. Maybe she'd never eat again. Certainly not offal and certainly not those Lebanese lambs' testicles ever again. How boring to be mistaken for Jancis, she thought; she'll be tickled pink when I tell her.

Not that Jo moved in the other Robinson's circles with any confidence or regularity. They met at wine-tastings and Jo's dull autumnal clothes would contrast vividly with Jancis's florid displays of age-defying bravado and celluliteless, figure-hugging adornment. It was hopeless being a food and wine writer, Jocasta thought, when you lived in Maidstone. The title of food and wine editor of the Kent Hop Picker, and odd articles on wine in women's magazines, and an occasional consultancy on apples – her speciality – was hardly enough to keep body and soul together. What she really hankered after was a juicy consultancy with a wine merchant or a shipper. But the men, the predatory male members of the Circle of Wine Writers, grabbed most of those. She giggled. Male members! She sighed. It had been a singularly impressive penis. Whose could it have been? Those damned men! How come they got all the consultancies going? She knew as much about wine as the late Pierre Dupré but had she ever managed to have some of the liaisons that he had enjoyed over the years? Not a bit of it. She had a finer nose and palate than him. If only she'd… She stopped thinking.

The woman was waving a salami at her. Or was it another set of genitals? She shook her head. She covered herself more closely with the blanket, even though it was stifling in the room, and tried to steady her nerves. The giggle had helped. She accepted a glass of the merlot. It was like chewing an old leather armchair. She drank most of the bottle. She fell asleep.

ooooo

"Thank God you are all in one piece," said Ludmilla Vengerov. "How are your foots?"

Jocasta, as she had during the rest of the trip, ignored the interpreter whom she regarded as a silly cow. Feet? What was this about feet?

The acting chairman of the Bulgarian Vintners Association embraced her. Jocasta did not flinch. He was absurdly young and very good-looking. She noticed, as they touched, that he was staring at her feet.

"I cannot begin to apologise for this…this episode." (His English was so beautiful, thought Jocasta.)

"It has happened before," she said tartly. "No-one warned, us, that we were in danger on a trip like this. What about that poor Australian? Was he a flying winemaker? You know…the one who lost…"

"What Australian?" said the chairman. "I assure you that this is the first time anyone has kidnapped a guest of ours. And it will not happen again. I am so glad you are…all in one piece."

"Can I go to my hotel room now, please? I'd like to have a bath. And if you would be so kind…"

"Your colleagues will be thrilled to see you back amongst them," interrupted Ludmilla pointlessly.

Not all, thought Jocasta. She shuddered. Even though she loathed Trevor Pfister she would not wish castration upon him.

"They seemed to think I was Jancis Robinson, not Jocasta Robinson."

My god, thought the acting chairman of the Bulgarian Vintners Association, thinking about it for the first time, if only we could get the legendary Jancis out here! If only we *had* got the legendary Jancis out here – instead of this dried-up old cow. Seventy-five million would have been worth it. He wondered whose toe it had been. He thought somehow that he had been had.

"No matter. We paid the price."

"As I was about to say, Mr Ozstov, if you would be so kind as to arrange the first plane out of here for me tomorrow morning I would be grateful."

"But you haven't seen yet…" began Ludmilla. Ozstov waved his hands in the air and silenced her.

"Of course, Jocasta. I will meet you and your friends at the hotel and we will all have a great dinner together. Ask my secretary to come in would you, Ludmilla?"

ooooo

Fifty minutes before the time she was due to meet everyone else for dinner, Jocasta was telephoned by Ozstov who politely asked if he might come up to her room. Unusually, she noted, he had with him a large briefcase. After accepting her offer to sit down, he removed from it a bottle of Domaine Chivrun Oak-Aged Bulgarian Merlot 1999, two glasses, and a small sheaf of papers. He handed her the papers. Jocasta looked at the wine and felt ill.

"You'll have to work out the leva for me," said Jo after looking briefly at the contract.

"Twenty thousand pounds a year for the next five years. After that..."

"We'll negotiate upwards."

Ozstov sighed. Still, it was the Bank's money.

"Of course," he said, "we will expect some amount of genuine consultancy from you. Help with organising wine-tastings, input on the consumer front...you are an expert on consumers, aren't you?"

"For twenty grand a year I'm an expert on anything."

"Excellent. We can proceed to dinner. But first, shall we celebrate your appointment with a glass of our award-winning wine?"

Jo tried to keep the bilious feeling in her throat from rising to her mouth.

"What have you told my colleagues about this? Do they know the truth?"

"There is no such thing as truth. My father, who was a Marxist, said truth was a capitalist trick," he said, pouring out the wine. "Your friends know only that you were taken by a gang and that you were released when they realised they had got the wrong person. All a mistake. They need to know no more than that. Except, of course, that you were treated properly. If you insist, as I insist you do, that they do not make a fuss of this...slight misunderstanding...when they write whatever they do write about this trip, on their return, then who will ever know what actually took place? It can be...be our secret."

He handed her the glass. Her face was stone.

"Your health, Jocasta Robinson. And prosperity."

The smell of the wine, as she brought it closer to her nose, was of a cold claustrophobic room in which she was unaccountably sweating. She could smell only horror in the glass: the horrifically leathery aroma of a fearfully sweaty merlot.

She tossed the wine back in one, in the approved Bulgarian manner. Ozstov smiled.

"Now, I think, we can proceed to dinner."

"I'll get my coat."

She went in to the lavatory and was sick.

"Only a light coat, Jocasta. It's a warm evening," he called.

It's a wonderful evening, though Jocasta, a quite wonderful evening. It might just be the best evening of my life so far. She washed her face and told herself that for twenty grand a year, she could swallow anything.

ooooo

Tesco's Own-Label New Zealand Riesling 2000

Hartley Coleridge held up the bottle of Chilean wine in front of the customer's face. The man was a beetroot on legs with a tattoo running down one forearm of a devil brandishing a pitchfork.

"As you can read – I assume you can read? – it says 'local grapes'. But I can assure you that cabernet sauvignon is in the blend…and so…"

"What'ye mean I assume you can fucking read? You're a bit hoity-toity for a fucking supermarket greasy rag, ensch ya?"

Hartley took note of the muscles that appeared to quiver above the pitchfork, but the man made no move to take his hands away from the trolley he commanded.

"Just an expression, er, sir. Look, you say you like Chilean cabernet but we've had a run on that…but this wine is almost indistinguishable." He coughed at this lie but soldiered on: "And if it's not to your liking you can easily return it for a refund…"

"If it's not to my fucking liking, mate, I'll return all right and knock your fucking block off."

Hartley placed the bottle in the man's trolley.

"I'm a bit more than a greasy rag, sir. I'm the wine advisor at this branch. Wine is my…my…"

Life, Hartley was going to say, but the man snorted and moved off. How long a time lies in one little word [1], he thought.

Ten minutes later the assistant manager, a young woman dressed as for a state funeral, appeared in the wine aisles.

"A customer has complained that you were rude to him, swore at him, and questioned his literacy, Mr Coleridge. Is this true?"

Hartley, who wore his fifty-eight years with dignity but with no attempt to artificially conceal his ragged edges and melancholy battleship colour and demeanour, let his years of wine merchanting rising to the surface of his smile, took the young woman, who wore a badge saying Selina Ahmed, lightly by the arm and drew her away from the elderly couple who had just emerged in the wine aisle.

"The customer to whom you refer, Miss Ahmed, was a thug. I merely offered to read something for him. He was totally unreasonable. You know the sort. I was as diplomatic as I could be. He went away with a wine he will enjoy, of that I am sure."

Selina Ahmed gave Hartley Coleridge a searching glance, as her first-class degree in catering management studies had taught her to do in situations like this, and, finding nothing but sincerity in the man's face, nodded. And the customer *was* a thug; she didn't need her catering degree to demonstrate to her the truth of that.

"I didn't think there was anything in it, Mr Coleridge," she whispered, as the elderly couple drew closer. "But at Tesco we must investigate every complaint."

Then investigate mine, he cried inside himself, investigate mine. He said to her retreating back: "Thank you, Miss Ahmed. Now, madam, how can I help?"

One half of the elderly couple was lunging at him with her teeth. It passed for a smile.

"It says Wine Advisor on your badge. You know about wine? Then my husband and I require three or four bottles for lunch this coming Sunday. We already have the lamb, and there'll be thirteen of us, including a couple of children, but we want something special...red...fruity...bit special...do you know the sort of thing?"

Hartley Coleridge knew the sort of thing. He propelled them along to the Australian shelves. No-one, he thought, will ever investigate *my* complaint. Be my heart an ever-burning hell [2], he muttered half-audibly. The woman turned and looked at him and wondered if he had said something to her but she was more taken by the bottle of Woolpunda Cabernet Sauvignon he was waving at her.

ooooo

He would explode Tom Reece. At his tea-break taken, as usual, alone in the canteen with his Times crossword, he thought of Tom Reece. He thought about Tom Reece often. Tom Reece was the reason he kept going, doing this humiliating job in this vast commercial cathedral. Oh cruel irreligious piety [3], he muttered half aloud. The employees around him, thinly scattered on a dozen tables at this time of the mid-morn, heard nothing. They treated Hartley Coleridge as they would a virus from Mars: to be looked at from afar but hardly to be touched or gotten close to.

Tom Reece would have to be exploded. That would be a fitting end for a man who had blown apart Coleridge & Trelawney – wine merchants est. 1889. Trelawney had departed to an insane asylum in 1917, never recovering from the loss of his third son in the battle of Passchendale that year, having lost his second at Loos in 1916 and his first in the Festubert offensive in 1915. Hartley's great-grandfather, whose son had emerged from four years of combat with merely an eye out and the loss of his left hand, kept on the Trelawney name not only for memorial considerations (which brooked no contrary argument) but for sound business reasons which proffered the view that two names were sounder than one.

It had not been an easy business birth. Coleridge & Trelawney had opened on May 22nd in '89 brimful of confidence: Coleridge had come from Fortnum & Mason and Trelawney from Victoria Wine, a much humbler establishment of course (and indeed there was a suggestion of this difference in the way each man spoke), but they had immediately gelled on first meeting – an event which took place at a Vintner's Ball to celebrate the Queen's Jubilee celebrations in June 1887, and had struck up a friendship since they discovered they lived within quarter a mile of one another in the burgeoning suburb of Highbury, north London. Both married, both wives expecting their first children, they had a lot in common. Two years later, though young for this sort of enterprise, their fresh-faced energy convinced a County Bank Manager that they could make a go of it in the expanding county of Berkshire where a superb premises had become available fully equipped with capacious cellarage. They had not reckoned, however, on the monstrous Great London dock strike of August 15th that year, which saw vital supplies of wine from Europe and the colonies held up by socialist-inspired stevedores until late September.

Having survived this horrific political and economic irruption, Coleridge & Trelawney imagined they could survive anything. The Boer War came and went (with no cessation of later supplies of excellent Cape brandy and fortified wines), the First World War came and went (as did Trelawney, of course, along with the popularity of German rieslings but the latter recovered by 1923), the slump of the late twenties and early thirties saw belt-tightening by customers but the firm never looked likely to collapse, and it saw out the Second World War, the restrictions of '40s' and '50s' rationing, the excesses of the 1960s and '70s, and it was all set to sail through – hatches battened, every sail furled – the recession of the late 1980s and early 1990s. The Berkshire village in which the firm had originally set up had become the prosperous town it always promised (foreseen by that original bank manager); the firm was famous throughout the county; no-one of any note in Berkshire bought wine anywhere else. The recession of the late 1980s and early 1990s proved not just stormy, however, but produced monsters from the deep. Turnover dropped dramatically; the finance tied up in expensive bordeaux and burgundy, with vintage ports and champagnes lying there begging for customers to buy them, was met only by trimming every excess from the business including two long-serving members of staff.

"We've been through this sort of thing before," Hartley said, addressing his wife's tombstone, no celestial yawns forthcoming (as in life), as, not for the first time, he reeled off the pedigree of the firm's indomitability in the face of crises.

Until Tom Reece came along. And with him, by malign divine coincidence, the opening of a giant Tesco superstore on the by-pass that skirted the town. A still growing town, in 1991, with its original village centre boasting abundant boutiques, antique shops, small food emporia such as two butcher's and three bakeries (one also a tea-shop), and, prominent by the clocktower, the imposing edifice of Coleridge & Trelawney – wine merchants est. 1889.

Hartley sat there struggling with twenty-two down ("Side of a taxi, six letters", which he had so far reduced to e something, e something, e something) and thought of it all gone: most of the boutiques (three knocked into one in 2000 and turned in to a single Gap outlet), one butcher's (to leave just the game specialist), two of the bakeries, most of the antique shops (though several had returned by the late nineties). He thought bitterly of that recession and what it had wrought. Thank God Peta had not been alive to see it (cancer had carried her off in 1986 after nineteen years of marriage) and thank Him there had been no progeny to witness his disgrace. This inability to conceive of the Hartley Coleridges had dogged their marriage and Peta had, after nine fruitless years, offered him a divorce since no heir was possible with the current arrangement. But Hartley loved her more than he loved the business; or rather more than he loved the idea that his own son or indeed daughter would succeed him, since when was it automatic any more that sons or daughters took over when their fathers left off running family businesses? Hartley now regretted his father's spurning of the chance to expand and open up branches in Reading and Newbury, not to mention his own caution at not trying for expansion into Oxfordshire and Bucks and indeed further down in to Hardy country.

What is this bloody side of a taxi, he asked himself, conscious it was the end of his tea-break and he must return to his beat. He stood up, put on his green vintners apron, checked that he had the foil cutter and corkscrew in the large front pocket, then went out to the locker room and put the paper away in his personal compartment.

He shuddered. As he always did when he contemplated the past years of C & T. The crash of the firm had been spectacular. The receivers had auctioned the wines, an antique shop had bought the fixtures and fittings, the premises were now a Waterstones, and the proprietor...and he gritted his teeth...had been snapped up by Tesco. He reluctantly headed for those enervating aisles, each step a minor torture down from the canteen, and thought of how he would blow up Tom Reece. I grant him, Hartley foamed inwardly, bloody, luxurious, avaricious, false, deceitful, sudden, malicious, smacking of every sin that has a name.[4]

ooooo

He could forgive Tesco opening, with wines so much cheaper than his own had been. That was progress. It was Tom Reece who has stabbed him in the back, the front, the side, and, regarding the bleeding corpse, had stripped it of its most enticing assets like some crazed Iliad warrior. Tom Reece had purchased many of the wines auctioned by the receivers. That was the more insufferable indignity.

Tom Reece had once been Hartley Coleridge's part-time employee and then friend. He wrote a column once a week in the Berks Bugle, the largest county newspaper in the country, and he broadcast regularly from BBC Radio Oxford. Indeed, nowadays he wasn't just published in the Bugle but had a syndicated column in hundreds of local newspapers. He was a national star. And all because he had been the first wine critic to devote a column solely to supermarket wines.

Hartley laid firmly at Reece's door the demise of the old firm. Who was it that had made shopping for wine in supermarkets respectable? Reece. Who was it who that had forcefully written of the delights of £2.29 a bottle Romanian pinot noir whilst scorning the £10 Nuits-St-Georges at wine merchants like Coleridge & Trelawney? Reece. Who had then conceived of the idea of turning this small local success into a regular radio programme and annual wine guide devoted to supermarket wines? Reece. The abominable Reece.

Of course, the irony was not lost on Hartley that he was now employed by a supermarket and not just any supermarket but the largest in Britain; furthermore, it was the largest and most successful wine merchant in the world since he estimated that last year they had probably sold well over 700 million bottles of wine. Only Sainsbury's came close, and then Asda, and Safeway, and Somerfield, and....and the list went on.

Hartley had no doubt that had it not been for Reece trumpeting the virtues of supermarket wines at the onset of a major recession, Coleridge & Hartley would still be in business. Think of the present day value of all those bordeaux and burgundies! The same wines which now lay – certainly the choicest specimens of – in Reece's vast cellar under the mansion he had purchased in Aston Clinton on the strength of his royalties. And where had Reece learned his job? It is not difficult to guess where: during his Saturday stints at Coleridge & Trelawney whilst studying for a degree in art at Newbury. Hartley had even helped the lad with his first wine column, a small enough endeavour in 1989.

Small wonder, then, that Reece (and Reece *was* a small wonder, Hartley smirked to himself as he entered his aisles, being a mere five feet three inches in height compared to his ex-boss's six one) was the object of Hartley's schemes for satisfaction on a scale that was truly poetic.

"Look here, I bought this wine two days ago and... goodness! It's... it's...um...I know you...! You had the wine merchants in town, the big place…um…Coleridge & Trelawney."

Hartley suffered these encounters once or twice a week. He didn't recognise the man and from his dress and his manner didn't suppose he ought to, however much he might have patronised the old firm years back.

"Ah yes! You must remind me of your name…I…"

"I see from your badge you are H. Coleridge. I am V. Belsham. I used to buy your Fine Old Medoc. Tesco put paid to that, though. Couldn't afford your prices. Fancy you working here."

"I advise Tesco from time to time. It's keeps my hand in. And it's local. How can I help, Mr Belsham? Victor, isn't it?"

"Why yes!" said the man. "You're an old pro and no mistake. Well, you can take this filth back and find me something that tastes as if is made from grapes…this stuff here…"

"Permit me, Victor." Hartley took the bottle, as V. Belsham struggled to come to terms with Hartley's familiarity with his name, and pulled out the cork, which was loosely inserted in the top. He smelled the wine and grimaced.

"It's corked. This is a pretty decent drop of stuff usually. Have another bottle to replace this one and have a second bottle for your trouble."

Victor Belsham hesitated and shook his head.

"Once bitten twice shy, I'm afraid, er, Hartley. I'll have something Australian for the same price. I'll take a refund."

"You'll need to go to customer services for that. It's opposite checkout twenty-three."

He escorted the man there, waited whilst he got his money refunded, and accompanied him back to the wine aisles. What fates impose, that men must needs abide; it boots not to resist both wind and tide [5], thought Hartley. All those Coleridges, all those Trelawneys (two of them military heroes) – were they looking down at him from their heavenly clouds and wondering just what sort of spineless wimp had been the last to inherit the family throne?

Hartley helped Victor select a bottle of £5.99 Coonawarra Cabernet/Shiraz and made up his own mind at the same time. He would contact the man who said he knew a man who knew a relative who claimed to be friendly with an ex-IRA bomb-maker, living on amnesty in Southampton, and see if he could be persuaded to inculcate him into the mysteries of constructing untraceable explosive devices. With a bit of luck, he could organise a few cases of wine and do a quid pro quo.

ooooo

He heard the woman's voice before he saw her. Some minutes before he saw her, in fact, as he was taken up with advising a customer as to a suitable wine to drink with hedgehog. Was it a wind-up? Hartley supposed so at first then decided the man might be some kind of extreme rustic and hedgehog was regular fare. But if so, why did he need advice as to what kind of wine went with it? As this last thought trickled in to Hartley's mind, and he tried not to be deflected by the woman's accented English further along, it was answered:

"Normally, I have cider – I make it meself – with me hog but…well, the son and his new wife are coming over tomorrow and I reckoned I'll show 'em! I'll show 'em I can put on a show, you know…so wine it is."

Anything above £3.99 being ruled out of court, Hartley, and his customer, settled on a very vibrant, slightly sweet red, reduced to £2.99, from Puglia in southern Italy. Hartley sighed as the man bowed-leggedly wandered away with his basket containing its two bottles and thought how much he missed Peta at times like this: who was there to whom he could spin out the improbable tale of the customer who wanted a wine to go with roast hedgehog?

He examined the aisle and its sole remaining customer. The woman with the intriguing throaty accent with its rich clipped vowels had disappeared: the young man looking diffidently, or perhaps shiftily, at the sparkling wine shelves was definitely the sort who might try to nick a bottle.

ooooo

But she had not disappeared. She had acquired several loaves of bread and was pushing her trolley down the aisle with, he was relieved to note, a determined air of indeterminacy. He had liked her voice. He had, in his days as a loftier wine merchant than he was now, always been intrigued by customers' voices; it was a sort of game he played with himself. Could he guess from the voice what sort of wine the customer would eventually settle for? He tried to shut his eyes to the person pushing the trolley, a not especially fetching bottle-blonde with fat ankles and a somewhat hysterical line in lurid blouses, and reckoned she would, with a voice like that, go for something sweet from Germany.

He pretended to busy himself with the bubblies. He looked up. She had, quite improbably, stopped by the New Zealand selection. She caught his eye.

"I won't bite, little man. Come here and help me if you would."

Little? Him? He strode over and stood to attention by her trolley which contained, he noted approvingly, several of the more unusual unpasteurised cheeses and various large wrapped items from the fresh fish counter, a mass of fruit, and a great many vegetables – on the top of which lay half a dozen baguettes. Hartley held his back straight. In spite of the funny accent he knew a lady when he saw one.

"The girls like Kiwi wines, you know. I've got these two big salmon here. No brai, of course. Not in this blasted climate. I can bake 'em. Back home..." She paused and Hartley realised it was a colonial accent he was hearing, which always sounded posher than it really was.

"Well? It says Wine Advisor on your badge. Stop gawping and advise. Twelve of us. Two salmon. Baked. I want a sauvignon blanc. Not from the Cape or anywhere where it's too bloody hot. I want..."

"Madam wants subtlety in her sauvignons. From a cooler climate."

"Got it in one, Hartley, old sport. In one. Now you're motoring."

Indeed he was. He persuaded her that Tesco's Own-Label New Zealand Riesling 2000, at a mere £4.99, was a better bet, since eight bottles were on the cards (it was for the dinner after the all-girl bridge party finished its last hand), than the Jackson Estate Sauvignon Blanc 2000 at £8.99. Madam declared she wasn't made of money, that she would trust his judgement (especially as there were only four bottles of the Jackson and many more of the own-label wine), and that he was a real sport. He accompanied her to the check-out.

It was a quiet Wednesday afternoon. He offered to see her out to her car and help with her bags. There was no-one else needing surgery in the wine aisles.

ooooo

"You seem a funny sort of bloke to be working in a supermarket, if you don't mind me remarking on it." He had opened the boot of a Mercedes soft top. Something about the number plate struck him.

"Sorry? What did you say?"

His head emerged from the boot and he glanced down at the number plate again. She repeated what she had said. He meticulously packed all her bags away and the cartons he had carefully stowed the wine in. He slammed the boot shut.

"I try to cultivate a sense of humour, madam."

"What? Oh, yeah, I get it. I see. No. I meant you don't seem…" And she stopped, her hand in her handbag juggling with her loose change. She thought better of completing this gesture and shrugged. He opened her driver's door for her.

"…anyway…thank you for your help. I don't normally get help like this at a supermarket. Britain has sure changed."

"I can vouch for that."

She sat in her seat and finally found the pound coins she was searching for in her handbag.

"Thank you," she said, and made to present him with the coins and then, as she did so, withdrew her hand – not because the expression on his face made the donation unnecessary, if not insulting, but because she had just remembered something.

"Oh shit! I'll need this change. I forgot to get my car park ticket stamped at the check-out."

"Give it me. I'll run back and get it done for you. Won't take me a jiffy."

He came back after a few minutes to find that she had driven round to the front of the supermarket so he wouldn't have to come all the way back through the car park. He got a full view of her number plate now. It was fate. He could have kissed her.

"Here you are, madam," he said, a trifle breathlessly but triumphantly. "Stamped as required."

"That's very decent of you. Here is a toke—"

"That won't be necessary madam. You have already given me that which I have sought the answer to all day."

"Sorry?"

"Your number plate. QWT 11. I can't thank you enough. I must get back. Had a sudden influx of punt…of customers…"

And Hartley Coleridge was skipping across the forecourt and back inside the supermarket.

Bloody barmy British, thought the woman, as she studied his retreating back with its disjointed strides. They reminded her of a giraffe's way of locomotion. She piloted her vehicle out of the car park and wondered whether to tell the bridge girls about the curious old bugger on Tesco's wine aisles. On balance, she decided she should keep the incident to herself.

ooooo

Two days later, cycling in from the flat he now occupied a quarter-mile from the old high street C & T premises, he was surprised to see QWT 11 in the car park. The flat had been forced on him when the house went; he had raised a second mortgage on it to stave off bankruptcy but the sale of 60s' and 70s' first growth Medocs he had banked on, to a Far East customer, never materialised. The bank sold the house, with its grass tennis court and wealth of mature oaks, to an adman who, Hartley later noted, had butchered it.

He apologised for his lateness to Miss Ahmed but he still had to clock in. When he reached the aisles she was waiting for him, leaning against a trolley, barely half a dozen items lying in it, reading the Telegraph.

"Late this morning, Hartley."

"Good morning, madam…good Monday morning."

"Which justifies your lateness."

He saw no point in not agreeing with this perfectly accurate observation. He had overslept. He had had a frustrating weekend phoning people, and he had got absolutely nowhere. The ex-IRA bomb-maker did not exist.

She returned his compliant smile.

"The girls loved that Kiwi white wine. Got any other hot little numbers like that up your sleeve?"

They toured the shelves, selecting a variety of bottles. Then:

"What was it about my number plate?"

He laughed. It was the first time he had given full vent to a proper laugh for some weeks. She felt even more attracted to him.

"You will think me a trifle barmy but…I have this obsession each day…had it for years…I must finish the crossword puzzle in…the newspaper." He was going to say The Times but felt this sounded like boasting. For some reason he didn't want to be seen to show off in front of this woman whose hair colour he now realised was not artificial or her ankles fat, and indeed did not resemble the first impression she had created. "It was the word eleven in your number plate. That was the answer to the clue." Good luck lies in odd numbers [6], he thought.

"Eleven?"

"Eleven."

"Sounds a pretty easy crossword. I do them myself."

"Oh. I wouldn't say it was easy. Today's looks an absolute swine."

She departed after ten minutes with twenty bottles of sparkling and white wine.

During the mid-morning break, as he sat there with his tea and a truly porcine crossword, Althea, who stacked some of the wine shelves, came over and sat down. Althea was a strange person who worked three days a week only – for unspecified medical reasons he had never been able to work out. She put a glass of milk in front of her and regarded him. He waited for her to speak. He knew the best way to treat Althea. The skin of her face, it struck him, seemed as angelically wan as the drink in front of her. Why did angels have such white skins? A racist concept? Or some metaphysical construct beyond him to unravel?

"Mr Hartley. Mr Hartley...Mr Hartley, I ought to warn you about that customer Mrs Van Rensburg...er..."

"Who?"

It was a mistake. No-one said 'who?' to Althea without it being seen as a provocation. However, at least the needs of expeditiousness were served. Althea did not mince her words.

"Don't play the inn'cent with me. You've helped her twice with her wine. Seeing her to her car, that swanky pervertible..."

Hartley's eyes goggled. He put down his pen. Truth to tell, Althea was a welcome distraction. He'd hardly done but three clues. The blasted puzzle was an eliminator for the annual Times crossword puzzle contest and it was indeed more than usually fiendish. He could hardly believe what he was being told as Althea burst her banks. Why the warning? Was the angel jealous of the Van Rensburg woman's unholy tan?

"Mrs Van Rensburg's the widder of that man in South Africa who blew up all those protectors...and he's in prison..."

ooooo

Sitting on the lavatory straining to do fifteen across, Hartley also struggled to sort out what Althea had told him. If Mrs Van Rensburg was a widow then her husband was surely dead, but Althea seemed to think he was also a prisoner. How did Althea know all these things? Or become so confused about them? Mrs Van Rensburg had appeared, so Althea said, in a minor way in Hello! magazine. Hartley had seen it displayed on the supermarket's magazine racks. How did he acquire a back copy? Or was such research necessary?

Would she even know how to construct a bomb? She was the man's widow, or as good as, not his accomplice, he reminded himself. "Art thou afeared to be the same in thine own act and valour as thou art in desire?" [7] he reminded himself. He could do with some of Lady MacBeth's resolve. He already possessed her bloody inclinations.

ooooo

He found the address by surreptitiously accessing Loyalty Card data on one of the computers. Her house, as he regarded it from the cover of the copse besides the adjoining cricket pitch (an allotment during the war, now the subject of a tussle between a developer in cahoots with the water board which owned it and the local council whose members were hugely enjoying themselves regularly being entertained at Manoir aux Quatr' Saisons by the developer's PR consultant), was the smallest in the semi-circle beyond long off but he would have known it was hers because of the car, hood down, lying like some large eviscerated gaming trophy in the drive.

What he could not have imagined in his most fevered nighttime dreams – and he had these too – was that she was regarding him from an upstairs window with the pair of vast

Safari binoculars her late husband had owned. She could not be sure, though, whether it was her or her house, or indeed her automobile, that was the object of his attention or, more excitingly, the precise reason for his presence under the beeches. He could just be out for a stroll or taking a look at the state of the grass before the match next Sunday. How she hated cricket.

Hartley walked around the pitch, adopting the air of the *flâneur* on no particular mission. As he reached her gate, he bestowed on the car a brief glance, and carried on. She recognised the act. There could be no doubt of his motive. She tripped across the short lawn and popped her head out of a gap in the hedge. He started and looked genuinely surprised to see her. But then he *was*. Where had she sprung from? He hardly had time to examine the proposition that she might have been spying on him just as he had been spying on her.

"Hartley! Hello. Are you local?"

He felt peculiarly naked without his apron on. He assembled his thoughts in coherent order, best able to mislead, and responded that he often wandered this way on a Saturday afternoon if the weather was fine and, yes, he lived in King William Street.

She looked at him. He looked at her. He ran his hands down the front of his hips. Without his apron on he was undone. Without the slight weight of the corkscrew in the front flap pressing again his flesh he was unarmed. It had never struck him before that the donning of the vague uniform of his profession gave him the armoury of…deception? No, not deception exactly; it was more the ability to unfurl the silver tongue. This was an exciting and also an unnerving discovery. He would wear his old C & T apron when he exploded Tom

Reece; ironed and folded away, it was in a box of his father's effects.

She saw all this – or rather she saw something like saintliness cross his face and inferred this without the analysis. If she hesitated about the next move, she realised, there would be not be a mere silence between them but an irreconcilable gulf.

"Would you like a drink? I have a bottle of that Kiwi riesling you recommended open. Come in and have a glass. Very refreshing on a warmish day like this."

Thinking, as she uttered the last, that it was not really warmish at all but only what passed for warmish in these parts. It was as cool as a Cape winter in truth.

Incapable of uttering an immediate yes or demurring with a hesitant no, he found himself walking along to the gate and passing through it and past the car in the drive and under the eaved front door of the house and sitting on a sofa in the living room. A cockatoo croaked at him from a large cage in the corner and she introduced it as Nelson (a crude joke which no-one local had yet twigged). In part it was revenge for her husband's secret life; the life she had only discovered when he shot himself before being unmasked as the apartheid government's assassin he had been for fifteen years.

The room was like a furniture showroom compared with his own small living room. Sofas and armchairs, all covered in varieties of small flowers and beasts, seemed to sprout everywhere. She sighed; handed him a glass of the wine; wondered how soon, like everyone else, he would remark on all the soft furnishings and seating. But…

"I thought," he said, smelling the wine but not drinking it, "that Nelson had been released…"

She stood up, threw her arms wide, laughed, and sat beside him on the morass of springbok and lion and wildebeest minutely depicted on the sofa. He took a draught of the wine.

"You know how long I've been in England?" she said. "I'll tell you. It's eight months. You're the first person in that time to have been in this room and understood…"

"Understood…er…Mrs Van Rensburg?"

"Oh no! None of that, Hartley. I'm Lavinia Pascoe again now, though it's not the name on my charge cards until a few legal niceties have been sorted out."

"I…"

"I think you and Nelson will get on very well together, Hartley. You understand him so well already. Have some more wine. Call me Lavinia please. Mrs Van Rensburg is dead." She laughed. "Whilst I awhile obsequiously lament,"[8] she added, with more laughter.

He looked at her in astonishment. He was truly done for in that moment.

"Lady Anne," he muttered admiringly.

ooooo

Mr and Mrs Hartley Coleridge lived to a ripe old age, as did Nelson. Hartley never thought to tell Lavinia why he had been so keen to talk to her in the first place and she never asked, though the suspicion that it was something other than simple attraction did briefly weigh on her mind when they honeymooned in Provence and she told him about her husband's explosive peculiarities and he showed uncommon interest in this.

But of course the Windsor Amateur Shakespeare Theatre Group consumed most of his time, as it did hers. When Tom

Reece's popularity waned and even the local paper fired him, Hartley didn't even think to gloat. When Reece's wine guide failed, he didn't even register a frisson of glee. Not even, ten years later, when, idly filling up his trolley with wines from the Tesco shelves, a small shrunken figure of a man, with barely a respectable hair left on his head, came up and feebly wondered, without recognising Hartley (who had become plump and glowing), if he wanted any help. Hartley looked at the man, the shadow of the man he had once known, and shook his head; felt nothing approaching *schadenfreude*. So we profess ourselves to be the slaves of chance, and flies of every wind that blows [9], he thought. He never came back to the Tesco, preferring henceforth to do all his wine-buying online from Corney & Barrow.

ooooo

Note: references in text refer to the following characters in the following plays:

1 Bolingbroke, 1-3-213. *Richard II*

2 Marcus Andronicus, Act 3, sc 1, l.242. *Titus Andronicus*

3 Tamora, Act 1, sc 1, l.129. *Titus Andronicus.*

4 Malcolm, 111-58. *Macbeth.*

5 King Edward, 111-57. *Henry V1, Pt 3.*

6 Falstaff, Act 5, sc 1, l.3. *The Merry Wives of Windsor.*

7 Lady MacBeth, Act 1, sc 7, l.39-41 *Macbeth.*

8 Lady Anne, Act 1, sc 2, l.3, *Richard III*

9 Florizel, Act 4, sc 4, l.539-541, *The Winter's Tale.*

Domaine de Crachat Assortis 2001

These were the smoothest tastings, he always thought: quiet room, no-one else in it. He stared out the double-glazed window at the traffic. Little interference from this direction, either. He sighed; raised his arms above his head. He stared at the wines on the table. Should see them off in a couple of hours; another retailer done and finished with. He only had to wait for the PR girl to return with the list and he could begin his routine.

He noted the clean glasses, the platter of dry biscuits, two large vases containing fake flowers, the flagon of water, the little pot containing half-a-dozen biros, a sheaf of clipboards. No spittoon though. Into what did he expectorate?

"Here we are, Ed. All in order. And with enough space between the wines to write proper notes as you requested."

Edward Severn stood up, inwardly wincing at the Ed. He took the wine listing from her. The PR agency girl, April Knights, was a little taller than he and she wore the regulation black trousers of her fraternity. He didn't like Ed until Edward had been formally exhausted. Was she fuckable? Or take-outable at her or her client's expense?

She picked up on the cursorily predatory expression of the male unable to suppress the sudden force of his primitive hormones; she smiled. She was not unused to it. Her regular receipt of it was one reason why she had been taken on as a PR girl; her recognition of the power it gave her was one reason why she might succeed at the job.

"Vanessa will just be a moment. She apologises for not being here to greet you, but she had to take an urgent call on her mobile from head office...dynamic changes afoot at Berryman's, you know!"

Edward, who had met Vanessa only once since Berryman's had taken her on, tried to remember what she looked like. He selected the Oxford blue clipboard from the sheaf, a black biro from the pot, a glass from the tray...and raised his eyes up to April's.

"Into what exactly do I spit?"

She uttered, "Oh yah, I forgot" and left the room to return a moment later with two champagne buckets with the word Bollinger on their sides. Edward was already nosing the first wine, a pinot grigio, as she placed one of the buckets near him on the table. April smoothed her trousers, fiddled with the back of her hair, and sat down on one of the director's chairs against the wall. She examined her nails, threw him a glance, sighed; he missed none of this though he seemed intent on gargling with the pinot grigio which, after seven seconds or so (long by his standards), he ejected, without moving his head, dead centre into the Bollinger bucket, where it made a ploshing sound well above the low growl of the traffic outside. He scribbled down a note; moved on to the next wine; performed the same ritual. By wine four, an Australian-made Sicilian blend of inzolia and chardonnay, April had issued several more sighs and had examined every cuticle on both her hands. He was about to remark that if she had things in her office to attend to, more pressing than her nails, he would quite understand if she left him to slobber in peace. But Vanessa surged in on billowing green pleats, apologised for her absence earlier, and made as if to greet Edward Severn with more than the usual flutter of colliding hands by offering a cheek to be pecked. Damned cheek, he thought, unconscious of any pun; I've only met the woman once and she wants to show this April creature that we're on continental kissing terms. There followed a formal handshake and Vanessa explained what she had done to the range since "coming across" from First Quench to "face the excitement" of being Berryman's wine buyer. She gave him a well-rehearsed litany of reasons why Berryman's was irresistible and Edward perfunctorily nodded: hmmming and arrring at suitable moments in lieu of yawns. He knew full well, and she knew he knew, that all the buyers at First Quench were jumping ship and any one of them would be happy to grab any job – even wine buyer for a cross channel ferry line – if it meant getting out of a wine chain (Thresher's, Victoria Wine, Bottoms Up, Wine Rack and God knows what else) which had just been flogged off and whose future was uncertain. Only yesterday lunchtime Edward had had lunch at Pasha Ali's with the director of a large importer and been told that the entire wine buying team of First Quench had been in to see him for a job – all of them in one week. Berryman's was hardly a career move up for Vanessa Holden-Bragby but then neither was it exactly a move down. She was barely into her thirties and had plenty of time yet; and if she managed to turn a conservative franchised chain of grocers like Berryman's into an interesting place to buy wine, then who knows? Sainsbury's might come calling, or Adnams, Laithwaites, or one of the more successful dot com wine merchants.

She rattled off her strategy to improve Berryman's wine range but Edward had already sussed what it mainly consisted of: branded wines to fill out the shelves between £3.99 and £5.99 and for everything less concentrate on the big co-ops in southern France, Italy and Spain, and some of the bigger players in eastern Europe, always making sure of course that hotter and more chic spots like Chile and Australia figured as well (on shelves as well as on the buyer's essential travel itinerary). What am I doing here? he thought. But he knew the answer.

Edward Severn, in spite of his comparative youth in the noble profession (several wine writers still gargling and spitting well into their seventies), and in defiance of a crippling education at a minor public school and a stifling one at Durham University (the traditional choice of those who fluff their Oxbridge interviews), wrote an annual wine guide which sold in its tens of thousands. He might feel disappointed at failing to have gotten a first-class French degree but he could always brush aside any suggestion that he had been less than scholarly by pointing out, mainly to himself, that had he not started 'Fiver-and-Under' in his second year at Uni then he would not be in this position now. 'Fiver-and-Under', from its humble student beginnings, had become the biggest selling wine guide in the UK, published no longer with help from the Students' Union and the Agamemnon Press of Newcastle but by Random House, who were proud to number Edward Severn amongst their best-selling authors. The fact that the guide did not now entirely limit itself to wines under a fiver, but regularly listed bottles costing £2 or £3 more and considered by the author to be stupendous bargains, did not frustrate the book's annual rise to number one in the book sales charts over the Christmas season.

Vanessa should have asked me to extend my foot for her to kiss rather than proffering her cheek, he jossed to himself. The fact that he bothered to cover a down-market franchised grocer at all was only due to his and his publisher's boast – which he was obliged (often taking jibes from fellow wine writers for his pains) to live up to – that his was the only wine guide that covered *all* the major retailers.

This meant not just the Tescos and the Oddbins but the Spars and the Aldis and the Berryman's; this latter having several thousand off-licences and licensed grocers and small supermarkets, independently run, all signed up and buying from the Berryman's central purchasing office which directed wholesale operations.

Vanessa had some clout; her employer would sell over a hundred and fifty million bottles of wine, if she was on target, in the coming year. Edward had to include them in his aptly priced £4.99 wine guide from which he received a little short of 40-pence for every copy sold. Last year this had been 367,789 copies.

He was living very nicely on nigh-on one hundred and fifty grand a year and he was widely considered to be the most envied, oft loathed, member of the Circle of Wine Writers – for every other member believed that she or he could write a much better guide than the upstart Severn who had never had a day's training in the wine trade, had never worked in wine journalism or had a column in even a local newspaper, wrote in clichés and mostly wretchedly, and extolled the virtues of cheap wine. What Edward's green-eyed colleagues never appreciated was that extremely few of them, perhaps none, would have cared to get out of bed on so many mornings to taste such wines as Berryman's might offer.

His stamina was to be admired; but it was not of course. It was held against him. Indeed, there had been rumblings of late from members that he ought to be thrown out of membership or disbarred because of what he wrote. His encouraging of others to believe in the ethos of cheap wine went against the true spirit of wine writing, some thought. It was misleading the consumer: pandering to the common herd's ignorance and prejudices. Such heresies were in contrast to, and in defiance of, the true wine writer's duty, which was surely the enthronement and worship of £50 bottles of white and red burgundy from growers with barely a hectare (two and half acres) of unirrigated vines to their names. How could anyone prefer £3.99 bottles of Australian chardonnay or £2.99 Romanian pinot noir made in stonking great stainless steel wine factories from grapes grown in hundreds of unromantic acres of well-watered soil?

Had any of these other writers descended from their garrets with their double-ring baby Belling stoves and their small stocks of claret and burgundy given them free by wine merchants proud to call them friends and seen Edward Severn's Chiswick house with its cellar and Guggenhau kitchen; were they to be miraculously invited to sup with Edward Severn and his five foot partner, Rachel, who had a way with fish; were they to even be permitted a glimpse of the Severn lifestyle then they would find it entirely in contradiction to the one they imagined from his books. Indeed, his readers (but not his publisher, who regularly consumed Edward's rare burgundies and old clarets at the Chiswick address) would be equally astonished. But Edward's sojourn at King's Canterbury, neglected by a lubricious mother and an army office father who liked serving in deserts, had instilled in him not only selfish ambition and self-reliance, almost solipsistic in intensity, but the shrewd means to shield such traits from general view and understanding. Rachel loved him and cooked for him when she got back from her advertising agency job and bore his occasionally flirtations and strayings from the path with the stoicism which the fledglings of the Thatcher generation had somehow been granted as their birthright. As adults they were formidably self-possessed and arrogant and Edward moved amongst them with the ease born of familiarity – he *was* one.

Edward directed his gaze at Vanessa's nose as she waited for some response to her speech on her range of wines. He muttered some conventional expression of understanding and bent his head to the next wine along. Ninety-two wines; he'd be out of here in less than two hours if he didn't have to stand here and listen to her spiel.

"I'll leave you to carry on tasting. Any questions, please don't hesitate to ask."

Wines five to eight were middlingly interesting and priced and reaching the mainstream European whites, he began to get in to his stride. Vanessa went and joined April and they both regarded Edward as he unerringly hit the middle of the Bollinger bucket each time. They suppressed yawns; they looked at each other and bent their heads and whispered a few words. Then:

"Well, I don't know about you, Nessie, but I hate those early morning commuter trains…"

"I'm with you on that one, April. I always use the car for early meetings in Town. Well, like today."

"I try to get a lift with my boyfriend but since he got clamped the second time – only dropped in here to help me with a computer problem and he got done – he tends to use the tube, you know."

"Ah, tube. Yes. I meant, er, um, British Rail or whatever it's called now. Being based in Birmingham we don't have tube problems…"

Edward glowered in their general direction but they were now oblivious to him and his concerns.

"No, course not. But you know I'm using the Jubilee line now and it has its fair share of monsters and…" – dropping her voice for decency's sake but with an insufficient diminution of decibels for it to fail to reach Edward's ear – "…creepy feely men – know what I mean? – and they *are* a problem, you know? I don't know why it's the Jubilee line. You'd think it would be the Northern…"

The Scouse accent struck him again. Merseyside, he thought: mers-i-cide. We have suicide and infanticide and regicide: would not mersicide be perfect for the strangling of a Scouse PR girl? He grimaced; forced himself to concentrate on making legible notes for his typist to transfer to disc but it was difficult. He had to taste several of the Spanish whites twice to confirm their status in his mind; and how was he supposed to provide a witty one-line summation of their charmlessness or, as in one case, the opposite, if he was fighting against the middle-aged man with the posh striped stockbroker suit who had perfected a remarkable style of close-contact female fellow-straphanger massage whilst holding The Times? Mersicide!

Edward gritted his teeth and soldiered on to the sauvignon blancs, chardonnays, and the odd viognier…and accompanying them all were the various tube lines and their resident gropers…and then there was a line-up of less conventional whites, like the riper, cheaper new world rieslings…and the conversation turned less *sotto voce*.

"Southern Italy this year. Food's good, weather dependable…you know? Not too many British families with…with little brats…you know?"

"California for me…I…"

"California? Oooh. Smashing."

"Bit of a busman's holiday. The supplier of the own-label Cal zin and Chard has a place, a ranch would you believe, and so I've got that for ten days. Everything all right, Ed? Something wrong with that chenin?"

The Severn cheeks, puffed out with the wine, vibrated as he shook his head. He had been regarding the wine in the glass overlong. He spat in to the bucket. It would require emptying soon.

"No. Nothing," he lied.

"You know I'd love to get out to California…"

He reached the last bottle of the white wines, which turned out to be from the State on April's tongue. It was quickly on his own and though he did not regard it as necessarily bad he took some delight in giving them low marks and a harsh sentence. Vanessa may have enjoyed the ethically dubious privilege of accepting the free run of their maker's ranch but in accepting the wines she would have to pay a price. Edward took some satisfaction in that; sixty points out of a possible hundred ought successfully to sour her disposition when she reached the United States of America section in Berryman's entry in his wine guide. Perhaps, he conjectured wildly, a director of Berryman's might ask why such poor rating wines were on Berryman's shelves only for it to be revealed that the buyer had spent ten days at their maker's ranch…

"Ev'thing all right, Ed?" called Vanessa. "Not as funny as all that is it, that Cal chardy?"

He shook his head and spat out; turned his back; he was struggling to contain his laughter. "No, lovely wine," he said, "lovely. Didn't know you get such quality for £4.99 out of California."

Vanessa beamed; returned to her theme and April, whose nail varnish shade she much admired.

Pointedly, as he worked through the reds, listening to further details of April's boyfriend's ambitions and the life Vanessa was leading as a newcomer to Birmingham, he employed the two flower vases – which he ostentatiously emptied to no audience response – as spittoons since the Bollinger buckets were full. Neither woman shifted from their conversational posture and as their litany unfolded he felt it was as if it was he who was intruding on them, rather than they on him. It was like, he thought, a small focus group of Cosmopolitan readers in to which he had inadvertently strayed; and he knew all about the natures of such readers since he had been this magazine's wine columnist for three years before falling out with a new editor who objected to his portrayal of a certain extremely buttery Aussie chardonnay as being "perfect for attaining multiple orgasms". He pointed out that the successful reaching of such things was the aim of the magazine, was it not, but was rebuked for being frivolous about a serious subject and so they appointed a forty-five year old Canadian, completely bald and with even less of a palate (in Edward's opinion). He was not entirely displeased to depart since the pay was pitiful and he never once met a decent tart via the mag's good offices – not once.

"…I had thought about joining a dating agency until I met Nigel…"

"I know a Nigel…"

"…and so I'm settling down in Brum…"

"…or rather I used to know a Nigel, you know."

Why didn't he just give the whole bloody lot a sixty out of one hundred score? This was as near minimal as his scoring system allowed since a wine got fifty points merely for being in a bottle. He had filled up the two flower vases by now. He was done; tasted the lot. He ripped off the tasting sheet from the clipboard. He stood there regarding the two women.

"…course I don't mind if it's only a question of a little slap and tick…oh, you finished, Ed?…you know that comes with the job, you know what I mean?"

They fussed about him now like a pair of mechanics worrying over the driver at a pit stop. It was established he would take a sandwich with them. Vanessa wanted him to take a look at the new Berryman's website, where she had a wine page.

"Do you mind coming through to the other room? We have the computer set up there and we have some sandwiches…"

"…from Patisserie Raoul, you know…"

He did know. He'd had them before. He might eat several sandwiches if they were from Raoul's.

They retired to the office with the computer. He made soothing noises about the wines he had tasted. The sandwiches arrived.

"Would you like a glass of wine with your meal, Ed?" said April.

"Well, er…"

"I know I would."

"Yes, I think I can manage a glass. What do you suggest, Ed, now you've tasted my fantastic new range?"

He sat back; regarded the ciabatta with mozzarella with mountain ham, tomatoes, roasted courgettes and basil salsa.

"Or shall I just grab a few bottles?" said April.

Edward stood up, feeling inspired.

"No, ladies, you must be my guest. Let me bring you the greatest wine on display today...see if you can guess what it is..."

"Oh that's easy," said Vanessa. "That's the Cactus Ranch Zin. Be great with this...whatever it is..."

"That's fenzuela leaves with croeken tomatoes and toasted sesame seed on bar...barbouzia chicken...er...on rye bread... I think..."

"I know just the thing. Get some decent sized glasses, April, and I'll be back with something that'll be perfect with that...that sandwich."

He went into the tasting room and emptied a bottle of the Californian chardonnay and filled it with expectorated wine from one of the vases. He gave the full bottle a good shake; took one of Berryman's carrier bags from the pile in the corner and wrapped it around the bottle. He picked up the bottle of Cotes de Castillon at the end of the row.

"Here we are," he said, coming in to the room with the glowing computer screen, which he had yet to view.

"Ah, that claret...amazing I could pick up a ninety-three..."

Because every other retail buyer knew it was on its last legs, he thought.

"No," he said. "You'll have to guess what wine I've chosen." He brandished the carrier bag at them.

"Oooh," said April.

Vanessa smiled. "Great," she said. "A blind tasting."

He poured out some of the masked wine, hoping the strange head of bubbles it produced as he poured would soon subside as it filled the glass.

"You're not having any?" said April.

"Well, I know what it is. Besides, I must see just how well this claret goes with my sandwich."

April was the first to take a sip, then a draught. Vanessa regarded the colour, smelled the wine. Seeing this, April did likewise.

"Smells a little of garlic…you know."

My God, thought Ed, the girl has a palate. He'd had a lot of garlic with that Indian lunch yesterday. He prevented his guffaw by making a leap with his mouth at his monstrous sandwich.

Vanessa sipped and then looked up at the man who entered. He was wearing a dark suit with broad stripes and an even broader smile.

"Ah! The famous Edward Severn. Mr Severn, I am a great fan of your books…never go to Tesco…er…or indeed a Berryman's franchise…without a copy of the latest edition in my hand…"

You've never been to a Tesco in your life, thought Edward. He stood and shook the man's mackerel-like hand (an accurate enough reflection of the suit, he further thought). April introduced him as Russell Parminter, one of her directors. Mr Parminter made a comment about the sandwiches – that Raoul's was reserved strictly for special occasions and special guests – and April asked if he'd like a glass of the red.

"Well, never usually drink at lunch time, of course." He laughed at this joke as April expostulated and he went to examine the Cotes de Castillon.

"Have some of this instead, Russ. Try and guess what it is."

Edward, the bottle by his side, grabbed the top to ensure the bag's handles did not slip from where he had tied them round the neck and went to say that surely Mr Parminter, Russ, didn't want to engage in games like this but the man rubbed his hands and nodded. "Oh yes," he said. "Oh yes." He left the room to return with a large glass and Edward found himself filling it a quarter full and then, as the man gesticulated that this was insufficient, he filled it half full.

"Well, I can see it's red," he said, plunging his nose in to the glass. "Ah, Bill…and Matthew…come and meet the famous Edward Severn…we're trying to guess what wine this is…camouflaged by that exquisitely designed Berryman's carrier bag…produced by our own design group, I might add…"

More glasses were brandished in the direction of the carrier bag and Edward poured out wine. It was Vanessa who spoke.

"I simply can't make out what this is, Ed."

"But you bought it, Nessie!"

"Yes, bought it and brought it, but it tastes like no wine in the line-up I presented today…oh, of course…Edward, you sneaky devil…you've blended that zin with some of that Cotes du Rhone…"

Edward produced a smile he hoped was enigmatic. It succeeded, in Vanessa's eyes, in making him appear saturnine.

"Well," he said, thinking he must say something.

"Do I detect cardamom? By George, yes…cardamom." This was Parminter.

Edward squirmed, keeping a firm hand on the carrier bag.

"Tastes pretty vile to me I must tell you, Miss Holden-Bragby…" said one of the men. "I'm getting poppadums."

"I didn't buy this wine! Edward's made up a little blend all his own."

The truth of this could not but force the enigma to erupt into a full-blooded grin. How did he get out of this?

"I thought so," she said, regarding him.

"Let's get Hugh and Seb in on this, they fancy themselves as wine buffs," said April.

Edward no longer felt hungry. He pushed away his plate with the uneaten half of his sandwich.

The room was soon full, the website forgotten, the sandwiches disappearing as fast as the contents of the carrier bag.

"Why are you not drinking any of this wine?" said Parminter. "It must be almost empty…that mystery bottle…"

Edward stood. "I, er, really must be going now, um, I, er, have another tasting…this afternoon." He moved towards the door, the carrier bag firm in his hand.

"Well," said Vanessa, "at least tell us what two wines you blended…or was it three? Couldn't be more than that. You were gone only a few seconds."

"Show us the bottle, Ed!" said April. "Put these guys out of their misery."

Edward took his bag containing his notes and his mobile phone and threw it over his shoulder. He thanked April and Vanessa and waved at the men. "May I use your loo before I go?" he said. "I can tell you that the wine…the wine is Domaine de Crachat Assortis 2001."

"But…" said Vanessa. "What?"

"Strange bloke," muttered Parminter, taking a draught of the wine. "Domaine de Crachat Assortis 2001? It doesn't taste like a French wine."

After five minutes, when Edward had not returned, April went to investigate. The little group followed her – all except Vanessa, who sat there with a wondering expression on her face. They found the carrier bag in reception. The receptionist confirmed that the guest had deposited it there before exiting and going down in the lift. April picked up the bag and took it into the room where Vanessa, rather pale of countenance, sat there regarding the glass in her hand like a phial of poison. April gave her the bag and as she did so it slid away to reveal the bottle.

"That's a white wine bottle!" said Parminter.

Vanessa stood up and rushed out. She was being sick in the loo. When she returned, to regard a group of puzzled faces, she sat down and asked for a glass of water.

"What's happening?" said Parminter.

"You alright, Nessie?" said April.

"If you go into the room we used for the tasting," said Vanessa slowly, breathing hard, "I think you will find that one of spittoons Edward…that bastard…used…has less wine, less expectorated wine…than the other…Domaine de Crachat Assortis 2001!"

She sat back as though exhausted from the effort of speaking. April and the men left the room to return a moment later to explain that there were four spittoons in fact but that one of the vases, the one in Parminter's hand, had only a film of wine at the bottom. Vanessa looked in to it; a wave of nausea passed over her.

"This was full," she gasped, "this was full when we left the room…to come in here…I noticed he used the vases…"

"I didn't see him doing that," said April. "Really? He just chucked out those origami flowers?"

The realisation of what Vanessa was saying was slow to dawn fully on Parminter and his colleagues. There was a general folding up of lips and puzzled glances at the glasses they had drunk from. Then:

"Yuk!" said Parminter.

"Some fucking guessing game that was," said one of the men. "That was a really shitty thing to do."

"Are you telling us that that bastard…that Edward Severn character filled this bottle with his own…?"

"Look at it! That's what that funny scum on the surface was. It was all his spittings out!" screamed Vanessa. "Domaine de Crachat Assortis 2001, he said it was. Work it out for yourself!"

"That cardamom was for real then?" said Parminter, who had felt proud of his olfactory sleuthing.

"Can we sue?" said one of the men.

"I don't get it," said another. "Domaine de Crachat Assortis…or whatever it's called…isn't it one of your wines, Vanessa?"

April sat down and picked up the remaining morsel of Raoul's extra-special honeyed pastrami with shrimp paste. She regarded it hungrily. Vanessa furiously rummaged in her bag to see if her filofax contained Edward Severn's mobile phone number.

"Domaine de Crachat Assortis 2001 is not *one* of my wines. It is *several* of my wines," she said, discovering she only had his office number. "Domaine de Crachat Assortis 2001 is several of my wines…plus Edward Severn's…spit!"

April laughed and bit into her sandwich as the room emptied of males as they sped off to the loo.

"It went okay with my sandwich, you know. Whatever it was called. And you know he never saw the new website, did he? Shall I contact him and see if he wants a personal run-through?"

ooooo

Chateau Lafite 1953

Ralph Guiseman, he of the flamboyant hair, was on the 113 bus from Finchley Road to Baker Street when he noticed that The Times, being read by a clubby-looking fellow further down the top deck, had a major article, the headline of which he could dimly make out, about himself. To make matters worse it displayed that unflattering photograph of its subject taken when it was looking the worse for wear after its last divorce. Guiseman was shown clutching to his bosom, a sordid composition of crumpled shirt, five opened bottles of wine and he wore the sleazy grin of the recently liberated.

Ralph did not read newspapers on buses (or anywhere else, truth to tell), though he was the wine correspondent of one. On buses he composed *haiku*, or more strictly *senryu,* on the backs of the tickets. It would have been cheaper to get a travel card or a seasonal bus pass, but that that little printed receipt was, for him, the ticket to more than a physical destination. He had just scribbled down his latest *senryu* when he caught sight of himself, black and white and lit by flashlight, in his fellow passenger's reading matter.

Appetite.
Finchley Road
Like a squat toad
Stretches and yawns

And gobbles cars like flies.

Prawns instead of flies was a possibility but that would have made it a half-clerihew and possibly inauthentic, though a frog would presumably happily engulf a prawn if one came along. Flies would have to suffice. It was adequate as an aide-memoire to the final version, always faithful to the form's obligatory seventeen syllables, which he would inscribe on to his ancient word processor's database. Indeed, not only would it adhere to the principles of the seventeen-syllable form but be composed of three lines of precisely five syllables, one of seven syllables, and then a further five-syllable line. He was aware, however, of the advice given him by a Japanese acquaintance that the western idea of a seventeen-syllable *haiku* or *senryu* was utterly fallacious since in Japan, where the *haiku* has been a poetic form for many centuries, the language would admit of only twelve. "Western haiku," further advised Gheiso Tanada, "are childish drivel and have as much to do with the real thing as a buttercup with a bonsai." Admiring of this metaphor from someone whose first language was not English, Guiseman was persuaded. Why was it the Japanese devoted so much of their intellectual passions to miniaturisation? Guiseman didn't know. But he did know Anthony Sykes-Eden would publish his *senryu*, authentic or not, and that was enough. Sykes-Eden had impressed Guiseman with his clear understanding of the difference, spiritually, between the moment of nature the *haiku* celebrated and the human collisions depicted by the *senryu.* Guiseman felt at home in either genre.

For he was a deep, ironic fellow, in spite of his surface, irresolute charm. When people asked him the name of the brand of his software system – with the absurd manner (he always thought) of someone enquiring the make of his non-existent motor car or the address of his ex-university – he always replied "cuneiform" and the response, invariably, was "Really? That's Mackintosh, isn't it?".

It was this irresolution of his forceful charms that had got him into so much trouble. He had been divorced but eight months and, fuelled by the last fifty-nine sexless months of his childless marriage to Candida he had, upon divi-ing up the proceeds of the house sale, embarked on a series of high-level seductions which had resulted in precisely eight 'romances' yet precisely nil genital engagements. He had made these eight romances, one following upon another each and every month with the remorseless precision of a menstrual cycle, the subject of scores of bus-bound *senryu* which, after each dedicatee was deposed, or departed, or the frenzy of lust had diluted into casual friendship, became severely edited down so that the book they would eventually compile, *Omniverse & Worse*, was of a publishable (£5.99 paperback) length. It was in Caernarvon that he had found the sympathetic, reputable, non-vain and obviously psychologically deranged Sykes-Eden, who had, on the basis of Guiseman's renown as a writer of wine articles and books, been prepared to take a punt. Mitchell Beazley, which had published his *Revolution in the Ribatejo* and *Iron Curtain Grand Crus*, was hardly in the poetry publishing line. He conjectured that he would be the first member of the Circle of Wine Writers to be a published poet. Or maybe not. That humourless phasmidiac creature Clifford was rumoured to compose agonised, rhymeless verse but had any been published? In book form, that is? Guiseman couldn't say. He wasn't, when all was said and done, especially competitive and he certainly wasn't expecting to make the

Laureate's nomination list on the basis of 250 *haiku* and *senryu* all composed on the backs of bus tickets (thousands of them, lovingly mounted in albums like philately specimens).

Shirley had been the first. Imogen the last. He was currently girlfriendless, though this term was not his preferred one. He was, he supposed, between divorces – though the thought of getting married for a fourth time frankly appalled him but could not, given his record, be discounted.

As is fairly obvious by now, Guiseman was an orderly, not to say taxonomically obsessed (anal is the Freudian preference), kind of a person. His habits were ordained, ingrained, and neatly laid out; only to be breached by anything resembling spontaneity when a woman he fancied, and whom he reckoned might, given a little cajoling, fancy him, came along. This was frequent in the wine trade and had become urgent during the fading – those oh so agonisingly long drawn-out – months of his marriage to Candida; but he had not felt able to consummate any of the flirtations then embarked on because he had a horror of others' beds and the thought of hotel or one-day bed-sit liaisons filled him with disgust. He was not averse to kitchen floors or even lavatories, but sitting rooms were the favoured locale, on a sofa or, better, within the confines of a deep armchair. This was his pet sexual congress site. In bedrooms he read and slept.

Candida did rather get in the way of these kind of ambitions. He had had to have his own place to pursue his desires properly – not only with regard to women, but with much else besides. Candida had discovered the gulf between them included much more trenchant predilections than vegetarianism (on her side), Sunday worship followed by tennis (her side also) and a violent antipathy to the other half's friends (his side). Naturally, sex was abandoned – when it had been pretty good, he thought, in all the rooms of the jointly-owned Hornsey house in which this activity had been pursued – after a mere four years and ten months of marriage. He was on his own now. Much better that way. Candida, comparatively young at forty-six, could "go and marry a racket-carrying, root vegetable-obsessed born-again Christian", which was his departing piece of advice to her. The house, once sold, had seen both of them able to site themselves elsewhere: Candida in Dulwich and Ralph in West Hampstead (though he would have preferred Hampstead proper).

He edged closer to the clubby-looking fellow but the man folded the paper and got off at Lord's just as Guiseman was near enough to have read it. Had he been imagining things? Had the paper really had a piece about him? He thought he might be hallucinating. He slunk back to his original seat and composed another *haiku*, or rather one came to him as he peered at the young man opposite whose cheeks, lips, nose and ears were perforated with a least twenty (he estimated) silvery metal studs the size of pin-heads. How did he shave with all those hurdles to negotiate? Surely electric razor blades would buckle under the assault? Maybe he used a wet razor. The poor chap was reading a book, and it was this that set Guiseman off. He would sort out the poetry of the studs later.

Loss.
Beside me he reads:
'Doctor Atkins New
Diet Revolution.'

It was only last night that had he worked out that his women, thus far, composed a *haiku*, or rather, and more strictly, a *senryu*:

Shirley
Abigail
Tabitha
Sharon
Ruth
Tsai
Carole
Imogen

He was superstitious enough to reckon that though his next pursuit of the Ideal would, then, result in the disarray of this syllabic perfection, he would achieve what he was seeking. This consideration was rather heartening. Who would it be? He was dying for a shag. He had, rather uncomfortably, begun to realise that he had taken to dawdling near phone boxes and idly running an eye over the carded whores blue-tacked inside. He shuddered at the horror of what a whore's bed might be like, even though such a thoroughly commercial artiste would probably be game for sex anywhere.

Shirley, forever a *haiku*'s first line, had been far too young for him. Twenty-two years! She could have been his granddaughter. He had met her whilst he was slurping and spitting his way around forty wines at the offices of a PR company representing a group of Oregon wineries calling themselves The Argyle Select Eleven. She was a temp, anxious to get into the wine trade. She had magnificent breasts and lips like mountain bike tyre treads and she readily fell in with his suggestion, whispered in her ear when the two biddies who ran the PR company left her to empty his spittoon, that they meet for a drink, near his home, the following evening. She appeared forty-five minutes late for this rendezvous and said she had forgotten his mobile phone number. She removed her top coat and sat down, her mammalia jostling like live puppies inside her blouse. She drank a glass of merlot. He was enraptured. A few evenings later, when she consented to have dinner chez Guiseman and try his particular brand of home cooked Thai food, he seized, gently it must be said, one of these puppies – looking to stroke it – and was rebuffed. The heavy-duty pneumatic lips offered polite pecks but further exploration was discouraged. Within ten days, with Ralph several hundred pounds lighter (thanks to Le Gavroche and Bibendum), she admitted she had a nipple problem and was unable to accept caresses. Also on the horizon a lout of a boyfriend appeared. Guiseman lost interest. As did, very soon afterwards, the PR company, which fired her for, Guiseman later learned to his fury, making sexual advances to a client. She vanished. *Haiku* number eleven would be her memorial (not *senryu* for she was, Guiseman argued, a freak of nature).

Abigail was much classier (also in wine PR) and much older. She had a beautiful way of walking, as if she glided rather than moved the conventional limbs. He did manage to touch her tongue with his, didn't especially like the taste, but this triggered a furious bout of clothes disposal on her part. Embarrassingly, when she finally lay naked on his sitting room floor, she was not only all skin and bone, like an emaciated supermodel, but the smell of bitter clove he had discerned on her tongue was more emphatic. Alienated, he failed to get anything resembling an erection. Instead of being sympathetic, Abigail was angry and stormed out without booking a cab. She rang his doorbell, forty minutes later, said she couldn't find a taxi anywhere, wasn't prepared to risk the tube, and could she spend the night with him. Guiseman immediately called West End Lane Express Minicab service, making no show of gallantry, and they endured fifty minutes of mutual torture before a car turned up. He had seen her twice at social events since and she had been coldly not to say icily professional. He couldn't abide the taste of cloves. It was the horror of boarding school apple pie, crust like concrete, all over again.

Had he undergone some curious hormone interchange or redevelopment during his marriage? Even if Abigail had put out off-putting pheromones once naked and had appeared skeletal once divested of clothes, she was still pretty and had ample entablature but even the pressing of his lips to this apparatus had not succeeded in exciting his member. Was he simply too old for adventures like this?

He sought solace with Tabitha, a red-haired body discovered at the annual Marks & Spencer tasting. But when, two days later, he took her to the opening of a new Indian eating club in Westminster and found himself eyeball to eyeball with her, he also discovered her disconcerting predisposition to kiss everyone who came within her orbit in exactly the same suggestive way she had impressed her lips upon him. His member, that once-eager prick of a thing, died a death with this realisation.

How had he ever, given his anti-viral defences, contracted Matrimony? He wondered. Matrimony was the disease with no known cure, which no physician was even working upon relieving let alone trying to eliminate. He suffered from this diagnostically obvious condition to the extent that he was incorrigibly infected by it and was not just a random temporary victim struck down by a chance passing virus. Who can, though, cure *la condition humaine*?

Sharon cut his hair. No more need be said. Well, Guiseman and Sharon at least exchanged words but not bodily fluids.

"God, I fancy you, Sharon."

"I know."

"I've struggled with it for six years, can it be six years?"

"You came to me first in 1996. Yeah, gettin' on six years."

"You understand!"

"I've seen your erections under the cape as I snipped. And as I washed your hair. Nothing new."

"You mean…?"

"I mean I noticed you were a randy old bugger. Why has it taken you so long to get around to…to this…? Anyway, d'ye want more off the top?"

"I just want to get off with you."

"You can fuck me for a grand. You can afford it."

Guiseman left her flat, where he had ritually gone every six or eight weeks for a ritual snip, and wished he had kept quiet. Who else was going to tackle every six weeks his unruly mop for eight quid, including shampoo and tip? From where had she got the idea he could afford to pay £1000 for a fuck? If he could, why was he the customer of so cheap a hairdresser? A hairdresser who was a single mother working from a shabby apartment block of metal-windowed 1930s flats overlooking a neglected cemetery in the Grey's Inn Road?

Strictly he had not had a romantic relationship, in the forensic sense, with Sharon but he had in the metaphysical one and he had mentally undressed her a thousand times – especially when she had leaned over him to riffle her strong almond-skin coloured fingers through his hair and he had absorbed her perfume, always the same, of tobacco, tea and cabernet franc. He sometimes brought a bottle of wine and opened it with the wooden handled corkscrew personally given him by Miguel Torres and she would accept a glass, presumably drinking the remainder after he left. He never saw her smoke but he knew she did. It was her resemblance to Eva Marie Saint, smoking so sexily as he remembered from *North By Northwest*, which made her so tempting. Sharon had the retroussé button nose of Ms Saint and just as that American actress had become an embroidered figment of his imagination with that smile like ice, so had he transferred one fantasy upon another. As Sharon cut his hair, invariably wearing one of her sleeveless jumpers (winter and summer), he would imagine travelling up her arm, that strong brown arm at the end of which were the scissors (able placidly to cut hair, he reflected, as well as stab and maim), and along her shoulders with his tongue…but of course there was the child to consider and the fact that the father was believed to be a pugilist of ungovernable temper. Guiseman had been introduced to Sharon by the racing correspondent of his newspaper, who gave him inside information on certainties in exchange for bottles of wine. It was confusing to consider that Sharon had not been among these certainties and that he had also lost as much money as he had won – though he bet on horses barely three or four times a year. He supposed it was the exquisite ears, like Eva Marie's, he found most compelling; those ears like the shells of a small rare mollusc, edible, strangely khaki-coloured with a pink interior…how he longed to lead his tongue to find that interior after its journey along her arm.

He also knew that these fantasies had begun when sexual relations with Candida had declined to zero. All those little chats they had had over a glass of wine before Sharon would invariably say "I've got another client in twenty minutes" and he would trot off to Kings Cross station or to a wine-tasting in the centre of town.

Guiseman got off the bus at the top of Baker Street, just across the road from the ridiculous Sherlock Holmes museum, which, in the tourist season, was sentried by a phonily uniformed police constable so as to beacon the existence of the place to the gullible. The idea that a wholly fictional character could have given birth to such a miserable, tackily exploitative 'museum' caused strong objections in Guiseman every time he passed in the bus and he would invariably grimace in distaste as he glanced at it. But not this time. This time he was preoccupied with acquiring a copy of The Times and so he walked down to the station instead of turning into Melcombe Street, which was his route today. What was the newspaper doing featuring his person so prominently? If indeed it was him and not a trick of the light as he suspected it must be. He knew a lot about tricks of the light. Had not Sharon, scissors clicking away in that crepuscular flat lit by a three-bulb make-up mirror behind his head, been a trick of the light?

Then there was Ruth…

…but here was The Times, that disgusting Murdochian – he had heard it applied to Iris so it surely could be used to demystify Rupert – imprint for which he once been proud to write. Guiseman could reflect on his own ruthlessness but it was insignificant compared with that of the man who owned that shitty news-sheet. Guiseman disliked jumping on fashionable bandwagons but he was happy to be aboard the one that held the view that The Times was nowadays a shoddy, scandal-mongering shadow of a once great paper. It was this latter consideration, scandal, which had caused him some unease in the bus and he was busily racking his brains as to what he might have done to cause his name to merit so much space. He hoped he was wasting his money buying the oily rag as he took his change and left the newsagent's.

He felt a sense of dread, excitement, and anticipation. He needed to visit the lavatory. His bowels felt like rice pudding. He would open the paper in the seclusion of one of the Landmark's luxury lavs.

He walked up Melcombe Street and crossed Dorset Square. He noted the late-arrivers streaming out of Marylebone station and entered the venue of today's wine-tasting, the Landmark Hotel. Once the HQ of British Rail (now as antiquated a notion as the Raj, it occurred to Guiseman), the Landmark was becoming a favoured spot for wine-tastings amongst the premier division wine merchants.

The lavatory was marbleized and tomb-like and barely well-lit enough to close-read type, but it would do for now. He dropped his trousers and opened the paper. He noted his hand did not shake as, on page five, his face taking up one fifth of the page, the headline "Prominent wine critic admits 'I took bribe'" shouted at him. He evacuated his bowels instantly as he further made out the by-line "Times wine-correspondent Topsy Aylesberry" and the caption under the photograph: "The Custodian's wine correspondent, Ralph Guiseman, grabs all he can get."

Topsy! He had always loathed her smugness and each Christmas he wrote scornfully of her annual wine guide, which always faithfully appeared during the festive season and sold in its thousands. But when had he ever admitted to her, or anyone else for that matter, that he had taken a bribe? He wiped his arse, buttoned up his flies, and washed his hands with that scrupulous delicacy often noted by his colleagues when he was tasting. He fled to a remote corner of a small ante-room in the hotel, where the light was better and began to read Topsy's revelations…

The trilling of his mobile phone interrupted and when he looked at the number on the screen he recognised it as the direct line of the consumer affairs editor, Virginia Malan, under whose aegis his weekly column was published.

"You silly bugger, Ralph! You've really landed yourself in it, haven't you, and no mistake. Is it true? Don't tell me. Of course it's true. Even the slimebags at The Times couldn't make this up…"

"…well…er…"

"Ralph? This is you, isn't it? Have you read this morning's Slimes? I've been waiting for you to call, as has his Highness Lord Plowright, but since you didn't…and it is ten forty-five now…we, I that is, thought…"

"Hello, Ginny. Good morning. How are you? I…er…"

"Ralph, honey…you do know what I'm taking about here, don't you? How I am is somewhat less relevant than how *you* are, though since you asked I can tell you I am not best pleased to read about my wine critic in this way."

Ralph, who rather fancied Ginny Malan but had never proceeded further than the odd glass of wine with her at Groucho, said he had been trying to read the article when she called. She said: "Read it and call me back in five minutes. No later." The line went dead.

Was his career in a similar state? He felt in need of the loo again but quelled the artificiality of the feeling and steeled himself to read what Topsy had written. It took him a little longer than five minutes and when he dialled Ginny's number it was engaged. He took a deep breath and read some of the key paragraphs again.

"Readers will remember a column of mine some months back when I reported on the seamy side of wine journalism. Writing, at the time, in the Circle of Wine Writer's own closed-circulation magazine, Ralph Guiseman confessed that 'the very nature of the relationship between the wine trade and the wine writer means one influences the other' and he went on to admit that he has all his overseas trips paid for, receives regular cases of wine from supermarkets and wine retailers, and enjoys lunches and dinners at their expense almost weekly. Is it a conflict of interest? he was asked. He said, and I quote, 'by the highest standards of journalism you can only say yes. Yes it is a conflict of interest and I admit it.'

"Tesco confirmed it sent Ralph Guiseman at least two cases of wine a week. This retailer features strongly in Guiseman's column, analysis reveals.

"These shocking revelations will cause the proprietor of The Custodian, Lord Plowright, acute embarrassment. The Custodian is noted for its holier-than-thou, self-proclaimed 'enemy-of-sleaze' approach. Yet it has a wine critic who sees no shame in accepting gifts of wine, free trips abroad, and lunches and dinners in Michelin-starred restaurants, in exchange for featuring certain wines in his Saturday column. Further, he is accused of making advances to young women in PR companies by offering their clients space in his column if they make room for him in their beds.

"Shirley Grossman, who has since left the PR industry, said: 'Guiseman fondled my breasts, or tried to, and said how easy it would be for me to make it big-time in PR if only I took my clothes off.'

"Abigail Threale, leading PR consultant, revealed that Guiseman once propositioned her. 'He said,' claims Miss Threale, 'that if I accompanied him on a trip to California as his wife, he would ensure my client had his wines featured in his column. I was shocked and left his flat immediately.'"

ooooo

How odd that reading it for the *second* time made Guiseman feel sick. His hand *was* shaking when he dialled Ginny's number for the fifth time and got through.

"This is, Ginny, simply an attempt to have a go at the Custodian. You know how it rankles at the Slimes that we're now considered the top quality daily..."

"Ralph, honeybun, we know all that. But you are accused of specific misdemeanours. Did you write what they say you wrote in that wine writer's rag...what's it called?"

"Circle of Wine Writer's newsletter. Yes, I did write that. Partly tongue-in-cheek, of course. Stupid of me in retrospect. I don't really believe it's a conflict of interest because it's how the business works. I'm still free not to write about any wine whose maker's hospitality I have enjoyed. All wine writers accept free wine and free trips abroad. Would his Lordship take kindly to my expenses if they took into account me buying all the wine I need to taste in order to write my column? And what if the Custodian had to pay for all those trips to vineyards...?"

"Hold on...a mo—"

"No, Ginny. Listen. This whole article is sleaze from first word to last and Topsy Aylesberry knows it. God, she's been itching to take a swipe at me..."

"Oh yes, your annual review of her wine guide is one of the funniest things you send in..."

He didn't like "send in." It suggested a less than solid relationship between him and the newspaper. He was the wine correspondent, after all, and he had a contract.

"If you and Lord Plowright would like to redraw my contract so that all my expenses for wine samples are met..."

"She says you receive two cases a week from Tesco! Is that true?"

"Of course. Even so, it isn't enough. Do you know how many different wines there are at Tesco? Over a thousand. Do you know how many bottles of Tesco's wines Custodian readers bought last year? I'll tell you because Tesco itself estimated it and told me: between thirty-five and forty-eight million bottles. I recognise that our readers patronise that supermarket and need to know about the wines there."

"I see that."

"Good. Then also see that this article is sheer artifice. I'm no different from any other wine critic. Even Topsy Aylesberry has to get her wine samples given her and the same goes for her foreign trips and lunches with winemakers."

"I take it, then, that she also offers her body to young PR men in return for…"

"Oh, Ginny, that is unworthy of you. That—"

"I know. I'm sorry. I'm really sorry I said that, Ralphie. But tell me, because Plowright wants, needs, to know: is there any substance is what those women are saying?"

"Yes. And no. That Shirley creature I did make a pass at. Absolutely. And she was not averse but it didn't lead anywhere and yes, I did fondle her tits, they're the size of Vesuvius, Ginny, no-one can miss them, and now that it's in print I did say to her that she could make it big in PR if she took her clothes off, but it wasn't said to promote my own lust but merely to point the fact out. Christ! I might say the same of you, Ginny, that if you wanted to make it big, or even bigger at the Custodian, then you only had to sleep with Plowright… and…"

"Don't be disgusting. He's eighty-six."

"All the more reason to consider it, Ginny…"

"I take your point. What about that Threale woman?"

"She needed no encouragement to take her clothes off, unaided by me. I wasn't exactly overwhelmed by her. I admit I treated her badly or rather somewhat brusquely…"

"I know your brusque, Ralph. It can be crucifying."

"She left my flat in a huff, tried to get a cab, couldn't and came back and I refused to sleep with her…for various reasons…and I got her a cab…"

"What about the holiday in California accusation?"

"Her word against mine, Ginny. She represented a Californian winery, which I wanted to visit, and she was organising a trip for me and a couple of other journos. The usual deal. It was her idea that after my visit to her client she joined me and, at her client's expense, we toured the State together. I never took the suggestion seriously. In the end I went alone, or rather I went with two other wine writers. But how can I prove she's twisting the truth?"

"There's nothing in this article then? Nothing at all?"

"I'll write up a complete rebuttal when I get back home later this afternoon and e-mail it to you by…"

"By four at the latest, Ralph. The lawyers need to read it. We need a point-by-point demolition of that article. Plowright wants a lead piece on page three in tomorrow's paper ideally, or he'll simply ask you to resign. If what you have told me is what we can carry in tomorrow's paper, more substantially vindicating your good name in other ways as well, of course, then fine…we, you, can weather this."

ooooo

Guiseman sat in the small annex only dimly aware that around him a large hotel revolved and from distant corridors and rooms came the faint sounds of voices, wheels on hard floors, and the clunk of plates. On one floor here the wine-tasting was being held to which he had been invited. He had to face the wine trade and face it today. Everyone would have read the article. Doubtless it was being passed around the offices of everyone in the industry as he sat there. Was this fame at last? The fame, or rather faint celebrity, his column brought him was limited to Custodian readers and his books were purchased solely by wine magazine enthusiasts.

The paragraph that really stuck in his gullet was this one: *"Guiseman was recently divorced, for the fourth time, from a daughter of Lord Glenroth, Candida Connaughton. It had lasted almost ten years, well above average for the wine critic."*

Well above average! The fucking bitch. He felt such hatred of Topsy Aylesberry that he had to stand up and walk around the room. A waiter, certainly a youth in a starched white jacket, poked his head round the door and then withdrew. Was Guiseman talking to himself? He often caught himself doing it now, increasingly so in the years past fifty. He put his hands in his jacket pocket to keep himself from punching the air in mock combat and moved to gather up his overcoat and scarf and briefcase. He pulled the 113 bus ticket from his pocket and read the *haiku*. It was rubbish. He walked out to reception.

"The Uglow tasting, sir? Just up the stairs there and up on the balcony."

He had initially experienced – shaving, strolling up Lymington Road, slumped against the bus-stop – some small excitement at the Uglow prospect. Uglow was a royal-appointee said to have supplied George the Third with the port that addled the King's brains and caused the 'misjudgements' which lost England its American colonies. Uglow had an inside track with the House of Hanover due to the original Uglow (changing his name from Ullrich-Neus) having some kinship with Handel. An eponym, Barrington Uglow, was still in charge of the firm which, with its three branches sited in the sveltest parts of London and its ownership of the big selling international Scotch whisky brand Tavish Rare, had survived the onslaughts of the supermarkets, the various recessions, and the changes in fortune that had seen dozens of firms like Uglow go to the wall. Guiseman knew Barrington, had even briefly met him when both were at the same college of the same university though not in the same year. Uglow's was an annual tasting, normally put on for a discrete group of journalists (no regional johnnies got invited and certainly not the less well-connected members of the Circle) in the plush upper rooms of the main branch in South Audley Street. But this tasting was the first the firm had organised outside its own environs because it was celebrating some obscure anniversary: the royal George and Ullrich-Neus's first meeting? – something trivial like that, Guiseman recalled vaguely. Thus not only had the usual wine hacks been invited but various food writers and social journalists.

As he trod up the stairs to the mezzanine floor he felt it was a tasting pregnant with unpleasant possibilities. He paused, his hand on the rail. Should he quietly sneak out the front? Surely he should be consulting his lawyer? He had to write his piece for Ginny. But then he thought of what he would miss. Uglow's was not just showing the usual line-up from its portfolio but masterpieces from the past, including a flight of ancient d'Yquems as well as various old burgundies. Most incredible of all, however, was the flight of Lafites including 1926, '34, '45, '49, '51, '53, '59, '62, '66, plus a couple from the seventies and eighties up to '89.

How could he miss all that? Especially the '53. It had been the wine that had made his head spin, his world turn, and his mind go giddy with excitement. He had first tasted it at the Randolph Hotel, after his graduation in 1968; a wine purchased by his parents in celebration of their only son's survival of the university and the respectable degree it had conferred on him.

He paused on the stair. My God, that '53! Wine had been merely a perfunctory libation, champagne apart, until then. But that wine with its sumptuous fruit, its gentle spiciness, its amazing rich marzipan-like undertone, and above all that texture like liquidised satin, had overwhelmed him. He had never forgotten its bouquet – like cassis and roasted walnuts. He had tasted it only twice since, both bottles not as memorable as the first though still pulsating with life, and here he was within a few feet of yet another '53 and a chance to revisit the memories of that Oxford hotel, the musty odours of which had failed to mar the aroma of the wine. The holiday he had planned with a fellow new-graduate to climb in the Pyrenees had its itinerary rearranged so he could visit Bordeaux. His French (and indeed his German) was more than passable. When he returned to Leamington and Mum and Dad, he had no doubts what he wanted to do with his life and their protests dented his enthusiasm not one jot. His father proclaimed his regret at having paid for that Lafite if it had been the inspiration for his son becoming a grocery clerk. For what was going to work for a wine merchant in Bristol other than a clerkship? The old man had fondly imagined his son becoming a professor of literature perhaps, or a writer of biographies of continental celebrities. When, after a few years in the trade had convinced young Ralph of its shortcomings, the meagreness of its financial rewards, its creative nullity (though plenty of opportunity to swig wines beyond the capacity of his pocket legitimately to acquire), he found employment at a London magazine, the father felt a little less aggrieved – but it was many years before he felt his son acquired the success his intellect promised. This came with the hiring of Ralph by a national newspaper as its wine correspondent and, hard on the heels of this, publication of *Revolution in the Ribatejo*. Not quite, as Henry Davenport Guiseman had dreamed up for his son in his more extravagant moments, *The Secret Life of Balzac* or *The Machinations of Metternich*, but it was a start – and then he died.

Thank God, Guiseman reflected, that the old man was not around to take, as was his normal habit, his own daily dose of The Times. His mother, in a nursing home, read nothing any more. Distant cousins, of whom he saw extremely little, could be forgotten.

But he could not forget the wine trade. It was waiting at the top of the stairs. He removed his hand from the rail and ascended. He turned the corner and there was Barrington Uglow, the same Leachmore & Traherne suit and purple Packmore bow-tie, detaching himself from Rosemary George, the chairwoman of the Circle, and coming across the room to greet him. Guiseman steeled himself for the usual effusive handshake but was rewarded with an arm around the shoulders. Was it sympathy? Guiseman decided in that moment that *sang froid* was the only course, indifference to anything but the wines he was here to taste and, he hoped, find sufficiently moving to fashion into his weekly Custodian article.

Not taken middle age in his stride, thought Guiseman of Uglow, as they swapped the usual greetings. He'd cut quite a figure at Oxford, he remembered, but he was three stone heavier now. Gifted with so much excess, and expensively acquired, flesh had given Barrington a manner to match. There was always a suggestion of a secret life about the man (he had had the reputation, Guiseman knew, of being a devoted spanker of female bottoms at College). He had never lost the distinctive aura of the roué, Guiseman decided, as Uglow handed him the tasting sheets and showed him the various tables where the wines stood so invitingly. So far, only a dozen or so people had arrived. Guiseman nodded at the various people he knew and he could tell by their demeanour that they had all seen the Times piece. He would affect disdain. He would get on and do his job with his nose in the air.

Uglow only let his guard slip when he said in a low voice, as he gave Guiseman a clipboard: "Glad you had it in you to turn up this morning, Ralph old sport. Always good to see you, you know that."

"What," said Guiseman, twirling his tasting glass, "makes you say that, Barr? What are you glad about specifically? What have I had to have in me to make it here? A quid on the 113 bus was all it took."

Barrington laughed. He deflected the questions with: "Custodian sniffy about taxis, are they? I thought you broadsheet journos had unlimited expenses."

Guiseman could hardly explain to Uglow about the *haiku* on the bus tickets. He remarked that he often took the bus because he liked the view of Lords from the top deck as it passed that hallowed spot; and, he added, even the speediest taxi wouldn't have done the journey much more than five minutes quicker. Not for the first time it struck him that he lost expenses money by keeping the bus tickets instead of adding them to his usual monthly sheaf of receipts; but it was, he told himself, part of the pain of poetry. Hardly a great sum in any event. And if it led to the publication of *Omniverse & Worse*...

"I'll leave you to get on, Ralph. The Lafites have just been decanted. Ready for you when you are."

ooooo

It was difficult to concentrate. He was aware that several people who would have engaged him in conversation merely permitted an exchange of pleasantries to take place rather than a swap of the customary clichés. He tried to keep his head down as he went through the burgundies. It was difficult.

He wandered over to the Lafite table, spotting a sudden gap. The room was filling up. It was becoming quite a crowd and glances were definitely being cast in his direction. When he got to the Lafites, several tasters looked up, seemed as if to snort, and left the area. Was he imagining things? He tried the younger Lafites, thinking how hard and disappointing they were, and then, avoiding the '53, he tasted some of the pre-war vintages. Not holding up especially well, he considered, trying to be as generous as he could. He looked at the special prices, reduced for the occasion, Uglow was charging for the oldest wines. It was obscene. Who could afford £28,500 for a case of wine? He sighed. He scribbled. He felt the warmth of others' eyes on his back.

He finally had the '53 poured for him by an Uglow assistant. He twirled the glass and inserted his nose in to it. Were there still roasted nuts coming through? Hmm...possibly. However, it was a marvellous aroma, whatever it might be. It was a sumptuous liquid…even at £36,000 the case. He tasted it but did not spit out. The walnuts, which he decided were definitely present, had become like roast chestnuts now, the cassis sweeter, the tannins, inevitably, less grippy and not as striking as when he last tasted the wine. Can anything live up to The First Time? It wouldn't last but a few hours in the decanter, he reckoned, perhaps only thirty minutes. He glanced at the Uglow rep, a chap called Sebastian, if memory served, and waited for him to serve a glass of one of the other vintages to someone else. In a sudden move, Guiseman reached over and took the bottle of '53 and filled his tasting glass as full as he dared. He glanced at the spitoon as he did so. It had barely been used. Everyone was drinking the stuff. Only the real pros, like Rosemary George, were spitting out. Sebastian frowned at Guiseman's manoeuvre but said nothing.

He took the glass over to the sofa, by the grand piano and the spread of luncheon cheeses, and sat down. The spittoon here had been more liberally taken advantage of, but Guiseman had no intention of using it. He nosed the wine in his customary, hound-dog manner. He sipped, gargled, breathed in…and swallowed. It was pretty remarkable, even if it was beginning to show faint traces of arthritis as the tannins melded with the acids. All the memories of that afternoon at the Randolph came back and he thought of his father and his mother and their huge pride. What would they think of him if they could see him now? What would they say if they had read this morning's Times?

He slowly took a little more of the wine. The smell was beginning to make him tearful. All those years ago. All those parental sacrifices to see him through that minor public school and then university. For what? He would drink this '53 and then get himself another glass. If he was being judged by these buffoons here on the basis of what they had read in that newspaper, if he was as corrupt as alleged, then he would live up to it…

But there was a small commotion at the top of the stairs. There was a sudden visible rise in the tension in the room, in the level of sound; a shift in the amiability of the atmosphere. Topsy Aylesberry had arrived and was striding into the middle of the room with a vast grin on her face. She didn't see Guiseman sitting there but she did when he stood up and, seized by a daemon he knew not he possessed, confronted her and stopped her progress. She looked startled. It had simply never occurred to her that she might run into Guiseman on today of all days. She was a fairly tall woman, in her middle thirties, and she always dressed with a swagger even if she didn't walk with one. Her long black hair was tied in a bun behind her head and her eyes struck Guiseman, as never before, like some kind of weaponry; the kind that is sharp and can he hurled.

"You fucking miserable bitch! How dare you write that utter tosh, those absurd lies, about me!"

Topsy's face took on colour. The assembled tasters pretended nothing was amiss but could hardly turn their backs on the arena the room had suddenly become. Barrington Uglow began to wave his arms, meaninglessly. Topsy looked at Ralph and tried to smile. It was the expression, Ralph concluded, of the rat who is about to whine "What, can't you take a joke?"

"I have something to offer you, Topsy Aylesberry. A glass of 1953 Chateau Lafite. Here."

He aimed the contents of his glass at those eyes. Five hundred pound's worth of old claret splashed on to Topsy's mascara and eye shadow and ran down the nose, and she screamed and attempted to swipe him but he was not there. He had leaned over and picked up the spittoon and as she was wiping her eyes and trying to get away, he aimed the contents at her face. However, he couldn't find the strength to lift the spittoon high enough and so the wine hit her blouse, which was green, and quickly it turned crimson and then black. There was a crowd about them now and Topsy screamed again and fled, to be followed by Uglow as Guiseman stood there, the wine glass at his feet, the spittoon emptying its last dregs on to the carpet at his feet.

To his astonishment, and delight, applause broke out. Several of the male tasters came over and muttered their congratulations. The women, by contrast, seemed less impressed. Uglow assistants tried manfully to mop up the wine on the floor. Several waiters appeared. Then an under-manager.

"I'd better go," muttered Guiseman. "Where did Barr put my coat?"

He was directed to a room off the tasting hall and as he turned a corner, Barr nearly crashed into him coming the other way.

"Not quite the excitement I planned, Ralph, for today. Couldn't you have…no, I suppose you couldn't, could you? God, she's a bitch that one. I saw The Times this morning. She was out of order and everyone knows it. But did you have to…?"

"Where did my coat go?"

"Waste of a bloody fine glass of '53, Ralph. I can only afford to open two bottles."

Uglow threw up his hands and walked back to the tasting room. Guiseman continued down the corridor and threw open the door of the one he thought was being used as a cloakroom and lavatory. He opened the door and stepped inside and there was Topsy Aylesberry, blouse discarded, skirt down to her knees, removing her bra…

"You bastard! Get out of here, Ralph…I could sue you… you…for damages."

"I can sue you for libel."

He had never realised before what attractive breasts Topsy possessed. She realised her semi-nakedness at that moment and went as if to hide her top but then, running her fingers through her sodden hair and letting it fall down, she groaned and fell, gently, on to a pile of coats on the sofa.

"Lock the fucking door, Ralph, for God's sake. Lock the fucking door!"

He turned the key. She stood up and came towards him and, before he could stop her, she had grabbed his hair and kissed him and then twisted her hands into his shoulder blades. He winced, felt the erection soar in his trousers, and found himself fighting to get his tongue as far down her throat as humanly possible.

"You fucking bastard, Ralph," she whispered.

"You too, Topsy."

And they fell on to the coats oblivious, some minutes later, to the knocking on the door and the cries of "Are you alright in there, Miss Aylesberry?"

He could definitely taste 1953 Lafite on her neck as he traced the pattern of her larynx with his tongue.

ooooo

Argentinian Malbec 2010

"I having trouble," said Enrico, "with the word 'steeple-chasing'."

"Ah," said Crossman sagely.

"Something to do with the Church. Yes?"

Crossman (no-one ever called him Ted) was an ascetic-looking, pebble-glass-eyed individual whose mien invited intellectual interrogation. Enrico was more rotund, prided himself on his languages, and was in love, unusually for one of his following, with tobacco.

Enrico noted Crossman's furrowed austerity of feature and let his hand pause over the computer mouse. On the screen was a document entitled "Biographias de delegadoes."

Crossman nodded confirmation in response to the question.

"He says here," added Enrico, "his also hobby is ornithology. Does this sit happy with steeple-chasing?"

"Matter of opinion. Matter of opinion. Steeple-chasing is a rare sort of theological game. It has no Spanish equal. No easy translation in any language, I would say. Steeple-chasing is, well..."

"Chasing steeples?"

Thus encouraged, Crossman did not so much warm to his theme as volcanise.

"Yes. That exactly. It is the sport, I mean, um, hobby or rather not so much hobby as…as science…of following the sermons…held in various churches on Sundays…our day of worship…"

"Sunday is a day of worship in all Christian countries, Edward. Even here in Mendoza."

"Yes, of course. But steeple-chasing…" and now he was fully saddled and raring to go "…is the devotion to the idea that in order to fully understand the mind of God one must attend every church, every church where there is a regular preacher, and listen to every sermon…but not only hear the sermon but listen to the bells, which are in the belfry situated at the base of the steeple…"

"Ah!"

"…and so the steeple-chaser is called what he, or indeed she, is because they…chase steeples. Every Sunday they are to be found outside a different church, listening to the bells which summon the faithful to prayer, and then going inside and listening to the sermon. It is not a hobby followed by a huge number of people in Britain nowadays, Enrico, but…"

"I would not think Nigel had so a hobby. But there it is. He lists it. I guess ornithology can be conducted in the vineyards, I mean churchyards."

"Oh indeed. Yes. Of course."

Enrico's pudgy fingers danced over the keyboard; he manipulated the mouse; he stared intently at the screen. He felt pleased with himself, for he suspected that Crossman was being a little sly with him in that he was sure steeplechasing had a simpler religious explanation but that it was the English way to be ambiguous with words. He also suspected that Atherton's hobby was not as serious as it sounded;

nevertheless he was pleased to have got the word nailed down so beautifully even though it took seventy words in Spanish to describe it instead of the two in English. Crossman, the difficult old fart (an expression Crossman had taught him and which Enrico loved), had his uses.

Crossman wondered what it was Enrico had written to translate what he had said. Enrico fiddled with a pack of small cigars by the mouse pad and Crossman coughed theatrically to remind the Argentinian that the Englishman hated smoking. Enrico glared at the pack and let his fingers return to the keyboard where he began a gentle rat-a-tat. They discussed some minor points of Nigel Atherton's background, all faithfully transposed into Spanish on the screen, and then Enrico said:

"Next is Janet Bolsom-Windgate…da da da…yes, that all make sense…oh yes, she put here that she is bridge correspondent of Country Life as well as wine critic for Waitrose Magazine…"

Crossman could hardly believe his luck.

"Dear Janet has that distinction, yes. Bridges are a big thing in Britain. Several millennium bridges have been constructed…"

"…Ah! Yes…!"

"…the notorious one which spans the Thames between the Tate Modern and City of London Boys School, where I myself had the misfortune to be incarcerated, you will know about because of its tendency to swing on its day of opening, which caused it to be closed for stabilisation repairs to great ridicule in the world's press. Then there is the amazing tilting Millennium Bridge between Gateshead and Newcastle, which is designed to swing…"

"I get the point."

"Not with the Gateshead Bridge. It is semi-circular so there is no point to be got. Unlike steeple-chasing, eh?"

Enrico dutifully laughed, pretending to have fully grasped the subtleties of Crossman's wit. He bashed away at the keyboard, queried a date (an obvious error which Crossman could further embroider and make the egregious Bolsom-Windgate fifteen years older than she was) and then it was Hugh Johnson's turn. However, there was little biographical detail here Crossman could turn to his advantage until Enrico asked: "It says here 'his seminal book entitled Wine' but it gives no publication date. Do you know it?"

"1952," said Crossman promptly.

"Really? He was very young when he wrote it then."

"Hugh was a prodigy. He was 29 when he wrote Wine. I was barely a twinkle in my father's eye."

Enrico stared at Crossman. What sort of joke was this? Twinkle? Some kind of fairy? He said nothing. He would remember the phrase and use it when next an opportunity presented itself, though he was not entirely sure what it meant. If indeed it meant anything.

"So Mr Johnson…"

"Sir Hugh, please."

"Oh! He is a sir. He is…has been…what you say? Benighted? Knighted?"

"Oh yes, yes. Queen's birthday honours list."

Enrico made changes to the screen.

"So he 87? Really?"

"Keeps himself fit, does Hugh."

Enrico nodded. Several more British delegates' names were scrutinised, minor adjustments made to their details as certain words required, and it was only when the wine correspondent of the Independent's name came up, Flora Benedict, that opportunity again presented itself.

"...after medical school where she had studied to be a paediatrician Flora was inveigled...inveigled?...into doing a wine course at the Central London Poly and...ah, let me be clear here..."

"Not many people study paediatrics nowadays. You can take pills for it now and..."

"Edward, I know what is a paediatrician. It was..."

"Really? I thought only we Brits had fart doctors."

The word made Enrico's face light up. He knew about these obscure British obscenities. He kept a straight face.

"Ah yes, of course, a fart doctor. No, it was not that, it was..."

Crossman laid a hand on Enrico's upper arm, just the briefest of touches. It was sufficient to enhance the bond between the two men.

"I wonder, Enrico, with your superb command of English why you need me to help you with this...this list."

"That is kind of you but, as you have seen this afternoon, even I find certain terms requisition of lucidating."

"Even so. My father was stricken with farting. That's why I know about paediatricians."

"Aren't they doctors for children?"

"A common mistake. No, no. A paediatrician specialises in irritable bowel syndrome, diseases of the gut, and of course their expulsion as gas via the anus. It..."

"I did not know this."

"Flora had a glittering career ahead of her. Instead she chucked it up to become a wine writer."

Enrico was furiously turning over and over in his hand the packet of little cigars. "I can see the root. We use the word *pedo* for a fart...in Spanish."

"Is that so?" said Crossman innocently.

"I wonder how I can put this in Spanish..."

"*Medico di pedoes*?"

Enrico smiled indulgently. "Something like that." He thumped the keyboard and clicked the mouse several times. Then he turned to Crossman and looked serious.

"I hear you have problems with paedophiles in your country. What is the connection here? Surely not people who... who love...er?"

"...farting. Love farting. Indeed, yes. It's a problem." He leaned across the mousepad as if imparting a great confidence. "For those of us with sensitive noses, well, I can't tell you what a disgusting thing it is. Paedophilia has quite a following in the UK. You can't walk along a major thoroughfare, Oxford Street for instance, without hearing them and smelling them. Many cyclists wear masks."

Enrico Riccardi looked amazed. He made a gesture of solidarity with his hands. He banged away some more on the keyboard.

"But then *suus cuiquie crepitus bene olet*," added Crossman softly.

"Euh?"

"Everyone thinks his own fart smells sweet. Erasmus."

"Erasmus?" Enrico toyed with a further question, but desisted. He sighed. "Thank you for these insights. Miss Benedict's previous profession will be of great interest to some of the physicians who attend this conference in their capacity as wine consultants. But...it was the word Poly which concerned me."

"Oh! Of course. It's an old scholastic term. It refers to a college where things are learned parrot fashion…"

"Parrot fashion?"

"Parrot fashion, yes. A polly is a parrot…"

"Ah si! I yes. We say *como un loro.* Same think, I thing."

"Doubtless."

"British educational methods are a mystery to me, Edward."

"I assumed you had studied in Britain…"

"Had I done so I would have experienced all your lovers of farting for myself." He shuddered and congratulated himself on his narrow escape in not winning the Berlitz language scholarship he had hoped for, which carried a year in Birmingham as its prize.

More furious acrobatics with the cigarette packet and further changes to the biography under review took place. "How do I translate this? This poly?"

"You do not have polytechnics in Argentina?"

"That is the full term? Polytechnic? I thought that was something to do with er…er…fireworks?"

"That's pyrotechnic, Enrico. Dear Flora studied wine at a College of Parrot-Fashion Learning. You can translate it literally if you like. Though I appreciate that the term may not be precisely translatable."

"I thank you for your advice. I will do as you say. Our national delegates are intense interested in foreign delegates' blackground details."

"Of course."

"I am grateful for your assistance, Edward. We are done. All nine British delegates accounted for. I can release you. I can rely on your discretion, I hope."

"Absolutely, my dear Enrico. I was never here this afternoon. I was watching the polo match."

"You might catch the last pukka if you hurry. I am so happy you have helped me with this document. I am relied upon for my English, but if the committee thought I needed assist…they might…"

"You don't need assist, senor. I have merely smoothed out a few wrinkles anyone would find…bumpy."

"Thank you. Enjoy the polo. Manuel is in the car outside and can get you to the field in ten minutes. I have my cigar now."

Enrico watched his new friend depart. Fumes from the large Ecuador cigar between his lips wafted over the computer. Who could afford Cubans nowadays with all Argentina's problems with the peso? He hoped the polo match had not been cancelled. Polo horses too were expensive luxuries nowadays and there had been talk in some circles that such animals would be better used to feed the poor. As for the luxury of holding a conference on the malbec grape when times were as they were, well…

He puffed and watched copies of the document flow out of the printer. It was a sign how seriously the country was taken as a player on the world wine-making stage that so many prominent wine writers, commentators, producers, marketeers and wine buyers were pleased, at Argentine Wine Guild expense, to fly out and attend the conference. The Chileans, he was aware, were jealous as hell, though there were three delegates from the neighbour across the Andes.

Once the government civil servant who had been delegated to observe the conference saw how smoothly he, Enrico Malvares Tarrico, had organised things, paying attention to little details like immaculately translated biographies of the leading delegates, he was sure, even with the peso in the state it was, that further funding would flow. He gathered up the pages of each document and slipped each into a plastic spine. He couldn't wait to distribute them on the morrow, nine o'clock sharp, to each delegate. It would be a delight to watch them reading his perfect English when even to himself he admitted the written side of the language was hell for him.

What a sweet man Edward Crossman had proven to be. And his services had come free, what's more. Enrico reflected that had not Crossman been English then he would have had to pay several hundred dollars for the input the English wine writer was pleased to provide free. Crossman thought himself very witty, Enrico thought, but he had lacked the wit to ask for the usual brown envelope.

The English! Would he ever understand them? If only he had won that prize of a year at Birmingham, the centre of England. He gathered up the documents, all thirty-six of them, and put them into a large leather case he had selected for the purpose.

Birmingham was cold and filthy, he had been told. It was better he had never gone, he thought now. His future was assured anyway, wasn't it? Tomorrow morning, nine o'clock sharp…

ooooo

Somerfield Own-Label Mexican Sangiovese 2001

The metallic clang of the letterbox opening and closing woke him even though there was a floor between the bedroom and the front door. It was ever thus when Hortense left for work early and he tried for an extra bit of shut-eye. It was an extremely expensive brass contraption which Hortense had insisted upon when various neighbours were robbed by ingenious felons poking bits of wire, often straightened coat-hangers the home beat copper said, through conventional letter-boxes and snaring front door keys left on hall-side tables and gaining admittance. It won't happen to us, said Hortense, and came back from Home Base the next day with the blessed thing, fully confident that her dear Dennis would have it up and fitted by the time she got back from work in Newcastle.

But he failed to fit it. What did he know about DIY? He got the local handyman to do the job and only when she came to pay the bill did Hortense complain. She was always telling Dennis he ought to make more of himself, cooped up scribbling and tasting wine all day.

He peered at the alarm-clock. It was 8.11. He got up. On Hortense's side of the bed there was an envelope on the pillow. He grimaced, went off to pee, returned, thought about tearing the envelope up since he knew exactly what it contained but then, since he was not entirely a stranger to the fear that one day she would leave him for someone more glamorous or simply more cash rich (or even, heaven forfend, better in bed) and that the news of it would come contained in an envelope lying on a straightened pillow, he opened it and was rewarded with several terse sentences, of the sort with which he was entirely familiar, reminding him that Cloris and Dover, Winston and Cherie were coming to dinner and he must not forget to prepare, as he had promised, that marvellous ground-rice ice cream with stem ginger for dessert. It was to Winston, after all, that she owed her job with its sleek BMW which transported her to and from the office in Grey Street; and it was to this job and the woman whose brainy head had been on that pillow not an hour before to whom Dennis owed his citizenship of Durham, his shared tenure of this delightful property, and the freedom to write on wine.

He gathered the letters – most of them the usual stuff from PR companies, he noted – washed perfunctorily, shaved electrically (and coarsely: he would give his face another going over early evening), and threw on some clothes. The doorbell went as he was preparing his shopping list. He had already cooked the pheasant casserole and he removed it, in two large plastic tubs, from the freezer. He thought he might do scallops to begin, if the fishmonger had them in, and apart from the salad stuff and bread, that was more or less it as he had all the ingredients for the rest of the meal. On the sideboard in the dining room stood four bottles of 1966 Clos René Pomerol and a bottle of port to decant. Hortense might grumble at Dennis's stuck-in-the-mudness, as she put it, but she had no beefs about his arrangements for the food and drink at their dinner parties. He was a more than competent cook.

Reminding himself he must get the cheese out of the larder and bring it up to room temperature, he opened the front door. An unshaven man of prodigious elevation stood there clutching a parcel. His breath came out like a steaming kettle's. There was no let-up with the snow, Dennis observed, though he was indifferent to such meteorological niceties of the season.

"Hallo, Mr Jervis."

"Oh! Roy! Even on New Year's Eve you come? Is there no respite for the bibulous scribbler?"

"Happy New Year to you too. Just sign here. Oh yeah. This was stuck in your letterbox."

He waited until Dennis had signed for the wine, for that was what the parcel contained, and handed him an envelope. Dennis saw it was addressed to one George Leblanc, care of Express newspapers, but had been forwarded on.

"Oh, thanks. No hiding from my readers either. Well, happy New Year. Thanks for this. And this. And, er, be seeing you."

"Cheerio! Make those resolutions count now!" And Roy crunched across the driveway to his panting van.

ooooo

After an hour fiddling with his computer, mainly spent scanning irrelevant, often childish, almost invariably pretentious missives from crapulous fellow wine scribes, he descended to the ground floor and opened the parcel. There appeared a bottle of Mexican Sangiovese 2001, from Somerfield, with a letter from Angela Mount, the store's wine buyer (about whom Dennis had once had an erotic dream), informing him, after wishing him well for the season, that this was the store's 2002 new year bargain, only £2.97. He put it aside and noticed, just as he was disposing of the cardboard the bottle came in, that the letter Roy had given him was stuck to the sticky tape on the side of the box. Bit of luck, he thought; another second and the squashed box would have been in the bin. He retrieved the letter and put the kettle on. He didn't get many letters from Express readers. He didn't want any. His work for the Express was his best-kept secret.

Sitting there sipping Lapsang, he examined the envelope. Was it the third or the fourth letter in three years George Leblanc had received from an Express reader? He rather thought it might just be the third. Not an especially glittering record, if one's success as a wine columnist could be measured that way. But then Dennis measured his success by another paper's yardstick. He noted the immaculate typing and the PERSONAL AND CONFIDENTIAL – PLEASE FORWARD injunction. He saw that the postmark was Kensington, W8. Posh reader then, thought Dennis; might even be literate, hopefully friendly. The stuff he got from Mail readers was mostly garbage, which he forced himself politely to respond to.

With a little giggle he opened the envelope and to his utter astonishment saw that the letterheading was Associated Newspapers…The Daily Mail, no less…and…and…that the signatory was his own Gloria. The tea in his mouth suddenly tasted like ashes. His heart fell to his sneakers. His blood ran cold. Every cliché in the book of horrors found expression in his face, heart and arteries.

"*Dear Mr Leblanc,*" he forced himself to read, "*Forgive me writing to you at the newspaper but I do not know your office address and it would obviously have been unwise of me to enquire. Can you telephone me as soon as possible please at the direct line number above? There is something I wish to discuss with you, which I think you will find most attractive. I have been aware of your excellent wine column in an opposition rag for some time and your approach, fresh and juicy, is just what we need here – but on a much larger scale than you presently enjoy at the Express. If you can, and you receive this letter promptly, I would appreciate you calling me before the new year as I have plans I must firm up soonest. Yours sincerely, and in eager anticipation, Gloria Vincent, editor, Consumer Affairs."*

What could the ugly old hag want with George Leblanc except to offer him Dennis Jervis's job? *His* job. What else could "most attractive" and "I have plans" otherwise portend?

He felt physically sick, when he knew he should be laughing his head off. The job at the Mail was pretty thin gruel by world wine writing standards of fare but it gave him some kudos in Durham and indeed in the Circle of Wine Writers and, not least, it gave Hortense something to boast about when she was twitted that wasn't she the only financial advisor in the north-east with a house-husband? He had a job. He wrote for a scurrilous rag, true, but loads of Hortense's clients read it, as did the neighbours. He was the star speaker at the annual Tyneside Wine Buffs dinner and he had once proposed the notion at the local university students' union debate "that this House believes the only way to a man's heart is through his stomach". He lost the debate and now it looked like he was going to lose his job.

He took the letter upstairs to his study and stared at the telephone. "*If you can, and you receive this letter promptly, I would appreciate you calling me before the new year as I have plans I must firm up soonest.*" Gloria was in the office, he would bet on that. The bitch. The miserable, lousy bitch. Only last month he had had lunch with her, taken her out to Le Gavroche and treated her to her annual feed, and here she was touting his job to all and sundry. For surely, "*on a much larger scale than you presently enjoy at the Express*" could mean only one thing: she wanted to expand the column with a new columnist.

Only Horteuse knew that Dennis Jervis and George Leblanc were one and the same person and she kept schtum. It wasn't much of a column, the Express one, just a Bargain of the Week piece, two hundred words, every Sunday. When he had been offered it he had said he couldn't write for a rival newspaper, his arrangement with the Mail precluded it, but he was told don't be silly, just do it under another name. George Leblanc was born on the spot and the income was useful even if he couldn't put the credit on his Circle of Wine Writers members CV listing, though a few of his pals down south suspected it was he who was the mysterious George. And now the pseudonym was being offered the chance to supplant its creator! It was intolerable. It was grotesque! He had been doing the job for the past eleven years and Gloria, who was the third editor he had worked under in that time, had never complained about his style or that she craved an "approach, fresh and juicy". He was frozen in indecision. How could George Leblanc telephone? How could George Leblanc be interviewed for Dennis Jervis's job when they were one and the same person?

But maybe he was panicking unnecessarily. What if the Mail was launching a new supplement and wanted another wine writer for it? That was it. Surely that was it. Only one way to find out. He picked up the telephone.

He put it down. She would recognise his voice. He couldn't ring. Maybe he could get away with a slight French accent. He had chosen Leblanc because it sounded French and George, though it was the English spelling of the name, because it had, by merely inflecting the first syllable a little more throatily, a French intonation and the Express people had been delighted with the class that implied. It was just past eleven o'clock. He must go and do the shopping. He was already late if he wanted the best scallops. But he had to call Gloria. How could he not? How could he spend the next day, new year's day, with Hortense at home, perhaps the next week if Gloria was off on her annual ski trip, not knowing what was in the woman's devious, treacherous mind?

He rushed down stairs and poured himself a large slug of Armagnac and swallowed it in three gulps. He refilled the glass. He returned to his study and dialled the number he hardly had to refer to the letter to recall.

"Yes? Consumer Affairs."

"Ah, bon jour, er, good morning, Miss Vanson, er Vincent. My name is George Leblanc and I was pleased, just this morning, to get your letter..."

"Monsieur Leblanc! Bonjour. Comment ça va, monsieur? Euh, je suis enchantée de faire votre connaissance. Merci pour votre appel. Bonne Année!"

Oh God, he had forgotten about Gloria's bloody French. She had been embarrassing enough at Le Gavroche, insisting on speaking it to all the waiters who had been collectively polite enough to pretend to understand every word she uttered via that fleshy throat of hers. Dennis panicked and took a quick slug of the Armagnac.

"Goodness, what fine French you speak. But I think you would prefer me to speak in English, no? After all, if I infer your thinking correctly from your letter, you would like me to write in it for you."

"Exactly. And what you have just said is exactly why I contacted you. I love your little column in the Express. Disgusting newspaper run by a sleazeball, but you know that, but your little thing is a gem. Your approach is just what I'm looking for in a makeover of the wine and food pages on Saturday…"

"But you 'ave that excellent fellow Jervis, Dennis Jervis. How could I follow such a brilliant writer? He knows so much about wine. He is a giant of 'is profession. He has…"

"Your attitude does you credit, George, may I call you George? I feel we're going to get on splendidly. Look, I've got nothing against Dennis Jervis personally, he's a reasonably amusing fellow but he's gone stale, stuffy, tired. He's been stuck in a rut for years. He is, as you say, *vieille chapeau*…"

It's masculine, you ignorant fish-brain! Dennis wanted to shout (pleased he could still pun* under such pressure). He took more of the Armagnac. Stale? Tired? Him? Only a 'reasonably amusing fellow'? And as for 'stuffy'! He felt his head boil in Armagnac-inspired rage. Who was it who had objected to Fat Bastard Chardonnay's inclusion in his column? It had been Gloria Vincent, the stuffy bitch, on the grounds that "Mail readers are not ready to see such words in print even if they do refer to a white wine they can see on a shelf." He dutifully excised the wine. This recollection made him momentarily drop his guard.

"I see," he said flatly.

There was a silence for a moment, less than a second. On the phone, however, such lacunae stretch like eons.

"We've never met have we, George? Your voice suddenly sounded familiar. I note, by the way, you spell your name the English way. Nice touch. Mail readers are more sophisticated, of course, but we should keep it ambiguous. Not overwhelming lovers of you Frogs, our readers, even though thousands of them have homes there and go there for their holidays. Oh yes, your voice suddenly sounded familiar. We haven't met, have we? The year before last Dennis took me as his guest to the annual Circle of Wine Writers Christmas party and I met several members then. You, perhaps?"

Dennis felt his legs go cold. He finished off the Armagnac.

"No, we 'ave never met, Gloria…but…"

"Then we must make arrangements to rectify that situation immediately. Have you your diary handy?"

"Er…yes…yes."

"Right. Kensington Place, one o'clock, next Wednesday the ninth. Suit you?"

Of course there was nothing in his diary. There was never anything in his diary until the wine-tasting season began after the twelfth.

"Is that convenient? Do you live in London?"

"No, I live in Durham…I mean…"

Oh fuck!

"Durham? But…did you say Durham? Near Newcastle, you mean? But…that's an extraordinary co-inci—"

"Durram is a little village in Kent."

"Right. Of course. That's a relief."

"Vraiment? Does it matter to the Mail where I live?"

"No. Not at all. Of course. It's just that…never mind. See you on the ninth then? You know Ken Place?"

"Of course. Merci pour tout, Mademoiselle Vincent, et Bonne Année."

ooooo

There were no scallops at Harvey's. They were all gone. It was New Year's Eve. There was some fresh squid left and some crab. Could he summon up the will to make fishcakes with grilled calamares on the side? He would have to. Hortense could not be disappointed tonight.

He made the cakes immediately on getting home, adding his special touches of cardamom and harissa oil to give them some punch, wrapped them in cling film, and put them in the fridge. He knocked up his specially requested ice-cream. He noted the already casseroled game birds, out of the freezer, were barely room temperature but he could always bung them in the microwave before he warmed them up properly.

It was getting dark. Hortense was bound to be home early. He shaved properly and ran a bath. He sat on the loo seat and stared at the steam and wondered how, within a little over a week, he could transform himself into George Leblanc and somehow contrive an address in a village called Durram he didn't even know existed. Maybe he could write the copy and sent it to his old friend Zack, who taught at Westminster University and did live in Kent...but of course there was e-mail nowadays. Who would know, or indeed care, where he lived? That much deception was simple to achieve. But how did he turn up at Ken Place and ensure he kept his job for the foreseeable future until Gloria, or her replacement, got bored and went hunting, always on a whim, for new columnists as these capricious Mail editors habitually did? It was second nature to Mail editors. They fired columnists. They hired them. It was the grown-up procedure. He knew the score. He still felt slightly drunk from the Armagnacs. Had he overdone the spices in those crab cakes?

Could he grow a beard in a week? Get his hair cut drastically short? Maybe just cultivate a moustache? Change his glasses? Rub on some Man-Tan? Get a new wardrobe? Sport an earring, perhaps? Walk with a stoop? On the other hand, could not Dennis Jervis show Gloria that her wine columnist was no longer stuck in a rut? This, surely, was the move dazzling prospect.

He put on his bathrobe and went downstairs. He opened the fridge used to store samples he had to taste and rummaged around. At the back, something sent to him years back but which he had neglected to open, was an old bottle of Veuve Clicquot, '85, if he remembered. He was keeping it, vaguely, for a special occasion...but...wasn't this...?

He laughed to himself and opened the bottle. It took some twisting, the cork, for it was well-established in the neck and resisted removal. It finally came out and he put it to his nose. It was fine; none of the mustiness he had been half-expecting. The wine was old, a touch, but then he was no spring chicken any more either, was he? He took a cooler and a long-stemmed glass and went upstairs. It wasn't every day, he thought, that he enjoyed a bath with a widow, or rather The Widow.

He began to sing in the bath, his favourite bit of Le Nozze de Figaro:

"*Se vuol ballare,*
Signor Contino,
Il chitarrino
Le suonero.
Se vuol venire
Nella mia scola,
Le insegnero.
Sapro...ma piano,
Meglio ogni arcano
Dissimulando

Scoprir potro.
L'arte schermendo,
L'arte adoprando,
Di qua pungendo,
Di la scherzando,
Tutte le macchine
Rovesciero."

"Goodness, Dennis darling, you're in a good mood."

Hortense had come home. He hadn't heard her car. But then he never heard her car. It was practically noiseless. She was standing by the bathroom door.

"*Ah, cor mio, che accidente*!"

"Dennis! Are you all right? I've never seen you like this. Dennis..."

"Call me George," he lisped and he approached her, suds hanging from him like fluffy crustacea, and as she tried to back out he grabbed her and kissed her and...

...moments later they were in the bath together. Her protests that they didn't have time faded under a double attack of bubbles. They lay there in the warm suds, sipping from the same glass of Veuve Clicquot.

"I've made a new year's resolution, Hortense dearest, starting early. It's time I made a new man of myself. Time indeed I became a new man altogether. Isn't that what you've always wanted? What you've always been telling me to do?"

"Shut up and make love to me then, Georgeous. You know, I've always liked the name George."

ooooo

* *The fish called bass, aka loup de mer, is also referred to as* 'une vieille' *in France.*

Domaine Ostertag Riesling 1984

"...can you write..."

"Yes?"

"Can you...er...put... to Paul with best wishes for a speedy recovery from writer's block?"

G. W. Darke scribbled this on the frontispiece and inwardly winced at the pun (her own). *Righter's Block* had been the first novel; light years away from the one under the pen now. Underneath the dedication to Paul, Darke added a signature. The full first name and surname too, not some arachnoid ideogram. ("How different from other authors," had exclaimed a woman in Wimbledon Waterstone's some years back, "who only scribble a set of initials. My shelves bulge with feebly initialled firsts.")

"It's my son, you see," explained the reader. "He never writes."

Darke switched on a sympathetic expression (thinking: Be Patient. He will grow older and wiser). The expression was unempathetic at source. How could G.W. Darke know what it was like to have a son who never wrote?

The queue shortened. The wine was almost gone as far as could be seen. Darke took a circumspect slug of the Chilean merlot the bookshop had supplied and held the pen up invitingly. The queue looked at the author either in silence or with whispered reverence.

The author, it must be said, was a figure deserving of quiet homage: a state of grace which, at the comparatively young age of forty-two, Darke did not yet feel comfortable in acknowledging. She had, after all, cornered a market all her own: the psychological wine thriller.

Darke thought of Gregory Righter now as another reader offered her book for inscription. Poor Greg and his block. It was a condition his creator had suffered from until the dazzling solution was found and then came, dizzyingly, the raucous critical success of that first novel and, richly in its wake, its attendant notoriety and the chance to spend the autumn months each year on a circuit of the nation's most prominent bibliotechs as well as English-speaking markets overseas and, now that translations were forthcoming, even the odd foreign tour. What the publisher never realised was how much Darke depended on these vacations from normality.

"Can you write happy birthday Jeffrey?"

"Of course. Is that with a G or a J?"

"Ah…J, I think. Yes, J. Though he was christened Geoffrey with a G, I'm sure. The J version is more contemporary though devalued by that disgraceful creep Archer. Thank you! I love your work. *In a Deeper Vein* is my favourite. Such an original idea! It captured my own relationship with my father and his blessed wine cellar precisely! Isn't this wine delicious?"

"There isn't any more about, I suppose?" said G. W. Darke hopefully, closing the covers of the book.

Jeffrey's friend leaned closer. She picked up the book and stroked the cover.

"When I've paid for this I'll go and see for you."

"I'll be in your debt."

"As I am in yours," said the reader, wandering off.

Darke looked at the dwindling remnants of the queue. Sixty-five people had turned up and forty-one had bought a book, one woman three copies for "Christmas presents strictly for close friends". Darke had been able to have a good look at these readers, many with young scrubbed faces and guiltless eyes, but only two candidates for later preference seemed suitable and neither had yet presented themselves with a book for signature.

There was a carelessly tall young woman with a sexy mole nudging her upper lip (a small rich currant, as Nabokov would have put it, thought Darke) and with extraordinary black glossy hair and deep-set eyes. The lips were significant adornments to her face. Perfect age, sighed Darke and, seeing Jeffrey's friend appearing behind the ragged throng with a fresh supply of the merlot in her triumphant grasp, finished the wine in the glass.

The other candidate had been male, subtly exotic. (Darke thought Portuguese from the accent revealed by the stock question "Has anyone objected to your use of living people in your works of fiction?"). There was, however, a suggestion of brilliantine about the scalp and possibly after-shave on the skin – even, horror of horrors, deodorant which Darke, somewhat quaintly bearing in mind her comparatively young vintage, considered one of the twentieth century's most repulsive mal-refinements.

"It masks true character and, worse, it interferes with the bouquet of wine," said Darke in answer to Melvyn Bragg's question, who went on to remark that Darke's feudal attitude to the flesh was perfectly represented by several characters in the novels – some of whom, Bragg controversially added, were sometimes cruelly based on individuals who were alive and kicking (themselves at being portrayed cruelly yet insufficiently libellously to invoke forensic action).

On balance, Darke thought the tall girl more acceptable and fingered the small pieces of card, printed for the purpose and secreted specifically for easy retrieval, in the pocket of the jacket hanging behind the chair. It was the way the girl moved her limbs; not in any clichéd feline way, it was more casual – as if she might express surprise, and perhaps delight, that she even had a living relationship with the limbs at all.

Bragg had pressed the handsome Portuguese's point more firmly: "do not the living relatives of the real people, the living and not-so-long dead, who dot your works of fiction ever take offence? What of the persons themselves? What about, for instance, the unpleasant incident the fictional protagonist has with Norman Lamont and Jancis Robinson on the Central Line in *God's Lioness*? Or the depiction of Hugh Johnson in the same novel?"

Inevitably, the interview covered Darke's early double-career as the Spectator's wine and cinema critic. Surely, this latter field was the reason the novels themselves were so cinematic? Even, perhaps, the reason Darke used real people in fiction?

The reader filled Darke's glass with more wine. She was a fidgety creature with a hedge of white hair and wearing a smart astrakhan-collared overcoat.

"Shall I leave the bottle?"

"How kind, but no. A second glass is enough. Thank you."

"Can I…can I just ask one question before I go?"

"Of course."

"Is it true…did you really mean what you said in that interview in the Guardian supplement? You know. About the reason why you bring real people in to your novels?"

"What did I say?"

"You said it made up for the total lack of real sex in the books."

"Then I must have meant it. There is no sex, of course. It is an impossible thing to write about."

"Th…thank you."

More merlot was consumed. Darke's colour rose and with it optimism. The tall girl was now more firmly in evidence, drinking wine by the windows and in her hand was a copy of the new novel. Was she alone? Were those her friends she was talking with or just acquaintances she had made during the evening? Darke pondered. Was the older, smaller woman by her side her mother? Darke rather hoped it was. The suggestion of oriental flair to the nostrils was common to both women. Mothers, in Darke's experience, were easily detachable appendages in such circumstances.

The novel, the new work, which Darke had read from this evening, was "the Darkest book yet" in the Telegraph's critic's view. Darke thought that apart from the consideration that the irresistible pun had been used not to make a point but to stretch a banal joke, the novel had lots of humour breaking through to the surface. The gathering in the bookshop had laughed in the right places.

"Can you just sign it please?"

It was the tall girl. She was elegantly boned and firmly fleshed and the hair did not seem so black now. It had a hennaed sheen to it close up. Darke could smell no perfume, no clumsy fragrance. The skin was clear. The lips, now they were closer, were like a great wound. Darke experienced a sudden ache to heal them with a kiss. A line from a half-remembered Laforgue poem surfaced in Darke's mind. What was it?

Something like "*...be mine that mouth, that prudish furrow where longings grow...*". Darke suppressed a sigh at the youthful memory and concentrated on the wrist at the end of the leather jacket; it dangled thin and unadorned and the equally unringed fingers suggested finesse. There was a languorousness, Darke noted, to her movements close up.

Darke briefly chewed the end of the pen and toyed with just writing 'please' and handing the book back but it would have been a poor joke, though she had used it once before when confronted by a customer but one who had inspired antipathy. The pen had an unremarkable intestinal sac of blue ink but the exterior was black with a gold-coloured clip and bands and it was marked Rudding Park, a hotel near Harrogate whence Darke had filched it after spending the night there during the first week of the current season's tour.

The signature, under Darke's elegant, octave-and-a-half span hands, formed itself with a serene flourish so that the girl could see every slow line and each curve form themselves to confer on the book a talismanic magic it had not possessed a moment earlier. Yet it was the same book.

What excruciating complexities dictated that an author's signed copy was more valuable, more exciting, more personal than an unsigned one? Darke knew the answers to these questions.

"I hope you enjoy the book," said G. W. Darke with a face poised expertly between serious enquiry and jocular optimism.

"I have never not enjoyed your work. May I say it provides liquid inspiration?"

Darke refrained from closing the covers and took the girl's hand in a light grip and kissed it.

"Thank you."

The girl looked utterly astonished, slightly alarmed; then, as Darke had hoped, pleasure, like a tide returning to stain and reclaim the shingle, spread across her face.

The signature, especially elongated and etched with a Chinese clarity, was scrutinised by Darke and a further line added and then, in a rapid practised movement, before closing the hard covers, Darke took a card, scribbled something on it, and inserted it before handing the book over. The girl appeared puzzled, then she smiled and her tongue poked through her teeth.

Darke felt a spasm of lust. The girl bared more of her small sharp teeth, a flicker of amusement on her features lightening the pitiless eyes, and she placed the book under her left breast and moved off to the till. Those eyes, thought Darke with relish, were enormous eddies of danger.

ooooo

Darke began a routine examination of the authorial features in the lavatory mirror. The thought had often occurred: how is it that a writer can delve so deeply under the skin and travel along the bones of a fictional character yet be baffled by the ones closest to hand? The ones more familiar to the sight, more at home to the touch, than any other? I am a mystery to myself, murmured Darke, rubbing a knuckle across the left eye, the green one, and staring at the reflection of the nose, an instrument, in this instance, of notable Scandinavian rectitude and, to some observers, lack of excitement.

The Roman nose was more fascinating to behold because it described more perfectly the job the organ did; it was a more architecturally satisfying shape, Darke thought. The nose on the tall girl was ever so subtly retroussé. The writer began a close inspection of the skin's pores, checked the right eye, the brown one, and pulled the hair behind the ears; considered the lips, dark enough; bared the teeth to see if a surfeit of tannin in the wine had stained them unattractively; combed the hair, vigorous and brown with the few, very few, grey ones submerged and invisible to all but the most intimate perusal; ignored the birthmark.

Darke emerged from the bookshop lavatory and wondered if the tall girl had read the card yet.

ooooo

"Will you be alright walking? Mortimer's is only half-a-mile away but the streets twist and turn. Ipswich is like that. I could call a taxi. Or one of my staff could accompany you..."

"Thank you, but no. My booking is not for twenty minutes and I've already been to the restaurant and reserved a table... and a bottle of wine..."

"Goodness," said the bookshop manager, "how efficient." Thinking: this author is quite as mad as all the others. Darke regretted mentioning the wine. It was out of character. Had the excitement of the tall girl inspired overconsumption of the merlot?

In fact, Darke had not only reserved a bottle of restaurant wine but had purchased it, smelled it to ascertain its perfection of health, and had ordered it to be decanted and left to breathe until it would be consumed two and a half hours later. After taking a taxi at the railway station upon arrival, Mortimer's (selected from the Good Food Guide) had been visited and approved of after inspection of menu and wine list. It was a Darke routine. The publisher paid for the tour's expenses but never knew the meticulous extent of the author's arrangements to ensure good victuals and, where possible, intriguing company. The publisher had no inkling of anything else his author might get up to when she was let loose on the world at his office's expense.

Only the publisher's publicist felt hard done by since Darke was the only author on the firm's books who toured without a minder, preferring to travel alone, by train, scorning even the chauffeured limo. The reasons for all this were never guessed at and the novels hardly offered clues; but how, Darke thought, not for the first time, could one tolerate, night after night, being in the presence of someone likely as not not fully baked and witlessly charming? Even if he or she was the most devastatingly witty and responsively sensual individual upon earth, not to mention a first-rate publicist, more than one night would be impossible.

More than one night was impossible with anyone – except, of course, her fictional characters.

ooooo

"I hope the wine is alright. It's been open now for several hours and, as you requested, we kept the decanter outside on the sill."

The manager of Mortimer's – far too young for such a post, thought Darke – placed the decanter on the table. It was nicely chilled with December's help. Darke nosed the top of the wine container, from which the manager deftly pulled off the sheet of muslin Darke had requested be tied there, and was greeted with the smell of limes and plasticine.

"Everything's perfect," said Darke. "I won't order for a few minutes. Someone might join me."

Mortimer's was on the quayside, fish its speciality and though said to be the best restaurant in Ipswich (which could simply mean, Darke thought, the least disgusting), it looked to the novelist's eyes like a transport cafe with its plastic tablecloths with bright bunches of embossed grapes, its preponderance of straggly green potted plants, and waitresses who, apart from the one who waddled about with the glum-legged mien of a school dinner lady, appeared young enough to be pupils at the same school. It was packed. Older diners too, noted Darke with satisfaction; that meant no cigarette smoke adhering to clothes from alfresco puffing. Darke poured a glass of the decently mature Alsace riesling into a glass and began the ritual of close-up smelling and tasting. It was a treat finding wine like this to look forward to and the menu promised fresh Dover sole, grilled with smoked salmon butter. It would suffice for supper.

Darke examined the volume the bookshop had offered as thank you for the signing which, the manager said, was one of the best attended they had ever had. Not all bookshops were so thoughtful as to present a book as a gift but branches of Waterstone's invariably did and Darke always insisted that the staff dated and signed it, much to their surprise, and over the years these tomes were swelling the spatial resources of a special shelf in the author's study.

The book was V. S. Naipaul's *Letters Between a Father and Son* and it would provide anticipated delicious companionship to the riesling and the sole, if they had to be consumed without a living talking human opposite.

Darke was more than pleased to have been given the Naipaul book. Naipaul's novel *A House for Mr Biswas* had formed a significant part of her degree in modern literature obtained – or perhaps snatched just in time might be a more accurate description of its bestowal – twenty-one years before at an infamous drug-ridden provincial university, where Darke had studied desultorily, as much interested in the discovery of the pleasures of the table and the epiphanal revelations of the flesh as with the excrescences of poets and novelists.

Darke considered Biswas one of only three first-rate fictional characters created in literature in English since the Second World War. The others being, of course, Geofrey Firmin and Humbert Humbert. Darke, circumspectly, did not include in this overview any characters from any G.W. Darke book but hoped that other literates, compiling their own shortlists, might feel obliged to include Seb Brewer or Stella Harkness. Of the new novel, *Third Person Singular*, Darke had great hopes but no firm belief that it contained any character, to be brutally honest, so moulded as comfortably to fit any list of the unquestionably most memorable fictional characters. The fictional humans in the book were – a fact Darke was beginning to appreciate since the critics unanimously alluded to it – overshadowed by the appearances of General Pinochet (no chance of a libel suit), Oz Clarke (small chance of a libel suit), and Monica Coughlan, Jeffrey Archer's infamous prostitute (no chance of libel suit from poor Monica but possibly one from Archer if Darke's memory could be proven faulty, as the woman had died since the book's publication).

Darke smelled the wine, tasted it in a theatrical slurping and gargling action, and let in trickle down the throat. It was a beauty; furthermore it was not outrageously priced. Some of Darke's restaurant and hotel food and wine bills caused comment amongst the easily ruffled feathers of the fledglings in the publicity department but no-one dared comment – not to the author's face. Darke took out a notebook and began to write.

"I got my mother a taxi at last. You've got a nerve."

Darke looked up. The voice was friendly yet far more confident and richer than it had been in the bookshop. A waitress was taking off the tall girl's coat. In her hand was a Waterstone's bag, which she placed on the table. She went to sit, then hesitated. Darke saw in her other hand the small printed card. She had also brought with her something new: the very faint smell of melissa oil and lemon, doubtless components in some *eau de Cologne* applied since their last meeting. Darke was not outraged by this innovation.

"You are expecting me?"

"Another wine glass please. Immediately, if you would. Oh yes, I'm expecting you, though I must admit I didn't dare hope you would come. Sit. Please sit. Have a glass of wine."

"This card…"

"Shameful strategy," said Darke. "One day I will be too respectable to carry on like this. The essential chutzpah of the process is…"

A glass arrived. Darke poured the girl some riesling, hoping, when the second bottle arrived (if another was necessary, as it sometimes was), that it was in as healthy and sensual a condition as the first.

"…is?"

"Is invigorating. Life-enhancing. Plot-forming. Character-building."

The tall girl looked alarmed, fascinated, wary.

"Am I to become a living character in one of your novels? Is that a nice thing to be? Is that what this is all about? Oh, isn't this wine…quaint."

"Yes. Quaint sums it up perfectly. Now what will you have to eat?"

"Well, Miss Darke…I…"

"Please. Call me Grace. And you?"

"I'm Naomi. Naomi…Yorath."

And what Naomi had wanted to say was that she wasn't very fond of fish.

ooooo

"But…the sheer nerve you have! I could never, God willing, do such a thing."

Assuming God, thought Darke, you wouldn't do much if he wasn't willing.

She said, "Naomi, Naomi, you are not a writer. You are a pharmacist. You don't lead a lonely existence confined to an ivory tower, but strive to stay sane in an overrun, overpopulated camp for the temporarily unhealthy. Are you greedy for sensation? I am. I'm starved of it for months on end. You are engulfed by it every day."

G.W. Darke chewed the remains of one side of the sole and expertly removed the whole of the skeleton before attacking the other. The wine was almost depleted; the restaurant temperature rising. Darke was pleased to note Naomi was not a disappointment after an hour's intense microscopical consideration three feet away and she wondered what Naomi thought of her own shortcomings; not the conversational sort, since Darke admitted no superiors in this department at restaurant encounters, but in the discovery of the fine lines beginning to edge along Grace's eyes, if the discovery of one green and one brown eye was not disconcerting, and if the burgundy birthmark, visible only with prolonged gazing since it was concealed by most of the hairline, was despoiling once spotted.

Naomi's face was like a face reflected in a pool, Grace thought. There was a pleasing suggestion of a cleft to the chin, unusual in a female, and her manner was easy and getting warmer. They had briefly touched hands once, an accidental brushing to be sure, but one which struck neither of them as unwelcome or unpleasing.

"What I'm thinking," said Naomi slowly, "is how deliberate, contrived, set-up…well, heartless all this seems. Or rather *seemed*…now I've talked to you…to *you*…to an author…like you…your work…your work has…"

"You said it inspired you. In the bookshop. But then you didn't know you would ever see me again, let alone be sharing dinner with me."

Naomi laughed. Drank some mineral water. Ate a little halibut.

"I mean…Grace…that this card…"

"Forget the card. Just an introduction device. Tell me about all the drugs you handle at work."

"Do you hand it to someone at every book signing? When you're recognised in the street and take a fancy to someone? It's being a printed card that takes the breath away…yes, that's what it is!" Naomi took the card from out of the book, lying on the table under the salt and pepper, where a waitress had, to the amusement of the two diners, placed the condiments with a sniff of reproach at the book daring to mess up the table arrangement.

"It's being printed that does it!" repeated Naomi.

Grace took the card. "You're the first person to make that observation," she said, looking at the card. It said, in Helvetica italic: *Please join me, just you, for dinner. I have a table booked at 9.15.* And then, in G.W.Darke's own hand was added, from that stolen pen whose membrane of ink, had it a memory-bank that could be squeezed, would ejaculate a stream of still-fresh purloined experiences: "*I will be at Mortimer's on the Quay.*"

"Don't you see?" said Naomi. "Isn't that why you did it that way? Had it printed, I mean? It means…"

"I had it printed years ago. On an impulse whilst waiting for a train in Bradford."

"It's like a summons, being printed like that. Has no-one commented on the difference it would make if it was just a hand-written note? This is like an official ticket. It's irresistible. Do you hand one out at every tasting? Aren't you ever bitterly disappointed? Don't you find yourself with a nut, or a bore, or a potential mad man? I take it you don't only invite women…"

Naomi realised something as she said this. Was this just a sexual thing? Was Grace Darke to be trusted? Was the author mad? Foolhardy? Or just brave? Would she end up as just another Darke character (perhaps eviscerated, likely as not stuffed), either disguised or as a real person acting out the role already assigned by society? *The Pharmacist*, thought Naomi, wondering how long she would have to wait for an answer to her questions. *The Pharmacist.* Not a G.W Darke title at all.

She tried again, as she had many times during the dinner, to fix Grace Darke with a gimlet stare which might force some betrayal of motive, the true reason for her receipt of the card, but she saw only that fine display of bone and taut flesh and the startling eyes, one brown, one green, and she thought how serenely uncluttered of feature the author was; vibrant, elegantly composed, with a bodily form like a musical instrument to be plucked or stroked or fingered, like one of those incredible creatures in a Meredith Frampton portrait at the Tate.

Out of time, thought Naomi. That's it: Grace Darke doesn't seem to exist on the same time scale as the rest of us. She stared at the novelist's fat notebook with its protective rubber band discouraging instant access. Is this where I will end up? Between the covers of a memorandum prior to elevation to the finished work? She suppressed a giggle.

G.W. Darke fondled the card, kissed it, and replaced it within the pages of the book, thinking the giggle was motived by something else entirely. She smelled the wine, appreciating the almost feral aroma of old Alsace riesling with its sense of worn stones and rich soil and expiring minerals.

"That's a lot of questions. Why does it refuse to go away?"

"Why does what refuse to go away?"

"Your suspicion that I've only invited you here so I can go to bed with you."

"If you haven't," said Naomi Yorath, taking a chance which, on balance, she felt the evening so far merited, "then *I* will be disappointed."

ooooo

I am reminded, thought Naomi Yorath, of a scene in one of the books. Which one is it? It involved a TV personality, of that she was sure, but she couldn't pin the precise scene down or who the person, someone certainly real, was. Hadn't it been the father of the Dimbelbys? She was sitting on the restaurant's lavatory peeing. Too much fizzy mineral water. The wine had been odd and not especially nice and she'd only sipped at it. Grace had offered something else but Naomi had declined. Three glasses was her limit.

What other limits were to be circumscribed in the present situation? Did she take her signed book and leave, thanking the novelist for an enthralling evening and a pleasant meal?

What happened now? She felt less brave by herself in this upstairs lavatory. Why had she been so bold? The situation she found herself in had made her act that way; contrived to compel her to act out of character. She was not unused to being propositioned by medical staff, but they were all men, the inevitable older randy surgeon (brain ones were the worst), and she had gone through mild flirtations at college with women friends and had indeed been positively propositioned, in her final year, by a female chemistry lecturer. But nothing like this. It was like a dream; it had all the ingredients of one: the celebrity of the novelist, the bizarre nature of the invitation ("like a portable lonely-hearts ad," she had remarked over dinner and Grace Darke had applauded this observation, which only made matters more complicated; whereas if Darke had become ruffled at the unhealthy suggestion this implied of an inability to form natural relationships, it would have been easier to handle), the food and wine, and, most pressing of all, the weight of those eight previous novels and, lying on the restaurant table, the ninth, as yet unread but with its calling card nestling inside.

Did Darke do this all the time? Was she a sexual predator and nothing else? *Was* she mad? Was she a psychopath? All those questions about her work and the details of drugs – research for just another fictional character? What would happen next? Those eight previous books had not a single sex scene in any of them. It was much commented upon by critics but it had never occurred to Naomi that it mattered or that it carried any significance – if it did.

She suddenly felt she had been sitting, with her face in her palms, for rather longer than manners or indeed comfortable micturition dictated. She stood, adjusted her knickers and tights, looked at herself in the mirror and had this surge of expectation. She was reminded of the first time she had faced a ski slope of unusual precipitation and length. Hadn't she just taken a deep breath and pushed off? She took a deep breath and opened the lavatory door and, when she reached the table, found Darke dreamily contemplating space.

"I began to wonder if you hadn't felt obliged to sneak off. But then I was reminded…well, never mind…Let's just say I knew you wouldn't go without saying goodbye."

Naomi stood over the table. The credit card receipt lay on top of her copy of the book. The fish had been surprisingly tasty, for a change. It was not all she was grateful to G.W. Darke for. Coats were brought. They moved towards the door.

Outside there were stars, the masts of yachts in the marina, and the distant echoes of traffic. A taxi waited; just the one (which invoked no comment from Naomi). Their breath came out in steamy billows. Plumes of grey fumes issued from the cab's exhaust.

"When you were gone so long in the loo I found a solution, for which I have you to thank, to a wicked conundrum. It relates to the novel I'm working on."

"Your tenth. Is it so unceasing?"

"I cannot not work."

"But you do this book-signing tour…every year, you said. Is that work?"

"It brings its own rewards." Grace placed a hand on Naomi's and was rewarded with a grip of firm fingers on wrist. "Even a stream of consciousness is a rut. Tours take me out of the one I write in, the one I revel in. I can, sometimes, glimpse answers to problems which I wouldn't normally be able to solve… and…with you tonight I was able to see something concerning an important element in my idea for a novel…"

"Does this approach always work?"

"Oh my God! I didn't mean. I didn't…"

"I know you didn't. But it's worked. Shall we get in the cab? It's bloody freezing out here."

ooooo

As Grace paid the driver Naomi said: "Does it always work out that the person in my place always feels at this point that it is she who has done the picking up and not the other way round?"

Grace: "Absolutely. Can I have a receipt please? Make it five pounds."

The hotel was not plush but it ran to a minibar. Grace opened it and extracted a small bottle of Moet & Chandon.

"You have this glass. I'll use the one in the loo."

Naomi found herself agreeing to this. She took off her top coat and removed the jacket beneath. Grace's things had already been flung on the bed along with the D&G shoulder bag with its small umbrella handle protruding.

The room went beyond the realms of anonymity to a region where only the certified non-dangerous inmates of a house of correction could feel at home. True, the bed was large but the headboard was composite and veneered in plastic walnut, the pictures seemed like prints taken from a weekly colour supplement, the carpet was one step above coconut matting, and the furnishings looked run up by a carpentry class the day before. There was a shallow, almost sinister gleam from every surface.

"Sometimes," said Grace, pouring the champagne and looking around the room, "I am forced to stay in hotels which provide a new twist on the word 'grot'."

"Perfunctory is the word. You would know."

"Melvyn said I knew too much. What a sweet man."

"Did you hand him a card?"

"Too old, my darling, far too old and, don't forget, a novelist himself. I make it a rule. Never sleep with novelists."

Naomi said nothing. She felt out of her depth; not for the first time this evening.

"How," said Grace, "did you get so subtle a henna affect with such black hair as yours? It's striking." She ran a hand through the short stiff locks, let it lie for a moment on the neck. "Though not as striking as those eyes of yours. You must have to fight the docs off with a club at work."

"I use this," said Naomi, and from the bag on her lap she took out a gun. It was brown and black and glinted like the other things in the room.

"What a surprising girl you are, Naomi."

Naomi pointed the gun at Grace and pulled the trigger. There was a plopping sound and a black flag emerged from the barrel. It said, as Grace discovered when she rolled across the bed to read it, "**FUCK OFF. PLEASE**" in white capital letters.

Grace, who had experienced a moment of real fear as the realistic toy revealed itself and the barrel turned to face her, stood up, shivered, and threw the coats and her bag off the bed. Naomi pushed the flag back inside the barrel, put the gun in her bag, and pushed it under the bedside table. The two women looked at one another and then they were kissing, using their mouths to stem their torrents of laughter.

"Am I?" Naomi had asked, with sibilant emphasis on the personal pronoun.

They were naked, covered by a single sheet on the bed. Only after some effort had Grace managed to turn the radiator thermostat to a high setting in order to permit such meagre coverage on a chilly night.

"Now you are," said Darke. "A very special friend."

They merged into one another again, Darke congratulating herself on her judgement as Naomi, learning fast, used lips and fingers and even knees and elbows to such stunning physical effect. By two o'clock they were asleep, only to be rudely awoken, as Darke had planned, by the seven-thirty wake-up call and, in the middle of a joint shower, interrupted by the arrival of what passed for a continental breakfast delivered to the room.

How easy it would be, thought Darke, to spend more of the day with this creature in this room, only pausing for wine and food, but then she remembered she had met the chef, or certainly a young unshaven representative of the species (wearing a pristine *tocque blanche* and a stupid grin), in the foyer of the hotel as she dropped off her suitcase before proceeding to the bookshop and this cretin, she recalled, had, in answer to her question "What's cooking tonight", replied "Don't rightly remember. The menu's over there", thus confirming the impression created by the hotel's atmosphere and dire design taste that one would need to be starved or utterly devoid of sensibility to put one's palate and stomach in the hands of so vapid a cook.

"I must tell you," said Naomi, as they parted outside the hotel, "that I first read your writing when I was at school, before you had written any novels..."

"Published any..." corrected Darke.

"My father used to take the Spectator. I was fifteen, I think. I read a review you wrote of...of some film...some French film and I went to see it and I loved it. I would never have gone to see that film if you hadn't written what you did."

"Was it '*Sais-tu faire de la cycle?*'?"

"I don't remember."

"You do know how I got that job as film critic of the Spectator? I fucked a friend of a man of influence at the magazine and he introduced us. I had only been out of university a few years. I was desperate to write for it. It was a style leader in those days."

"Like you now. Are you totally immoral?"

"Naomi, my darling, you do yourself no favours asking such an asinine question."

"Which invites me to believe that all this is just research for a novel…a novel you will have to write one day."

ooooo

The Intercity picked up much later at Birmingham, after a route via Ely and Bury St Edmunds, boasted a buffet car and she had a sandwich, but Naomi was not as easily disposed of as the wrapping of a tuna and sweetcorn. This was nothing new; as a sensation; as a mental aftermath. Darke had developed a strategy for dealing with people she felt especially drawn to; mental acupuncture was how she characterised it.

By sticking pins in the parts of the brain which might go soft on the deal and start to kindle emotions about what was nothing more than a night of food, wine, conversation and sex, with a vital person eighteen years younger than she, a cauterisation occurred. These pins were cast from the sharp reminders of where affection – which some imbeciles called love – inevitably led: to ennui firstly and then, disastrously, to revulsion. There was also the reverse side of this coin, that the other person him or herself might become too attached, and indeed on a couple of occasions over the years of these book tours the publisher had received anxious letters and phone calls beseeching a contact address.

Darke was not a flawless picker of the right person with whom to spend a night; at times the evening ended with the serving of the restaurant's coffee or a peck on the cheek as the taxi dropped the novelist at her hotel and the other party sped off home; but this occurred more often with men than with women. Sex with men was such an animal affair; sex with women had an aesthetic dimension which took it completely out of the realms of mere lust (though lust had to play its part) and into a mysterious, uncharted territory, Darke thought, where the arrival at a climax was not the whole point of the business, though one, often two, sometimes three, four and five, inevitably did. Sex with a man is like consulting a map or a list of instructions, she reasoned. *Mode d'emploi,* as her French translator had put it (who, though attractive and probably willing, Darke had resolutely refused to get physically involved with because it would likely as not mar future translations and project her into a relationship she could not control or sever without loss of more valuable things than cross-Channel sex).

Men had pursued her. One had threatened her; another had tried blackmail; both dissolved under Darke's refusal to be intimidated (she was stronger and could be more brutal than most men anyway and had no fear in such situations). One man, a don her own age discovered at Blackwell's in Oxford, she felt she might have loved but she applied red hot acupuncture needles to the exact place in the cortex, a particularly easy exercise once his infamous rancid apologia for T.S.Eliot's racism was published, and she cured herself of him completely. The year before last there had been a painter in Edinburgh who had shown great tenderness and exhaustive inventiveness but in spite of promising to meet him again, for lunch at Valvona & Crolla's café before she took the train to Newcastle, she never turned up.

It was for these reasons that one year's schedule of bookshops was never the same as the previous year's. True, this did not stop the odd one-night-stand individual from making the trip to a bookshop out of the area where Darke was signing but only one of these had ever occasioned an embarrassing or violent incident. She did not relish these occasions; abhorring violence unless it was necessary to prevent herself being physically injured or essential to eliminate someone wholly deserving.

ooooo

The train had been moving some minutes, she realised, and the station it had stopped at was slipping away. A shoddy aqueous landscape glowered out of the window under a feeble sun, with a threat of rain contained in the mournful stratocumulus. Her mobile phone vibrated.

"Hello. Darke."

It was the publicist. Of course it was. She always rang up around this time. How had the signing gone? Was the hotel all right? Did she manage to get a decent meal and a decent bottle of wine? Was the roundabout journey proving too arduous? Wonderfully; yes; yes; no: the answers. She didn't comment on the implied criticism of her eccentric route to Manchester.

Darke was brief. Yes, also, to the invitation to take part in a Granada TV book show during the late evening. The publicist, swallowing the feeling she always had after a phone conversation with G.W. Darke that it had somehow been prematurely cut short, made encouraging noises about a projected American tour in a year's time and the possibility of one in New Zealand and Australia in the coming February. This latter tour (it was always relatively simple to get a rich US university to sponsor most of an author's tour) required assistance with external funding and the publicist hinted that this was now a distinct possibility.

ooooo

Sophie Grigson, the cookery writer, was talking and signing in one of Waterstone's events rooms and, when Grace learned this from the poster stuck up in the bookshop's entrance, she felt momentarily that with such fragrant competition on this winter night she was in for a poor attendance; but the other event room, hers, was packed as she entered and a way had to be cleared for her. It was expected of her to be fashionably late, though no-one asked why. Who except an imbecile asks an author why she is late?

Piles of *Third Person Singular* lay on a table, there were bottles of wine, expectant faces (for the free wine or the free speech she couldn't say); a short introduction, a patter of polite applause, and she was on her feet, a copy of the book in her hands with her left thumb inserted between the pages where she intended to start reading. She apologised for her few minutes' lateness, explaining with utter truthfulness that it was the tortuous route she had insisted on taking from Ipswich. She scanned the faces; nothing but sympathetic eyes gazed at her: middle-aged married couples (he in an anorak, she in quilted plaid), a gaggle of female students (far more neatly turned out than in her day), a few solitary oddballs.

When she had first undertaken readings at bookshops she had been not nervous in any conventional sense but wary of selecting a passage that was boring or meaningless out of context; but now she felt she could open any of her books at any page and babble away and it wouldn't make any material difference to the result: the impressing of her signature and a dedication, the taking of her book to the cash till, the satisfying *clunk clank* of a financial transaction concluded. Did she write for money? She hadn't been asked that question for years. Questions went the rounds; maybe it was money's time to come round again.

People began to sip from wine glasses as she spoke. Grace had already tried the wine, an unremarkable French red, and decided she would go easy on it, saving herself for the treasures within the vast and complex list at the Midland Hotel. The usual table was booked, nine-fifteen. She could see no-one, as yet, who looked interesting enough to invite. But then she also knew she had only ninety minutes for dinner before the Granada limo arrived.

"*Third Person Singular* is the most concentrated novel I have written. It is the shortest, by thirty thousand or so words than all the others, yet it took me longest to write. This is not to suggest it is better than the others, I have no opinion of the relative merits of my fiction books, only that it is thicker, denser, more packed. A second reading will reveal much that is not necessarily evident from a first. There is little dialogue, another departure for me. Less wine in it. You may have read some of the early critical reviews. I am surprised to see so many people here if you have all read those wretched reviews."

There was a dutiful, polite gentility of sniggering and chuckling. The room knew what she meant. G.W. Darke always divided the critics, it was said. She often responded, when this came up, with "I am happy to diminish journalistic critics, though complete annihilation to nil might be preferable to a mere halving. As an ex-critic myself, albeit in a different medium from the one I work, I know how shallowly and sometimes falsely those paid to criticise creative work can see things." Bad critics, she had said in an oft-repeated phrase, confuse the pole with the pole-vaulter; the good critic sees immediately the height of the bar.

"In many ways, the novel has been gestating in my mind for decades. It is the story, the biography, of a marriage as written by the person, the third person singular, who is created when two people, a man and a woman, developing a relationship and living intimately together, become married. Being married is not an affair between two people, it is an affair between three. The third person is the creature manufactured by the coming together of the two parties. It is not noticeable at first, the birth is secret and concealed, but the impossibility of marriage is the theme of the book, the monster created when Paul, a wine writer, marries Roberta, who after their honeymoon becomes teetotal for reasons I won't reveal, and it is this monster who narrates the story. It is this genderless creation's story, *Third Person Singular*. I hope it is funny in places. I have never been a writer who has lived up to her name, though many critics, reaching for the obvious, have said there is nothing but bleakness in my novels."

She shrugged. She took her thumb from between the chosen pages. She felt like taking a chance.

"I had intended to read from chapter four but I think I'll just open the book at random and begin from the first complete sentence on the recto. Shall we fill our glasses first?"

A stir went around the rapt room as assistants poured out more cabernet. Grace took a sip from her own glass. She opened the book, stared at the two pages revealed; wondered, not for the first time, if she wasn't soon going to need reading glasses. She moved the book further away from her so as to bring the type, Monotype Fournier, into sharp focus.

"*Rachel came, in black, every Sunday morning to sit there on the turf and spit at Gerald Warbeck's gravestone. It was a duty. It became, like all duties, a habit – come rain or shine. Even come, as it did, disruption or postponement to the number 53 bus route. After seventeen years (17 x 52 not forgetting leap years) it added up to a fair bit of spit. This was no casual expectoration, or even one expressed singly. She spat often at the stone over the hour she sat there, sometimes longer if the weather was clement or she felt particularly spiteful; even on stormy, cold, vengeful winter mornings she was there condemning Warbeck's spirit to eternal, insulting unrest. She never took a holiday. She never missed a Sunday. She never got anything but grim satisfaction from the missile gobs she directed at the various parts of the stone she decided to deface; mostly the name, of course, but also the date of birth. The date of death she religiously left dry if she could help it. At first this had been difficult because spit does run and it took a few years for her to become so practised that she could fairly hit what she aimed at. Only once had anyone stopped and queried what she was doing and the old gentlemen had been seen off with one filthy look and a cuss. Checking on his last resting place, thought Rachel as the old man shuffled off; and then she shouted, wishing it had come to her sooner, 'You'll be down here yourself soon enough!' She took a gulp of wine from the bottle she always carried on these trips. It was red wine. You could tell it was red by the pink spotting on the gravestone. It was a deliberate choice of colour, that wine. It was always a deliberate choice of bordeaux, a minor chateau, for the tannins in such a wine made such beautiful stains on a tombstone.*"

There had been some titters during this, and one outright bellow. Darke approved of these reactions. Surely, Rachel was a comical figure. Tragic figures do not take the 53 bus route, thought Darke. Even Warbeck's tragedy was diminished by Rachel's unceasing campaign of salivated hatred. She turned the open book over, to rest against her chest. She had read an extract that hardly revealed the nature of this third person singular, she realised, but she must soldier on.

"This will," she said, "eludicate, perhaps, those reviews that said the book was grim and also intensely cinematic. The latter is often used to describe my work. Perhaps because it is an easy association. I was a professional film critic. I was always taken with how film editors often made a good film great and a not-so-good film bearable. The way they cut scenes, using small details, cutaways. In the passage I have just read it is easy to see how cinematic is a descriptor which fits my work..."

"Are you saying, Ms Darke, that you do not write consciously visually or that you do? It seems to me that you always have. It characterises your work. The use of the dramatic close-up." The voice was that of the passionate devotee, and young. Surely she was not quite yet set text or prescribed reading for modern English literature undergraduates?

"I didn't want to get in to this area of my working style, right now. I should have chosen a passage which more directly or helpfully illustrates the theme of the book. I think you're right, by the way..." She waved a hand in the direction of the questioner. "I like close-ups, used sparingly amidst long shots or long drawn out scenes."

The man who had interrupted acknowledged the compliment paid. He was too old to be a student, to young to be...a man? Darke wondered at the livid necktie he wore.

"I should explain that the woman in the cemetery is someone whom the central male character gets to know...and the cemetery, like a house in a Compton-Burnett book or the milieu in a Sybille Bedford, is a protagonist in itself...well, it's difficult here because I don't want to give things away upon which the tension of the story depends...but I can say that Rachel and her relationship with Gerald are crucial because through it the male character, who is called Paul, as I said, realises the impossibility of his own marriage, of his loving a person with whom he cannot share his greatest obsession – which is wine, of course."

"May I ask a personal question?"

A small dark woman with a Tesco carrier bag beside her held up her hand. She was taking off a headscarf as she spoke. She was the sort, Darke thought, who only turns up having wandered in at the last minute...but then she remembered that tonight's event had been ticketed well in advance and was obviously sold out.

"Of course."

"Why does marriage fascinate you so much? Almost as much as wine. You are famously unmarried, are you not?"

Darke thought she detected a faint foreign accent. Middle European? She said nothing; waiting for the woman to continue, which by her stance, she was keen to do. There was the trace of a moustache as the light caught her lips.

"All your books have featured failed marriages. Is there a successful one in any book? A truly happy marriage? Are you really, as that little racist shit at The Times put it, the 'laureate of separation'?"

The assembly chuckled at the "racist shit" bit.

"Marriage is a compromise. I've never seen or heard of a happy marriage. A happy long marriage, that is. In *Third Person Singular* I have tried to write an entertaining and possibly original view of a marriage that tries to come to terms with the third person who evolves within it. Shall I read a little more? Yes, let me."

Darke turned the book to face her and flicked over several pages.

"Can you just confirm for me your unmarried status, Miss Darke? It seems important. To me," said the woman with the accent.

"I am unmarried. I have never been married. My single claim to fame."

The audience laughed. Not the woman.

"Thank you," she said. "Please. Continue with your reading. You read beautifully, by the way."

This praise stunned Grace. No-one had ever said that before. Maybe the woman was a witch and in the carrier bag was a head she was going to boil up for her supper when she got home. Maybe the extravagant compliment was a plot to unnerve her, to make her try too hard. She took a gulp of the wine, swilling it around her mouth before swallowing. Was Trevor Healy a racist shit? She had never thought so. He was rather dishy in his pseudo-donnish way.

Come the signing, the woman with the carrier bag bought ten copies, to Grace's amazement, and Grace dedicated every single one – in each case to a woman who was receiving the book as a Christmas present. For a moment, Grace fingered the card. But no. Not that the moustache was off-putting. It was those ferocious black eyes. Grace had

had enough of encounters for one day. Besides, she had the TV show to face yet.

ooooo

As was normal when she returned home from anything longer than five days away, the front door of the flat was wedged against a pile of post. Later, after dinner, she sorted it out in her study (she abominated the term "work-area" on the grounds that in the case of a novelist, this was the entire universe). There were the usual dozen or so letters addressed to her publisher and forwarded; mostly stuff from readers or an invitation from a university debating group or literary society. One envelope addressed to her care of her publisher, however, was different. It addressed her as Grace. She was compelled to open it.

It revealed a postcard with a view of the Norfolk Broads taken just after the last world war. It was from Naomi and when she turned it over and looked at the small handwriting, with its sharp decliners and fiercely tight loops, she could not from this calligraphic display discern the character of the person with whom she had spent the night. The card was laconic:

"*I had intended to put behind me our evening. As you, no doubt, intend to do the same. But I was compelled to just say…thank you. It was a privilege and a pleasure to meet the only inhabitant of Planet Darke. When you return to Earth, and discover it is love you crave, you know where to find me. Naomi.*"

Grace held the card over the waste basket and then, with a tetchy toss (of hair and card), consigned it to the file marked "Rdrs Lttrs" which hung from a row of twenty files on a portable, ball-wheeled frame. Eight further envelopes, unopened and all suspected of being from readers, followed.

Planet Darke. She liked that. Did she know where to find Naomi? Then she remembered the girl had written her telephone number and address, unasked, in her notebook. When she looked at this the handwriting was wildly dissimilar to that on the card. She thought: we have one style for communicating sober facts; another style for conveying the stirrings of the heart. Was this a human norm?

A fragment of Shakespeare floated in her consciousness: "*when like spirits embrace total they mix and obstacle find none of membrane, joint or limb.*"

She shivered. She didn't care to be the only inhabitant of her own planet, like one of those creatures in *Le Petit Prince*. She also felt rather irritated to be told she craved love. Love was the opposite of what she demanded…wasn't it?

She went to the kitchen and took a bottle of white wine from the refrigerator.

As she sipped the riesling she thought about what Naomi had said. Were these book tours merely research for a novel she would one day have to write?

Not a novel, she concluded, but maybe a short story…

ooooo

Domaine du Vieux-Télégraphe 1992

"Now you were of course an expert on science fiction before the wine books arrived."

The interviewer had warned the interviewee that old, though perhaps not filthy, washing might be publicly aired.

"You make my books sound like babies," said Beryl Longman. "They do sort of tumble out, I suppose, all bloody and unable to fend for themselves, requiring careful nourishing before they can walk on their own two feet. Having to submit to interviews like this is part of the nourishment."

She wondered just who, at 11.30pm on a Thursday night in November, watched a programme about books. She was more taken with the possibilities of the baby analogy. She wished she could expand it. She wanted to note it down. Was that sort of thing done on television? On the Desmond Wilson hour surely anything was possible.

Desmond Wilson was a highbrow personality. Commercial TV employed a few. He was a poet of sixty-eight who had been touted for the laureateship. Wilson had been effusive in his introduction of Beryl Longman and made no bones about his delight at "snaring" her when the scheduled author, Rosalia de Francisco-Rodriguez, had been arrested, at Stansted Airport the day before, with a quarter-pound of cocaine in her luggage, thereby causing a diplomatic row to erupt between the

Peruvian ambassador and H.M. Government whose officers detained her pending deportation or possible imprisonment.

Beryl had not known this until fifteen minutes before she went on. Wilson, thought Beryl, as he explained the reason for the Peruvian novelist's non-appearance as make-up was daubed on her face, looked as if he was made out of the drug himself with his white hair, white eyebrows and, nestling like snowy owlets in a gnarled trunk, his startlingly avian white-haired inside ears – all of which were set in a clean-shaven face of impressively cracked maturity. She had once admired Wilson's unfashionable home-spun humour, only to be astonished to learn he was a TV presenter.

"For the richest life within dig deep.
As vine roots do, superior nourishment to seek."

How could she forget those lines? They had embellished the frontispiece of her *The Death of Liebfraumilch*. She helped herself to a glass of the wine on the table between them. There was always a bottle on the coffee table beside a small pile of books, on top of which was her latest.

("Please help yourself to the wine," had said the producer. "It all helps to foster the idea that this is a friendly chat between fellow intellectuals and artists. And we know you love great wine.")

Beryl was touched to see that the bottle was a ten-year-old Domaine du Vieux-Télégraphe. Wilson himself was sipping from a glass, as was the other guest, the American script-writer and film-maker Adair Webster, but Beryl was busy contemplating how good the wine *should* be before she plunged in.

Webster, she conjectured, might not care whether he was drinking Coca Cola rather than such a wine. He was younger than her, ascetically featured, an earring in his left ear, hair in a ponytail, a two-day growth of rich beard resembling ginger suede. Like a Silicon Valley internet-technology billionaire, she concluded (though she had never met one).

Wilson wondered at his guest's diffidence. The wine was delicious, he thought. Remarkable in fact. Maybe she just likes the smell of it. Early days yet, he thought, we've only been on air a minute; and he recalled, and could now confirm for himself, the researcher's view that "she's a damned tricky bitch".

He let the 'having to submit to interviews' remark pass and pressed his point about her early work. The science fiction area was surely fertile; a little exposed area of Longman. Webster, he reasoned, would surely find it sympathetic since he had turned two Philip K Dick novels into scripts and then into finished films and was busy on a third, though Beryl had not known this. She had lost her interest in science fiction about the time she discovered there was more to lunch than quiche Lorraine.

"I would never claim expert status," she responded, taking her nose from her glass. "Science fiction interested me at university, the history of it..."

"Your first book was called *Yesterday Men, Tomorrow Women* and it was based, I believe, on an uncompleted doctoral thesis. I should explain to viewers that it was not a wine book, of course, but...well, literary criticism?"

Beryl laughed and studied her wine glass further, seeing Wilson sucking up the contents of his own. She grimaced and Wilson, thinking he had touched on an aspect of her career she didn't want to talk about, congratulated himself. It was important to get tension in the show.

"You've done your homework, Desmond," she said. "It was a loose critical thesis. I got a decent enough degree to embark on a doctorate, but left before completing it. I did expand on it to make it fit for publication after I came down…"

"Came down?" muttered Webster.

"With the disease of graduation, Mr Webster. My thesis blossomed into a book, which I admit I was astonished to learn someone wanted to pay me to publish. My interest in sci-fi…dwindled…"

"I never use that term," said Webster.

"Dwindled is a harmless enough word," said Beryl.

"I mean sci-fi. Such terminology is childishly demeaning."

"Like so much of the genre it encompasses," said Beryl.

Wilson felt a warm glow inside. He took more wine.

"The title caused much offence, doubtless intentional. *Yesterday Men, Tomorrow Women* has a challenging ring to it," he said.

Beryl sighed. She supposed she had to get into this; get it out of the way.

"I took the view that the writing of science into fiction was a male thing based on severely male fantasies. Jules Verne, Poe even, H G Wells, Olaf Stapledon, C.S Lewis, Wyndham with his ludicrous Triffids, the early Vonnegut, Simak, Aldiss, Sturgeon, Leiber, Ellison, Harrison, Moorcock, Arthur C Clarke, Asimov, Dick, of course…whoops, sorry to laugh… even people like Alfred Bester, who transcended gender and the genre, unlike Ursula le Guin, who simply portrayed messiness, as did Tolkein, though he is more properly, if we must be rigorously taxonomic about it, a fantasist as Poe, strictly, was a spiritualist. There were university contemporaries of mine who shone at showing how the Brontes were masculinists, if you can credit the term, and one, who now has tenure at Oxford, built a career out of the dazzling proposition that Mansfield Park was the first anti-colonial novel and that Jane Austen prophesied Marxism. I just joined in the fun…"

"You left out Orwell," said Webster.

"And what about Mary Shelley?" added Wilson.

"Orwell, like Kafka, was a political and social satirist. Not relevant. But Mary Shelley underlines my whole point. She rewrote the myth of the mittel-European Jewish monster-brought-into-life-from-clay, the Golem, and the mythologies of male power are everywhere evident in this and indeed are the inspiration for Frankenstein's created man. She couldn't write it otherwise in 1818, I suppose…"

"What the hell's this got to do with Tomorrow's Women?" said Webster.

"Nothing," said Beryl. "That was the bit I had trouble with. But for the feminist press my weakness in this area didn't matter. I had proven that men write science fiction out of inadequacy…"

"Now hold on there, sister!"

"…and it was merely enough to progress from this, since science itself had developed in broad and spectacular ways no-one thought would ever happen – artificial intelligence, limb replacement, cloning, DNA manipulation, the internet, for example – and this had been done with women's help and connivance and of course professional involvement as scientists and technologists, and thus I could from this develop the line that what men had started women would finish and make reality."

"Have you," said Wilson gently, feeling that this had gone far enough, "been tempted to develop the scientific prophesying or 'what-if' syndrome in your wine novels?"

"No. Never."

"I was thinking about genetically modified grapes, for example, or the biological tampering with certain insects to assist vines in fighting pests."

"Wine is certainly a more scientific subject now than it has ever been, though it was Pasteur who was the pioneer, of course. The other things you mention are, well, routine. I left sci-fi behind once I saw through the hollowness of writers like Dick."

"Philip K Dick wrote great literature…was a literary giant…a science fiction visionary," Webster protested, taking a huge draught of the Télégraphe.

"That last is tautology. Don't be so sensitive about an average writer. Dick wrote so furiously fast he never became anything more meaningful than a small time sketcher of small-town American life. Raymond Carver does it, did it, much better."

"Carver didn't write science fiction!"

"He wrote social fiction. So did Dick in his way. Look, Mr Webster, the difference between literature and sci-fi, or SF if it'll make you feel less pissed off, is that one is infinitely flexible and the other is fixed. SF, as with any kind of thriller or *policier,* develops plot; literature develops character. Think of it like two houses. The SF house is a one-storey job, all on one level. You cannot move the furniture about or redecorate the walls without ruining the design and there are no stairs. The great book, on the other hand, is a great rambling multi-storied construct, imaginatively and fluidly designed with mobile characters. You can live in it. You can even re-hang the pictures. In most novels, like all SF, everything is nailed down. The furniture, the ideas, the characters' emotions, are fixed. SF, however visionary or exploratory, is always like that. Just like spy books. A hero like James Bond, say, serves a fixed purpose in a staid setting, he's just a wooden bench that speaks. A knight's errand-boy like Sancho Panza takes you, me, us, the readers, around a dazzling edifice and if you want to rearrange the pictures, feel free."

"The great book gets a blue plaque then?" offered Wilson, the wine perhaps going to his head. "The mediocre stuff just has a house number?"

"More or less," said Beryl, wary that the piss might be being taken here.

"You guys slay me. What does plaque have to do with anything? James Bond is *a wooden bench*?"

"Nothing is what it seems," said Wilson. "Reality is what other people see, as Goethe put it."

You made that up, thought Beryl. Wilson saw her expression. He took more of the wine to cover the grin spreading over his face.

"By the way," said Beryl, "this wine we're drinking, or rather you're drinking, stinks to buggery. You haven't another bottle by any chance, have you?"

"Now I know you're nuts," said Webster. "This wine is out of sight."

"I thought Télégraphe was one of your favourites," Wilson purred, thinking that this unexpected, and indeed unprecedented, turn in events was a useful diversion.

"Not when it's corked. It stinks of old engines."

"There's no cork or machinery in my glass," said Webster.

"Are you seriously telling me, Beryl, that the wine in this glass is anything but magic? It smells like a Provençal summer afternoon," said Wilson.

"Where do you spend your Provençal summer afternoons? Next to the petrol refinery in Vitrolles?"

Wilson was stunned by this and gabbled something. He picked up Beryl's latest book, on which pretext she had been invited on the show, and thought about throwing it at her but realised he should say something. Silences on television shut down shows, he had been told. He waved the book in the air and asked for a fresh empty glass to be brought to his female guest and as this was being done, he asked Webster to explain the difficulties of bringing a novel to the screen.

A midget in overalls sidled up to Beryl and presented her with a glass and she took it and smelled the bowl, as she always did (but hadn't with the other glass), and as she did so she realised what was wrong with the wine. Her glass was infected with washing up liquid.

Were Wilson's and Webster's? Presumably not, otherwise they would surely have felt as she had done. Why had she agreed to do this show? Television was so trivialising and stupid and in spite of her thinking that Wilson would rise above the norm he had insisted on going down the SF route and so her book, which her publisher was so excited about her publicising on Wilson's show, was being neglected. "Of course," she trumpeted, "I am in the lucky position of being a writer of books no-one would ever want to turn into films."

Webster, who had been in full flow about the differences between one medium and another, faltered and Wilson laughed, glad of her sudden reawakening, for the American had been a serious mistake, tedious with his whining accent and dogmatic in his assertions. Webster, though, was furious at Longman's interjection.

"Christ, woman, can't we go one second without you wanting to turn the conversation back to you?"

Wilson was pouring from a second bottle of Télégraphe into Beryl's glass.

"No we bloody well can't, you prick. That's what I'm here to do, talk about myself and my work, and it is patently clear that in your case your self is a bore and your work..."

She was not allowed to finish. Webster had stood and snatched the bottle of wine from Wilson's grasp and upended the contents over Beryl's head.

"Oh how lovely!" yelled Beryl and ran fingers through her hair and licked her fingers. "How lovely to be doused in Vieux Télégraphe! And it tastes perfect! Free from these contaminated wine glasses!"

Within a month her book, an account of the revolution in southern French vineyards called *The Frog Bites Back,* was at number one in its sales category and she had a weekly column in the Independent. And, of course, she was a frequent guest on TV celebrity quiz shows, radio programmes, and was regularly invited to be the guest speaker at corporate events where large fees were involved.

Many of us wonder, in later life, why we studied what we did at university or further education establishment and we conclude that, given our lives over again, something else ought to have been the object of our intellectual or physical enquiry. Beryl, who had often considered her three tertiary educational years a complete waste of effort, now revised her views. And naturally, every November 10th, she solemnly opened a bottle of Vieux Télégraphe (of what ever vintage was current) and toasted her good fortune.

Webster became a hero of the New American Male movement. Within two years, he was richer, happier and less anxious and he too every November 10th opened a bottle of Vieux Télégraphe and toasted his good fortune.

A bottle of the right wine in the right place at the right time can change people's lives forever.

ooooo

Nambrot Tenuta di Ghizzano 2001

Quentina Pears had lived in Bryanston Palace Mansions for twenty-seven years. She had inherited the flat as a student from a single, male, extremely elderly godparent whom she had met only once. On a mantelpiece of one of its five rooms was an old brass day calendar and it had never been changed since the day she moved in: January 17th 1975. The Mansions is a dapper block of some forty flats in York Street, off Baker Street, that tediously intent London argument for a boulevard which aims aggressively one-way south until it touches Portman Square, where it is abruptly swallowed up, only to be regurgitated the other side of the Square as Orchard Street, one of the Capital's shortest walks and remarkable solely for the glaucously binocular frontages of Selfridges food hall on one side and Marks & Spencer on the other. This whole stretch of thoroughfare, bakers and orchards left behind, is then tamely rolled up into the shattering rackets (commercial, auditory, sometimes both at the same time) of that first-floor-level architectural obscenity – Selfridges' extravagant front entrance excepted – called Oxford Street.

Though decently boulevardish in width – Quentina was prepared to admit that much – Baker Street is banal in temper and nondescript in endeavour (one adventurous Chinese dim sum restaurant apart and the Galvin bistro), and no local inhabitant ever happily walked up or down any length of it except when it was necessary to get to the tube station. I am, she often said to out-of-towners, domiciled – as perhaps was the previous occupant – like a disappointed character in an Anita Brookner romance (a role into which she felt she was increasingly fading, like some old Liberty print). The Pears readers to whom this was said, if they were Brookner readers also, often thought and occasionally said "surely that disappointed is a tautology", and QP would agree and think, but never utter, "perhaps just a pleonasm".

It was in the dim sum restaurant that Quentina Pears had her occasional Sunday lunches with Bry Meadowes. She kept him away from Galvin, which was superior in style and ambition, as she liked eating there alone. Meadowes shared her inclination for Alsatian wine with Chinese food, of which the restaurant, unusually, kept a list of exemplary specimens. Meadowes himself fed Pears, along with her agile memory and fat notebook, and had appeared in two separate fictional guises in two of her novels six years apart; but he had recognised himself in neither manifestation, in spite of once unburdening himself – Quentina choking on a mouthful of woo kok and Schlumberger Tokay Pinot-Gris as he spoke – of the revelation that "that Prigmore fellow in *The Man Who Wept Ants* reminds me strongly of someone I knew in advertising but since you cannot have known him because he died before we met, Quentina my dear, it must be a coincidence. We were briefly in partnership, Prigmore and I, I mean Dai Nunn and I – commercial partnership, that is – and he was exactly as you described him. A man who found a new hobby every week, dropped it the next week after spending a fortune on it and boring his friends with it, and yet criticised his wife for following exactly the same pattern of behaviour."

Quentina let the woo kok and the wine take their course and waited to have the contents of the chilli sauce pot, from which Meadowes was contributing a smearing to the chung fung on his plate, to be ejected over her head; but she realised, with even greater astonishment and indeed admiration, that Meadowes was even more shallow that she had ever realised or characterised in fiction. How could he not see far enough, that desperately short distance surely, to recognise himself in Adrian Prigmore, the prime minister's spin-doctor? Quentina had had a strategy prepared, once the book was published, to deal with Meadowes' recognition of himself when he idly wondered at the coincidences; but this was the first and only time the matter had been referred to, even though it had been Meadowes' brain she had principally picked in order to create the spin-doctor's election advertising campaign, which was an important refinement of the plot.

It was also Meadowes' brain from which sprang the names of the wines with which certain of her more tedious, and often evil characters, indulged themselves. Because Meadowes had met her when she was in possession of an uncommon wine, he assumed she was interested in the subject and knew something about it. In fact, she cared only for the odd bottle, sometimes splashing out for dinner parties or if her agent or publisher came for lunch. But Meadowes proved himself a valuable source of rare wines (rare to Quentina at least) and though he rarely purchased them for her to drink he did talk about them. How could she plausibly have had that spin-doctor possess an expensive predilection for something called Comtes de Lafon Clos de la Barre Meursault 1996 if Bry had not told her it was one of the best white burgundies in the world (adding "and now, Quentina dear, you know that too")?

Meadowes had a flat in the same mansion block as Quentina but lived most of the year in Provence, near his old friend Peter Mayle. He part-owned a vineyard there, Clos d'Abricots, which he claimed he had bought into purely because his name was pronounced therein. The old ad man was, in his own phraseology, not retired, just "largely disengaged." His wife and he had been separated for thirty years but still exchanged vitriolic postcards and, latterly, e-mails, which was how he kept up with her giddying profusion of in-and-out hobbies, from portrait photography, illustrating children's books, feng shui, Catalan cookery, garden design, libretto-writing, Japanese paper sculpture, along with carp-raising and bonsai-breeding, plus at least fifty other pursuits over the past decades, all of which he crushingly described to Quentina over these lunches along with, correspondingly, his own varied and richly-hued palette of up and down interests.

They had met one Saturday afternoon in the lift at the mansion block; the bottles of Alsatian wine which each had purchased from Selfridges wine department, his a very old *vendange tardive gewurztraminer* (an assault on the senses of honeyed peaches, lychees and crème brulée) to go with mango fool, hers a mere *edelzwicker* (a modest blend of chasselas, pinot blanc and sylvaner grapes, usually sold as jug wine in Alsatian cafés) purchased out of curiosity, causing mutual comment. If the sales assistant had not told her of the special offer on the edelzwicker she would never have dreamed of buying it, since she did not know what it was. But Meadowes seemed to have heard of it and was inspired to launch into a litany of praise for the wine he himself was carrying.

Three months later, on his next trip to London, Meadowes pushed a card through Quentina's door inviting her to join him for dim sum and "excellent Alsatian wine" at Ho Tan and Quentina felt: why not?

She fell under the spell of his hysterical superficiality and unknowingness of himself. He was sixty-four and still a child. He had felt compelled to buy a flat in this block, so he revealed, because his first name, Bryan, shared the same first syllable as the building. Until then, she felt sure, he had always referred to himself as Bryan but upon becoming a resident he had shorted his name the better to point up his residency. Such gems of inane superficiality delighted Quentina Pears. It was marvellous to behold, over the ten years of their acquaintanceship, how he neither aged nor matured and his interests, from deep-sea fishing to Provençal myth-collecting, built a vertiginous pyramid of current and past enthusiasms. It was impossible not to utilise his personality, or lack of it, in one of the novels, and then another. Two novels was, she felt, one too many; but for the author the friendship was entertainingly fertile since the conversation always turned to the amazing wines he drank in France and then, more intimately, to the separated wife and her maniacal pursuit of the hobby which would, finally (but never did), become the all-consuming life-long devotion. Once he did bring a bottle of his vineyard's wine for her to taste (a red, blended from grenache, cinsault and mourvedre) but she found the liquid so hollow as to be tiresome after one glass. Many months later he did ask how she had found the wine and her expression was more vivid than words.

"I understand," he said matter-of-factly (and the subject ended there). "Clos d'Abricots doesn't travel well, does it?"

Quentina liked Bry. She could never kill him off, however infuriatingly slight he was. One might as well plan the demise of a piece of thistledown. He was without a nasty bone in his body yet he could physically squeeze the life dry from a close relationship, a marriage or a commercial liaison, and then be bemused at how it all turned out. What sort of see-saw reality he had had with that Dai Nunn, of whom Meadowes thought the spin-doctor reminded him, she shuddered to imagine. Meadowes was a benign Frankenstein's monster, assembled from the accreted piecemeal emotions of his trade over the thirty-nine years he had practised it; and Quentina lived, and dined, in hope that one day she would meet the real Bry Meadowes, the boy he must have been before he left Salford College of Art and became an ad man. Bry's innocent if sun-soaked features, even at his age still roundly choir-boyish beneath a halo of lemon hair, no visible grey, had a perpetually puzzled expression enhanced by the prunish wrinkles around the eyes. Quentina thought he had a live-in girlfriend in Menerbes but the subject, when placed on the flash grill of conversation, yielded little aroma and almost no taste.

Quentina realised that when this woman was out of sight she was also out of mind. Meadowes had an immediacy of emotion which made her wonder if he had ever experienced love, even though he proclaimed his ability to fall in it at the "drop of a hat or, should it go that far, a skirt".

Quentina liked these fragile jokes; had even used one or two of them in the books. With his second fictional appearance, Quentina had felt she was surely on wafer-thin ice and Bry could not fail to spot the resemblances, but if he did he said nothing. She now knew he completely failed to analyse anything he did or read, not giving consideration to anything beyond what fed an immediate appetite. He had never made a pass at her. His appetite for her was simply as a convenient, entertaining and almost-always-available neighbour. She assumed she was too old now for old men like Bry, whose waning hormonal transmissions, she assumed, were mostly radiated at nymphets.

What happened when the day came, as surely it must, when a friend of Meadowes read one or other of Quentina Pears' books and brought up the uncanny likeness of certain characters to the disengaged adman? Probably, she thought, Bry would feel flattered.

Lunch, a terrific lunch at that, two or three times a year, or an occasional dinner, with the perennially tanned Bry was a small and very civilised price to pay for the theatre he unconsciously provided. She never lunched at the Ho Tan except with Meadowes and neither had yet seen the inside of the other's flat. My chopstick chum, Meadowes called her. He never asked her about her own interests, though he read the books (or said he did). He rarely commented on the reason why she might not be free for dim sum, mostly because of a lunchtime concert at the Wigmore Hall. He had no interest in classical music, and hardly any in any other form, proclaiming it to be "too contrived for my ear, since I discovered birdsong" and so another hobby would have the dust-covers taken off it and Quentina treated to a extraordinary disquisition on the repertoire of the nightingale. All this while his wife, from her house in Dorset, would be roundly castigated for saying in a postcard that "since discovering lepidoptery, I have lost all interest in impressionist art" and Meadowes' chuckle would turn into a cackle – which was about as vicious as he could get, Quentina thought.

ooooo

It was a short hop from Bryanston Palace Mansions, for the devoutly pedestrianised Quentina, to Selfridges shopping hall, where she bought her fish, rather than at Fish Works in Marylebone High Street; and a trip to the Wigmore Hall was a twelve-minute stroll. She was a regular feature at the Wigmore, a Schubert or Mozart or Beethoven (even Debussy) score on her lap. Interpretation interested her and had once caused embarrassment when, fortified one Sunday by an impressively alcoholic and extremely late lunch, she had been unable to contain a loud exclamation of protest when Heironymous Stark, deep into book two of the Well-Tempered Clavier, wandered preposterously far from Bach's written intentions in both the F minor and G sharp preludes. Quentina received fierce looks from others in the row and in a gesture that she hoped conveyed her feelings, she closed the score book with emphasis and sat on it, and left during the applause at the end. Quentina imagined a slow suffocation inside a Yamaha for the pianist. A Bechstein or a Steinway, let alone a Fazioli, would be far too good for the coffin of a musical butcher.

At one lunch Meadowes had confessed, with deadly seriousness, that his very part-time chairmanship of a London advertising film production company was under threat and for the first time in their relationship Quentina felt that now she might see the man beneath. And she felt she had, once Meadowes told her the sorry story of the company's imminent bankruptcy and debt-ridden status. Meadowes revealed that he was having to consider selling his London flat to meet his obligations and Quentina, unaccustomed to seeing men cry, felt sufficiently moved to pay for lunch, which had included an expensive bottle of a special vintage of old Alsatian wine. Was this to be the last lunch?

Quentina made useful notes after the lunch about the intricacies of company receivership and felt sorry for old Meadowes, who had aged since she had last seen him. Six weeks later she encountered him in the lobby, chatting to George the porter, and she took him aside, complimented him on how well he looked, and discovered, before he breezed off, that he had utterly forgotten the subject of their conversation over lunch the month before.

"How is the company business going, Bry? You know..." and her voice dropped, since it would not do for George to catch a whiff of Meadowes' financial embarrassment.

"Company business? What do you mean?"

And Quentina soon discovered the layer of Bry that had been hidden, or rather not so much hidden as so much on the surface that she had missed it for looking deeper. The threatened bankruptcy had passed away. The company had survived. Work had come in suddenly, a project of six commercials for Spain, and a large outstanding debt had been settled. Quentina marvelled at the man. The polish of Meadowes' superficiality was breathtaking in its sheen ("one can only polish surface", as Philip Larkin had pointed out). There was absolutely no substance to him beyond that conferred by the seeking and the satisfying of the immediate interest or desire.

Meadowes had altogether forgotten his tearful display at lunch. That had been last month's emotional mask. His mood was now so lifted that not only did he not wish to be reminded of the possibility that the film company might have gone into receivership, but he had genuinely removed it from his mind and mentioned the case of Domaine de la Romanée Conti

Richebourg 1998 he had acquired for his cellar in France. Thus it was that she saw for the first time that she had not, in his two fictional appearances in her work, drawn the man as he really was; he did have a dangerous side and she was glad their relationship went no deeper than it had or would do in future.

The nature of his personality was now revealed. He had no personality. He was simply a child of the moment. Now she fully grasped the significance of what he had said (on two separate occasions over the years and so this was the third):

"Advertising is like a Jewish mother. It stops you growing up and leaving."

After ten years, Quentina wondered if these lunches hadn't run their course. Bry Meadowes was beginning to repeat himself. His 'use-by' date had been well passed.

She had promised herself that the day he said "You know, I've just realised that one of your ears is larger than the other" would be the last time she would bother to see him. But he had yet to say it. And not because he felt too polite to point out the abnormality. He simply hadn't, Quentina knew, noticed.

ooooo

Quentina went to bed early with the new biography of Iris Murdoch. Dinner with Bry had been more exhausting than normal. It had not turned out as she had hoped or anticipated. Still, the wine talk had been good. The wine talk was always usable. So was Bry. His utter moral correctness was nauseating. He was evil compressed; surrounded by his civil shell. It is always thus, she reasoned. How did dear Ivy C-B put it? "*Patience is merely impatience contained.*"

ooooo

Madame Agace, the disappointed, widowed crone whose flat was on the opposite side of the corridor from Meadowes', had once (she claimed thrice but Bry considered this a possible exaggeration) posed nude for a famous picture of Lucien Freud's. Or was it Francis Bacon's? The dilemma interested Quentina more than the fact of the posing; it confirmed, in her mind, the utter hopelessness of Meadowes' intellect. She had long ago gathered that Freud and Bacon were the only two post-war British artists that Meadowes had ever heard of (or certainly whose work he had seen in any quantity over any period of time), in spite of claiming an interest in looking at pictures (later she was forced to add Hockney to the league). She therefore concluded that the actual painter of Mme. Agace's supposed pose was just as likely to have been someone utterly obscure, perhaps a 1950s' Royal Academy summer exhibition hopeful. Since she saw the woman rarely, usually in conversation with George in the lobby, possibly engaged in the fertile subject of the emptying of the dustbins and the collecting of the tenants' rubbish, she had never had the opportunity, or indeed great desire, to make a deeper acquaintance with her and so ascertain the truth. It was from these occasional sightings that Quentina formed a view of the woman's disappointed status and conceived an opinion of her position as most likely that of a crone. It was a cruel word to apply to someone who had never offered her a nasty word, Quentina conceded that. But the physicality of Mme. Agace fitted it (and Quentina was well aware of the etymology of the word, which derives from a parous ewe no longer able to bear lambs). There was mischief in the woman, of that Quentina was sure. Quentina was glad she didn't live on the crone's floor and could pass by her, issuing a mandatory good morning or good afternoon in her general direction, resplendent in the secret knowledge that she knew full well that she had once, or perhaps twice, taken off her clothes in 1956 for a British artist at a time when, so Meadowes would further reveal, she was involved in mysterious employment in the Charing Cross Road at a famous Marxist bookshop and was, therefore, likely to be a double agent. The munificence of the pension that enabled her to live on in Bryanston Palace Mansions, and dress with sybil-like severity, could only be speculated upon. Quentina was mildly curious to see what style the woman lived in but then she ought, by the same token, to have been more intrigued to see the inside of Meadowes' flat but had never been invited.

Mme. Agace did, however, exhibit one trait that Quentina found endearing and wondered if she should copy. But after mature reflection she decided it was something only couples went in for and coupling, in that sense, was not a Quentina Pears disposition.

Mme. Agace and Quentina one day found themselves in the same lift.

"When Bruce was alive," Quentina had been told in that portentous lift, "we had a summer arrangement and a winter arrangement for our flat. We lived for both transformations. It kept us young. At the end of April we would totally rearrange the furniture. It took us a day and a half, with the help of two of the porters – amply tipped, I might add. And then around October 15th, we'd move everything back to winter mode…the sofas nearer the heating…you know the sort of thing." Quentina didn't. She didn't move things, or buy much new. She had inherited old Firebrace's furniture with the flat and apart from replacing one sagging armchair, it was very much as he'd left it (apart from new curtains, recovery for a Chesterfield, a new gas oven and fridge, and a re-papering job – once she was established as a writer who made enough to live on and to acquire an overdraft).

When her agent phoned to say Alan Parker, the English film director working in Hollywood, was interested in optioning *Welcome to the Abattoir*, she did not go out and immediately treat herself to lunch at the absurdly pricey Orrery restaurant in Marylebone High Street (as she had promised herself). She waited. Nothing, surely, would come of it (it wasn't the first time a film director had shown an interest in one of her books). But something did – £100,000, to be precise.

Quentina was single, did not smoke, spent occasionally on wine, did not own a car, had one phone, did her faxing in the print shop in Crawford Street, and had never made more than £23,678 in a single year from her writings, though it was true that foreign translations were rumoured to be on the horizon, and increased sales in English-speaking markets.

When other authors at literary gatherings talked of the irritations of VAT, Quentina reflected she would like to earn enough to expose such complaints to her peers.

With the film money she opened an ISA, paid for some necessary repairs to the bathroom, including a new shower, bought some new shoes in Bond Street and stuck £80,000 in a two-year bond with the Britannia Building Society. What was left over was more than sufficient to give her a fortnight's holiday at an opulent villa in Ischia and develop the idea that she would go and splurge on a bit of wine. She would surpass herself and surprise her friends.

A carpenter came and fixed up a large wine cupboard and filled it with racks. An electrician installed a temperature control unit. It was her cellar. And she filled it with some 250 bottles clearly capable, in the words of the Hunt & Luard saleswoman with whom she concluded the deal, of "improving with keeping and possibly increasing in value, though we make no guarantees".

It was enough. She would indulge herself for once. Bry Meadowes had given so many of her fictional characters a taste for great wine when their creator had little knowledge of it that now she felt she should join them. Wine was something she enjoyed, though not with the reverence accorded it by Bry, so why not do as her characters did?

She especially liked the glass door the carpenter fitted to the cupboard so she could, when she felt in the mood (as she increasingly did these days), stand and regard the contents in their perfect conditions and, now and then, pull out a bottle for dinner. She might throw more dinner parties now.

ooooo

Quentina consulted her notebook. Once a week she did her sweep through her random jottings, where so many of Meadowes' conversations had become the rich fertiliser for a character's lifestyle, thoughts and wines. She made notes wherever she went.

"*Love is the only virus which once caught does not confer immunisation.*" This had been written whilst staring at the Canalettos in the Wallace Collection. She had often sat and made notes there in the half-rotunda fronting the Manchester Square side of the Collection and now the paintings had moved downstairs adjacent to a sofa, she could sit and contemplate them in more comfort.

"*What is the most prominent feature of all British urban landscapes? Curtains, blinds, frills, lace – things which conceal an interior, or confuse an interior's design and conceal its occupants to any passing spy."* This comment had been committed to the book after a drive in a mini-cab (Quentina could not drive herself nor wished to learn) through Battersea in order to fix the location for a projected novel.

"*Czeslaw Milosz, the Polish poet, writes of 'a river, suffering because the reflection of clouds and trees are no clouds and trees'.*" This after she had read his notebooks. It was a beautiful idea: a suffering river recognising its own emptiness.

How could she use this imagery in the work now under the pen?

The phone rang.

"Quentina, Bry here. Back in Town again! Just two floors up from you. You know I really do think you and me should have dinner together tomorrow. What do you say?"

"You mean you and I, Bry. And aye is my answer. I have news."

"I? You mean yes? And you have news? I thought I was the one always with the news."

"You make me sound like the staid old stay-at-home and workaholic that I am. Let's not meet in the restaurant as always do. Drop down and let's have a drink before we go…yes?"

"A drink? Um…well…"

"I promise you something you'll love."

ooooo

When she answered the bell there was Bry, as unchanging as ever. His tan was like crème caramel and the jacket and trousers were immaculate and matched his skin colour (his hands, she noted, were beginning to display liver spots the size of florins). Quentina thought he looked like an exotic toffee; a toffee that would definitely stick in the teeth.

They kissed in the British version of the continental two-cheek and he somewhat hesitantly stepped inside.

"I booked for eight-fifteen," he said. "We have ten minutes before we need to move off."

She often wanted to ask him if he had a station-master amongst his ancestors, or a clock-maker. She ushered him into the living room, across the parquet flooring. He ignored the exquisite Carnivalho prints in the hall, stepped on Firebrace's genuine 18th century Afghan rug without comment, and found himself in a room which in window placement and design was not hugely different from his own on the top floor. There was an ornate silver-lipped decanter filled with red wine by the Chesterfield and he gravitated towards this, muttered some perfunctory clichés about the attractiveness of the room (in truth rather gloomy and still distinctly Firebracian in epoque), and sat down. He slung one leg over the other to expose a perfect length of yellow sock and a prominent pair of mahogany-coloured brogues.

"Strange to consider we've never met in my flat before, Bry, or in yours."

"My flat's a mess, Quentina. No opportunity to have a cleaning lady with my visits being so unplanned. I entertain there purely for business. You know."

She poured him a glass of the wine. She poured herself a glass.

He stared at his glass for some seconds. He looked at the impenetrable crimson of the wine. He cleared his throat.

"Isn't this a Riedel red burgundy glass?"

"Why yes. It is. How clever of you to spot it!"

"But this is not red burgundy…"

"Oh dear. Have I committed some offence already?"

"Oh my goodness me…no, my dear. No. No. I'm curious, that's all. I didn't associate you with glasses like this. I must treat this wine with respect."

"I use these glasses for all sorts of wines."

He smelled the wine, sipped, looked astonished.

"You and wine seem to have come on a bit since we first met. Is this a special from Selfridges?"

"No, not at all. I, er, have a bit of this wine. Something I've acquired."

"Oh."

Quentina relaxed in the armchair matching the sofa in which Bry was sitting. He was trying, from the pained expression on his face, to work out what on earth the wine was. She had her hair up, as she preferred it in the evenings, and was wearing a pair of recently acquired Butler & Wilson earrings and a Miyake trouser suit, which for her was immensely sensational: she'd felt fifteen years younger as she looked at herself in the mirror..

"What a wonderful wine," he said. "What is it?"

"Nambrot," said Quentina, "2001."

"I must confess that means nothing to me. How astonishing a wine can taste like this, have this perfume, and I have never heard of it."

He stood up. The wine was making him restless.

"Can you show me the rest of your flat? I love these old Persian rugs. Must be worth a fortune."

Holding their glasses of wine, they went on a tour, though Quentina knew that nothing else in the place would come up to the splendour of the rugs, which a friend had urged her to put on the wall or sell to a dealer. She showed him everything, including a brief glimpse of her study where she wrote. The library, now two rooms with a connecting folding door, where Firebrace had accumulated three thousand volumes, had expanded to include at least half that number again, which Quentina had acquired from second-hand shops. Bry disregarded the books except to emit a low whistle at the extent of them. He didn't spot the rare Dickens set or the complete Lawrence, Waugh, Powell, Compton-Burnett, Pym, Norman Douglas, and Fielding (Costram & Wilkins, 1772).

Coming out of the kitchen and into the small communicating space between that room and the dining area, Bry stopped by Quentina's wine cupboard. He was looking at it as one might regard an exotic animal at a zoo, as if unable to tell whether it might bite or constrict.

"I'll go and get us some more Nambrot," she said and disappeared to return with the decanter in her hand.

"Incredible bouquet," said Bry, with an abstracted look on his face as she poured more. "It reminds me of a Chateau Ausone I once enjoyed."

"Nambrot is a merlot cabernet from Pisa. The man who sold it to me said it was not well known. I hoped you'd like it."

He was opening the door of the wine cupboard.

"My God, Quentina," he said. "I didn't realise…"

He took a gulp of the wine, forgetting, in his trance, to gargle before swallowing it.

"You have all these Schlumberger '89s and Meyer-Fonné '88s. And René Rostaing Condrieu! Guigal Hermitage! The '94! Sauzet's Montrachet and Batard. My God! You've got Domaine Leroy Clos de la Roche '94 too. And look at these clarets! I don't believe it. Quentina…I…er…this is '82 La Lagune and Beychevelle…"

"The '89 Coutets and d'Yquems are on the bottom shelves

along with the '94 Cristals and the '88 Dom Perignons. But all this is surely routine for you?"

She led him back to the sitting room.

"I wonder if they'll keep our table a little while longer or should you not ring and tell them we'll be half an hour late?"

"What? Oh, the table at Ho Tan. Yes. Um. Look, Quentina, I didn't know you had all this wine. Where does it come from? You're a strugg…a, um, novelist. You didn't know anything about wine, remember? All these years I've been trying to teach you…"

Quentina felt the colour rise in her face. But she kept calm and refilled his glass and her own. Was it the Miyake suit? Or the preposterous Butler & Wilson earrings? Or maybe just the wine? She felt a little heady.

"Teach me, Bry? Is that what you've been doing? You've been very generous, I grant you…all those lovely lunches and dinners with all those gorgeous wines…"

"Yes!"

"Well, here's looking at you, kid." And she raised her glass and offered him some more from the decanter, but he stood up and roamed around the Afghans.

"I feel I don't know the person I thought I did," he said.

Quentina was finding this a little too melodramatic. What was upsetting him so? She was beginning to feel a sense of mild outrage.

"None of us is precisely the person those who think they know us really know."

"I can't compete with the wines you have…all these years…all those incredible years…"

"Compete? What on earth do you mean? And by years do mean the years we've known one another or the vintages of those few bottles I have in the wine cupboard? That little larder of current drinking bottles. Goodness, Bry, you should see my cellar in the country!"

"What!?"

Quentina felt, as she drank more of the Nambrot, that any embroidery of this magnificent and surely implausible lie and she would burst, either in shame or in laughter at the absurdity of it all. She could recall the mansion of Norman Greer, the pop star who was so ingeniously murdered in *The Locust's Revenge*, and she could vividly remember the appurtenances of stardom she had given that social climber. Indeed, many of the bottles poor doomed Norman had collected had come from Bry Meadowes' brain, though in older vintages than the ones originally issued.

"Have I never told you of my house in Wiltshire?" she said grandly, pulling straight with her foot a kink in one of the Afghans. "Vintages there go back to the 1890s. D'Yquem '29 of course, Lafite '45 and '47, Vega-Sicilia '55 – oh you know, the usual old rubbish…"

"You have a house with wines like that?"

"But surely you knew I had inherited the title? And the estate? It was in the papers, extensive obituaries, when poor dear Lilith died…"

Bry ran fingers through his field of uncropped hair. He drank more of the wine. He got to his feet. Quentina felt how wonderful it was to lie so…so…ridiculously yet, best of all, to be believed.

"You know, I don't feel at all well. Do you mind if we scrub dinner tonight? I must go upstairs and lie down."

On unsteady toes he crossed the Afghans, put down his glass on a hideous gothic sideboard, and moved to the front door. Quentina, feeling unusually liberated by her torrent of fiction, followed him.

"I'm sorry to hear that, Bry," she said. "How wretched for you. But don't cancel the reservation, if you had thought of doing so. I have a friend I sometimes take to the Wigmore and she's always wondered what Ho Tan was like and so… well, it's a pity to waste the reservation when they're so hard to come by on a Saturday night…"

"Fine, fine," muttered Bry and he wandered out into the corridor like a man suffering from amnesia. "I don't feel much like Chinese food now. See you…when…"

"When I see you." And she shut the door.

ooooo

Quentina Pears never saw Bry Meadowes again for nine years, though Christmas cards, unreciprocated by her, arrived for the first three. The Parker film was a flop, seven more novels were published, she bought a small house in the Auvergne.

It was February when she saw him. He was getting out of a taxi, shrunken in form and heavily dependent on a tall younger woman, and he was going up to the entrance of Bryanston Mansions as Quentina, crossing the road, was bringing home the latest David Lodge from Daunts bookshop. She greeted him with some heartiness but he looked at her as if she was an oyster unfit to eat. He was the same burnished brown, though the yellow mop of hair was turning ashen.

"Have we met before? This is my wife Margery. Margery handles all my business affairs. She'll take care of you when she's settled me in," he said with a resonant quaver in the lower registers of his voice.

"No need," said Quentina to Margery. "My mistake. I thought your husband was someone else."

ooooo

Negru de Purkar 1969

Gilbert Carr was renowned as a travel writer but *The Rude Eye of Rebellion* was his only novel. Max had read it, often reflecting later, with a measure of irony, that had he not done so and enjoyed it he would never have considered Carr for the programme. He might then, Max thought, have been able to carry on performing on TV until the day he died.

It wasn't naked greed or lust for the limelight that motivated his ambition to carry on as the one great successful TV wine presenter. He had to defeat the monster, this debilitating loss of his sense of smell, and if he could hold out he would eventually defeat it. He had lost his olfactory powers but he could still pull the rabbit out of the hat.

In spite of the loss of his nose (effectively speaking), he had found a way to keep the myth of Max Cockburn, TV wine sleuth, alive. Or rather his ingenious producer Douglas Conquest had. The Bott Spot was the only serious rival Strictly Come Dancing and The Dragons Den, not to mention Big Brother, had in the TV ratings.The Bott Spot had been Conquest's idea. In the early days it had been a doddle. He had approached the bearded nonentity who wrote the wine column for the Hackney Gazette, having read his florid prose, and after three hours with him in the pub decided this was the man he was after. Off went the beard, out went the name (Norman Frears! It had to go), on went stripey jumpers and dazzling bow-ties. Max Cockburn – Conquest had the name already prepared – was perfect.

Norman, now Max, loved every minute of it. The show was a hit because Max was so unlikely a wine connoisseur and the camera loved him. He demystified wine. He brought celebs down to size and indeed wine personalities. The development of the celebrity element had scared Max at first but he soon, as his myth developed, was able to detect grape varieties at one sniff, though, cleverly, he seldom pronounced his findings too quickly.

However, celebrities were becoming more and more obscure with the wines they brought along for him to smell and taste blind (that is to say covered up so as to obscure the label) and identify. Max had grown up with French wines and those from other European countries. On the show, the odd South African cabernet or Israeli dessert wine was fine, and not impossible to pinpoint, but wine was pouring out of hundreds of new vineyards in scores of unlikely lands. A new world had come calling and Max Cockburn was being stretched.

It was a complete fluke that he guessed David Gower's bottle was the new sauvignon blanc from Marlborough. At first he thought it must be Cerbois-Dassault's Menetou-Salon, but when had this wine ever been so intensely herbaceous? A cricket tour destination gave him the New Zealand clue and he took a lucky shot.

It was a turbulent time. The TV show rode on through the worst recession since the thirties and Max was happy to concentrate on cheaper, more readily accessible wines as he had done as a local newspaper hack; but still the celebrity bottle slot was the high point of the programme, drawing the viewers to the goggle box. His fans depended upon him not just to rescue them from boredom on Thursday nights but to save them from bad wine, from overpriced wine, from wine snobbery, from wine lies, from having to put up with the rituals he was famous for demolishing and the bullshit he was renowned for exposing.

The new world of wine he was a vivid part of relied upon him: the man of the people. How could he abandon his fans because a small piece of scaffolding bracket had fallen on him?

ooooo

Why he'd insisted on going to Manchester that June, the 15th it was, was never clear. The producer thought it was because of a fantastic new Chinese restaurant opening up, a rarity in tough economic times, and it was suggested Max might film a quick piece on it and recommend wines to go with Chinese food.

Max thought he went up there to meet Alice, who was now making-up for Granada, and he missed her. Who else, in so many years, had he enjoyed such a lengthy relationship with? He often referred to her upper arm (encircled by a tattooed ring of tiny undefinable insects, possibly scorpions) as the sexist part of any female body he had ever kissed.

He never saw Alice that day, as it happened, and he never saw the lump of iron and brass that clouted him on the head as he was being warned to keep out of the Deansgate area by a squad of screaming policemen. He was unconscious for thirty-six hours but made, as far as the outside world was concerned, a complete physical recovery.

The only strange thing was that when the nurse brought in all the flowers that had been sent him, including a posy from Alice, he couldn't smell perfume on any of them and the nurse had no feminine odour whatsoever.

"What's happened?" he screamed.

"IRA bomb," said the nurse, not knowing that was not what he meant.

ooooo

He summoned sufficient wit not to remark about his loss of smell except to casually ask the doctor, as he was being discharged, if in cases of physical trauma certain senses could be temporarily curtailed.

"Oh yes," the doctor was pleased to reveal. "Deafness might be prolonged for a week or so, and in some cases there is short-term blindness and the use of a certain limb is restricted. I love your show, by the way."

Max managed to summon up a smile of thanks.

"Many times it's not a trauma, but a severe illness. A colleague of mine wrote a paper, not so much medical as literary, on the extraordinary metamorphosis undergone by Vladimir Nabokov – you know that Russian American who wrote *Lolita*?"

"I've read the book but I don't see…"

"Nabokov was a mathematical genius up to the age of seven and then he contracted pneumonia. His genius for numbers vanished. Just like that. But of course he recovered to become a literary genius and—"

"Yes, yes! But tell me…tell me…can olfactory sensibilities be affected by an accident like mine?"

The doctor was reassuring. Nothing unusual about it whatsoever. He even painted the horrifying picture that Max's sense of smell might be increased by the bomb.

"There are documented reports of war wounded," he said

airily, "who enjoyed an enhanced sense of smell after recovery. In London, during the Blitz, the opposite happened. Many people, even those uninjured, endured a temporary sense-loss of one sort or another but only in a few cases was it a permanent condition. You can smell this, can't you?"

He held a small flask taken from the trolley under Max's nose. Max inhaled.

"Ugh!" he lied. He had assumed from the look of the receptacle that it wasn't going to smell of roses. Did it contain urine? Some sort of solvent?

"Exactly!" the doctor cried. "You're fine."

ooooo

To be suddenly deprived of a world he wore like a second skin, a world whose language he spoke so fluently, was unnerving and deeply disturbing, then blind-panic producing. It was as alien, as shocking, as completely fantastic an experience as the opposite phenomenon had been all those decades ago when he had inhaled the perfume of the first great wine he had ever experienced.

How was he to conduct a celebrity bottle interview if he couldn't smell? He had nightmares about these things as the limousine took him to London. He tried to convince himself it was temporary. He'd be okay in a week, two weeks at the outside. The new series didn't start for several months.

But by the end of the first month, a month of misery, a month of pretending to enjoy wine he couldn't smell, his condition was no different. Not only was his ability to perform under threat but his whole existence as a human being.

He began to hate wine. It was no longer a pleasure. It was a torture. His nose sat there in the middle of his face, a useless lump. He could see it plainly, but it was completely bloody non-functional.

His tasting expertise lost eighty per cent of its potency, unable as he now was to discern aromatically one wine from another. He could no longer function as any sort of blind taster. The specialist he saw in Harley Street examined him, carried out tests.

"It'll probably come back just when you least expect it," the specialist said feebly.

It didn't.

And in a week's time, Max knew, he was due to confront Andrew Lloyd Webber with, so he had been promised, one of the most curious specimens in the deep and rarefied cellar of this avid collector.

The odd thing was that he didn't feel a victim. He considered his accident was a jolt. He had taken life too much for granted.

The accident was a transient blip, an inconvenient recession; a rebuke from the Gods for his shallow acceptance of his bounty; a reminder that the wealth and fame he enjoyed could, by violent modern means, be refashioned to torture him. It would pass. He would heal. He would overcome this temporary hiatus.

But how? He could no longer put off confronting Conquest. He had to come clean with the producer. Perhaps he would emerge from this ordeal stronger than ever. That, surely, was the right way to face it. He slept moderately well on that consideration.

ooooo

The producer of The Bott Spot, Douglas Conquest, was a small man with a big heart, which he never forgot to wear, Max once remarked, under his sleeve, a defence mechanism not uncommon in small people. The general opinion was that defensiveness was Douglas's art form.

His hair was always worn cut short, trimmed at great expense unusual in a BBC producer, and his immense tortoise shell glasses sat across his nose with a degree of pugnacity totally at odds with his avuncular dress, more often than not fawn slacks and a burgundy coloured cardigan (that woolly cardigan! Max would come close to strangling him with it).

Douglas Conquest had done very well from The Bott Spot. It had furnished him with expensive tastes to which he had not been to the manner born and these included wine. The show was his golden goose and he was not going to see the show scuppered – by "an inconvenient hiccup", as he put it to Max – if there was an easy remedy to hand.

Max invited Douglas to his house, saying he would cook something for lunch in spite of cooking having become a chore he no longer relished. Without a sense of smell, the pleasures food had once held for him were drastically curtailed. He could taste *something*, certain prominent flavours and textures, but all the sensuality and richness had been erased from eating and drinking.

He experienced hunger but no longer were there any aromas to excite it. Wine did nothing to titillate his appetite, which became perfunctory.

Max made a show of lunch. He opened two bottles of stupendous burgundy: Comtes Lafon Le Montrachet 1986 and a 1978 Mazis Chambertin from Domaine Leroy. Both wines from two Burgundy growers who deserved, in his view, their reputations. The wines had no need of doctoring, like so many burgundies, with sugar or acid, their makers were able to exploit local resources with something approaching genius.

The food was as simple as Max could stomach to make: omelette with wild mushrooms, a salad, and cheese. Conquest was open-mouthed with lust when he smelled the Le Montrachet and he gasped with something approaching hysteria when he got round to the Mazis.

It was only then, as they got on to the second bottle, that he looked at Max critically.

He pushed his considerable spectacles down his nose, and said: "But you've hardly eaten anything and…and you've not said a thing about these wines. Aren't they utterly…well, out of this world? This Mazis is one of the most dazzling red burgundies I've ever tasted. The fragrance is astonishing."

"Thank God they're not corked."

Conquest looked puzzled. He laughed.

"Well, you wouldn't have served them to me if they had been, would you?"

"Dougie, I can't tell if either of these wines are faulty or as magnificent as you say. Your kind remark, with the Montrachet, that 'here's to your narrow escape' is not quite accurate, I'm afraid. My escape may have been narrow but for my sense of smell it is a total loss. I can't smell a bloody thing, Dougie!"

Conquest put down his glass slowly, then picked it up, inhaled. He stood and went around the table to Max's chair and twirled the wine in Max's glass, one of those vast red burgundy glasses used for tasting on the show, and he thrust it under Max's nose.

"You mean," he said, slowly, "you can't pick up all the truffles and the wild raspberries and the…"

"…the long dead grouse!" Max snarled. "I know the litany. And no, I can't. Wine means nothing to me any more."

"We have a live series starting in eight days!"

"I know."

"It's temporary, Max. It'll go away. It'll clear up. I know about post-accident traumas."

"Good, then you'll be well prepared for the disaster that's shortly going to tax the imagination of the programme planners at the BBC."

They talked and argued for hours. Max had a further glass of the Mazis, which he was quite sure was as incredible as Conquest said because he knew that it should have been. He had predicted its medium-paced ascent to greatness some years before.

Now it just tasted of rather thick, fruity wine with some soft tannic richness. It could have been a pinot noir from Chile for all he was able to enthuse about it being one of the greatest red burgundies since the war and one of the very few to justify its appellated terroir.

Douglas Conquest rose to the occasion marvellously, an exercise greatly aided by consuming the major part of the contents of those two bottles.

"We can't have a temporary sensory loss jeopardise the huge investment my department and the BBC have in you, Max. We'll have to see out this series..."

"Twelve programmes! Twelve celebrity wines tasted blind! I can't do it. And what about all the other wines I'll be tasting and talking about and evaluating?"

"We'll just have to...to cheat a little, Max. No-one need know. You can busk it with all the other wines. You can make it up as you go along. You taste *something*, don't you? You can invent the usual clichés about the exotic fruit and vegetables you've discovered in the glass and as for the celeb bottles..."

Max was almost in tears. Somehow he had expected Conquest to reel off the name of the perfect doctor, possibly

Viennese, who knew all about conditions like loss of smell and who would put him right in a trice.

Conquest, however, was concerned with other things. Max could hardly blame him for that but wasn't Conquest being extraordinarily callous? Max wasn't a machine that had suddenly and mysteriously broken down. He was a human being deprived of his reason for living.

Such considerations went completely over the head of Douglas Conquest.

ooooo

The series was transmitted. It was a total invention from start to finish. There was not a single second in any programme, Max thought, where he was genuine. The programmes acquired more viewers than ever. Max acted his head, tongue and nose off.

No foreign medical specialist whom he saw – under yet another false name – was anything but optimistic yet, in the end, useless. The Cockburn nose was relentlessly uncooperative; its sense of smell was as good as nil, yielding no sensations whatsoever.

Nevertheless, the celebrities queued up to appear. Everyone – viewers, celebs, critics, the BBC hierarchy – applauded the change in presentation, which Dougie had devised, no-one aware that it also enabled Max surreptitiously to discover what the celebrity bottle was before each show went on air. It was an ingenious scheme and Max grabbed it; a temporary Faustian expedient; a life-line back to sanity.

In the past the bottle each celebrity brought was wrapped in brown paper and sealed with masking tape with an elaborate wax seal on it in a ceremony filmed in their own homes some days before transmission. It was broadcast immediately prior to The Celebrity Bottle spot in the show. This was so the audience in the studio and the viewers saw, in dazzling close-up, what the wine was.

Conquest now announced that this filming consumed too much time and in future the bottle would stay in the possession of the celebrity until arrival at the studio, where it would then be ceremoniously wrapped and sealed. The ceremony was not filmed, though Max had always to spin out the questions at the outset of the confrontation with the celeb to establish that there was no way the presenter could know what the bottle was, and that it had been sealed in complete privacy.

What no-one except Conquest and Cockburn knew was that there was a hidden camera in the room where the wine was wrapped up – Conquest had rigged it over a weekend – and it was connected via closed circuit to one of the several monitors in Max's dressing room.

Max now made it a habit to request make-up and continuity and any assistant producer hanging around to leave: he wanted to be by himself for ten minutes. This perfectly rational request was sympathised with and instantly granted. Max locked the dressing room door and switched on the monitor, and there was the resident bottle sealer (an ex-police sergeant, another of Conquest's demon new ideas) who solemnly sealed the wine in the presence of the celebrity.

Not a soul ever twigged that there was a camera lens, perfectly focussed, transmitting all this, and that the presenter was given more than a minute to note the name, the year, and everything else about the bottle.

Except Max would never know what it smelled like unless he knew the wine already. He would also be aware of only a small proportion of its taste. Robbed of the faculty of smell, which is taste postponed, it is surprising, Max was discovering, how little flavour things had unless they were uncommonly spicy.

Max began to enjoy the performances he put on. The perversity of it filled him with illicit joy.

He was like the ultimate doctored wine: one hundred per cent fake yet viewed as totally genuine. He was getting away with more than he had ever got away with in his life before and not one second of it was based on reality.

He didn't feel conscience-stricken about any part of it, just astounded that could get away with it. Surely, he kept telling himself, his sense of smell would come back? He asked himself this question daily: as he got up in the morning, as he cleaned his teeth, tied his bow-tie, bolted his breakfast; put his nose to the newsprint of the morning papers, which had once carried so much resonant odour.

Any pangs of guilt he exhibited, even the merest hint of doubt about the legitimacy of his deception, Conquest was there to smooth away.

"You're like a paratrooper who suddenly develops a fear of heights. Does he do a bunk? Or does he face his responsibilities, refuse to let his comrades down? I think you know the answer, Max. He waits for his courage to come back. He stiffens his sinews and soldiers on."

Max did. He soldiered on. He knew what all the wines he clandestinely watched being sealed would approximately smell and taste like and he could embroider their virtues, and on occasions their vices, like mad.

Not every wine might be in perfect condition, but the risk had to be taken. He could barely tell this from the taste; if a wine was subtly faulty he was sunk because he would be unable to smell the fact.

If there were any such wines, no celebrity commented on it as they explored the mystery bottle together under those bright lights. The celebrities invariably said it was marvellous or, with examples designed to add a little of the opposite spice to the proceedings, utterly dreadful. Even Max's handicapped senses could spot such wines as they went down his throat (the spitting out having been abandoned).

He made a few deliberate errors with the more arcane bottles; was a year out with the vintage, perhaps got a neighbouring vineyard instead of the real one, but in general he thought he would play the game according to his own rules and thus where the wine was one he reckoned he would have got anyway, he always gave the correct answer.

He was held in greater awe and esteem than ever before. He just couldn't repeat the performance on foreign live TV or when people out of the blue thrust a covered bottle at him or, at dinner parties, the host poured a wine from a decanter. In the latter instance he always said, "*...kind of you, but I'm not here to work, am I? Can't I just enjoy this amazing wine?*" And the host would beam, because the wine always *was* amazing because the world's greatest wine nose had just said so.

Then, out of the cathode-rayed depths of the competitive struggles of the various TV channels, a tug-of-war ensued between the BBC and the Commercial crowd for Max's services. Channel 4 wanted The Bott Spot and waved a very fat cheque book.

Max had never had an agent. Not a proper one. He had always left such matters to his accountant's office (the senior partner still balancing the books in Temple Fortune at seventy-three years of age). He was content to do so now; or rather, he left it to Conquest to be the man in the middle once he himself had expressed no problem about quitting the Beeb. It was just a question of money. Just A Question of Money. What a good name for a TV quiz show, thought Max.

Thus, much to the BBC's surprise, anger and ultimate chagrin, it was open season for The Bott Spot. And commercial money won. But not Channel 4's. It was ITV who triumphed, coming up with even more money than Sky had thought of offering.

Douglas Conquest cheerfully resigned from the BBC, set up his own production company just to make the programmes, and took home, so he said to Max, approximately five times more money than the BBC had been pleased to pay him (actually Max knew for a fact it was nearer twenty times more but who cared with so bounteous a cake to carve?).

The move to a commercial channel meant that the show could be sponsored and this was quickly accommodated by Le Vrai Belge, a mineral water company of international repute, the French Wine Institute, and Barclays Bank. Advertisers of appropriate products also insisted, Conquest was ecstatic to learn, on having their commercials in the breaks immediately before transmission and immediately after; the break in the middle becoming one of the most valuable on commercial television.

Max began to appear in TV commercials himself: for a fruit jelly, a series for a soup company, and several for the mineral water sponsor.

Max's sense of smell, nonetheless, continued to be stubbornly out on strike. He began to lose weight. He began to drink malt whisky. He could, at least, taste something as the stuff went down his throat.

The new set of programmes set viewing records. The secret camera never let him down.

For the next three years Max Cockburn was the most famous undetected con artist in Britain. He no longer bothered with ex-BBC make-up artists in Manchester. He threw caution to the winds and concentrated on all the mellow-breasted and shallow-eyed girls who populated the various layers of commercial TV. They prevented him from becoming completely unhinged, they drank his wines, and even as he mourned (silently) the loss of an essential element of their sexuality and naked sensuality, their aromas, there were compensations. Only in fleeting moments did he deplore his decline into complaisancy and corruption but every time he held a glass of great wine under his nose and sensed nothing but what he had forfeited, he found the resolve to continue; the means to stay controlled, keep his sanity. Life had been unfair. He had to pay it back.

Yet mad Max went in the end: courtesy of prize-winning author Gilbert Carr, the oldest living winner of the Booker and a man who had assiduously collected bottles of wine on his travels.

ooooo

Carr was reluctant to appear at first, though he'd seen the show and, like everyone who saw it, had, so he told Max, marvelled at the expertise of its presenter. When Max telephoned him and discussed his book Carr warmed up and relented and promised to turn up with a bottle that would tax Max's powers to the full.

Conquest had his secret camera switched on as Carr presented his bottle for wrapping and Max was, as ever, grateful for it. Would he have sussed this wine had his nose still been in perfect shape? He had to wonder. For what Max saw revealed was a bottle of Negru de Purkar 1969.

The crafty old sod! Max almost cried out aloud. What a wine to ask anyone to guess blind. Negru de Purkar, Max knew, came from Moldova and the '69 had been made twenty-two years before that country's independence from soviet Russia. He opened his wine encyclopaedia and quickly ascertained what the grape might be – separavi, a native of the region – and he also boned up a few more relevant details which might come in useful.

Max had tasted Negru de Purkar before and knew how extraordinarily complex and gamy such a wine could be. It would be gamble trying to describe this wine with an obvious connoisseur like Carr in the opposite chair (not a film actor with too much money and no taste or a TV personality trying to fool him with a duff vintage of a legendary vineyard), but at least he knew what the wine was. The biggest hurdle, thanks to Douglas Conquest's creative mind, was already well cleared.

He had developed a technique when pouring the celebrity wine (first in to the guest's glass, then into his). He waited for the guest to smell it before he put the glass to his own nose. The guest always did this and during these few moments Max could examine the colour, pass comments on it, and ask a few general questions about the wine, such as what the celebrity might have eaten with it last time a bottle had been drunk, and this gave him time to examine the guest's face; if the wine was faulty the eyes would betray the fact. For Max had become skilled at looking at eyes and detecting their hidden truths. Disappointment always showed on a celebrity face if the wine was badly out of condition or even if it was merely not as great as it should have been.

Carr came down the studio stairs with a jauntiness, Max considered, belying his years. The paper-wrapped bottle, like a baby, nestled in his arms. The two men shook hands and Carr sat in the guest's seat and answered an anodyne question about his interest in wine.

Carr had a halo of white hair, which gave him the appearance of a guru, and his face did not belie this exalted status with its folds and creases and suggestion of a life well-lived.

Max made much of taking the capsule off the top of the wine, flourishing the show's giant corkscrew and removing the cork. He took two of the large tasting glasses, which Conquest insisted on – preposterously bulbous for dramatic TV effect – and poured the wine out. He handed Carr a glass. He put the cork to his nose. It was the usual ritual.

It meant nothing to him now, of course, smelling the cork, but for years it was the routine beginning of any wine's evaluation.

It was then that Max first became aware of Carr's eyes. Max raised his glass and commented on the colour and how the browniness of the fruit and the near-orange or brick red of the liquid near the rim suggested a quarter of a century of age.

A polite ripple of applause went round the audience at this first correct response.

Carr's eyes were, Max realised with something like horror, exactly like his older brother's before he died: that cruel, deep, ancient amber. He suppressed a shudder but he could not tear his eyes away from Carr's.

Carr's face gave absolutely nothing away as he inserted his much travelled proboscis into his glass. With Carr's eyes averted, Max could turn his attention to pretending to smell the contents of his own glass. This he did, breathing theatrically as was demanded by the tube. (*"That electronic box in the corner of the living room, Max,"* said Conquest, *"has never had anything real ever come out of it."*)

Max was trying to forget those eyes. He regarded the colour as he looked at Carr again. Carr now smiled as he nosed the wine a second time, settled back in his chair and answered a question about the single incident in his novel involving wine. Max inhaled a further time. Was the Negru de Purkar in perfect condition? Max watched Carr smell the wine again; and again a tight smile irresistibly flitted across the author's face. The wine was in perfect condition. It had to be.

Max examined the colour again, pushing his glasses down to the end of his nose to get a sharper focus. He remarked on the brown tinge yet again. The usual stuff came out of his mouth. He twirled the glass and breathed deeply. He sensed nothing. Max could have been underwater for all the impression the wine's aroma made on him.

Was the wine perfect? Max waited for his guest, as they always did, to confirm the fact and Carr, after a moment, complied.

"You know," he said, his deep, almost mid-Atlantic accented voice as rich as some crusty old claret, "wines like this are glorious, rare I would say, artefacts. What a tragedy..."

"Yes...?"

"...what a tragedy it is my last bottle."

Max chuckled. Carr smiled. The audience tittered. Max relaxed. He could strut his stuff.

He exclaimed at the wine's richness of aroma, saying that it was perfectly concomitant with a wine of twenty-five years of age. He reeled off a list of the things the last bottle of Negru de Purkar he had tasted had exhibited. He said it reminded him of something French. Something like a Haut-Brion or a Chateauneuf-du-Pape. Cabernet, he declared, seemed more likely than any grapes of the Rhone. Or was the grape, or grapes, something extremely obscure?

Max posed the question. Tip of the tongue stuff. The audience was deathly silent. They loved, as Max and Conquest knew so well, the tense bits, the lead-up to when Sherlock finally, teasingly, unmistakably reveals the identity of the villain. For the viewers, who were granted close-ups of the two faces and the glass of wine, plus cutaways to the audience, it was compelling drama.

"Your powers of detection are enthralling me, Max, please go on."

The wine was a tricky customer, Max said. Carr's eyes continued to hold his and Max forced himself to bring the glass up and concentrate on taking a sip. The eyes of Carr were so uncannily like his death-bed brother's. He felt himself being sucked in, engulfed.

He muttered some perfunctory clichés about the extraordinary vigour of so relatively aged a wine. Carr smiled that tight smile. His eyes were enormous! They were strangling Max's usual powers of polished response. His lips were on the rim of the glass, but under Carr's blazing gaze he could not taste.

Finally, Max tore his eyes away from Carr's and threw out a complex litany of all the wine's riches, including such extravagances as Balkan Sobranie cigarette tobacco and Tia Maria. The audience lapped it up.

Max began now to dangle the possibility of eastern Europe in the air and he touched on obscure regional grapes. Then he plucked, seemingly from nowhere, the wine's magnificently obscure grape, the separavi, and soon he was raving afresh over the wine, which he began to realise Carr had not yet, for some reason, tasted.

Max could see, remarkably, the beginnings of anger and disgust creep across his guest's face, so he decided to wrap it up – with that practised finality which had become his style.

"I must go for Negru de Purkar…1970?" he said flatly.

Why did Carr suddenly look upset? Was he finding Max's theatrics too much? Too bad, thought Max. He shouldn't have come on television if he didn't like drama.

The studio audience burst in to wild applause as Max announced the name of the wine and a young woman dressed in a long silver lamé evening gown with a very low cut front (nothing greatly exciting concealed within – Max had explored it several times) appeared as she always did and snipped off the brown paper and the tape, to reveal a bottle of Negru de Purkar 1969.

As the camera zoomed in for a close-up, the studio audience became physical and raucous, as they had been taught, and the applause was thunderous. Max extended his hand to Carr but the author brushed it aside.

"I do not know how it is possible, Mr Cockburn…" where had the friendly 'Max' suddenly disappeared to? "…for any human being to have discerned the identity of this wine unless he knew beforehand what it once was."

His tone was icy. A silence fell over the audience; their hero was under unprecedented attack. It had happened only once before when, years ago and with his nose in fine fettle, Max had disparaged the bottle of 1955 Chateau Co d'Estournel bought in by a film mogul.

Carr's anger, however, was more substantial; more menacing in its measured hostility and derision.

"The wine is oxidised to buggery, you charlatan! You obviously have no faculty of smell whatsoever. It is vinegar, more or less. The cork smells of rancid cardboard and sherry vinegar. The wine is undrinkable. How could anyone get further than the cork? It is horrible. Smell it! Taste it!"

To say that an engulfing tide of dank, fetid horror gripped Max is an understatement. Why had he not tasted the wine? Because Carr's eyes, his older brother's dying eyes, had so gripped him. He had been paralysed, unable to resort to his routine tasting of the wine.

The wine had turned to nigh-vinegar? If only Max had tasted it he would have discovered this for himself. A man without a nose may not be able to smell vinegar but he can assuredly recognise it when it is in his throat.

The audience did not know how to react. Max could not see Douglas in the control room but he could glimpse an assistant producer, doubtless on Conquest's instructions, trying to divert attention elsewhere. But the camera would not desert Carr yet. He was unstoppable. The eyes of a dying sibling bored in to Max as Carr stared at the presenter, and he stood up, brandishing his glass of Negru de Purkar in the air.

Carr took his glass, before the assistant producer or Max could restrain him, and he stepped down to the front row of the audience and screamed:

"Taste this abominable once great bottle of wine. It is vinegar! Go on. You there!" He thrust the glass unceremoniously at a fat wine buff, a regular who always fought to get a front row seat. Max knew him to be a taxi driver.

"No, don't taste. It is unnecessary. Just smell. It is vinegar pure and simple. But didn't you, Mr Cockburn..." and now it was Carr who was all theatrics as he let the cabbie sniff the glass and go audibly "Ugh!", to which there was a gasp from the people around him "...describe this wine as glorious, gamy, rich and...what was that brand of Bulgarian tobacco...? Oh yes, and coffee! And chocolate! Chocolate!? Whoever heard of chocolate vinegar!"

Hands appeared from everywhere to try to take the glass of wine. It was passed around and the sounds of disgust were audible. Max, crucified, could not move from his seat.

The show went off the air as the audience became menacing and bellicose and two security men appeared and escorted Max through the throng to his dressing room. Conquest was waiting inside, shaking and pale, his glasses bobbing up and down on his nose. Beside him were the series editor, Rachel Green, and a stiff-shirted man in a herringbone suit and a bow-tie Max did not recognise. Conquest looked ashen, Green uncomprehending; the bow-tied individual wore a grimmer expression – murderous would sum it up, Max thought, and he wondered who the hell the man was. Dougie was yelling.

"What have you done to me? What have you done to this show? You thief! You cheat! You monster!"

Max was too stupidly dazed to respond immediately to this. The actual implication of Conquest's words didn't sink in. All he could do was look at each of them in turn, shake his head, gasp for breath; his lips were quivering with shock, he felt he might hyperventilate, even vomit.

Why had he never tasted that wine? Why had he let himself be led on by Carr? It was a tragedy, not because it was the author's last bottle and wonderful as Max had thought, but because it had oxidised over the years and become stale and vinegarised. No wonder Carr had never tasted it. He didn't need to.

Max sat down and picked up a bottle of chilled Le Vrai Belge, surprised to see how vibrantly his hand was shaking. Before he could pour himself out a glass the man with the bow-tie put his hand over Max's and, gently, as if taking a sharp implement away from an infant, prised the bottle from Max's grasp.

"I would prefer it, Monsieur," he said with only the faint trace of a Belgian accent, "if Max Cockburn was not seen drinking my water any more. Find another brand. Mine has received damage enough by being associated with your name."

Max felt relieved as the man caressed his bottle. It was all over. Max Cockburn would never have to smell another wine on TV again. He could retire and, as his cleaning lady pointed out the next day: *"You meet such a superior sort of person in Wormwood Scrubs nowadays, Mr Cockburn, you'll feel right at 'ome."*

ooooo

About the Author

Malcolm Gluck was wine correspondent of *The Guardian.* He wrote a Saturday column, Superplonk, between 1989 and 2004. His annual wine guide, also called Superplonk, was a number-one best seller for eight years. He wrote and presented his own BBC-2 TV series on wine, Gluck Gluck Gluck, has produced a Deutsche Grammophon double cd of music appreciation and wine drinking, and has written 39 books on wine. This is his first work of published fiction.